Praise for Sean D

"The legion of fans who have already discovered Sean of the South's heartwarming southern stories will be raving about this knock-out novel, and readers new to his work will find this tale strikes every perfect note. With relatable characters, comedic relief, sensory-rich descriptions, a dose of romance, and a fast-paced plot that keeps the pages turning, Dietrich has hit a home run with this one . . . a victory that would surely make The Incredible Winston Browne proud."

—*NEW YORK JOURNAL OF BOOKS*

"Dietrich imbues plenty of Southern charm and colloquialisms in a read that will appeal to people of all genders, and especially to fans of small-town living. Readers who enjoy well-developed, realistic characters similar to those from Charles Martin and Lauren K. Denton will want to watch for more from this author."

—*LIBRARY JOURNAL*

"Dietrich meshes mystery and romance beautifully in this moral tale about one man set on using what is left of his life to enrich the lives of others. Dietrich's fans will love this rip-roaring, dramatic inspirational."

—*PUBLISHERS WEEKLY*, FOR *THE INCREDIBLE WINSTON BROWNE*

"This poignant novel is about people, life, community, family, friendship, love, the day-to-day, even the mundane . . . Baseball fans and non-fans alike will enjoy this sometimes humorous, occasionally heartbreaking story about all that we hold dear, which gives us a timely reminder that we need to live in the moment, or life can pass us by while we aren't paying attention."

—THE HISTORICAL NOVEL SOCIETY, FOR
THE INCREDIBLE WINSTON BROWNE

"Sean Dietrich has written a home run of a novel with *The Incredible Winston Browne.* Every bit as wonderful as its title implies, it's the story of Browne—a principled, baseball-loving sheriff—a precocious little girl in need of help, and the community that rallies around them. This warm, witty, tender novel celebrates the power of friendship and family to transform our lives. It left me nostalgic and hopeful, missing my grandfathers, and eager for baseball season to start again. I loved it."

—ARIEL LAWHON, *NEW YORK TIMES* BESTSELLING
AUTHOR OF *I WAS ANASTASIA*

"Sean's writing is infused with the small-town South—you can smell the exhaust of the cars cruising down dusty back roads, and you can sense the warmth of the potluck meal on your plate. Make no mistake. [*The Incredible Winston Browne*] is a classic story, told by an expert storyteller."

—SHAWN SMUCKER, AUTHOR OF *LIGHT FROM DISTANT STARS*

"Sean Dietrich has given us an absolute treasure of a novel. Moving, powerful, and dazzling, *Stars of Alabama* is a page-turning wonder of a story."

—PATTI CALLAHAN, *NEW YORK TIMES* BESTSELLING AUTHOR OF *BECOMING MRS. LEWIS*

"Dietrich is a Southern Garrison Keillor. Fans of the latter and former will be pleased."

—*LIBRARY JOURNAL*, FOR *STARS OF ALABAMA*

"[*Stars of Alabama*] is a testament to inner strength, and the good that can come from even the worst beginnings . . . Historical fiction and mystery readers will find this to be a very satisfying book."

—*BOOKLIST*

"Sean Dietrich has woven together a rich tapestry of characters—some charming, some heartbreaking, all of them inspiring. *Stars of Alabama* is mesmerizing, a siren's call that holds the reader in a world softly Southern, full of broken lives and the good souls who pick up the pieces and put them back together into a brilliant, wondrous new mosaic full of hope."

—DANA CHAMBLEE CARPENTER, AUTHOR OF THE BOHEMIAN TRILOGY

"Set during the Dust Bowl, this pleasing, ambitious epic from Dietrich brings together unlikely allies all escaping dire situations . . . Though filled with preachers declaring judgment and prophecies of the end-time, Dietrich's hopeful tale illuminates the small rays of faith that shine even in dark times."

—*PUBLISHERS WEEKLY*, FOR *STARS OF ALABAMA*

"Mysterious and dazzling."

—*DEEP SOUTH*, FOR *STARS OF ALABAMA*

"Sean Dietrich can spin a story."

—*SOUTHERN LIVING*, FOR *STARS OF ALABAMA*

"A big-hearted novel."

—*GARDEN & GUN*, FOR *STARS OF ALABAMA*

"Sean Dietrich's *Stars of Alabama* is a beautiful novel, mesmerizing with its complex characters, lush settings, and lyrical language. It is, quite simply, Southern literature at its finest."

—*SOUTHERN LITERARY REVIEW*

The Incredible Winston Browne

ALSO BY SEAN DIETRICH

FICTION

Stars of Alabama

Caution: This Vehicle Makes Frequent Stops for Boiled Peanuts

Small Towns, Labradors, Barbecue, Biscuits, Beer, and Bibles

The Other Side of the Bay

Lyla

NONFICTION

Will the Circle Be Unbroken?

The South's Okayest Writer

Sean of the South: On the Road

Sean of the South (Volume 1)

Sean of the South (Volume 2)

Sean of the South: Whistling Dixie

The Incredible Winston Browne

SEAN DIETRICH

The Incredible Winston Browne

Published in Nashville, Tennessee, by Thomas Nelson. Thomas Nelson is a registered trademark of HarperCollins Christian Publishing, Inc.

Published in association with The Bindery Agency, www.TheBinderyAgency.com.

Interior design by Mallory Collins

Thomas Nelson titles may be purchased in bulk for educational, business, fundraising, or sales promotional use. For information, please email SpecialMarkets@ThomasNelson.com.

Publisher's Note: This novel is a work of fiction. Names, characters, places, and incidents are either products of the author's imagination or used fictitiously. All characters are fictional, and any similarity to people living or dead is purely coincidental.

ISBN: 978-0-7852-3135-6 (softcover)

Library of Congress Cataloging-in-Publication Data

Names: Dietrich, Sean, 1982- author.
Title: The incredible Winston Browne / Sean Dietrich.
Description: Nashville, Tennessee : Thomas Nelson, [2021] | Summary: "In Sean of the South's latest novel, a small 1950s town takes in a mysterious visitor whom they believe needs saving-but she might be the one who saves them"-- Provided by publisher.
Identifiers: LCCN 2020042112 (print) | LCCN 2020042113 (ebook) | ISBN 9780785226406 (hardcover) | ISBN 9780785231356 (paperback) | ISBN 9780785226413 (epub) | ISBN 9780785226420
Classification: LCC PS3604.I2254 I53 2021 (print) | LCC PS3604.I2254 (ebook) | DDC 813/.6--dc23
LC record available at https://lccn.loc.gov/2020042112
LC ebook record available at https://lccn.loc.gov/2020042113

Printed in the United States of America

HB 11.14.2023

To Jocelyn, of course. For getting me.

The First Inning

Winston Browne knew he was dying. He couldn't explain how he knew. He just did.

He removed his crumpled brown hat, exposing his prematurely white hair, and looked at the clear sky. He wondered what was up there. Behind all that blue. He sat on the hood of a truck, sandwiched between two men, listening to a tinny radio voice talk about strikes, inside pitches, and home runs. But his mind was on the big blue stuff above him.

The Floridian sun hung high over center field. The sky was empty and cloudless. What was up there? Was it friendly? Or the better question: Did anyone go *there* when they died? Or did they just become food for worms?

Winston lit a Lucky Strike cigarette and drew in a breath. He'd been smoking Luckys since he was ten.

The truck was parked in the left field grass, doors splayed open, grown men sitting just above the engine, leaning backward on the windshield. The Dodgers game was coming straight from New York, via WWLA in Mobile.

It was a good day, and good days had been hard to come by ever since the doctor started running Tests on him. Tests were just another name for systematic torture involving two-foot-long needles thicker than milkshake straws. The doc shoved these needles into his ribcage and removed plugs of pink lung matter. They called that a Test. In any other era, they would have called it medieval punishment. And even though the doctor hadn't come out and said it yet, they don't run Tests on people who aren't dying.

"You wanna beer?" said Mark Laughlin. "I got some in the cooler."

"No thanks," said Winston. "Technically I'm on duty."

"Aw, you're *always* on duty," said Jimmy Abraham, lifting a brown-bottled Dixie from the tin Dr Pepper cooler in the back of the truck. "You ain't in uniform, Saint Francis."

Winston hopped down, walked to the tailgate, reached into the ice and removed a bottle of Nehi orange, then popped the top using the edge of the truck bumper.

The three older men in sweat-laden T-shirts and jeans listened to every play with open ears and closed mouths and slippery longnecks in their hands. The game ended with pure elation. The small dashboard speaker crackled beneath the strain of the announcer's voice:

"Dodgers beat the Giants, folks! The Bums beat the Giants!"

There was nothing a Dodger man loved more than hating the Giants. Every game against them was a crucial one. The rivalry ran deep. Last year the Giants had squeezed the mustard out of the beloved Bums to win the pennant. And it wasn't the first time the Dodgers had been clocked by the Giants. The Brooklyn boys were the best losers in the National League. Sometimes they seemed to be better at losing than at winning. Nothing incites more loyalty among fans than losing.

Winston, Jimmy, and Mark all hollered after the win. The hollering was a necessary part of being a Dodger man. It was a temporary release of tension. It was decades of losses, wins, near-wins, season disappointments, and always being *this* close to the championship, but always blowing it. It was joy laced with the fear of more losses.

But for Winston, the yelling was simply to remind himself that he was still alive.

Only a Dodger man living in the miniscule town of Moab, Florida, could know the frustration that went along with his lot in life. It wasn't just the losing. It was the powerless feeling a man had when he realized the game did not involve him. No matter how much he rooted, no matter how much he cheered, it was all happening twelve hundred miles north, in some New York borough, which might as well have been the edge of the world to someone from a one-horse town like Moab.

Winston could hear the clanging of pots and pans in the distance from various houses in Moab proper. More Dodgers fans. Then he heard a few bottle rockets. No shotgun blasts—those were reserved for pennant races. He even heard a faint trumpet, probably played by old man Pederson, who was crazy as a run-over cat.

Dodgers sympathizers were everywhere in Moab. The town was nuts about them. Winston had persuaded WWLA to start broadcasting Brooklyn's games six years earlier, since Mobile's minor league team, the Mobile Bears, was part of the Dodgers farm system. It only seemed right that boys from the rural corn cribs and remote farm communities could hear about the fantastic, nearly mythological feats of the incredible Jack Roosevelt Robinson. The Dodgers were outspoken, open-minded, black and white, and they were going to change the world. Winston Browne believed that.

The old men in Moab who rooted for Jackie Robinson grew up not drinking from public drinking fountains after a black man. That was how they had always been.

But then Jackie Robinson came along. The old bigoted men would sit beside their radios with Dixie bottles in hand, listening to fantastic accounts of Jackie stealing home—nobody stole home—and these men were slapped by their own bigotry.

Baseball fever swept over the little town. Each summer the town's residents were serenaded by the radio shouting about Gil Hodges, Roy Campanella, Duke Snider, and the rest of America's most lovable "bums." Some rooted for the Yankees, the glory of Babe Ruth still the most talked about subject in boyhood. But the Brooklyn Dodgers were more than a team, they were family. Men referred to players like they were personal friends, rarely using last names. Outsiders might have thought the men were talking about nephews or cousins.

After the game, Winston clicked off the radio and the men resumed work on Moab's first community ball field. They finished hanging the giant halide lights over center field with punch-drunk smiles on their faces, oblivious to the dangerous sunburns they were developing. A good Dodgers victory will do that to a man.

Winston crawled into the hydraulic cherry picker basket and ascended forty feet into the air. Jimmy climbed the ladder over right field. Together, they worked as the sun went down, wiring lights while the sky turned purple. The outfield grass was covered in the salty, sticky Floridian dew, and the frogs were singing. It took two hours to install the giant bulbs. Once they finished, it was dark.

For the final hurrah, the men stood beside the large electrical panel. Mark, the electrician, did the honors and flipped the switch. The vibrant green ball field was illuminated beneath the bluish lights. Winston almost cried.

Not because of the field, but because life was moving too fast and there was nothing he could do to stop it. It was a runaway train. The boxcar would keep rolling until it reached the end of the line, or until it tumbled off the tracks.

His ribs hurt. The bandage over the hole in his chest needed to be changed. And his cough wasn't going anywhere.

But right now he was overcome with joy. The satisfying glow of the enormous lights made Winston Browne's eyes swell with saltwater, and he almost forgot every bad thing happening inside his body.

Jimmy slapped Winston's shoulder and handed him a mitt. "You wanna christen the field and embarrass yourself in front of Mark?"

"Where'd you get these?" said Winston. The heavy brown gloves were familiar.

"From Bill Lemons. He saved all the Gnats' old stuff in a trunk in his garage. I still remember how to call 'em if you remember how to pitch 'em."

"C'mon, Win," said Mark. "Pull a muscle for me."

Winston smelled the glove. "This was *my* glove." He could tell by the smell. Old bacon grease and axel grease.

"You don't think I know that?" said Jimmy. "It took Bill an hour to find our old mitts."

"Jimmy, I can't pitch anymore, I haven't pitched since . . ." He couldn't even remember when. Probably since he wore the Moab Gnats jersey, which seemed like a lifetime ago. After high school he'd joined the army as a wide-eyed youth, was discharged, then volunteered again like many able-bodied men had when Pearl Harbor changed everything. "You don't even have a mask. That ball could hurt you. Remember, we're old men."

"Speak for yourself. I'm fifty-two, same as you. Besides, I don't need a mask because you couldn't hit the south side of a north-facing barn."

Before Winston knew it, Jimmy was behind home plate. Jimmy punched his mitt and grinned the same way he'd done when they were Gnats. Back when the biggest, baddest, most evil things in the world were the Saint Louis Cardinals and Bob Feller from Cleveland. Long before Hitler became a household name.

And for a moment Winston thought his old friend looked like a boy at the plate. For a moment Winston half felt like a boy himself.

"C'mon!" shouted Jimmy. "Let's show arthritis what for!" His voice sounded more childlike than usual. His face looked almost smooth at a distance. Jimmy's hair was no longer quite so gray. Baseball can make a man young.

Winston dropped his shoulder. He threw the ball a few times until he and Jimmy were laughing after every pitch. He couldn't remember having this much fun. Not in a long time. He pitched until his shoulder was aching and he began to cough. The coughing did not stop. He doubled over and hacked until he felt his vision dimming from the exertion.

Jimmy trotted to the mound. "You're a lot older and considerably more decrepit than I thought," said Jimmy, slapping Winston's back. "But hey, cheer up, at least I'm still better looking than you."

When the cough subsided, Winston looked at the large lamps suspended over Moab's field like objects from another realm. They were bright white. Floating in the darkness. The sky was no longer blue but black. And no artificial lights could ever change that.

Jimmy pointed to the sheriff's shirt. "Win, you're bleeding."

Just below Winston's armpit was a small pool of dark blood, growing like an ink blot. Winston laughed at it. Laughing was all he could do.

Because Sheriff Winston Browne was dying.

The Exile of Jessie

Jessie sat in the front seat, watching Pennsylvania go past her at forty-five miles per hour. There were big trees in the windows, blurry from highway speed. No homes, just trees and swelling green hills. Sister Johanna was driving, both hands on the wheel, a stern look on the old woman's face. Jessie's three temple brothers sat in the back seat. They were dweebs.

Jessie had no idea where Sister Johanna was taking her, but she didn't care. Sister Johanna and Jessie's friend Ada had been conspiring for weeks; Jessie knew this. Several times Jessie had found them talking in secret. Wherever they were taking her, at least she wasn't going to be attending the temple school anymore.

She had only ever been on a car ride twice before in her life. The truth was, riding in cars was pretty fun. You went fast; you saw new things. The only things better than car rides were sneaking a game of marbles, eating Mary Jane peanut-butter taffy candies, and climbing trees. But not necessarily in that order. She was good at all three.

Her brothers were sleeping on each other's shoulders, jaws open, drooling like animals. She didn't know these boys very well; they were older than her by a few years. And already working on temple farms instead of going to school. In fact, Johanna wasn't really her sister and these weren't actually her brothers. That's just what temple people called everyone, brothers and sisters. People in the temple called everyone by family titles because they were stupid.

The things Jessie saw through her window were wonderful. After several hours a sign read Welcome to Maryland. Not long after was a sign that said Welcome to Richmond. Wherever they were going, people certainly were welcoming. And it was now a long way away from Pennsylvania.

They rolled past townships with pretty steeples, church towers, bell towers, and clock towers. Jessie marveled at all the big towers. She had never been this far away from the temple community before. She'd never seen so many towers in her life. All this time she had figured the secular world was dreary and ugly. But this outside world was nicer than the temple community. It was colorful, and the people wore clothes that weren't black.

"Where are we going?" Jessie asked Sister Johanna. Sister Johanna did not answer her. She only readjusted her grip on the wheel. She was not happy. In fact, she'd been silent with Jessie ever since they left. Sister Johanna finally responded to Jessie by saying, "I don't want to hear you ask questions. Ada is putting her life on the line for you. Do you realize that? That's all you need to know. Do you know what they would do to us if they found out?"

Jessie didn't have any clue what Sister Johanna was talking about. All she knew was that this woman was a grump.

"Her *life on the line*?" said Jessie. "What's that mean?"

Sister Johanna shook her head and swore in German. "They're probably looking for us right now."

The night before, Ada had been emotional. Ada was much older than Jessie, who would be ten next April. Ada was married with kids, but she always paid more attention to Jessie than all the other temple orphans. She'd held Jessie in her arms and cried hard enough to clog her nose. Then she'd given Jessie a wad of money and told her to keep it in her shoe "for the trip," and she told her to mind Sister Johanna for her own safety.

When Jessie asked where she would be going, Ada said nothing more, except that she would like it there and it was very pretty. She said it would be exciting and there would be lots of sunshine. Sister Johanna stopped at a motor inn. It was dusk. She went to check in but left Jessie and the boys in the car. She came back and said, "You sleep in the car tonight with your brothers; it's safer. If anything happens, we can escape quicker. I need to lay flat tonight."

Jessie didn't even give her a *yes, ma'am.* She just stuck her tongue out at Johanna. Two could play at this game.

"You ungrateful . . . ," said Sister Johanna. "If you had any idea how much I'm risking for you. Do you have any idea what is happening? I'm breaking the temple laws. If they find me they'll kill me."

Jessie put her tongue back in her mouth.

The night fell fast. Soon the whole world was black. Jessie didn't sleep in the car because her brothers stunk. Besides, this was a very big secular world. She sat on a large rock behind the motor inn, overlooking acres of farmland that spread for miles. A cow on the other side of a fence seemed interested in her, so she approached him. It stood in one place, staring at her while chewing. She named this cow Harold. Harold was a good listener. He let her talk about things as he whapped his tail against himself. She talked about everything that came to her mind. Eventually she realized Harold was a girl. So she changed her name to Harriet.

The next morning, when Sister Johanna found her curled up asleep on the rock, the woman marched across the field and grabbed her with both hands. She dragged Jessie into the vehicle by her hair. Jessie kicked and screamed, but Sister Johanna threw her into the front seat and slapped her on the face. Jessie stuck her tongue out at the woman again and said, "You don't slap very hard."

It was the wrong thing to say. Because Sister Johanna proved that she could.

"You're not my mother," Jessie added.

The woman didn't seem to care.

"And you're ugly," said Jessie. That ought to do it.

"I don't wanna hear another word outta you." Sister Johanna was beginning to cry. "Or I'm just gonna leave you right here, do you understand me?"

"I don't *care* if you leave me here," said Jessie.

The woman tried to slap her again, but Jessie caught her hand. Sister Johanna yanked herself free. "You stupid *Kind*. The *Bischof* wants to have you killed, Jessie. We're trying to save your life."

The Plains of Moab

Moab was located off U.S. Route 29, sitting on the grayish-brown water of the Escambia River, which ran downward through south Alabama, cutting into West Florida before spilling into the Gulf of Mexico. The town was covered in the last of summer's greenery, goldenrod, and purple asters. All storefronts, with their proud little awnings, tried to be so much more than they were.

The town itself was about as wide as it was high. Which wasn't very high. The nearby town of Layton was *much* higher—forty feet above sea level. Pensacola reached one hundred and two feet. But Moab was seventeen feet high. For some reason this was written on the town sign as though it were a point of pride.

But there wasn't much to brag about in Moab. To many, this part of the world was "Florabama." To others, it was "L.A.," which was short for Lower Alabama. To out-of-towners who had never heard of Moab, it was just a ketchup stain on the map while driving the old family heap southward for the annual vacation to the white beaches in Pensacola or Mobile.

To local residents it was covered dish socials, municipal meetings, and a bunch of people minding your business. To Eleanor Hughes, it was a river town full of millworkers, drunks, old biddies,

Sunday school students whose sole purpose in life was to make her life miserable, and women who got old many years before they became elderly.

But today was not a day for misery. Today was a day of matrimony. The white clapboard Methodist chapel looked beautiful done up in white flowers. The pews were adorned with white bunting.

Moab Methodist sat in the center of town like a mother hen with all its little chicks gathered around it. The Baptist and Methodist churches sat across from each other, separated by a single street, both swarmed with big-bodied, freshly simonized Chevys, DeSotos, LaSalles, Fords, and Packards. Friday evening was a popular wedding day in Moab.

People crawled from their vehicles and walked beneath the Methodist entryway dotted with white, yellow, and pink flowers and other intricate floral arrangements. A few stopped to take photographs of the flowers with Kodak Brownie cameras. The floral masterstrokes were Eleanor's creations. She was a lifelong Methodist and the long-time church beautification committee president.

She was always in charge of decorating. Being in charge suited her just fine because Eleanor was a bossy woman and a born leader. In fact, she was in charge of just about everything at Moab Methodist, including Sunday school and women's Bible studies, water heater maintenance, sometimes even choir practice. Eleanor Hughes did almost everything at Moab Methodist except preach the sermons.

The wedding decoration job had taken her four days with only one committee helper—a clumsy girl named Gwen, who knew as much about arranging flowers as a Labrador retriever. Still, the sanctuary looked like Eden with its magnolias and palmetto fronds. Eleanor had been gathering fronds near the river for weeks.

People found their seats and soon the ceremony began. When the piano played those four familiar chords, the congregation stood to face the bride.

Eleanor stood as well and smoothed her dress. The bride was her niece, Susan, who looked magnificent in her gown. Susan was moving unhurried, going a little too slowly down the center aisle. Way too slow, in fact. At this rate, Susan wouldn't reach the altar until the installation of the next U.S. president. So Eleanor motioned for Susan to hurry up. Susan noticed Eleanor making hand gestures and picked up the pace until Eleanor gave her the "okay" sign.

Where would this world have been without Eleanor Hughes?

Eleanor found herself sandwiched between her sister-in-law, Rose, her brother, Steven, and Jimmy Abraham. She had been Jimmy's steady girl since they were teenagers. Jimmy was one of the town's few 4-Fs, and thus one of the only eligible bachelors who didn't go to war. These days their romance didn't go any further than visiting the Chinese restaurant in Pensacola or attending an occasional ice cream social. She'd been waiting for him to marry her since Roosevelt was in office. But Jimmy never did. Because he was an idiot.

Jimmy elbowed her. "Some wedding, huh? I wonder who did all these flowers. They sure are pretty. I just love flowers."

She looked at him and smiled. But not with her eyes. Eleanor was fifty-two, and it had long since dawned on her that Jimmy wasn't interested in becoming much more than her glorified buddy.

Jimmy went on, "You oughta take notes, Eleanor. Whoever did these flowers is really talented."

She could have killed him with gardening shears. Once, Eleanor had adored weddings, but now they made her feel like a spinster. A girl spends her whole life thinking about weddings and marriage. She plays dress-up with her friends, forcing neighborhood boys to walk down imaginary aisles, burping make-believe babies, changing make-believe diapers. Her whole life had been aimed toward a day like today.

The wedding was a success. But when the vows were being exchanged, Eleanor heard a faint sound. A voice. A man's voice.

She pointed her ear toward the sound.

It was barely audible, but it was there. She looked at Jimmy, who was facing forward. He seemed to be overly involved in this wedding. That was when Eleanor noticed a thin white wire snaking out of his jacket, traveling upward toward his ear. And she could hear the faint words, *"There's a runner on first . . ."*

She elbowed him. When he turned to look at her, she could see the small earpiece tucked inside Jimmy Abraham's ear. She tried to communicate her disgust with the meanest look she could muster. Jimmy removed the earpiece, wound the wire around his fingers, then tucked it into his pocket. He whispered, "I was just checking the score."

Garden shears. Yes, that's how she would do it.

After the vows, the whole congregation was weeping, except Eleanor. Even Reverend Lewis had started to cry, which made the whole room weep and snort even harder. This, she could bear. But when Eleanor caught Jimmy wiping his eyes and nose with a handkerchief, she could have punched him in the mouth.

"What're you crying about?" she whispered.

"It's just so beautiful," he said. "Two people in love."

Her blood became hot. Eleanor Hughes lost control of herself. There were some things that insulted a woman's pride so severely they could not be tolerated. She shot to her feet and started to exit the pew toward the side aisle.

"Eleanor," Jimmy whispered. "Where're you going?"

"I'm going to find the flower lady so I can deliver your heartfelt compliment."

Eleanor Hughes left the church and walked home by herself.

The Bottle Tree

Buz Guilford and his best friend, P.J., spent all day looking for his grandfather. The sun was rising over the little shops on Hydrangea, making long purple shadows on the pavement. People were going about their business; a couple of fourteen-year-olds were searching for the town drunk. They searched the main streets and side streets, driving his grandfather's rusted Ford, a vehicle the old man never used. A vehicle with a carburetor that was always giving Buz trouble. Sometimes the truck would spew black smoke out the back end. Other times the truck wouldn't start unless you simultaneously turned the key, kicked the dashboard, gritted your teeth, and said exactly four swear words.

Buz rolled through the mazes of clean, manicured, board-and-batten neighborhoods dotted with modest off-white homes, searching for a shabby old man wandering like a vagrant.

"Has he ever been missing for this long?" P.J. asked.

"Once," said Buz. "But we found him in Layton."

But this time felt different. His grandfather had been missing for three days. Someone said they thought he had gotten so blind drunk he'd waltzed into the river and drowned. Buz didn't believe this. Not at first. His grandfather never would have done anything so careless, not when the Dodgers had just beaten the Giants. But he was starting to wonder.

For the past few days, Buz had been looking for the old man in all his old haunts, and he'd found nothing. They checked the alleys behind downtown shops. He drove as far as the highway and even looked in the ditches because he promised his mother he would. He checked every driveway. He checked the henhouse behind J.R.'s Mercantile. His grandfather was not above stealing chickens from the mercantile. Or sleeping with the chickens when he was too pasted to make it home.

The old man teetered between being a happy drunk and a thief. And sometimes he could be a downright beggar. Buz's family skated the poverty line. More than once Buz had seen his staggering grandfather approach people in town and say, "Can you spare anything to eat, brother?" What his grandfather really meant by this was, "How about some money, pal?" But people rarely gave money; they usually bought him some food instead.

They stopped at the hardware store to ask Mister Baker if he'd seen any sign of the old soak. Mister Baker said he hadn't seen his grandfather in a few days and reminded Buz this was not the first time the old lush had gone missing and not to worry. But Mister Baker's words sounded hollow, as though the old shop owner didn't believe this any more than Buz did.

So he drove toward Stahlman Creek, where the dirt footpaths weaved back into the woods toward the river. He leapt out of the truck and followed a dirt trail into the forest. Long ago his grandfather used to bootleg whiskey in these hollers, back during the days when the Drys ran the world and the Wets made all the money. Today, however, these woods were just a place where Moab's club of drunk old men would gather. There were about four of them. Men who lived on booze and hated the taste of straight orange juice in the morning.

When he came to a clearing, he saw the familiar live oak tree in the distance. It was huge, with massive arms that dipped low to the ground. P.J. waited in the truck while Buz roamed the area around the herculean tree.

"Granddaddy?" said Buz. He'd been saying that one word all day. But there was no answer.

Rusted patio chairs were positioned in a haphazard semicircle beneath the oak, as though they had been there since the beginning of life itself. Colorful bottles swung from strings overhead in the branches. Buz had always wondered how so many bottles had gotten there. There must have been a billion of them.

He sat in one of the chairs and stared upward at the brightly colored glass. Then he pitched a small stick at one of the bottles and cussed his grandfather. The old man had ruined their lives. It was because of the old drunk that Buz had had to quit school to take a job earning money so he could help his mother pay the rent. It was because of his grandfather that his mother worked double shifts at the mill.

"Who's there?" said an old voice from above, in the tree.

Buz stood. "Granddaddy, is that you?"

The man's voice was old and weak. The voice laughed. "I ain't your granddaddy."

Buz looked into the sunlight, using his hand to block the white glare. He could see the shape of an old man straddling a limb, just about to teeter off. "Mister Hank? Is that you?"

"The one and only."

"I'm looking for my granddaddy. Have you seen him?"

The old man didn't answer right away. "We're all looking for him, Buz."

"Where'd you see him last, Mister Hank?"

Silence. The old man took a swig from a flat bottle.

"Mister Hank?"

A few moments passed before the old man said, "It was frogs, Buz. That what it was."

Buz walked beneath Mister Hank. His feet were dangling about ten feet above Buz's head. "Frogs? What're you talking about?"

Sniffling sounds came from the tree.

"What do frogs have to do with anything?"

The man was crying now. He was sobbing in that pathetic, self-important way all drunks do. "It was all Adam's idea, going frog gigging at two in the morning. It was all his idea."

"Frog gigging?" Buz said. "Where?"

The response was so soft Buz could barely hear it. "Pine Basin. One minute he was there . . ." The old man snapped his fingers. "The next minute he wasn't."

Buz didn't wait for the man to add anything. Instead, he trotted back down the trail toward the truck.

"Anything?" said P.J. "'Cause I'm getting hungry."

Buz threw the truck into reverse. "No. That old drunk can't even remember his name."

Old Hank was faster than he looked. The old man had followed Buz down the trail and appeared at the truck window, rapping on the glass.

"Wait!" the old man called out. The man's face was swollen from tears. He was breathless. "Are you gonna look for him?"

"At Pine Basin? What am I supposed to do, rent a helicopter?"

The old man half laughed. He nearly lost his footing.

"You're drunk, Hank. Go home."

He stood before Buz with a red nose and distant eyes. "Can you spare anything to eat, son? I'm so hungry."

Buz gave him a dollar.

MOAB SOCIAL GRACES

BY MARGIE BRACH

Miss Jeanne Walters and Mr. Sam Allen are engaged and announce plans for a January wedding. They will honeymoon in Miami. This is Sam's second marriage.

Miriam Boswell is making Brooklyn Dodgers jerseys for boys interested. $2 apiece.

Miss Anna Jordan accompanied Mr. Richard Hackle to the VFW dance in Mobile.

The Boy Scouts returned from Lake Shelby on Sunday where Billy Simms and Radney Walker swam across the lake and back, a distance of two miles.

Miss Rosalyn Dudley was a guest of Miss Margaret Flood of Andalusia recently.

Emmet Threet has returned from Detroit, Michigan, where he visited his brother, Earl, who is ill.

The Women's Missionary Society social dance and fundraiser will be held at Moab Methodist on August 21 to raise funds for hungry Soviet children.

Mr. and Mrs. Lynn Straits vacationed at their cabin in Orange Beach this week and called on their relatives from Milton, Mr. and Mrs. John Roberts of Ensley.

Mrs. Sandra Green inherited her Eternal Reward last Friday. Memorial service to be held at First Baptist.

The Moab baseball field is nearly completed. Lights were erected last week by Mark Laughlin, Sheriff Browne, and Jimmy Abraham. Little League tryouts to be announced. Young men interested must visit courthouse to apply.

Miss Eunice Freeman of Hoyt was a guest of Miss Mattie Hicks. "The deviled eggs were delicious," said Miss Mattie. "I made them."

A donation supper will be served August 24 at First Baptist. Chicken salad and other good things will be served—with or without walnuts.

Mrs. Wiley Shelford was called to Bellview Avenue in Andalusia on account of the death of her father, Preacher John Murphy, former pastor of Moab's First Baptist. He died in Brewton, Alabama.

The wedding of Susan Hughes and Lawrence Roney was held last Friday at Moab Methodist, officiated by Rev. Lewis, assisted by former Rev. Richard Wentz of Washington County. "The flowers were real pretty," said Mr. Jimmy Abraham.

Peanut-Butter Taffy

Sister Johanna had stopped to buy sandwiches for Jessie's three brothers at a gas station but refused to buy anything for Jessie after she slugged one of the boys so bad in the kneecap that he was walking with a limp. Johanna told her she would just have to go without.

The boys ate in front of her and made a big show of it. They peeled the bread crust from their sandwiches and threw it at Jessie and called her names under their breath. They'd been acting like brats, and she was about sick of it. The oldest boy was the worst. He had been taunting her all afternoon. He was asking for it.

"You're a bastard," said the oldest in a sing-songy voice. "A bastard, bastard, bastard."

"Shut up, Jacob," said Sister Johanna.

"Look at the little bastard eat her bread crust."

Sister Johanna growled. "Jacob!" She looked tired and ragged. The woman had been driving since sunrise and her eyes were drooping. Nobody spoke to each other. Not even when Sister Johanna pulled over for everyone to use the bathroom in the woods.

Jessie walked into the forest to take care of business, far away from her brothers, and started to cry. She had considered making a run for it, but there was nothing around for miles. So she trudged back to the car, adjusting her black dress and trying to keep herself calm.

But when she saw her brothers digging through her open suitcase, splayed on the ground, with her clothes lying every which way, Jessie was through playing nice. And when she discovered they had found her three remaining Mary Janes and had eaten them, *and had confiscated her aggies and her shooters*, that did it.

Jessie marched toward them and tackled Jacob, who already had a mouthful of Mary Janes. Then she dealt with the others. She laid her fist into Isaac's nose. Blood came from his nostrils. Ishmael tried to pull her off Isaac, but she was stronger than he was. Much stronger. She was also a better first baseman than he was.

She landed a few shots into Isaac's belly and he went down under the power.

"Stop it, Jessie!" shouted Sister Johanna, who was trying to yank Jessie away, but she was too late. Jessie was not to be stopped.

Then Jessie straddled the taffy-chewing offender and used her hand to pry open Jacob's jaw. She reached her fingers into his mouth and removed a wad of caramel-colored peanut-butter chew, dripping with saliva, and she ate it in front of him. When she had swallowed it, she brought her nose close to Jacob's and said, "Nobody touches my stuff, do you hear me? Nobody."

Then, just because she wanted everyone to know she meant business, she pried the shooter free from Isaac's fingers and threw it as hard as she could at Ishmael. The shooter landed right where she intended for it to. And it would be a miracle if he ever walked upright again, or fathered children.

They quit calling her names after that.

Fifty-Four Points

Winston was drinking an orange Nehi, dabbing sweat from his forehead, trying with all his brainpower to find a way to use the triple-word score on the board.

Moab's summer mornings came with the heat of a veritable West Floridian hell. J.R.'s Mercantile was slow because it was a Tuesday, and Tuesdays were always slow. Jimmy was lucky if he sold so much as a Mary Jane on Tuesdays. The inside of the old brick-faced storefront was filled with sweating old men sitting in wooden chairs, busy doing what idle men in Moab did every morning. Which was . . . Well, Winston wasn't sure what exactly they did. But they did *something.* And whatever it was, they never skipped a morning of doing it.

Scrabble was a big deal in Moab right now, so this morning it was Scrabble.

Winston glanced across the street. Arty was lying beneath the old Packard, the county's second squad car, which had been parked in front of the courthouse since the close of the Civil War. Arty's shoes were poking from beneath the vehicle, bobbing to whatever music was playing on the Packard's radio. He would never fix that car. Arty never actually *fixed* anything. He always ran into a snag and told customers he had to order parts. So nobody ever got any automobiles fixed in Moab. They had to go to Layton or Pensacola.

The Packard would sit there for another hundred and fifty years, and Okeauwaw County would be down to its one patrol car, with a siren that didn't work and a moderately incompetent deputy, Tommy Sheridan, who ended every radio transmission with "Four-ten, Sheriff."

"Hey!" said Jimmy. "It's your move. I ain't gonna live forever, you know. The whole point is to *play* the dang game, Win, not *look* out the window."

Winston Browne stared at his letters. He rearranged the tiles a few times, then squinted at the board again. Scrabble was one of his best games, but he was a slow player.

"Come on," Jimmy said, patting the table. "While we're young, Win."

"Don't rush me."

He looked out the window again. Hydrangea Street was perfect in the sunlight. The multicolored awnings. The faded blue-and-white Miller's Drugstore sign, dangling over the sidewalk, unmoving in the breezeless purgatory. The two white clapboard chapels, competing for Glory. And of course, staring right back at Winston was the new neon sign over Ray's Cafe, which everyone hated with purple passion. Every night and early morning, the ill-favored sign glowed like neon-colored vomit in the dark.

"Winston, *go*! I'm gonna start using a dang timer."

"Watch your language, Jimmy," said Winston. "A man's character can be learned from the adjectives he uses in conversation."

"What's that supposed to mean?" said Jimmy.

"Mark Twain said that," said Winston.

Jimmy did not move a facial muscle. "Oh yeah? Well, what'd old Samuel Clemens say about punching a sheriff who takes too long to play Scrabble?"

Winston only rubbed his chin, lit another Lucky, filled the air with blue smoke, and rearranged his letters. "When was the last time anyone saw Adam Guilford?" he asked the group.

"Few days ago," said Alvin, who was leaning over Winston's shoulder. "Mister Hank and him bought some gigs and told me they were going frog gigging. You wouldn't have wanted to light a match within ten feet of those two."

Daryl said, "I heard he fell in the water while they were gigging. I heard Mister Hank looked for him but couldn't find him."

"Fell in?" said Winston. "Why hasn't anyone told me about this? I haven't heard that."

"Probably because Hank also claims he met Tennessee Williams once."

Jimmy let out a groan. "For the love of golf, Win! This game ain't supposed to take ten years. Veterinary school goes by quicker than this."

"Temper, temper," said Odie. "Maybe *that's* why Eleanor's so mad at you."

"Mad?" Jimmy said. "Who told you Ellie's mad?"

"Don't play dumb with us," Winston said. "Eleanor told Hilda Mae that she was furious with you. Hilda told Myra and Myra told Beatrice, who told me this morning."

"You never know with women," said Odie. "Maybe Eleanor's just having her *time of the year*."

"Time of the *year*?" said Alvin. "It's *month*, you dummy."

"Not with my wife," said Odie. "Her last mood swing lasted for almost twelve years."

Winston placed his letters onto the board. The men got silent. They puffed their leather-scented smoke and frowned in unison.

"*Bullock*," announced Winston, admiring his word. "Triple word score, fifty-four points." A new record for him.

Jimmy's face tightened. He had always been a sore loser, so

Winston didn't bask in his success for long. Instead, he stood from the table and stretched his arms upward in a yawn. He coughed several times until his throat felt like raw hamburger.

"Hey," said Daryl, "you're bleeding, Win. Under your arm."

Winston already knew he was bleeding. He'd forgotten to change the bandage this morning. "Got to go, fellas. Promised I'd help Tom Hicks frame his backyard fence today. Little League practice is tonight. Don't forget to bring the chalk bags, Jimmy. We're laying the baselines."

"You can't lay down a fifty-four pointer and leave the game," Jimmy said.

Winston reached into his pocket and put a golden foil-covered chocolate coin onto the table. "Here's your winnings, Jimmy."

"I don't want your stupid candy." Jimmy flicked it away.

"That ain't candy, Jimmy. That's a million bucks in sugar." Winston was already stepping off the porch and trotting into the street, half laughing, half coughing. He waved goodbye to the old men between coughs.

"What am I, twelve years old?" he heard Jimmy say.

Alvin said, "What's gotten into you, Jimmy? Is it your time of the *year*?"

The Packard sat in the morning light. Arty had already collected his tools and abandoned the broken-down vehicle.

Winston stopped beside the old hunk of metal and rested a hand on the car. It had been his faithful squad car for ten years, ever since he had accepted the role of a lawman for Moab after the war. "I know how you feel, old girl. The doctors can't fix me either."

Shirts and Skins

The scalped alfalfa field behind the Guilfords' dilapidated house was nothing but golden summer stubble. Dead stalks, dry and tough, ready for a game of baseball. Buz was working on the truck's carburetor, which had started giving him problems. It was always giving him problems. He leaned into the hood of the old Ford. Behind him was the wide pasture. Between turns of his ratchet, he watched the Roberson kids play a game after school, Shirts against Skins.

His house was empty, and Buz was alone. Same as usual. His mother was working late that night, his grandfather either vanished or dead. And if Buz couldn't fix this carburetor, this truck would be a goner and his mother would have to start walking four miles to work. And a woman whose legs were marred by the childhood effects of polio had no business walking four miles.

The Robersons always played ball in the field behind their house with their happy cousins, even if the alfalfa was high. It didn't matter to them if the grass came up to their shoulders. They were like everyone else in town, obsessed with the game. Buz loved baseball too, and would have enjoyed the luxury of playing it the way they did, with a kind of carefree spirit. But he was not like them. He was a dropout, and older than they were, even though they were the same age. He worked for Mister Arnold baling hay, feeding his hogs, or clearing fields while they sat in classrooms. Everyone's parents were bent out of shape that he was not in school, but a man had to do what a man had to do.

He couldn't have been more different from regular kids. They had real mothers and fathers and nice shoes on their feet. Buz had a working mom, a drunk who lived in the back bedroom, and a pair of black Chuck Taylors with holes in the soles. They played baseball for fun. Buz did man's work all day. Whenever he played baseball, he was playing for self-pride.

The Robersons were screaming and laughing in the distance, playing their game with loud mouths and happy voices. The rules were loose, and there weren't enough players to do anything more than hit, run, and repeat. They used big rocks for bases, which was just asking for a broken ankle. It also made it more interesting for Buz to watch.

Frankie Roberson noticed Buz under the hood of the Ford and came loping across the field. Frankie was a Yankee man. Buz was a Dodger sympathizer. The two were on opposite sides of the war. Even so, when the team was short a man, any player would do.

Frankie approached the driveway. The kids always sent Frankie; he was the most amiable. "Hey, Buz," said Frankie, scrawny and shirtless, covered in a thin film of sweat.

"Hey, Frankie."

"Wanna play with us?"

Buz shook his head.

"I heard about your granddaddy. Anyone found him yet?"

Drunks were the closest thing small towns had to legends. The only characters brave enough to have larger-than-life personalities and dumb enough to have the adventures to go with them. Everyone had heard *something* about his grandfather.

"Not yet."

"Gosh, do you think he's okay?" Frankie was being polite.

"I can't play baseball with you tonight, Frankie."

"We could use one more man. Then we'd be six on six. Nobody can hit like you."

"I gotta cook supper."

"Just thirty minutes? Won't be long. We need you. I'm sick of losing to my cousin Chad. He's always rubbing it in."

Frankie was laying it on thick because kids don't accept no for an answer. He sweetened the deal. "I have an extra glove, Buz." Everyone knew Buz didn't have his own glove.

"Frankie."

"Please."

Buz envisioned his grandfather, facedown in the mire. Or legless from a run-in with a railcar. He pictured the old man being torn apart by alligators or dangling from some tree. He wanted to cry. He thought of the waste the old man's life had been.

Buz crawled out from beneath the hood and wiped his greasy hands on a rag. "Thirty minutes," he said. "But that's *all*."

They played until midnight, beneath the glow of the nearby house lights, long after the ball had become almost invisible in the dark. Skins beat Shirts, 43–28.

The U.S. Male

Jimmy stepped onto the porch of the Wannamaker house carrying the mailbag over his shoulder. He was sweating through his blue mail carrier's shirt, and his pants were sagging. The Wannamaker home was a plump white house with green shutters and all the colorful flowers anyone could ask for. Its porch, with its ferns and rocking chairs, was an invitation into the world of gracious living. The two Wannamaker children were wrestling in the front yard on the trim grass. They waved to Jimmy. He tipped his safari hat to them.

When Mrs. Wannamaker opened the door, she was not smiling. She didn't even say hello. "Six days," was all she said. "Six whole days since I've had mail, Jimmy."

"I know, ma'am. I'm sorry. I've been a little behind. Staffing problems."

"A *little*?"

He presented her a stack of mail as thick as a Buick Roadmaster. He didn't bother to explain. There was no need; he'd been explaining himself ever since the U.S. Mail boats quit running the length of the Escambia River and had moved strictly to highway and train routes. Jimmy's workload as postmaster had tripled, then he'd lost two lazy mail carriers. He had gotten so backed up that all he ever did was sort mail.

People in Moab, even old high school friends, now wanted Jimmy Abraham skinned alive. Moabites took their mail even more seriously than, say, the threat of a Soviet nuclear war. "You got a card from your sister. She's pregnant. And your aunt from Andalusia says hi."

He tipped his hat once more and made a grand exit. Jimmy weaved his way through the quiet neighborhoods of single-story homes with manicured lawns and thick-bodied live oaks. Nobody waved to him except children. Which suited him just fine. He was doing his best to avoid contact with anyone, just in case someone tried to kill him with a length of piano wire.

Jimmy crept onto each porch, slipping mail into mailboxes and darting off the steps, half expecting to hear gunfire behind him. Occasionally someone would give him the stink eye. But—knock on wood—there had been no heavy artillery yet.

When he arrived at Eleanor's house, the last house on Evergreen Avenue, he removed his hat and clomped onto the porch for a rest. He always rested at Eleanor's house. Often she would have iced tea waiting for him. But not in the past days. He'd done something to tick the woman off, but he had no idea what. The only thing he knew was that whatever it was, it had something to do with flowers.

He sat on the steps and wiped his face. Eleanor's wraparound porch was swarming with children on roller skates. Her house was the best place in Moab to roller-skate. The wide, gray porch circled around the home, uninterrupted, like a racetrack. A group of teenage girls lingered on the porch swing among a jungle of potted ferns and daisies, still wearing their heavy skates. He waved at the girls. They waved back. They were growing faster than perennials. He could remember when they were toddlers, eating marmalade sandwiches. Now they were little ladies. One day they would even be old enough to hate him, just like everyone else in Moab.

He heard a voice behind him. Female. Monotone. "What do you want, Jimmy?"

Jimmy sprang to his feet. He approached the front door to find Eleanor behind the screen. She did not have any tea.

"Leave my porch, please, sir," she said.

Sir? Jimmy was no rocket scientist, but he detected a little hostility.

"How are you, Ellie? I haven't seen you in days. I've been worried about you. You don't return my calls, you don't answer the door, you don't—"

"You can put my mail in the box and go."

He put the letters in the box, but he didn't go. Not yet. "What time should we leave on Friday?"

Ice-cold silence. Not a good sign.

"I'm not going," she said. "You can leave whenever you want."

"Not going?"

"Are you hard of hearing?" Eleanor offered nothing more. She started to close the front door.

He lurched forward and placed a foot between the door and the jamb. "Come on, Ellie. You can't skip the social. You've worked so hard fixing up the church with all those chrysanthemums and Shasta daisies and daylilies, and did I spy some Japanese anemones in the fellowship hall flower beds?" Jimmy had taken out a book about flowers from the library.

She didn't answer.

"I promise," Jimmy went on, "once the social is over, you can go back to hating me again, sweetie. But give me a chance to make it up to you."

"I don't hate you. I just want to be alone right now."

"Can I pick you up at six forty-five?"

"I said no, Jimmy."

"Six forty-seven?"

"Jimmy."

"Six forty-eight?"

"Get off my porch."

"Ellie, I miss you." And he meant it. Nothing had been right since she'd quit him. "Please, I'll do anything to make things right. Tell me what I did wrong, and I won't do it again. Are those Boston ferns or Kimberly Queens?"

"You haven't *done* anything, Jimmy. And that's just the problem with you. You never *do* anything, at least not where I'm concerned."

This was code for something, but it wasn't penetrating Jimmy's frontal lobe. He knew enough to tread lightly, though. "Let me get this straight. You're saying I have done *nothing*? And you're mad about something I *haven't* done?"

"That's right."

This woman was speaking in riddles. The hidden language of womanhood was a mystery to him. He tried to think of anything, anything at all to say. But he kept coming up short. "Ellie, I'm such a fool. Can you forgive me?" This usually worked. Women loved to hear a man admit he was stupid.

"Yes, you are a fool."

"Does that mean you forgive me?"

Eleanor sighed. She nudged open the screen door and stepped onto the porch. She removed her mail from the box. "I'll make you a deal, Jimmy. You meet me in front of Miller's and you can escort me to the social. I'm not gonna be your date this year, but we can walk together. That's it."

"Walk together? Meet you at Miller's?"

She bid him good day, walked inside, and shut the door in his face, leaving him standing on the porch with nothing but the terracotta pots of Bellis perennis and Lilium orientalis.

Gold Buttons

The crowded train depot platform was orange in the late-afternoon sunlight. Swarms of young men in hats, women in floral-print dresses, and attendants in black uniforms with gold buttons were crawling all over the place. Jessie had never seen anything like it before.

Over the last few days the main thing she noticed were all the strange objects of the secular world. And too many smells, so many Jessie couldn't concentrate on any particular one. She closed her eyes and tried to take them all in. Hot peanuts, perfume, tobacco smoke, exhaust fumes.

Sister Johanna placed an envelope into Jessie's skirt pocket along with her train ticket. She looked Jessie in the eyes with an icy glare. "You are to destroy this letter and place it into the latrine when you finish reading. Do you understand me?"

Jessie nodded.

"I need to hear you promise, Jessie."

"I promise."

The woman was jumpy, looking both ways as though she expected sudden danger at any moment.

"Sister Johanna," Jessie asked for the hundredth time, "what're we doing here? Where're we going?"

She lowered herself to Jessie's eye level and said, "*We* aren't going anywhere, *you* are. Ada is my oldest friend, and if anything happens to you it will ruin her. Now, I want you to memorize the words I am about to say to you, Jessie. Are you listening?"

Halfheartedly, yes. Everything going on around her was thrilling and interesting.

"When you get off the train in Savannah, someone will meet you and ride the next train with you. It will probably be a woman named Sister Ella. She's tall and has red hair. She's Ada's baby sister, and she's going to take you somewhere safe. But they might send someone else, if it's too dangerous for Ella to come. Whoever it is, this person will say these exact words. Are you listening? The person will say, 'Isn't this a chilly night, kiddo?' Just like that. Now say it back to me."

Jessie said, "I'm scared. What's happening? Where am I going?"

Johanna gripped her shoulders. "Say it back to me, *Kleinerin.*"

"Isn't this a chilly night?" Jessie sighed. "This is dumb."

Johanna squeezed her harder. "'*Kiddo.*' Word for word, Jessie. '*Isn't this a chilly night, kiddo?*' You have to say the whole thing."

Jessie repeated it.

Sister Johanna released her. "If anyone says this to you and is off one single word, do not trust this person, Jessie. You run. Do you hear me? Run. Now say it back to me again, one more time."

She said it again, but it was more of a mumble.

Once Sister Johanna was satisfied Jessie knew the phrase backward, forward, and sideways, she pushed Jessie onto the steps of the train. The fear began to sink in. She'd held it at bay, but now it was overflowing the dam. They were sending her away.

"Where's Savannah?" she asked Sister Johanna. "Please don't make me go! I'm sorry! Please! I'll be good!"

People nearby were looking at Jessie, gawking. Sister Johanna did nothing, said nothing. She turned and began to walk away. It took the woman a few seconds to disappear.

"Sister Johanna, please!"

An old man in a uniform with gold buttons helped Jessie to a seat near the front of the train. He patted her head and said, "Don't be sad, sweetheart, you'll see your family again."

"No, I don't think I will." And they weren't her family.

He smiled, then sat in the seat beside her. He reached into his pocket and removed a fist. "If you quit crying, I'll give you a prize."

She was skeptical. She didn't know who she could trust after what Johanna had said. But then, he had said he had a prize. She quit crying and looked at his fist.

"Hold out your hand," he said.

She made no moves.

"Come on. Hold it out, I'm not gonna bite you. It's a long way to Savannah, so we might as well be friends."

Jessie held her hand open. He placed a Mary Jane into her palm, then winked at her. "Now don't let that taffy ruin your teeth, kiddo."

No News Is Good News

Winston Browne sat in the sterile white doctor's waiting room, bouncing his knees. He was about to vomit from pure nerves. He hated doctors' offices.

Music came from a radio in the corner, playing the stringy sounds of either Les Baxter or Henry Mancini, or one of those big-time musicians who looked like a car salesman or a dentist. The taste of disinfectant filled the room. People in chairs read outdated magazines. A receptionist refused to make eye contact with anyone.

Beside Winston sat a woman and a young boy. The kid swung his legs beneath his chair and read a comic book. Winston smiled at the kid. The child smiled back.

"What're you in for?" Winston asked the boy.

"Broke my ankle a few weeks ago."

Lucky kid. Winston would have much rather been suffering from an ankle problem right now.

Doctors' offices were their own kind of purgatory. He'd endured gunfire in muddy European trenches and he'd captained teenagers across acres of farmland littered with antipersonnel mines. But he was frightened by a little old man in a white frock coat.

He looked out the office window at Pensacola. It was the biggest city anyone from Moab had ever known, except for Mobile. Compared to Okeauwaw County, Pensacola was practically Chicago. The huge Gayfer's department store, the two movie theaters, the interesting foreign-food restaurants. In Pensacola, a man could eat at a Chinese restaurant every night of the week if he wanted. Astounding. In Pensacola, a man could get his car fixed on the *same day* he took it in. Unbelievable. He had almost moved here once, for a girl. She still lived on Brent Lane, not far from here. She had married a preacher while Winston was fighting in the war, carrying her picture in his sweat-stained photo wallet.

A woman in a nursing uniform appeared in the doorway. Winston smiled. She glanced at a clipboard and said, "The doctor will see you now, Mister . . ." She paused to check the page. "Browne?"

Winston stood, crumpled hat in his hand. He wore his civilian clothes today and hoped he wouldn't be recognized. He followed the nurse into the back room where she measured his height and weighed him on a scale. He had lost nine pounds since his last visit. This weight loss seemed to concern her. Before she wrote his weight onto a clipboard, she looked at his boots and seemed to be making mental notes.

"Outdoorsman?" she asked.

These kinds of forced pleasantries in a whitewashed doctor's office made him feel even more sick to his stomach.

"You've seen me three times in the last three months—you already know everything about me. I'm kinda surprised you haven't invited me to Thanksgiving yet."

She did not laugh. She just said, "What's your job, please? I need it for our records."

"Professional babysitter."

She shook her head in a way that suggested she didn't care. "You didn't list any immediate family members, Mister Browne. I have to list someone."

"I have no immediate family."

The words sort of stuck in the air.

She said, "What about a close relative or friend?"

"You know any who want to apply for the job?"

"Mister Browne, I need one emergency contact phone number. It's policy."

So Winston gave her the phone number of the Moab courthouse, which seemed to satisfy her. Then she led him to a tiny room. The walls were puke green, plastered with posters of the human skeleton and colorful illustrations of bodily organs. This made Winston uncomfortable. He hated this place, and he was uneasy around medical people. Doctors were always telling you that you were sick even when you felt fine. Doctors always needed to run experiments on you, the same way a little kid needed to take apart a wind-up toy using nothing but a sledgehammer.

Doctor Rogers came into the room. He was a polished man with thick-rimmed glasses. He wore a tweed suit beneath his lab coat, and his hair was glued to his head with Brylcreem. "Mister Browne, how are we doing today?"

We.

The man opened a folder and scanned it for a few minutes before he let his eyes meet Winston's. He wore a phony smile that made Winston's heart beat faster. Fake smiles were not good.

"How do you like this weather?" Doctor Rogers asked.

Winston laughed. "I don't wanna talk weather, Doc. Just get down to business and tell me what's wrong."

The doctor tossed the folder onto the nearby chair, then folded his hands. "Mister Browne, I'm afraid the test results came back not good. The biopsy was . . ." He paused. An entire lifetime went by. "*Malignant*, Mister Browne. The mass in your lungs is malignant. If the test results are correct, then this is . . . this is not good."

The air went ice cold. "Malignant," was all he could say. He said it a few more times.

"Mister Browne, that's just a medical word that means the cells are dividing uncontrollably, and they keep dividin—"

"I *know* what malignant means, Doc. I might be a hayseed, but I'm not a fool. How bad is it?"

"Depends. Let's start with that cough. Is it getting worse or better?"

"I asked how bad it was."

"Can't say how bad. I need one more test to be sure. And this one will be even more invasive than your last one. You didn't answer me about that cough."

"You're gonna stab me with one of those things again?"

"A trocar. Yes, just to be sure."

"How many more times are you gonna poke me in the lungs before you can give me a final answer?"

"Mister Browne, I just want us both to have all the facts before I tell you anything conclusive."

Winston placed a hand over his eyes. He was feeling dizzy. His ears were ringing. He had an uncontrollable urge to keep swallowing, which led to coughing. The doctor placed a stethoscope against Winston's chest, listening to his lungs. Then he looked at Winston's fingernails. Winston pushed the man away.

"Please just say it outright, Doctor Rogers. I don't wanna keep wondering for another eight weeks what's happening inside me."

"Okay, Mister Browne . . ." A long, pregnant pause. "Okay."

Crickets.

"Well, I'd say it's time to break the news to your loved ones, Mister Browne. The tumor is inoperable. I would suggest now is the time to get your affairs in order, maybe make some final arrangements with your family."

Inoperable. Winston covered his mouth and squeezed his lips in his hand. He tried to speak, but instead he began to cry. He didn't mean to; it just happened. Soon he was bawling into his hands, sobbing harder than he had in a long time. His palms became wet, and his nasal passages became so swollen he couldn't breathe.

"Family," said Winston into his hands.

Moab was still asleep, but Sheriff Winston Browne wasn't. Hydrangea Street was dark except for the pink-and-green neon sign above Ray's Café. Winston sat at his desk, staring at the hideous sign through the paned glass. He hadn't moved a muscle in a few hours. All he had done was sit. He was numb. He didn't know whether to feel scared, mad, or heartbroken. So he just did his best not to feel. Which was an awful lot like trying to ignore a hurricane while it ripped the world apart.

Winston lifted a hardback book from the courthouse desk drawer and thumbed it open. *Life on the Mississippi* was one of his favorites. Samuel Clemens always put him in a better frame of mind, but nothing was better than the man's memoir. He'd carried the book during a world war, marching across a foreign continent, watching nineteen-year-olds die. The book usually made him laugh, or feel something deeper than a laugh. And during wartime, this was nothing short of miraculous. He'd read it by lantern light. He'd read it in foxholes. It had kept his heart in America even though he was away fighting a European war. Even now, Winston could not—he *would* not—go to sleep unless he'd read a few pages by his favorite man.

But this morning the book seemed trivial. Stupid even. Besides, what good was a book to a dead man? Winston couldn't explain why the urge came upon him so abruptly. He threw the hardback against the wall. It came apart, splaying into a few pieces onto the floor. And almost as if on cue, he heard another smack on the courthouse door. The paperboy delivering the news.

The rolled-up *Moab Messenger* arrived each morning, not long after whatever time the delivery boy du jour crawled out of bed. Winston unfolded the paper and tried reading about the social happenings according to Margie Brach, but it all seemed so shallow. If there was one thing Moabites were fixated on, it was themselves. The rest of the world and all its issues were imaginary.

He flipped to the obituaries. He always read the obits, the announcements, and the gossip column. It was an elected official's duty to know who had been born, married, buried, nominated, praised, criticized, and honored. Of course, as Moab's coroner, he already knew who had died, how, and the exact time of death. But the obituaries were different. They were written by family members; they were heartfelt and dramatic.

One obituary read, "Sister Cleveland Hetta Gruene has inherited her Eternal Reward." Another stated, "Mrs. Jacqueline Gallard has gone on to Glory . . ." Winston stared at these sentences until he forgot he was even holding a newspaper.

Gone on to Glory. He'd read and heard that phrase a hundred million times in his life. That was how the preacher said it. That was how old friends would refer to it. The *Moab Messenger* obituaries always said it this way too. But what did glory have to do with anything? Take a big-city newspaper like the *News Journal* or the *Mobile Press-Register.* They never would have worded it that way. A big paper would have said something like, "So-and-So died of a heart attack and was survived by her husband and two children." Just the facts. No frills. Cold. Because to them dressing up death was like putting high heels on a donkey, slapping its rear, and telling it to do the foxtrot. No matter what the donkey did, it was still an ass. But not in Moab.

Not in this one-horse town. Here, nobody ever *died.* At least not in print. They went on to *Glory.* It was ridiculous. But then the *Moab Messenger* was the kind of paper that published recurring stories about Larry Herrington's prize red angus heifer.

Winston wadded the paper into a ball and chucked it into his wastebasket. No matter how they gussied it up, dying was the pits. Your casket was shoved into a pile of loose dirt and millions of earthworms made a buffet out of your body. There was no *glory* in it.

He walked to the edge of the room to pick up the floppy pieces of *Life on the Mississippi.* He felt so sorry for what he'd done to his faithful hardbound friend. He glued it back together, then sandwiched the book in place between *The Adventures of Tom Sawyer* and a few encyclopedias. Winston hadn't meant to be so cruel to old Samuel. In many ways, Sam was the only family he had left.

He walked outside to see the sun come up. It was an uncharacteristically chilly Floridian morning, fifty degrees and fogless. He breathed it all in, the sappy air, fragrant with the smells of foliage. The town was quiet but already humming with its pre-day energy.

Throughout his life and career, he'd seen enough senseless tragedies to know that wallowing in self-pity was a death sentence in itself. Some folks never quit wallowing once they started, and it killed them early. Self-pity was like a dangerous painkiller; it felt good somehow, but it turned you into its slave. So he made a promise to himself, right there, right then. He was not going to wallow. Not anymore. One morning of wallowing was enough. Winston Browne was going to live right up until he died.

He wiped two warm tears from the corners of his eyes, then jogged across the street to join his morning Scrabble game at the mercantile. On his way he saw a red dog trot past him, waltzing right down the middle of Hydrangea. It was Adam's dog.

"You," Winston said to the animal.

The dog trotted faster.

Winston whistled for the animal, but it ignored him. In some ways, it behaved a lot like the old drunk. Indifferent, a little oblivious. Winston followed the animal, hoping it would lead to Adam. He forgot all about Scrabble. He knew enough about dogs to know that if you chased them, they ran faster, so he tailed the dog, keeping his distance. The animal led him throughout the quiet neighborhoods and backyards, across the entire blamed town.

Soon the sheriff's ribs hurt, and his shirt was drenched in cool sweat. He had to stop to cough. The fit overtook him. The doc had stabbed him under the arm again, and it burned even worse than the last time. He leaned against a tree in Luke Jacobson's yard to catch his breath. Luke, who was watering his front flower beds, waved at him from the porch. Winston waved back.

"You all right, Win?" said Luke, killing the hose.

"I'm fine," hollered Winston in the cheerful voice of a politician. "Just getting old is all."

Then, for pride's sake, he squelched his cough and resumed following the red dog. His lungs felt like they were in a bench vise. This animal was going to kill him.

Now it had become a contest. He was locked in a battle with this dog. He had spent too much of his morning chasing the animal to give up now. Still, no matter how competitive Winston Browne's nature, his body was failing him. He followed the thing past Evergreen Avenue, Camellia Street, Peach Street, and clear over to Frond Circle. He'd been following the dog for almost two miles now, maybe more, and his airways were closing. His throat felt no bigger than a sippy straw.

On Lantana Avenue, he doubled over, gagging on his own wind. He'd never had a breathing attack this bad. He sat on the grass, looking up at the sky. He was wheezing to beat the band. "Forget it, you stupid dog. I give up."

When he caught his breath, he walked back to his house on Terrence Street. The little white house his father had built for his mother with his own two hands. His father, the German immigrant who came into Pensacola's port with ten bucks to his name.

The dog followed Winston home. When Winston reached his own porch, he collapsed in the rocking chair. He was just trying to breathe now. He looked up to see the dog.

"You dumb dog. You won, fair and square. Go on, you can consider this a legal pardon."

The dog didn't move, just sat beside Winston. So Winston ran his hands along its greasy red coat. The dog's fur was caked with mud and heaven only knew what else. The animal looked right at him, which was rare for a dog. Most animals wouldn't look a man in the eyes. There was something honest about this, something otherworldly. He fuzzed the dog's fur and said, "I'm dying."

He heard his own words with his own ears, and they cut him. It was the first time he'd said it out loud. And it felt good to say it because at least he was telling the truth.

"I'm dying," he said again.

Pretty Handwriting

It was almost too much for Jessie to take in. The green velvet curtains, the soft red seats, the golden trim work. She didn't want to forget a single moment of this train ride. She might never get another one. Her fear of the secular world and all its horrors had not disappeared, but so far she'd discovered the heathens weren't very different from sanctified people. But they wore loud colors, wonderful hats, and shoes that seemed to shine. In some ways the infidels seemed more at ease with themselves than the temple brethren.

She had been repeating the phrase Johanna taught her until she was tired of saying it under her breath. *"Isn't this a chilly night, kiddo?"*

The scenery outside the windows was full of trees, fields, horses, cows, barns, rivers, and valleys. She had no idea the secular world was so big. Her whole life had been spent surrounded by the sun-squelching woods of the temple community with its rickety homesteads and acres of fences. This was wide-open farmland and sunlight. It was so perfect it didn't look real.

A man in a gray suit was sitting beside her. He was asleep, his hat over his face. She could see his chest rising and falling. His clothes were magnificent. Much fancier than anything anyone in the community ever wore. His suit had a faint white striping. He wore a silver wristwatch. She had never seen one of those before, so she brought her face as close to the little watch as she could without disturbing him.

The old train attendant with golden buttons caught her looking. He tapped her shoulder and whispered, "If you wanted to know the time, all you have to do is ask." He removed a golden pocket watch and showed it to her. Jessie didn't know how long she had been on the train. It had stopped many times and stayed put for long stretches. People got on and off. There was lots of noise and rumbling. She'd fallen asleep for hours at a time.

Gold Buttons gave her a sandwich and a glass bottle of brown milk. She couldn't believe her luck. This was the third time he'd given her food. A girl could get used to this. "What's this brown stuff?" she whispered to Buttons.

He leaned in close. "Haven't you ever had Ovaltine?"

Oval-*what*? She sniffed it. Jessie had tasted chocolate before, certainly, and she was an appreciator of milk. But Ovaltine? She took a sip. It was like heaven in her mouth..

Sometimes Ada snuck chocolate into the temple school, but only for special occasions, like Jessie's birthday. If someone got caught with chocolate, it was worse than getting caught with a *National Geographic* magazine, even though those had naked pictures of tribal people in them. Nothing was as bad as a woman cutting her hair, however. Her friend Rebeka, who was seventeen, had been flogged with cane rods for getting her hair done at a salon when she was in town. The salon had cut eight inches off her hair. Rebeka was removed from temple school immediately, her head was shaved, and she was exiled. The last time Jessie saw Rebeka, the girl was tanned and leathery from working outside so much and covered in bruises. Rebeka wasn't allowed to speak to Jessie.

She took another sip of the Ovaltine and moaned. Jessie knew what she wanted to do with the rest of her life. She wanted to drink all the chocolate Ovaltine on planet Earth. She moaned again. The noise just slipped out of her. The sleeping man in the seat next to her awoke and gave her an ugly look. She offered him part of her sandwich, but he was uninterested. The man got up and stormed to the back of the car, where he slumped in a seat and placed his hat over his face again.

She smelled under her arms to make sure she didn't offend.

After she finished her sandwich, she wandered into the train bathroom. The room was tiny, and the little sink was no bigger than a gravy pot. She sat on the toilet, dug into her skirt pocket, and unfolded the letter Johanna had given her. She had already read it so many times she could have recited it. The dim light attached to the wall was not strong enough to read by.

The letter was in Ada's handwriting. Jessie would know that pretty handwriting anywhere; it was curly and feminine. Jessie wished she could write like that, but her handwriting always came out looking like she'd been holding a crayon between her toes.

Dearest Jessie,

I already miss you, but we shall be together again, my love. You are sleeping as I write this, and I am beside your bed. You are my beautiful girl.

Tomorrow morning you will leave me, but only for a little while. Do not be frightened. This is for your own good. There are those who would seek to harm us because of something sinful I have done. I will join you soon. We will start a new life in a new place. I ask the Almighty to preserve me so that I may be with you again. I'm sorry I could not come with you now, but it is safer this way.

There is something I want to tell you. I have yearned to tell you for your entire life, but could not speak it without endangering us both. If something bad should befall me, and I do not see you again, I want you to know the truth. I am your mother. You are of my flesh and of my own blood. I ask your forgiveness for hiding this from you.

Remember that I am with you always, even until my own life ends, and long thereafter.

Your mother,

Ada

Jessie folded the note. Her eyes were as wet as they had been the first time she read it. She made it very small, then tossed the letter into the toilet. She pulled the lever. A swirl of water washed it down the bowl. But it couldn't erase the words from her mind.

"Isn't this a chilly night, kiddo?" she said beneath her breath.

Nine by Twelve

Moab was flawless in the early evenings, when there wasn't enough daylight to see imperfection but just enough to see its beauty. The sky was dark red. Somewhere in the world a sailor was delighted because of that sky. The shop windows of Moab were curtained for Friday night. The sidewalks were rolled up. Hydrangea was vacant.

Eleanor Hughes sat on the bench outside Miller's Drugstore beneath the tin Coca-Cola sign swinging overhead. She was sweating even though it wasn't hot. She removed a bulletin from her pocketbook and fanned herself. The end-of-summer social would be beginning right about now, and Jimmy was late. She should have gone without him, but she had never been one to pass up a chance at martyrdom. An unmarried woman got so few opportunities for this.

These sweating episodes were happening more often. They were lasting longer too. It was miserable. Sweat dripped down her back and made her clammy all over. She willed herself to stop perspiring, but it wasn't working. It was as though her insides were being deep fried in peanut oil. Her face was on fire. Her nose was slick. Her hair was getting damp around the forehead. And she was miffed.

She wiped her forehead and cussed Jimmy.

Twenty minutes. Jimmy Abraham was twenty minutes late for their non-date, which she had barely agreed to. The pitiful man had all but begged her to meet him here, and now he had the audacity to be tardy.

Moab's streetlights flickered on. She felt a weak breeze come and go, not strong enough to blow out a birthday candle on a cupcake. She checked her pendant watch again.

Oh, Ellie, you fool.

She stood and paced to cool off. Eleanor caught a glimpse of herself in the reflection of Miller's window. She was wearing white gloves, a flowery hat, a floral-print dress, and coral lipstick, mail-ordered. She was carrying a nine-by-twelve casserole dish with a glass lid. Still warm. Hot chicken salad casserole. Jimmy's favorite. Her heart hurt. The only thing worse than being unloved was being unsure whether or not you were.

Ahead of her, Moab's water tower was spilling its overflow onto the sidewalk like it did at the end of every month. It was one of the only reliable things in life. Mister Wilbur would drain water, and in the summer afternoons children would play beneath the waterfall. The water slapped the pavement, saturating everything in its path. She remembered how it felt to be a child, innocent and happy about everything, instead of old and hot flashy.

Twenty-eight minutes late now.

Eleanor's niece, Susan, and her new husband were walking along the sidewalk, on the way to the social. Newlyweds, holding hands. They were back from their honeymoon in Miami. Wearing suntans. Newlyweds were always happy. Newlyweds always hooked arms with each other, even if they were just going to the bathroom.

She waved to them, and they waved back. Susan's dress was already clinging to her hips so tightly the seams were loosening. That girl had better watch out, or she was going to blow up as big as the Mickey Mouse balloon in the Macy's parade.

A deep voice said her name. It startled her. She turned to see Winston Browne, clad in a salt-and-pepper tweed suit, a red hand-painted tie, and his crumpled brown fedora sitting back on his head.

"Whoops. I didn't mean to scare you." A dog was with him, steadily by his side.

"Evening, Sheriff," she said.

"Oh, please," he said. "Don't call me that. It's not like I didn't sit behind you in third-period algebra." He eyed the casserole in her hands. "Lemme guess." He rubbed his forehead like a fortune teller. "Squash casserole, with bacon?"

"Hot chicken salad. Well, at least it *was* hot."

"Oh no. He stood you up?"

"I don't know."

"He's been so busy lately, you gotta cut him a break. Half the town wants him barbecued."

She gave him a look.

"Make that half the town plus one Sunday school teacher," he said.

Winston waited with her for a few moments. They both stared at the water tower spillage forming a huge puddle on Hydrangea. She noticed him looking down the street at Ray's hideous neon sign. He was shaking his head at the eyesore.

Eleanor said, "Can't you just make Ray take that horrible sign down? There's more of us than there are of him."

"Not according to Moab law. People got a right to put up whatever sign they want."

"Why can't we change the law?"

"That ain't the way it works. There's a whole process to it. We got some of the weirdest laws in the state. Did you know there's a law on Moab's books that says you can't drive a boat down Hydrangea Street?"

"A boat? On this street?"

"A leftover from the flood of '34. Ben Riley motored a boat up and down Hydrangea. The wake broke all the shop windows."

"I remember the flood, but I don't remember the windows breaking."

"We got another law that says you can't slaughter goats in town unless you have a permit."

"Who came up with *that*?"

"No idea, but if you see anyone with a goat out here, you better report them to me."

She laughed. It wasn't just a polite laugh either. It was sincere. Because for the briefest moment Eleanor had almost forgotten she'd been stood up, or that she was sweating like a politician in hell.

Winston removed his hands from his pockets and took the casserole from her without even asking. "Let me hold that."

"No," she said. "It's okay. I'm just about to head back home."

"Home?" he said. "I won't hear of it. Let me walk with you, Eleanor. I could use some company tonight."

Eleanor hadn't been escorted by a man other than Jimmy Abraham in years. Something about the sheriff's proposal felt scandalous and indecent. But also fantastic.

Winston held out his right arm. "Consider me Jimmy's pinch hitter tonight."

"Winston, I don't need your pity. Besides, Jimmy would be furious with you. You know how jealous he can be."

"We've been best friends since we were in grammar school. It wouldn't be the first time Jimmy got mad at me. Besides, I'm anxious to eat that casserole, Ellie."

Ellie. Mercy. This was more than indecent. This was downright illicit. She liked it. But civility and good breeding took over. "I'm a big girl, Win. I can go to a party alone. Don't feel sorry for me. I don't want your charity."

"Charity? You'd be doing *me* the favor, Miss Hughes, making a dog-ugly man look like he won a bet." He held his arm outward again. "I insist."

Eleanor took his arm. Because Sheriff Winston Browne was anything but dog-ugly.

Dixieland Bands

The Methodist church fellowship hall was lit with Chinese lanterns hanging from long ropes strung across the rafters. Everyone was here. Not just Methodists. Even non-dancing Baptists, who were incognito tonight lest they be seen making repetitive rhythmic movements. People swarmed the food table in the old gymnasium like bloodthirsty insects, fixing their plates, then zigzagging across the gymnasium to get more pound cake, chess pie, or congealed salad. There was no explaining mankind's repulsive taste for Jell-O salads that had become so popular in Moab. Some of these salads were luminous green, with black olives and cocktail onions embedded within the phlegm-like wretchedness.

Buz watched it all from a distance. These were the sorts of events his grandfather lived for. Free food was the old man's life pursuit. His grandfather would pilfer food from the tables, often shoving enough food into his pockets to last for three days.

Buz spotted her. A brunette. Not just any brunette, but *the* brunette of all brunettes. Becky Jernigan. He tried to wave at her, but his arm didn't work.

The very out-of-his-league, magnificent Becky Jernigan made her peers look like toads by comparison. She was the prettiest at the social. Maybe the prettiest in five counties.

He tried to speak to her when she brushed by him, but all he got out was, "Becky."

Becky stopped. "Hi, Buz."

She said his name. His consciousness wavered. The Dixieland band was playing in the background, and Buz was so nervous he was about to black out. He'd been in love with her for a long, long time now. Longer than he could remember.

He'd thought Becky didn't know he existed. Nobody seemed to notice the quiet, poor kid who worked for Mister Arnold. The uneducated nobody. Becky was the opposite. She was adored by all. Loved by all. And right now she was begging for someone to ask her to dance. Buz wanted to ask. He could feel the words stuck just below his sternum. He tried to force them out, but nothing was happening.

She stood before him, looking lovely. White dress, a green ribbon around her waist, hair in coffee-can curls. Eyes bigger than nine-gallon washtubs. He almost asked her, but there were two problems. The first was that life had a natural pecking order. She was an eagle, soaring in the clouds; he was a leghorn chicken. The second problem, which was an even bigger one than the first, was that Buz did not know how to dance. In fact, he had the same rhythmic grace as an arthritic jack mule.

As it happened, none of his concerns mattered. Buz was too late. Dan Conroy appeared out of nowhere and approached Becky, offering his hand. "Wanna dance?" Just like that. No hesitation. No self-doubt. Just confidence. Dan was everything Buz wasn't. A cocky little first baseman who wasn't a great hitter but played decent infield.

Soon Dan was twirling Becky on the dance floor to the song "When You're Smiling." After that, the band played "Saint Louis Blues," whereupon Dan Conroy dipped Becky Jernigan. What a dweeb.

Winston Browne walked up to Buz. The white-haired man held a plate filled with deviled eggs, coleslaw, and anything else involving mayonnaise. "You're a sight, Buz, standing over here by yourself like a puppy dog."

"Me?"

"Why don't you go ask her to dance?"

"Ask who?"

"You've been standing over here like Little Orphan Annie all night. I think everyone in this room knows *who*."

Tommy Sheridan sidled up beside Winston. The deputy was still in his khaki uniform, holding a plate with a mountain of food so tall it had its own climate. Tommy took a swig from a small pocket flask, then tucked it back into his pocket and chased it with a deviled egg.

"Tommy," said Winston. "I oughta fire you for that. I can't believe the nerve."

"What're you, Hatchet Annie? I'm off duty. Besides, nobody else wants this job. All I do is deliver groceries to shut-ins."

"That's a dim view of law enforcement," said Winston.

"Is he gonna ask her to dance?" said Tommy with a mouthful. "The suspense is killing me."

"I don't know how to dance," Buz said.

In a few minutes, the sheriff and Tommy had walked outside the fellowship hall, dragging Buz along with them. The sheriff stood beneath the oaks on the church lawn and removed his jacket. Tommy sat on the hood of the squad car. The music from the band drifted into the night air, and the sheriff struck a graceful pose. Feet together. One arm out. One arm holding an imaginary waist. "C'mon, Buz," he said. "It's never too late to learn."

Buz made no move.

"There's nobody out here to see us, Buz."

Tommy shoved a piece of pound cake the size of a brick into his mouth. "Sheriff's a good dancer."

"I can't dance," Buz reminded them.

"Don't be silly. Anyone who can fog up a mirror can dance."

The music changed to a waltz. Through the hall's windows, Buz could see the dance floor filled with people who all seemed to know how to move in three-quarter time. White-haired couples took the floor, sauntering back and forth. Reverend Lewis and his wife were cutting a rug too.

"C'mon," beckoned the sheriff. "I'm a beautiful woman, Buz."

Buz squinted and tried to imagine the sheriff as an attractive woman, but it wasn't working. He wandered toward the sheriff like a pig going to the processing plant.

"Okay," said the sheriff, guiding Buz's arm. "Now, put this arm around my waist and this one holds my hand."

"This feels ridiculous," said Buz.

Tommy hollered, "You should see it from where I'm sitting."

The sheriff talked Buz through the steps, counting with each side, forward, and backward move. Whenever Buz stepped on the sheriff's foot, the man just laughed. It didn't take long. Pretty soon, Buz was actually getting the hang of it. Tommy showed his appreciation by applauding. They were moving back and forth to the distant music like a couple of pros.

"It isn't as hard as I thought," said Buz.

"See?" The sheriff laughed. "I told you so. Anyone who can fog up a mirror can do it."

When the music finished, the sheriff was winded. They released each other. The old man leaned forward to catch his breath. "Buz, I've been meaning to talk to you for a while. Why aren't you on my team?"

The band began playing another song. Buz searched for an answer but had none. "Everyone knows you're a great ballplayer. One of the best. Come play for me."

"I work for Mister Arnold," said Buz.

"That doesn't mean you can't have a life. Now, I'm gonna ask you again, why aren't you on my team? I could really use you."

Buz didn't answer. He was flattered, of course. Buz bled baseball blue. He worshipped Roy Campanella, Duke Snider, Gil Hodges, and Jackie Robinson. He went to bed each night listening to radio scores and game summaries from out-of-town stations. If he could have tattooed "Ted Williams" onto his upper arm, he would have. But poor boys like him did not play baseball. That's just how it was.

The sheriff went on, "What if I could fix it with Mister Arnold so that you could get off work early for practice?"

"I can't, Sheriff. I just can't."

The sheriff nodded toward the fellowship hall. "Dan Conroy might be able to dance, but he can't swing a bat for spit."

The sheriff had a point.

"You don't have to give me an answer now, Buz," the sheriff said, sliding his arms into his jacket. "I know your granddaddy's missing, and things aren't great at home. But at least promise me you'll think about it. That's all I ask. After all, you owe me for those dancing lessons."

A Chilly Night

Jessie got off the train and a blast of hot, humid air hit her in the face. It was an elaborate train station, even more crowded than the last one, with arched windows and brickwork as far as the eye could see. Wherever this place was, it was like being in a giant steamy bathroom after someone had filled a tub with hot water. The man in the gold buttons had announced this was Savannah. She was about sick of layovers. And Savannah was pretty hot and miserable compared to Pennsylvania. Even at night.

She stepped off the train onto the platform, holding her suitcase with both hands. She was angry all over. Why had Ada let her be raised by the horrid temple sisters as an orphan? What kind of woman could live with herself for doing such a thing? And to her own daughter? Jessie could have had a family, she could have been happy, but instead she was a motherless nothing.

Before she left the platform, Gold Buttons inspected her ticket and reminded her not to dawdle but to get on train number six. He punched her ticket, then handed her a new one. "This one is for the Pensacola train." He pointed to the train across the yard.

"Pensacola?"

"In Florida."

"Where's that?"

"You'll see soon enough, you lucky kid. I wish I was going with you right about now. I could use a vacation."

"What's that?" she said.

"A vacation? It's like going to heaven for two weeks and still getting paid." Then he handed her one more Mary Jane as a parting gift.

She tucked the candy into her pocket and promised herself she would save it for a rainy day.

On her way across the train platform, a man with a mustache began following her, his hands in his pockets. The closer he came, the more she walked with unsure steps. Should she go toward him or away from him? No matter. Mustache wasted no time gaining on her.

"Jessie," he finally said in a free and easy voice, like they were old pals. "Are you Jessie? Wait up!"

She stopped walking and faced him. She kept her mouth closed and her eyes moving.

"How was your trip, Jessie? I've been looking forward to meeting you."

He wore a tan suit with a matching hat. He had nice shoes with spats. The faintest accent in his voice. He offered to carry her suitcase, but she took two steps back. She could smell the temple all over him.

"What's the matter?" he said. "I'm not gonna bite you, *Kleinerin*."

The train behind her whistled. "Now boarding passengers for Pensacola!"

"What's your ticket say?" he said to her. "Which train are you getting on? Is it that one?"

He stepped toward her. She stepped backward again.

Mustache smirked. He grinned at her and said, "Oh, right, you're probably waiting for me to say the magic words, huh?" He paused and seemed to be thinking. "Warm night, isn't it, kiddo?"

She felt a jolt go through her. It was all happening too fast. She needed a few more seconds to figure out what she would do next. She took another step backward. He took one step forward.

The train behind her was starting to hiss. It had started to move forward, gliding along the tracks at a turtle speed. The giant rods were struggling to turn the great wheels. The sounds of metal and steel filled the station. Hundreds of people flitted behind Mustache, who was looking at her like he was going to eat her. Apparently the man was done messing around. He lunged at her and reduced the distance between them. He grabbed her by the arm. "Relax, *Kleinerin*," said the man. "I said, it's a warm night, isn't it?"

Jessie kicked him in the leg. Hard. The man stumbled backward, jumping on his good leg, then fell on his rump. She ran after the train, which was chugging away from them. When she got close enough, she threw her suitcase into an open doorway and jumped aboard the steps. When she turned around, she saw the man running alongside the train. He gripped the rail and pulled himself onto the moving machine, and she kicked him again. He lost his grip but regained it. Whoever he was, this man was not going away without a fight.

He caught her by the skirt and she heard her dress rip. He was stronger than she was. She fought against him, but she couldn't get him to let go. The man was going to drag her off the moving train. She was on all fours in the stairwell, blindly kicking like a mule behind her, hoping a foot made contact with him. "*Du kleine Bastard!*" he shouted.

She managed to wrap her hand around the suitcase handle. Jessie used it as a weapon and swatted the man until he began shouting more profanities. The final blow came when she landed the case on his jaw. Upon impact, the case opened and her clothes spilled outward, strewn all over the tracks and into the night.

The man fell backward. She saw him tumble beside the tracks, then he leapt to his feet and started chasing after the train and soon was running beside it again. But he was not fast enough. The train kept picking up speed until the man became a tiny mustached dot in the distance. And she was left in the doorway watching the world go by.

Florida. That's where she was going. She could use a vacation.

Gene Kelly

The county Hudson struggled along the dark dirt roads on the east side of town. Winston and Tommy drove toward Pine Basin, taking long-forgotten back roads, weaving through the woods, past the old LaValle house and the vacant Pearson home. The car bounded through a series of enormous puddles on the pockmarked roads, paths that hadn't been regularly maintained since the Crimean War. Nobody used these roads anymore except the few farmers who still lived back here, town drunks, and teenagers looking for a secluded place to neck.

The red dog was in the back seat, looking through the back window at dust rising in the night air. Tommy offered the dog a cookie from his paper plate. The dog ate it in one bite.

Tommy asked, "You think Adam Guilford really drowned? I heard some kids say Adam fell asleep on the railroad tracks and got run over."

"Why else would Fletcher have called us at this hour?"

"Because he's a lunatic. Do you know how many times he's called me to complain this month alone? Mister Hank stopped by to say something about Adam, but he was so smashed I couldn't understand a thing he was saying."

But Winston didn't answer; his mind was still miles behind them, at the Methodist social. He just stared forward. He was wearing a kind of permanent smile that only dancing can put on a man's face. He was still out of breath from all the twirling, sidestepping, two-stepping, waltzing, and foxtrotting with Eleanor Hughes. It had been an entire night of dancing. He was thinking about the way he'd held her, the same way he'd held a young fiancée a hundred years ago. It felt good, holding her. Very good.

"Hello?" said Tommy. "Anybody home?"

Winston was still thinking about the peculiar look on Eleanor's face when he spun her. A look that was worth its weight in hot chicken casserole. A little bit of surprise. A little bit of caution. A little bit of unexpected excitement making an appearance. In other words, youth. It was the feeling of youth. Winston had almost forgotten what that felt like. Even though his pleasant thoughts were cut with the recurring word *malignant*; even though each cough was a nagging reminder that no dance lasted forever; even though he knew life's music eventually would stop playing and it would be time to go home, he was nineteen again.

Tommy finally quit talking and let Winston alone. Which was a borderline miracle. Tommy hadn't quit talking since Sherman arrived in Atlanta. They rode for several minutes. Winston had always thought dying would be a mournful thing, and in most ways it was. But there was another feeling he hadn't expected, the one he was experiencing right now. Certainly life seemed cruelly short, but it also seemed so much more vivid, wilder, and more in-focus than before. It was as though he had been asleep for his entire existence, then, without warning, pushed out of bed.

He had a little time left to live. And so he was going to do exactly that.

The sheriff coughed into a hanky. There was the dose of reality.

"That cough sounds nasty," said Tommy. "You really should get that looked at."

"It's just pollen," said Winston. "It's been bad lately."

The county roads couldn't have been any bumpier if they'd been manufactured by the National Washboard Company. Winston held the wheel with a firm grip to keep from losing control. Everything in the car rattled. Except Tommy, who was too weighted down with deviled eggs inside his belly to move.

Winston slowed the vehicle to a crawl and drove around a large puddle. The Hudson picked up speed again. When Winston gunned the engine to ascend the hill before them, he slapped the gearshift, and soon they were flying straight upward.

"Slow down!" said Tommy. "Why're we going so fast?"

Winston wasn't sure what had gotten into him tonight. When they reached the top of the hill, he hit the gas again. His foot wasn't even touching the brakes. The car zipped downward, rattling like a tambourine.

Tommy was pressing his hands against the Hudson's ceiling, one foot jammed against the dashboard. "What're you doing, Win?" he shouted.

The Hudson made a sharp left when Winston spun the wheel as hard and fast as he could. The vehicle veered so that both dog and deputy slammed against the windows. They came to a stop. Winston yanked the park brake and appreciated himself with a light chuckle.

"What in the name of Fred has gotten into you, Win?"

The laughing had turned into a cough now. Winston held his handkerchief against his mouth. He had no idea what was going on inside him. Not the faintest clue. His emotions had escaped from their little holding area and were calling all the shots.

The Fletcher cabin sat in the distance, perched on the edge of the Escambia, surrounded by pines as big around as Chevys. The tall trees suffocated the moonlight and made the night even blacker. It was a crude board-and-batten house with a rusted roof and broken shutters. A glorified shack.

Tommy appeared by Winston's side, holding the lantern that shone into the deputy's face.

Winston sniffed his deputy's breath.

Tommy said, "It was just gin. You keep forgetting, I'm off duty."

"You're never really *off* duty, not in Moab."

"That didn't seem to stop you from having a good time, Gene Kelly. You were dancing all night with that woman."

"That was just dancing. Dancing ain't the same as drinking."

"Spoken like a true Methodist."

They walked onto the porch, careful not to put their weight on the rotted planks that looked like they were about to disintegrate. Tommy knocked on the door, and Mister Fletcher appeared behind the crud-covered screen. The old man was small, slight, with wisps of white fuzz covering his bald head. He held a frog gig that was big enough to bale hay.

"Evening, Fletch," said Winston. "Just who do you plan on using that pitchfork on?"

The old man was upset. The rims of his eyes were red. "He's in the back, Sheriff. Better come with me."

"Wait," said Tommy. "Are you sure it's Adam?"

But Mister Fletcher didn't have time for conversation. He had already left them and headed for the rear of the house. Winston and Tommy exchanged a look, then followed the man through what could have been loosely called a junk heap with a roof. There were mountains of dishes on every surface, splayed magazines, and molehills of cigarette butts. Some in ashtrays; most on the floor.

The old man tossed open his back door and pointed the spear into the dark. "Over there, Sheriff. He washed up a few hours ago. I've been having to fight the cats away from him."

The red dog followed Winston across the soggy marshland behind Mister Fletcher's house toward a shape on the shore. A few cats seated beside the lump in the distance were staring at it. When he got close enough to shine the light on the thing, he felt hot tears swell in his own eyes. The old man was familiar but swollen like a balloon, the morbid trademark of the drowned. But even though the old man was dead, he looked somewhat the same as he always had. Except this time Adam Guilford was sober. The dog sniffed the corpse and began to whine.

"You rowdy old man." Winston tried to make the man's eyelids shut, but they wouldn't close. They were too engorged. "I'll look out for that grandson of yours, I promise."

Four Small Oranges

Jessie stayed in the water closet for the entire train ride. Whenever anyone knocked on the door, she would shout, "I'm not done!" She could hear the sounds of disgust on the other side of the door when passengers realized she wasn't coming out. Eventually the knocks stopped.

She spent half the ride sitting on the closed toilet, thinking about the letter Ada had written her. She wished she wouldn't have thrown it away. Each time she thought about it, it both grieved her and infuriated her. She was wayward now, and it was all Ada's fault. Jessie had no idea where she was or where she was going, let alone what she would do when she got there. She started to cry.

For Jessie's whole life she'd been an orphan in the temple. Ada had always been her friend, but nothing more than that. Jessie wasn't sure she could bring herself to call this woman who had betrayed her "Mother." You didn't just start throwing that word around if you'd been raised an orphan. As she thought about the note again, she could feel the weight of Ada's sadness on the page. She tried not to make too much noise in the water closet with her crying.

Another knock on the door.

"I'm still going!" she shouted. "How about a little privacy here?"

She gathered herself together and tried to figure out what to do next.

She briefly considered returning to the temple. Maybe if she apologized they'd let her back. But she was no dummy. She knew that no matter what happened, she could never go back after this. Jessie wasn't even sure Ada would make it out of the temple alive. Ada was like most young temple women, always under a tight watch. Always within a few feet of her much older husband, who kept close tabs on his woman and his children.

When the train stopped, Jessie could feel the screeching beneath her feet. Next, she heard sounds of people rustling through the car like the sounds of cattle.

She opened the folding door of the water closet. Standing outside the door was a man in gold buttons, like the one from the other train. Only not as friendly.

"Well," he said. "You must be very sick or something, to be stuck in that bathroom for so long."

She didn't know what to say, so she grabbed her stomach and moaned. She wedged her suitcase out from the tiny room, but he stopped her.

"Let me see that ticket." He inspected it, then handed it to her. "Welcome to Pensacola, kid. I hope you feel better soon."

"I doubt it," said Jessie.

She left the depot with her suitcase in hand, passing men who were loading a large truck. They were wearing shirts with no sleeves and flat caps, and the air was rich with cigar smoke. She passed men in sailor hats and stark-white uniforms. She saw young couples embracing.

Across the street from the depot was a small café. Jessie decided against going inside because she didn't want anyone to ask questions she couldn't answer.

She found a truck in the café parking lot stocked with wooden crates filled with potatoes, which were too hard to eat. In the back of the same truck, she found a crate of oranges. Jackpot. She used her fingernails to peel the bright citrus skin and ate four small oranges in a few seconds. A gray cat was seated on the roof of the truck, watching her with a look of condemnation in its little eyes.

"What're you looking at?" she said to the thing. "I can't starve to death, now, can I? Get lost, cat."

It yawned and started licking itself.

When she finished eating, she tossed several more oranges into her suitcase. She took to the road and began walking toward lights in the distance. Pensacola, she assumed. The shoulder of the highway was covered in empty soda bottles and cigarette butts, which were hard to see in the night and made her stumble a few times until the moon broke through the clouds above. She stopped and sat down on her suitcase to look at the moon for a few minutes.

A truck was approaching, headlights blaring. It was the same truck with the vegetables and oranges. The truck slowed down and pulled to the side of the road in front of her. The driver was a young man, handsome, with a smoke dangling from the corner of his mouth. He leaned out his window and said, "Need a ride, kid?" She considered bolting the opposite direction, but the driver seemed nice enough.

She stood there for a few moments, not knowing what to say. She was too afraid to trust anyone, but she was also afraid not to. The young man was halfway through his cigarette when he finally said, "You waiting on someone? I can give you a ride wherever you're going."

She thought long and hard but did not speak.

"It's almost midnight, kid. You shouldn't be out here by yourself. Where in the world are your parents?"

She would have given anything to know the same thing.

"Where're you heading, kid?" the man said.

She looked at the sign across the road. A few cars sped past them, causing great rushes of wind to blow her hair sideways. A sign on the opposite side of the highway read "Moab 10 miles; Layton 32 miles."

"Moab," she said.

The young man's face lit up. "Oh, Moab. I'm going right through it tonight. It's just up the road. Get in."

She tossed her case into the truck bed. The gray cat stared at her, hidden between two crates. "You," she said. "I thought I told you to get lost."

They drove through the dark, across the long, flat landscape. She didn't answer a single question the young man asked her. She kept her hand on the doorknob in case the company got unsavory. The young man didn't seem to mind the lack of conversation. He listened to strange music with a throbbing beat that made her uncomfortable. The only music she'd ever heard was communal singing. Once, she'd heard a banjo, but when the sisters found it, they chopped it with a garden hoe and burned it. Instruments were frowned upon in the temple.

The truck passed a tall wooden sign with an illustration of a white flower upon it. The sign read "Moab, Pop. 912, Elevation: 17 ft."

Neither Rain nor Heat

Jimmy Abraham was still working in the back room of J.R.'s Mercantile, sorting mail. He had been sorting mail since eight in the morning and his eyes hurt. He checked the desk clock. It was almost one in the morning. His eyes were tired and he had a headache. He hadn't eaten all day. No lunch, no supper, no nothing. All he'd done was sort, sort, sort. Odie had helped until eight, but then he left. Said he had something pressing to do. He never said what exactly, just that it was very pressing. Jimmy suspected that whatever the pressing matter was, it involved beer. He didn't blame Odie for leaving; this was godless work.

He stopped filing envelopes and stared out the window to refocus his eyes. He rubbed his temples. All night he'd been having this feeling he was forgetting something. It was a nagging thought, underneath the surface. What was it? Had he forgotten to restock navy plug behind the counter? No, he did that yesterday. Maybe the Dutch chocolate? Nope, Odie did that this morning. He resumed sorting, then stopped again.

He checked the miniature calendar atop his desk. He hoped the calendar would remind him of whatever it was, but nothing was coming to him.

The sound of the screen door opening and slapping shut interrupted him. He heard footsteps on the floorboards. "It's Robbie," a voice said. "Robbie Allen. I saw your light on."

"I don't care if it's Harry S. Truman. We're closed, unless you brought supper."

"Ain't got no food." Robbie patted his belly. "I couldn't eat another bite after the deviled eggs I ate at the social. Geez, Jimmy, it's one in the morning. What're you doing still working?"

"The mail, it never stops, Robb—" Jimmy's tired mind was barely processing the words Robbie had just said. "What'd you say?"

"I said it's one in the morning. What're you doing up so late?"

"Before that."

"I said I had too many deviled eggs. You know how those things can really lay on your belly."

Crime in Italy. Jimmy buried his face in his hands.

"What is it, Jimmy?"

"She's gonna mount my head above her fireplace."

"Who?"

"She'll never forgive me."

"Are you talking about Eleanor?"

He lifted his head. "Was Eleanor there? Did she look mad?"

Robbie shrugged. "Eleanor seemed like she was in a good mood to me. She certainly danced a lot. I didn't even know she knew how to dance."

"Dancing? What're you talking about? Eleanor doesn't dance; her father was Baptist."

"She did tonight. She was cutting a rug with Sheriff Browne. Those two never came off the dance floor. The band was packing up, ready to go, and Eleanor was pleading for one more tune. Kept the band there another hour."

The words sort of hung in the air like sparks drifting from a fire.

Jimmy's temper rose. "Robbie, are you gonna stand there and tell me that *Winston Browne* was dancin—" Jimmy was interrupted by a loud noise. A clanging filled the back room, followed by the loud clucking of chickens. And it got louder.

"What was *that*?" said Robbie.

Jimmy shushed him. More clattering. The chickens were screaming now. The clanging was sustained now, almost like a handbell.

Jimmy clapped his hands together and laughed. "I've got that chicken thief red-handed now."

Queen Anne

Branch Reinhardt, the funeral director, stood on the back porch of the Queen Anne home beneath the glow of a single dim porchlight dressed in a robe and slippers. The red dog sat in the Hudson's back seat, curled in a ball where Adam's wet body had been lying. It was almost like the dog knew something.

Winston and Tommy carried Adam Guilford's heavy body through the rear entrance of Reinhardt's Funeral Home. The lawmen were covered in mud and river water. Adam was a lot heavier than he looked.

"Sorry to wake you, Branch," said Winston, holding Adam's shoulder section. "Apologize to Tibby for me."

"She knows the drill, Win. This ain't the first time someone died after hours." The undertaker peeled back the bedsheet and let out a sigh. "What a shame. I heard old Hank telling everyone Adam fell in the water, but I guess I didn't believe him. I thought Adam would live forever."

"Me too," said Tommy. "He's survived everything."

They laid Adam on the table. Winston removed his crumpled, chewed-up hat out of respect. Tommy removed his cap too.

"Tommy and I have been looking for him all week," said Winston. "We'd almost given up on finding him."

Adam lay beneath the powerful lamp hanging from the ceiling of the sterile room. The body was draped in the blue-and-white striped bedsheet they'd borrowed from Fletcher.

Tommy said, "I never woulda guessed this old drunk could weigh so much."

"It's all the water," said Branch, touching the waterlogged skin. "Closed casket for sure. I won't even bother with makeup."

"Charge it to me, Branch," said Winston. "The Guilfords don't have a plug nickel to their name. I want lots of flowers. All the flowers you can fit in the room."

"Sure," said Branch. "I'll have Tibby do it up nice."

It seemed so final, Adam on that table. Winston couldn't help but feel hypnotized by looking at him. He was gone, really and truly. This was not his first dead body. But tonight it was personal.

Branch inspected Adam's feet and legs with the official curiosity of an undertaker. The old man's feet were as big as footballs. His hands looked like giant salamis. "Back when I was a kid, Adam took me frog gigging with my buddies after school all the time."

"Me too," said Winston. "Think he took all us kids in town frog gigging at one time or another. He was good with a gig."

"He didn't drink so bad in those days," said Branch.

Branch and Winston shared a weak smile in Adam's honor.

"I still remember when Carolyn got polio," said Branch. "It almost killed him to watch her suffer like that. Can't imagine what it musta been like to see your daughter in an iron lung."

"People can say what they will about him," said Winston. "But he was ours. That man came to every game Jimmy and I ever played. He was always front and center."

"Oh," said Branch. "He loved you boys. What were y'all called again?"

"The Gnats. Adam was our biggest fan. Maybe our only fan. We were terrible."

Memories were getting a little too heavy. Winston went outside to light a Lucky and rehash a few of his greatest hits. The smoke made his throat burn and his cough flare up. He removed the cigarette from his mouth and looked at the thin line of white smoke rising from the coal. He'd been smoking since he was a kid. Since that fateful day, he'd never been more than six feet away from a pack of Lucky Strikes. He took another drag. He wondered where Adam's soul had gone off to. Or did he just mix in with the soil and become pH, minerals, and dirt?

Tommy appeared on the back porch and placed a hand on Winston's shoulder. He let a few moments pass. "You gonna tell Carolyn and Buz, or should I?"

Winston flicked the butt end into the night air, then coughed. "I'll do it. After breakfast."

Winston stared at the spires on the Queen Anne house, the ornate windows, the gracious porch, and the magnificent circular windows. "Why is it that funeral homes are always the prettiest houses in town? You ever notice that?"

Tommy frowned. "Huh?"

"Lamberts and Sons Funeral Home in Layton, that's the biggest, nicest house in town. Look at Branch's, it's perfect. What's it all about? What's it all for?"

"I don't know," said Tommy. "I've never thought about it. Was your old team really called the Gnats?"

Winston laughed. "Yeah, it sure was."

To Catch a Thief

Jimmy flew off the back steps of the mercantile. He ran through the dark and Robbie followed him. The metallic rattling was coming from the henhouse, loud and clear. Jimmy carried a rifle in one hand and a lantern in the other. He dodged holes and exposed roots in the ground heading toward the coop in the distance. He could hear Virgil, the rooster, screaming louder than the other chickens.

"I've got that fool now!" said Jimmy with a crazed smile.

His ankle was acting up, and he was pretty sure he'd pulled his groin. He hadn't moved this fast since he wore catcher's gear. By the time he reached the chicken house, he was limping like a lame horse and his ankle was throbbing. Whatever was making the noise was tangled in the homemade booby trap of pots and pans. Before he opened the door, he handed the lantern to Robbie. "You hold the light, I'll scare him! Whatever you do, *don't* let him get away!"

After a few deep breaths, Jimmy cocked the rifle and kicked open the door to the coop, useing such force he almost brought the little building down.

Chickens screamed. Virgil fluttered his wings like he was possessed by the Devil. White feathers went everywhere. Jimmy barged inside, rifle in both hands. Robbie stayed beside him, holding the lantern outward.

Jimmy dropped the rifle. He expected to see an old drunk, or a few teenagers, or a hobo tangled in wire and tin pots. But it was no man.

"*That's* your chicken thief?" said Robbie.

It was a little girl. Before Jimmy could say a word to her, the girl shot to her feet. She kicked Jimmy's shin so hard he fell backward. She shoved Robbie, then bolted for the door, dragging behind her a train of pots and pans.

"Don't let her go!" shouted Jimmy.

But the girl was already making her getaway. She was climbing the back fence like an acrobat. Pots and pans weighed her down, clanging behind her like a glockenspiel.

"Stop!" Jimmy shouted, limping after her. "You thief! Stop!" He fired his shotgun straight up into the air. The noise startled the child. She lost her grip and fell backward. Her head hit the ground and bounced once.

He dropped the rifle and ran to her. She was bleeding. He held her head in his hands. "Honey, can you hear me?" he asked.

She wasn't moving, but she was breathing. Thank heaven. His hands were dotted with red from her wound, and if there was anything more terrifying than holding a limp, bleeding child, Jimmy didn't know what it was. Finally, he looked at Robbie and said, "Were they fast dancing or slow dancing?"

A Dodgers Man

Buz listened to the tinny sound of a radio broadcasting the baseball scores before getting dressed for work. The Philco radio sat on the nightstand beside his bed. The radio was his window to the world of the Brooklyn Dodgers. His grandfather had given him this small radio for his fourteenth birthday a few months ago. It was about the size of a brick, portable, and ran on batteries, and the audio it produced hissed and crackled as though the little speaker were choking on something. But it was his lifeline to the world outside. There was no way to be sure, but Buz figured his grandfather had stolen it. His grandfather never told him where it came from. And Buz never asked.

The scores were bouncing through his room while he got dressed. The Cardinals were sounding good this year. The Cleveland Indians weren't having the season they'd had last year. The Giants had also fallen from grace. But there was still a half season to be played. If the Dodgers ever made it to the World Series, one thing was certain: Buz was going to do everything in his power to help them win it.

Kids in Moab chose allegiances early in life. A boy decided which team he would root for on the day he was born. The majority became Dodgers men, but some traitors rooted for Mantle and Berra. After battle lines were drawn, the kid was forever checking box scores in the papers or listening to radio game summaries. You had two main groups in Moab: the Yankees fans, who always bragged about Mickey Mantle, Bill Skowron, or Whitey Ford, and the Dodgers fans, who were always crying. Because, historically speaking, the Dodgers had a way of breaking your heart when it mattered most. A Dodgers fan learned early: disappointment was the very melody of life. "You don't get what you want in this world. You get squat." That was always the Dodgers motto.

Buz was an authority on the Dodgers. Since games were always played during the daytime, none of the local schoolkids could listen to them unless they smuggled transistor radios with earpieces into their classrooms. Boys rarely did this, because among the faculty at Franklin D. Roosevelt School, this was considered worse than bringing a firearm into class. Dropouts like Buz, however, could listen whenever they wanted. Buz's boss, Mister Arnold, didn't mind if he listened to games while he cleaned out the hayloft or mucked the cattle stalls. Thus, Buz brought that little Philco radio with him wherever he went. He had invested too much money in batteries. But they were worth it. He did not miss a Dodgers game. He idolized each player. And if catcher Roy Campanella would have started his own major world religion, Buz would have bought a tunic and joined.

The announcer's voice cut through the static. *"Could this be the year the Yanks go down? Could the kingdom of the Yanks be in peril? Could it be the year the Bums do the unthinkable?"* The announcer was simply filling up dead air at this hour of the morning.

Buz buttoned his shirt and noticed headlights moving into the driveway, stabbing through the early dawn and the foggy glass of his bedroom window.

Buz went to the curtain. The county Hudson pulled into the gravel drive, crunching rocks beneath the tires. Buz got excited when he saw the car. The only thing this car could mean was that the old man was home. It always happened like this. The sheriff would drive his grandfather home, lead the old man staggering up the footpath and onto the porch, and everything would go back to normal. Whatever normal was.

"Mama!" Buz shouted. "The sheriff's here!"

In a few moments Buz and his mother were on the porch. Headlights shined at them for a few seconds until the driver dimmed them. Buz could hear the sound of screen doors slapping from across the street as people gathered on nearby stoops to gawk. Moab was nothing but nosy people.

Sheriff Winston Browne stepped from the car. The red dog followed the lawman. The sheriff removed his hat when he saw Buz and his mother. When he did this, Buz felt cold all over. There was no need for a man to remove his hat outdoors. Not even in the presence of a lady. The sole reason a man removed his hat was respect. For either God or the dead.

"Carolyn," said the sheriff, looking at his shoes.

Buz could hear the radio announcer's voice coming from his bedroom. *"Could this be the year the great Mickey Mantle and the Bombers go down? Will the invulnerable Yanks ever lose, folks?"*

Buz didn't even wait for the sheriff to speak. Buz left the porch, walked into his bedroom, and shut the door behind him. He yanked the radio from his desk, held it above his head, and hurled it against the wall. He fell facedown on his bed and cried into his mattress. Because Buz did not want to be the man of the house. He wanted to be fourteen. He wanted to be normal.

But a Dodgers fan doesn't always get what he wants in this world.

Almost Doll-Like

Jimmy stood beside the door of his bedroom above the mercantile, watching the girl sleep in his bed. The cat lay on the pillow beside her head. It wouldn't leave her side. The child was out cold. She had not moved since Jimmy placed her there the night before. Her black dress was torn, her legs and arms covered in chicken claw marks, courtesy of Virgil and his girls.

At that very moment Virgil was crowing at the morning from his fencepost. Virgil always started hollering a full hour before the sun came up and quit crowing around lunchtime. Everyone in Okeauwaw County could hear Virgil and hated him.

Jimmy and three elderly men stood outside the bedroom door, looking in with great curiosity. Odie was the first to creep into Jimmy's bedroom. The bedroom was a junk heap, old wooden crates and empty brown bottles that doubled as ashtrays in a pinch strewn about. Odie stood beside the bed, puffing his pipe, enveloped in a blue fog. He studied the girl. "How'd she hit her head, Jimmy?"

"She was trying to climb the fence but got tangled up in my trap."

"I'll bet she's a runaway," Odie said.

"What was your first clue, Doctor Holmes?"

Jimmy felt her forehead. "She's lucky she didn't hang herself. Took us ten minutes to cut her free with tin snips."

"I don't recognize this kid, do you?"

"No. Could be from Layton. Maybe McDavid."

"Hey, what if she's from the circus?" said Odie.

Everyone looked at the old man who was puffing a stubby pipe, arms folded.

"Does she *look* like a circus person?" said Jimmy.

"Never know, she could be a mind reader or the weight guesser maybe. They start 'em young. Ask her how much I weigh."

Tommy said, "I don't think she's missing from anywhere around here. I woulda heard about a missing kid on the APB. That's a nasty bump on her head, Jimmy. We'd better get Doc Howard."

Jimmy came closer. The gray cat started whipping its tail while keeping its eyes on him. He inspected the knot on the girl's head. It was covered in dried blood. He hated himself for causing harm to a child. He felt her cheeks, which were warm to the touch. And dry. Dehydrated, probably.

He brought himself eye-level with the girl. "Sweetie?" he said. "Can you hear me?" She was breathing through her nose, mouth closed. "Please wake up."

Nothing.

She had smooth features, almost doll-like. He was hard pressed to remember seeing a prettier child. He patted her cheeks. "Sweetie, just open your eyes so we know you're okay."

The girl's eyelids opened.

"Well, well, well," said Alvin. "At least we know she'll live."

Odie said, "Can you tell us how much Jimmy weighs?"

The girl yawned, then cleared her throat.

"She's gonna say something," said Alvin.

"What is it, sweetie?" said Jimmy. "What do you need?"

The girl said in a weak voice, "Would someone please shut that rooster up?" Then she went straight back to sleep.

Red Cheeks in the Sunset

Eleanor opened her eyes and heard the sound of knocking on her door. She was disoriented for a moment. She hadn't meant to fall asleep in this chair, but apparently she had. She was still wearing the dress from the social the night before, and she was still basking in the memory of it. Her muscles were so sore she felt like someone had flogged her with rubber hoses. She had not danced since the USO dances during the war, back when she and her girlfriends would get gussied up and drive to Pensacola in her father's jalopy to dance with a hundred airmen or navy men. That seemed like ages ago. Back when she was young. Back when men found her attractive. Before she started feeling like a homely church spinster.

The way Winston had held her made her feel something she hadn't felt in a long time. It wasn't romance. It was more than that. She felt important. And feminine.

She stretched her sore legs and thought about how funny it was. Life. It could change so quickly. One minute you were an old maid, the next minute you were being dipped on a dance floor by a sheriff in a salt-and-pepper suit.

Knock! Knock!

She shot to her feet, then inspected herself in the hall mirror.

Her reflection was godawful. Eleanor's smashed silver hair made her appear as though a mutilated rat were clinging to her head during a flood. She limped to the door. Her lower back was so sore she could hardly stand upright.

"Hold on!" she shouted. "One second!"

She rubbed the sleep from her eyes, fixed her hair, and pinched her cheeks. When she was a girl, her mother had always said the key to looking vibrant and healthy was pinching one's cheeks to make them redder. The redder the better. That was her mother's view on life.

Knock! Knock! Knock!

"For crying out loud! I said I'm coming!"

She placed a hand on the doorknob, smoothed her dress one final time, then swung the door open. On the opposite side of the screen was Winston Browne. Tall, lanky, a mane of white. He still wore the salt-and-pepper trousers and the white shirt from the night before, no tie. His shirt was covered in mud. "Eleanor. I hope I didn't wake you."

"Of course not, I was just baking a cake. How are you?"

Behind the sheriff Eleanor saw a group of gawking neighborhood children straddling their bicycles. She hoped they were getting an eyeful.

Winston removed his hat and muttered, "I guess I was just . . . Well, ever since the social . . . It's just been a rough morning."

She didn't know what to say, for she was still waking up.

They stood on opposite sides of the screen, staring at each other while early morning crickets serenaded them, along with the distant squealing of Virgil, the psychotic rooster. She tried to think of something, anything to say, but she was coming up short. She kept recalling the dizzy feeling of dancing.

"Win, would you like some coffee? I'm just about to make some."

"I'd love some. Can I pay you for it?"

What an odd thing to say, she thought. "Pay me? Don't be absurd."

Winston reached into his pocket and placed a golden coin into her hand. It was large, thick, and made of chocolate. "That's a million dollars in sugar."

She could feel her face getting warm. "If you'll just excuse me, I need to visit the restroom." She sped down the hallway and into her bathroom, leaning against the door and reminding herself to breathe. She looked into the mirror and fixed her hair again.

Then she pinched her cheeks until she nearly bruised.

An Ocean of Pillows

Jessie awoke. Her head was throbbing. She felt the bump behind her left ear. It was big. And her legs were on fire, covered in bloody scratches and cuts. A mounted fish stared at her from the wall across the bedroom, a pair of long underwear hanging over the fish's tail. The fish had a wooden tobacco pipe sticking out of its open mouth. Wherever she was, this room had not been cleaned in many years.

Beside her was the gray cat.

"What're you doing here?" But the cat didn't acknowledge her; it just preened itself.

Jessie pieced together the events from the night before, and all this intense thinking made her head feel very tired. In fact, her head felt so heavy she wondered if it would fall off and roll on the floor. She was unusually tired. Also foggy and confused. The one thing she knew for certain was that this was the biggest bed she'd ever seen. And soft. Like an ocean of pillows. It was nothing like the tiny cots in the temple school basement.

Even though she fought it, sleep overtook her again like a warm blanket. She was having weird dreams. Like the kind that accompany a fever. She forced herself awake again. Jessie opened her eyes and let her weary gaze rest on various things in the room. She could feel the vibrations from the cat purring in her armpit now, fast asleep. It sounded like a little machine.

She shoved it away. "I told you to git."

That was when she saw the collection of shoes gathered near her bed. Shoes of all colors. All shapes. Pointed toes, rounded toes, black, brown, even white. She sat bolt upright to see a group of old men staring at her. Each of them with pale hair. Her vision was double. Her eyes hurt something fierce. She couldn't focus on any one man—they were swirling around.

"Easy, honey," said one man, stepping closer. "Take it easy. Nobody's gonna hurt you." He had a cotton-colored handlebar mustache. "I'm a doctor, and I just wanna look at your head."

"Don't come any closer," she said.

He laughed. "Relax, darling. We're friendly."

Jessie knew she had to get out of here, and fast. Which was what she intended to do. Only, the light-headedness gnawed at her. It was a sickening feeling, and she was growing more nauseous by the moment.

"You'll be all right," the man said. "You just have a minor concussion, nothing serious, but you need your rest." The man flicked a needle in his hand. "This'll help with your headache."

She blinked to bring the man into focus, but it did no good. "Get away from me," she said, swatting at the double-imaged man. She tried to crawl out of bed but fell flat on the ground and landed on her stomach. It made her ribs hurt.

"Hold her still," the man said.

She felt herself get stabbed in the shoulder with a needle. She screamed, then fell asleep. The gray cat was curled up beside her right ear. The rooster outside was still going strong.

The Bottle Tree

The bottles hanging overhead in the branches of the sprawling live oak looked like pure crystal in the setting sunlight. It had been the worst weekend of Buz's life. He sat beneath this bottle tree and watched them twist and turn, making multicolored designs on the ground. There were thousands of bottles. Maybe more. It was a wonder the tree was still erect.

He found a green bottle on the ground and chucked it into the air toward the tree. Bull's-eye. A bottle shattered above him, sending a spray of blue glass into the air.

He climbed the tree until he was straddling one of the tall branches, the way he used to do when his grandfather brought him here. He studied the bottles up close and noticed some were antiques. They must have dated back to the days of traveling medicine salesmen in horses and buggies. Others were Coca-Cola bottles. Who was the first one to come up with such a foolish idea? The high school seniors in town had a tradition of tying bottles in this tree upon graduation, but who knew how long people had been tying bottles to this tree.

To one side of the tree were chairs that had been placed in a large circle. Rusted patio furniture, positioned in a ring so that anyone who visited could stare at the world's biggest pile of suspended trash. In the center of the ring was a smoldering campfire featuring melted Dixie cans and old Allstate tires. The seniors had been here. Either that or a group of rowdy drunks. There wasn't a big difference between the two.

Some things about dead men you could never understand. Once a man died, his life became part mystery, part folklore. Nothing anyone said could undo this. There were things Buz would never know about his grandfather now. There were pieces of Buz's own life he would never know. He hated his grandfather for leaving them in such a fog of unknowing.

He also loved the old man and missed him so much his stomach had gone sour. It was a riddle, how a boy could love and hate someone at the same time. Especially someone who wasn't even a someone anymore.

The old man had started teaching Buz how to throw a baseball the moment Buz was old enough to fill a diaper. And how to hit. Because of Adam Guilford, baseball was perhaps the one thing Buz could do well. In every other field of life, he was a failure. But when he held a ball, he was almost like everyone else.

"Don't be afraid of the ball." That's what Buz's grandfather said a hundred thousand times. "Fear of the ball was what ruined a man," he said.

Despite these memories Buz despised the old man. He'd also made their lives a tedious nightmare. For crying out loud, the man had no morals and siphoned gas for spare change. And when it came to booze, he was unstoppable. Nobody else mattered when the old man was in search of a bottle. He had once seen his grandfather, in a moment of desperation, drink all-purpose alcohol from a tin can purchased at the hardware store.

Buz selected a stick and tossed it at one of the bottles. It clanked against a purple bottle and knocked it sideways. One bottle hit another, which hit several more. Then more. And still more. The direct hit rippled across the entire choir of glass until most were clinking together, making a marvelous sound.

When the sound died, he tossed another stick. Harder this time. It hit one of the bottles, and soon the whole tree was singing again. The sounds were sharp, loud. He closed his eyes. And for a moment he tried to feel the arms of his grandfather wrapping around him.

"I miss you," he said. "But I'm glad you're gone." He felt guilty for saying this. But he was telling the truth.

The Whole Can of Carrots

The little girl was holding a spoon like a weapon. She waved it back and forth at Jimmy like she was going to stab him. He held up both hands and said, "Just what're you gonna do with that spoon? Eat me for dessert? The doc was just trying to give you a tetanus shot."

The girl said in a low-pitched growl, "*Geh weg von mir!*"

Jimmy and the doc exchanged confused looks. "There's no call for foul language," said Jimmy. "Put that spoon down and get back in bed."

The girl did no such thing. Her chest heaved like a scared rabbit about to be cornered. She sprinted out of the room, tore down the stairs of the mercantile, and headed toward the front door.

"I think that child's gone nuts," said Jimmy.

The doc was replacing his glasses. "I can't believe she slapped me. I think she broke my syringe."

Jimmy chased after her, limping down the stairs of the mercantile, hobbling one step at a time, like a man trying to remember how his knees were supposed to work. At the bottom of the staircase was the table of old Moab men, chewing the fat. Odie and Daryl were watching the Scrabble board. Winston was adjusting his letters, his hat sitting back on his head, legs crossed.

"Stop her!" said Jimmy. "Don't just sit there and let her get away."

"But, Jimmy," said Odie. "She's got a spoon."

"Win," said Jimmy. "You're the law. Get her."

"Nope," said Win, readjusting his Scrabble letters. "Everyone needs to calm down and quit trying to poke that girl with needles. Leave her alone. If you keep scaring her, she's liable to hurt someone."

But Daryl had already risen from his seat, hitched his pants, and moved to block the exit before she made it to the front door. Before she reached the door, he had positioned himself with his feet shoulder-width apart, like a very old and decrepit defensive lineman. "You'll have to level me if you wanna get outta here, sweetheart."

The child wasted no time. She jogged toward him, picking up steam with each step. Daryl screamed. The child ran shoulder-first into the man, planting herself into his ribs. Daryl landed on his back and almost went to be with Jesus.

"My ribs! I think she broke my ribs!"

The girl shot past Daryl and straight out the front door. She almost got away until she saw Tommy clomping up the steps. The girl turned and bolted back into the store. She ran through the aisles of canned goods, past the rice, sugar, and flour, toward the other end of the mercantile.

Jimmy was closing in from the rear, Tommy flanking her from the other side. The little girl lowered her center of gravity and stared right at Jimmy. "If you try tackling me, you'll be sorry, kid. I played two years of varsity football."

He had really only played one year. And he was a benchwarmer.

She took a few steps back. The girl picked up a can of carrots from a nearby shelf. She paused for a beat, then looked at Jimmy and Tommy, who were getting closer. She seemed to be weighing the can in her hand.

"Now, just hold on a doggone minute," said Jimmy. "This has gone far enough. Put that can down, sweetie."

Winston stood from his seat and said, "*Ich sagte, lass es fallen, Kleinerin.*"

She turned to face Winston. Meanwhile, Jimmy crept toward her, moving as quiet as he could, but not quiet enough. Jimmy must have spooked the girl because in one graceful movement the child cocked her arm behind her head, kicked out one leg, then pitched the can around her own foot at Jimmy's head. It was one impressive pitch. The can hit Jimmy square in the temple and he fell to his knees.

And that was the last thing Jimmy remembered.

Unchained Melody

There was enough piecrust on Eleanor's table to cover someone's front yard. She was humming, and her arm muscles were limp from rolling dough. She had rolled lumps of dough all morning, flat on the dining room table since it was the singular surface in her home big enough to handle so much dough at once. She had agreed to make twenty pies for the missionary fundraiser that week. Five apple, five lemon icebox, and ten chess pies. The chess pies took the longest. She could make icebox pies in her sleep.

She was in the perfect mood for assembling pies, which was something you really had to be in the mood for. It was mindless work, but it required a good attitude. Which was why she was bouncing her bottom up and down to the rhythm of music in her head, twirling now and then. She'd been dancing a lot when she was alone lately. And sometimes, when a song called for it, she would dip herself. She had forgotten how much she loved to dance. Now it was all she thought about.

Eleanor caught a glimpse of herself in the dining room mirror. She was shocked at how dowdy she looked. Never before had she realized what an old woman she was. She touched her hair. Jimmy had aged her. He'd given her an excuse to stay frozen in 1902 like

Ma Kettle. No more. Eleanor Hughes was finished looking like a dishwashing, pea-shelling old biddy.

Pie making was also good for getting aggression out. A woman could bang her fists on a lump of raw dough all day and pretend it was the body of, for example, Jimmy Abraham. This alone made pie making much more fun than, say, needlepoint. When she finished draping the dough over each tin, she trimmed the excess with scissors, then gathered the remnants into a ball, flattened it with a rolling pin, and gave the lump a stern warning not to mess with her. Then she went to town on it, laughing like a villain in an old movie.

Who needed dumb old Jimmy anyway? All he ever did was take her to the same places. Ray's Cafe for the two-for-one special. Or to the China King in Pensacola, with their stupid little fortune cookies. Her fortune once read, "Nothing is impossible to a winning heart." Which was obviously baloney. Because Jimmy's fortune had read, "To truly find yourself, play hide-and-seek alone." She hated him for this. She wanted his fortune to say something like, "Ask the woman across the table to marry you, you big dummy."

But who cares? she thought to herself. She was done with him now. She had come to the end of a very long chapter in her life. He'd toyed with her long enough. She was her own woman. Eleanor Hughes: proprietor of her own life. She decided she would do what she wanted, live how she pleased, even change her hairdo, maybe go a little crazy and buy a new girdle.

She took a break from making pies, rested her arm muscles, and lit a cigarette. She sat in her wingback chair and shook open a newspaper. She scanned the gossip column of the *Moab Messenger*. Every woman in Moab was obliged to read Miss Margie Brach's social column, even though it was dreadfully written and equally silly. Eleanor did not participate in or condone gossip, and in truth, the column disgusted her. She only read the column just in case Margie Brach had written about something or someone she needed to know about. Who was stepping out with who. Who was going to the movies together. Who had a baby. Or how Larry Herrington's prize heifer was doing lately.

The first item of gossip was about Jeanne Walters and Sam Allen's engagement. Her heart soared when she saw those names. Jeanne was at least one year *older* than Eleanor. The article stated that Sam was going to take Jeanne to Miami for their honeymoon. How marvelous! Miami! *Ay amor!* If Jeanne Walters could find love at her age and manage to finagle a trip to Miami, it meant the universe was on the side of the spinster.

Eleanor made a note to buy a bathing suit this week. Something a little sassy but not too revealing. It was important to keep the mystery alive.

She folded the newspaper and went back to piecrust. Her mood had improved. She couldn't explain why. She could never explain her recent moods. One minute she would be sort of lethargic; the next minute she would be ready to murder a grown man with a pair of salad tongs.

She rolled more dough on the dining room table, this time leaning harder onto her rolling pin, using her body weight to flatten the face of Jimmy Abraham. "Take that, Jimmy," she said to the dough. "You've never danced a day in your life." She smacked the dough a few more times. It made her laugh. She laughed until she cried. She was either losing her mind or finding it.

Eleanor used her apron to wipe the tears from her face. She placed an old record on her turntable, then touched the needle to it. The console hummed to life with a Strauss waltz. She couldn't remember which waltz this was, but it was about as interesting as a glass of mud. So she removed the record and placed another on the turntable. It was brand new. Les Baxter and his orchestra. Precisely what she needed.

The room filled with sweet sounds of strings, exotic voices, and bongos bouncing through the speakers. She closed her eyes. Eleanor imagined she was with a man. In Miami. A handsome man. Maybe even Les Baxter himself, who from his picture looked like an insurance salesman. Maybe Les had written this exotic tune for her and her winning heart. Maybe he was a dashing bandleader whose fortune cookie once read, "You will meet a Methodist woman with chubby legs who makes great pies and owns, not one, but two very sassy but also modest bathing suits."

She dipped herself once. Twice. Then a third time until her hair came undone and fell into her face. She kicked off her shoes and sashayed across her kitchen, shaking her Blessed Assurance for all it was worth. When she reached her living room, she screamed and stopped dancing.

Because Winston Browne was standing before her.

"I didn't mean to scare you, Eleanor. I let myself in."

"What on earth are you doing here?" she said, fixing her hair.

"It's Jimmy. He's hurt."

Bringing Home Baby

The woman's house was the nicest house Jessie had ever seen in her life. Actually, it was the first real house she'd ever seen that wasn't one of the plain, ugly buildings of the temple. The temple community was nothing but shacks with tin roofs, wood floors, white walls, and wet basements. The pictures on the walls at the temple school were paintings of praying hands.

Jessie hadn't gone with the woman quietly. It had taken a lot of doing on everyone's part to calm her down. The woman finally earned Jessie's trust with her soft, low voice. Jessie felt a little ashamed of how she'd acted, flailing her arms, kicking her feet at anyone who came near. She felt even worse about the man she almost killed with the tin can. She hadn't meant to hit him on the temple. She had been aiming for his nose.

This woman's home was a palace. The furniture was ornate, framed pictures covered every surface, and every corner was peppered with flowers. Wonderful flowers. Jessie could not recall ever seeing flowers indoors unless it was a funeral for an elder. She couldn't help but stare at a painting in the living room of a woman. Beautiful. Blonde. Jessie asked who the woman in the painting was.

"That was my mother," said the woman. "She was about sixteen in that picture. Beautiful, wasn't she? She was named Eleanor, just like me."

Jessie nodded but kept her mouth shut. Her strategy was to be quiet. She wasn't going to give away anything about herself. If these people didn't know where she came from, they couldn't send her back to the pits of Hades. And she might finally have a chance at . . . Well, she wasn't sure. But something.

Eleanor guided her down a hallway that featured even more paintings lining the walls. When they reached a bedroom, Jessie felt pain in her head something fierce. She set her suitcase down and placed her face into her hands, pressing on her eyes. The sensation shot from one side of her head to the other.

"Are you okay?" said the woman.

Jessie didn't answer. She felt sick. It was as though the world were moving sideways again. It came and went. Her vision would go blurry, and she would see two of everything. Then it would go back to normal.

"It must be the concussion," Eleanor said. "Do I need to get the doctor?"

"No. I'm okay."

"Are you sure? Let me get Doc Howard."

"No, please." She was done with needles.

"At least tell me who we can call. Your parents, family, or someone. They're probably worried sick about you."

Jessie ignored this question. Nobody was worried about her.

Eleanor placed a hand on Jessie's head and felt around her hair. She was a gentle woman, Jessie could tell right away. If it had been one of the sisters, say, Sister Maria, feeling her head, it would have been about as gentle as a slap.

"That's quite a bump," the woman said. "You need to lie down."

Eleanor fixed up the bed, fluffing the pillows. She explained to

Jessie that this living arrangement was going to be *temporary*. She said it in a stern but kind voice. She reminded Jessie that she had better behave or she would be sent to the courthouse jail, and that living arrangement would not be temporary. The woman really enunciated her words as though she thought Jessie might be either hard of hearing or a foreigner. So Jessie nodded often to show that she understood her.

Eleanor stopped talking and lowered herself to Jessie's level. "You're very pretty, do you know that?"

Jessie had never been called this before. These were vain words, and vanity was a sin.

"I can't see good," said Jessie. "Everything's sorta double and such."

Eleanor brushed a strand of hair from Jessie's face. The woman smelled so sweet all Jessie wanted to do was inhale her. Like vanilla and spices. And just when Jessie didn't think the situation could get any better, the woman reached into her skirt pocket and removed a foil-wrapped chocolate coin. Things were definitely looking up.

"Please tell me your name," said the woman.

Jessie looked at the pictures on the walls and thought about this. Names were not the kind of information that needed to be getting around. If they knew her name, that would be the end of it. She would be back at the temple before she knew it, scrubbing some concrete floor. So Jessie remained mute.

The woman didn't push the matter. "Okay, suit yourself. Can you at least tell me whether you're hungry?"

"Yes, I am hungry."

"Good, you rest for a little. When you are ready to eat, wash your hands in the hall bathroom, *with soap*, and meet me in the kitchen."

Before the woman left the room, Jessie had a change of heart. "Jessie," she said. "My name's Jessie."

Eleanor smiled. The woman seemed to be waiting for the other half of the name. But there would be no more.

Adam's Big River

The funeral was poorly attended, and Reverend Lewis was late for the ceremony. Winston stood by the graveside, hat in his hand, staring at the sky, hoping the weather would hold off. The sky threatened rain even though it was half blue. You could tell these things if you'd grown up in Moab. Most of the time.

Winston had been listening to the Dodgers game before the funeral, and he was beginning to believe the Bums were actually going to do it this year. They were strong and healthy, and this year's team wanted it. Yes, they were going to do it, there were no two ways about it. Even so, Winston could find little joy in baseball while wearing funeral clothes. It just felt wrong. So after he'd put on his suit he'd spent the rest of his afternoon with the game on low volume while he called every township from here to Georgia, asking about missing children. It turned up nothing. So he widened his search radius and put out bulletins as far as Tennessee and Mississippi. That was a lot of sheriff's offices and police stations to call. His elbow hurt from holding the phone for so many hours, and the county's long-distance bill would be horrendous.

Winston checked his watch. Pastor Lewis was almost twenty minutes late.

"I could strangle that man," Eleanor whispered to Winston. "Being late to a funeral is unforgivable."

"Let's give him another ten minutes," said Winston.

Sometimes Winston felt as though his primary job in Okeauwaw County was dealing with dead people and attending their funerals. He was too busy to deal with lackadaisical preachers too.

"Winston," said Tommy. "We'd better get on with Adam's service before it starts raining."

Winston and Tommy were in church clothes. Winston wore his only suit, salt-and-pepper, with a hand-painted tie. Fourteen adolescent baseball players stood next to him, all wearing blue serge sport coats and khaki trousers. Winston had made them come to the service because funerals were good lessons about respect.

Buz stood to the side with his mother, who leaned on a cane and held Buz's arm for support. Her skirt was long, but Winston could still remember what her polio-stricken legs looked like from their youth.

The boys were running low on reverence today. And Winston couldn't blame them for it. They were all talking about one thing. The same thing all males in town were talking about. Many females too. "The Dodgers are gonna do it this year," they'd say. Old Adam would've loved to have seen the boys in blue have a chance at the pennant. Even when he had a snootful, the old man never wandered more than six feet from a radio when a game was on.

Eleanor Hughes stood beside Winston. Jessie stood beside Eleanor. Two elderly men attended as well. Winston knew them, but not very well. The men were dressed in ancient suits, their bellies bursting out of their buttoned vests. The men were relics from 1918, white-haired, feeble, living memories. The red dog sat beside Winston.

They had all been waiting for half an hour near the open grave.

"I'll bet Lewis got confused," said Winston. "Bet he accidentally went to Union Cemetery instead of Moab Memorial."

Then it began to rain.

"Just great," said Winston.

It was not an easy rain. It was a hard rain. When it picked up tempo, the workers began lowering the pinewood box into the ground. They were rushing, and the ropes were slipping from the wetness.

Everyone's clothes started to hang funny, and the boys began to fidget in their wet jackets. The rain was getting louder, like the sound a radio makes when it's tuned to static.

One of the cemetery workers had already started shoveling dirt. When the sheriff heard the thuds of earth hitting the casket, he felt his temper swell. "Stop shoveling. This is a funeral. We have to say *something* before you bury him, for crying out loud."

In some ways, if you removed the shame connected with Adam's darker habits, you almost had to admire him. He lived hard and didn't apologize for it. And now he didn't even have a preacher to say a few words over his casket. It was staggering how fast a person could be forgotten.

Winston walked toward the cemetery worker and yanked the shovel from his hands. "Do you mind?" he said. He couldn't have been more different from Adam Guilford if he tried. Adam had been a slave to pure impulse. Winston was a slave only to obligation. County work had dominated his life. Okeauwaw County was the only family he'd ever known. All he'd ever done was serve papers, remove corpses, settle disputes, and fetch stranded house cats from high trees.

"Buz," Winston said, "do you wanna say anything about your grandpa?"

Buz shook his head.

"I'll say something, Win," said Tommy.

"Go ahead, Tommy."

Tommy shuffled forward and looked at the big wet hole. "Adam, we loved you." He stepped backward into his original spot.

Winston had hoped for a longer speech. He lifted his head and waited for more spiritual inspiration to hit the group, but nothing happened, so he whispered to Tommy, "Do we still have a Bible in the glovebox?"

Tommy said, "I don't know."

The rain was crashing like a waterfall upon the earth, pounding the trees. The sheriff's white hair was matted into his eyes.

Winston hollered over the sound of the rain. "Tommy, would you please go look for the Bible? I would very much like to have something to read in honor of the departed."

Tommy, who finally seemed to grasp the deeper meaning of what the sheriff was suggesting, jogged toward the Hudson. He was gone for several minutes. When he returned, he was carrying a hardback book that was clearly not a Bible.

"Sorry," said Tommy. "This is all I could find."

Winston held the book in both hands. It was Mark Twain's *Life on the Mississippi*. "I can't read from this. Where's the Bible? I keep one in the glove compartment."

"Guess I took it out when I cleaned the car."

"You never clean the patrol car."

"Had to clean it. I took the fourth graders on a field trip."

The sheriff turned the book in his hands. Eleanor held an umbrella over him while he thumbed past the first few pages. Winston Browne knew this book almost by heart. He flipped to chapter nine, then browsed the text with his wet finger.

He began to read in his loudest voice.

"'Now when I had mastered the language of this water and had come to know every trifling feature that bordered the great river as familiarly as I knew the letters of the alphabet, I had made a valuable acquisition. But I had lost something too. I had lost something which could never be restored to me while I lived. All the grace, the beauty, the poetry had gone out of the majestic river!'"

Winston paused to look at the boys who were saturated with rain. Their white shirts were translucent. Their blue serge coats were black with water. They were being respectful, and this made him proud.

"'No, the romance and the beauty were all gone from the river. All the value any feature of it had for me now was the amount of usefulness it could furnish toward compassing the safe piloting of a steamboat.'"

Tommy wiped his face with both hands. So did the two very wet old men. Winston closed the book. He offered a mute apology to Adam. No matter his choices, he deserved Scripture, singing, tears, and all the other things that went with a funeral. What he got was a few paragraphs from required reading material for Moab high schoolers.

"Thank you, Sheriff," said one of the old men. "That was beautiful. I don't remember that part of the Bible. What book was it from?"

"The book of Mark," said the sheriff.

Lightning sounded. The entire sky lit up electric blue. It sounded like a tree had been struck. Everyone scrambled to their vehicles.

"The Dodgers are gonna do it this year, Adam," he said to the hole.

Mein Bischof

Before Sister Maria entered the *Bischof*'s office, she adjusted the black missionary veil over her head with bobby pins. Her pocket mirror was about the size of her palm, easily hidden. It was forbidden among temple sisters, but she carried it with her everywhere. She touched her hair and indulged in momentary vanity since nobody was looking. Maria hadn't seen her brother, Noah, since they'd promoted him to *Bischof* after their father's funeral.

A young man opened the thick door to the all-mahogany office. He was barefoot. He told her to remove her shoes. "The *Bischof* will see you now," he said.

"Thank you, Heinrich," she said.

She slipped off her shoes, then placed them against the wall. She tried not to marvel too much at the finery in the office, but it was incredible. Since taking over the office, Noah had installed golden trim work and hung large paintings with people who were unclothed, wearing bedsheets and eating grapes. These surroundings were a far cry from the humble white walls of her father's office. It made her white hot with anger. Mainly because if Maria had been born a boy, she would have been the one sitting in this office, carrying on the mission of the temple brethren. She was stronger than Noah, and smarter. But rules were rules.

Heinrich led her into another room even finer than the first. With carpet—actual carpet. She found Noah standing in the corner beside a large bookshelf lined with her father's leather-bound books. He wore jeans and a T-shirt. This was different from the plain garb of the temple brethren.

Noah wasn't looking at her. He was too busy flipping through the pages of a *Look* magazine with the image of a swimsuit-clad woman on the front. He closed the magazine quickly and tossed it onto his desk and acted as though he wasn't looking.

Maria said, "Do you find it to be educational?"

He was obviously embarrassed. "I've just never seen one before."

Maria smirked. "Neither have I. I only confiscate them from the boys. When did you start wearing jeans, Noah?"

He shook his head at her and exchanged a knowing smirk with Heinrich. "*Bischof*, Maria. I am not Noah anymore; you must call me *Bischof*. It is my heavenly station in this world." The young man glanced out the window and shoved his hands into his pockets. "Tell me, Maria, do you know this Ada? Ada Müller?"

"Ada? She works in the kitchen at the school and cares for the orphans."

Her brother collapsed in a chair before the large desk. He placed his bare feet on her father's desk. They were dirty. He was disgusting.

"Take your feet off that desk," she said.

"You have not *heard* about Ada or else you would have known why I asked you about her."

She did not say anything.

Noah said, "Wait, wait. Do you mean to tell me that I know something you don't know? How marvelous. You are not Papa's favorite anymore, are you, Maria?" He laughed.

"What do you know about Ada?"

He held up his hands. "Hold on. I want to enjoy this feeling for a little bit. Is this how you felt all the time, being Papa's prized little girl? Knowing everything but telling nothing?"

Maria was infuriated.

"Ada has run away," said her brother. "She killed two men while trying to escape last night. One of them was her husband, Deeter."

"Killed them?"

"Poisoned Deeter and beat Jonas Schaffer with a crowbar."

He looked Maria in the eyes. He put his feet down and leaned forward onto his desk, trying a little too hard to be dramatic. He said, "Do you *know* what this Ada had been doing with your precious papa?"

Maria fell silent again. She had known all about her father's private harem of young women who were all eventually turned out when they got too old. Their heads were shaved, and they were never seen again. But Maria was among the few who knew these things. Secrets were kept tight in the temple community.

Noah went on. "Your foul papa was not the holy prophet you believed he was, and Ada Müller was one of his harlots." Noah threw his hands into the air. "He had dozens of harlots, and twice as many children. Some were even masquerading as temple children *in this community*. He was a dirty man, and his children were an abomination unto God."

She felt her blood run hot. This infant behind the desk knew nothing of the sacred mantle of her father's leadership. Neither did he deserve to inherit it. Maria marched toward her brother and slapped him. Not lightly. "You'll be damned, speaking against your own father like that. You know nothing of the burden he carried for us all."

Noah spit on the floor. "He was a liar, and he's gone now. I have dealt with his orphans and his harlots."

"What do you mean, 'dealt with them'?"

"Never mind." He reached into a drawer and removed a folder. "Ada's child is missing." He tossed the folder to her.

"So? What do you want me to do about it?"

"We know she was in Savannah."

"You *know*? If you know where she is, then why don't you have her? Why do you need me?"

"She's not in Savannah any longer. She was sent to one of Ada's relatives somewhere in the Mobile-Pensacola area. We know they were former temple brethren."

"How do you know all this?"

He smirked. "Ada's friend Johanna. She tried to escape as well, but we caught her and her three brats. She was very forthcoming with her information—once we persuaded her."

Maria could only imagine. "But you still don't have the child." She shook her head. "That little abomination got away from you, didn't she?"

"Yes, but we know roughly where she is."

Maria stared at the magazine on his desk. The young blonde in the swimsuit was sitting on the beach, her hair scattered by the wind. Men were vulgar, and their lewdness brought nothing but problems.

"So what do you want me to do, Noah?"

Noah came from around the desk. He held Maria's face in his warm hands. His eyes were ice blue, just like her father's had been. He kissed her forehead and held his lips in place a little too long. "I want you to find her and bring them back. Or you will be an abomination too."

MOAB SOCIAL GRACES

BY MARGIE BRACH

Mrs. and Mr. Sam Allen eloped last week to Pensacola, long before their planned January wedding date. "We're not getting any younger," said Mrs. Allen. They are honeymooning in Miami. This is Sam's second marriage.

Bill Tyler and Fred Jackson returned from visiting family in New Brockton.

Miss Mary Whipple has almost completely recovered from her cold. "Thank you, everyone, for the chicken soup," said Miss Mary. "I could not eat it all."

Miss Agnes Fourson visited her friends in Jay last week.

Mr. Mark Waller escorted Miss Emily Chaseman to the movies in Pensacola.

Mr. Joseph Flats has moved to Ferry Pass, where he has secured gainful employment.

Adam Laurel Guilford has gone on to Glory. Funeral was held on Friday at Moab Memorial Cemetery.

Postmaster Jimmy Abraham says mail is backed up due to issues in staffing.

Howard Jacobson was called to Daphne, Alabama, on account of the engagement of his daughter, Elsie. This is Elsie's third engagement. "I hope this one works out," said Howard.

Mr. and Mrs. Lawrence Roney returned from Charleston where they honeymooned. "Charleston is nice," said Lawrence.

The Women's Missionary Society dance and fundraiser raised $423 for hungry Soviet children.

Mr. Charles Barns danced with Miss Paula Macy. Mr. James Gregory danced with Miss Sarah Madison. Sheriff Browne danced with Miss Eleanor Hughes. Mr. Leo Martin danced with his mother-in-law, Mrs. Wanda Barkley. "My mother-in-law can really foxtrot," said Leo.

Mr. and Mrs. Don Robinson had a baby girl. They have not chosen a name.

Fall Ball

There were no other lights around except the glowing tower lights suspended over the ball field in the distance. They looked like a dozen celestial eggs floating in the cold black sky, levitating over mankind and all their problems. The bleachers were littered with people who were all shouting and clapping for the teenage boys practicing on the field. It was only a practice, but people in Moab came out to see the boys play three times a week because they were bored small-town people and they would have come out to watch paint dry if there had been nothing good on the radio. Even people who didn't have kids on the team had started coming to practices, ever since the team got their new uniforms. And it didn't hurt that the uniforms had the word *Dodgers* emblazoned on the fronts.

The town had gone extra crazy for baseball in the last few months. The World Series was around the corner now, and the Dodgers had beaten the Giants to take the pennant. Nobody could believe it. Not even the blue-blooded Dodgers fans.

Major league fever had hit. People who never cared a lick for baseball were becoming dyed-in-the-wool fanatics. When something became popular in a small town like Moab, it seeped into the drinking water. You couldn't go to the corner store without hearing the name Jackie Robinson on someone's lips.

“I don’t wanna be doing this tonight,” said P.J. It was cold, with visible clouds exiting his mouth. A novelty in Florida.

“Just hush and keep an eye out, you big baby.”

“I ain’t no baby. This was a lot easier when your granddaddy was with us,” P.J. said. “We’re not nearly as fast as he was. Someone’s gonna catch us and we’re gonna end up in the courthouse.”

“I don’t like it any more than you do. Maybe you can think of a better way to earn fifteen bucks.”

P.J. seemed to actually be considering what Buz said. “Nope. I can’t.”

“Then shut up and hold the gas can still.”

Buz crouched behind a Chevy Impala in the parking lot. His hands stung from the cold when he unscrewed the Impala’s gas cap. There were about thirty cars surrounding the ball field parking lot. It was a gold mine of gasoline because baseball practice could go on for two, maybe three hours. And since everyone was being so noisy cheering for fools in stupid uniforms, there was little chance of anyone hearing them.

P.J. held the empty gas can steady on the ground. Buz inserted the long hose into the tank, then brought the other end to his lips. He sucked once, then spit onto the dirt.

P.J. whispered, “What’s it taste like?”

Buz answered in the same way his grandfather would have answered when Buz was an eight-year-old, learning how to siphon gas from the master himself. “Like whiskey, only better.”

The crowd cheered. They screamed. They applauded. The voice of Sheriff Winston Browne was shouting, “Hustle!” It was the word of the day. The sheriff said it every few seconds. Buz glanced into the distance. He could see the red dog creeping along the perimeter of the field, sniffing for food, getting closer to the Impala.

P.J. picked up a rock and hurled it in the dog’s direction. The dog didn’t move. He started walking toward them.

“Just leave him alone,” whispered Buz. “He ain’t hurting nobody.”

"Why didn't your granddaddy ever name that stupid dog?"

"Principle."

"What?"

"That's what he always said when people asked him why he never named the dog. Principle."

The night was filled with sounds of happy people. Occasionally Buz could hear familiar voices among the crowd. Mister Acre, the banker. Miss Simpson, who used to teach the third grade at Franklin D. Roosevelt Elementary. The same woman who once told Buz that he was talented when it came to writing. The voice of Becky Jernigan, like a sonnet, riding on the night air. They were all cheering for the Moab Dodgers.

"Listen to them cheer," said P.J. "You reckon we have a good team?"

"They stink."

"My aunt says they're pretty good."

"Your aunt wouldn't know a baseball if one bit her in the butt."

"She never misses a Yankees game."

"I rest my case."

P.J. peeked above the Chevy again. So did Buz. Mark Fields was trotting the bases. The kids in the dugout were clapping for him. Then P.J. dropped as low as he could. They heard footsteps. Buz plugged the hose with his thumb to stop the trickle of gasoline, which had started spilling on the ground.

"Who got the big hit?" P.J. whispered. "I can't tell from here."

"Mark Fields. He ain't on the roster yet. He's not even from Moab. Will you hold the can steady, please?"

"How do you know who's on the roster? I thought you said they sucked."

"Just hold the can."

Buz peered around the tailpipe of the Chevy. He couldn't see anything from this angle, but he could hear enough. Footsteps. Two sets of feet, crunching on gravel. He dropped to his belly to look beneath the cars. He could see shoes. Nice shoes. It must have been Reverend Lewis and Mister Acre. Nobody else wore shoes like that. He could hear their voices, their light conversational laughter, their clicking lighters.

"They're gonna catch us," whispered P.J.

"They will if you don't shut up."

P.J. lifted himself a little and eased above the hood for a better look at the game. When he did, he lost his grip on the can. The can dropped and made a clanging noise. Gasoline began spilling from the hose onto the dirt, making a river that soon turned into a small pond.

Buz whispered, "You idiot! The can!"

They tilted the can upward before they lost the entirety of Buz's rent. Buz kept an eye on the shoes. The men didn't seem to notice the sound. They just kept on talking.

"This is my last can for the night. I wanna go watch the game."

"But we've only done two cars. That's not enough money to buy peanuts. We need at least ten gallons to make three bucks."

"So we'll hit the truck stop when the game's over. I wanna see the fellas play."

"The *fellas*? What's wrong with you? Those are a bunch of dweebs. You're not going anywhere. You're gonna stay right here and hold the dadgum can."

"You're not the boss of me."

"P.J."

P.J. stood and brushed off his trousers. He did not like to be told what to do.

"It's just a stupid practice," said Buz. "It ain't even a real game. Besides, when did *you* start caring so much about stupid baseball?"

"Since when did you quit caring, Buz?" P.J. walked away.

Franklin D. Roosevelt

The hallways of Franklin D. Roosevelt Elementary had white-painted brick and mint green tiles. There was no vibrant color here. It smelled like a combination of disinfectants, cookies, and little-kid stink.

"I'm scared," Jessie said to Eleanor, who was walking beside her.

"Oh, hush," said Eleanor. "There is nothing to be scared of."

Eleanor had dressed Jessie in nice clothes for her first day of school, and she had fixed Jessie's hair. Jessie didn't even recognize herself in the mirror. But then, mirrors had been forbidden among the brethren, and Jessie wouldn't have recognized herself anyway. She wore pink today. With matching pink shoes with little white flowers on the toes.

Eleanor squatted before Jessie to adjust her collar and straighten her dress. Then the woman licked her own palm and used it to fix Jessie's hair.

"I don't wanna do this," said Jessie. She'd already told Eleanor this several times that morning. And Eleanor was not exactly being very understanding about it.

"Quit being ridiculous," said Eleanor. "This is just a school."

"Please don't make me stay. I can help around the house. I'm a good cleaner."

"Quiet," said Eleanor, licking her hand again. "No child in my care is going to be uneducated. Now don't slouch. And don't chew your nails either. Understand?"

The clicking of quick footsteps came down the hall. A large red-headed woman with a floral-print dress and thick glasses was smiling and heading straight for Jessie. She introduced herself as Mrs. Plum, then took Jessie by the hand and was escorting her through the long passage of classrooms.

Jessie turned to wave goodbye to Eleanor, but Eleanor flashed a polite smile and a brief wave, then gave Jessie the "go on, shoo" gesture.

Mrs. Plum brought her to a door with a big window in the center, and Jessie could see into the classroom. The place was full of children who were fidgeting, working at desks, laughing, and a few were chasing each other. Mrs. Plum threw open the classroom door and showed her to her desk.

Jessie sat down and couldn't help but notice that every kid in the classroom was looking at her with large eyes. She couldn't help but gawk at them too.

One of the boys had a very strange haircut. His dark hair was shaved on the sides and level on top like a table. She marveled at this. Did he have this haircut on purpose? Had he had an accident with a frying pan? More than anything, she wanted to touch his fuzzy flat hair. The boy adjusted his thick glasses by pressing the nosepiece. He said, "Hi."

"Your head is flat," she told him. Just in case he didn't know.

"I know."

"Why?"

"I like it this way."

In the months that Jessie had been a guest in Eleanor's house, the child had been the quietest soul Eleanor had ever known. Even now, after her first day of school, Eleanor couldn't get her to talk about her day or the teacher or anything she had learned. All she got were short responses.

The only time the girl came alive was when Winston Browne turned on the radio and discussed baseball with her.

Baseball was unladylike, and Eleanor didn't think Jessie should be listening to a boy's game. But then, it meant so much to both Winston and Jessie that she never said a word about it.

She kept her mouth shut when Winston and a few boys from the team began teaching Jessie how to throw and catch. Though she didn't need lessons. The child was obviously a natural athlete. That's what they all said.

The truth was that she was growing attached to this little girl. She saw herself in Jessie. The child had her same inclination to be stubborn. If for no other reason than because it felt good to swim against the current.

When Jessie was dressed in her nightgown, Eleanor turned down her bed and patted the mattress. "Fold your hands, and let's say our prayers."

Eleanor bowed her head along with the girl but did not close her eyes. Often, Eleanor watched the girl and listened carefully in case she said something important that might reveal something about her family or where she had come from. But the girl never prayed for her parents or for any siblings. She never asked God to watch over aunts or uncles. She always just repeated a few prayers Eleanor had taught her.

Eleanor kissed the girl's hair. "I want you to know that you can talk to me."

The girl just closed her eyes.

"Dear God," Jessie said, "please take care of Duke Snider, Sandy Amorós, Johnny Podres, Roy Campanella, Gil Hodges, Tommy Lasorda, and Jackie. And, God, please watch over Ada." Eleanor stood and helped the child into bed. She tucked her in and kissed her forehead. "Were those your friends you were praying for? You must miss them."

Jessie shook her head. "Those were my favorite Dodgers."

But Eleanor was no fool. She had never heard of a Dodger named Ada before.

The Unreachable

Winston Browne was sitting on Eleanor's porch wearing a soggy soft-brimmed hat and sipping a mug of hot coffee. The late autumn rain was coming down hard, and a small river was flowing down the pavement of Evergreen Avenue, collecting in the gutters, rushing toward the end of the street. The frogs were singing in the happy way that north Floridian frogs do when it rains. The sounds of the night were like a symphony.

He had been traveling to Pensacola for oxygen treatments every morning. He hated being in a room filled with dying people wearing nasal cannulas. And it wasn't even doing any good. He had been spending the rest of his free time at Eleanor's house. Sometimes he came over for coffee before heading into work. And he started coming over most nights for supper. He didn't draw attention to his visits, for Jimmy's sake, but he couldn't help himself. It had started out of duty, to check on the runaway girl. But now it was just a dying man seeking his sanctuary.

He enjoyed Ellie's house. Maybe a little too much. It was more than a house; it was a refuge. Ellie had maternal powers. A man's life was not complete without a motherly person in it. His own friendship with Jimmy could not compete with what he felt when he was with this woman.

In the recent months, Jimmy and Winston had been on the outs. Probably because of pride on both ends. Jimmy had quit coming to ball practices. Winston had stopped playing Scrabble in the mornings. It was the first time in their lives that their friendship had waned to a standstill. And the worst part about it was, Winston knew he should feel guilty about it, but he didn't.

The knowledge of death changes the way a man handles guilt. Guilt is sometimes more about what other people think of you than about what's right and wrong. But when you're dead and gone, it doesn't matter what anyone thinks about you because you are worm food. All that matters is heart. Who gave a cuss if they had a beef with your choices? What were they going to do? Dig up your coffin and smack you around?

Eleanor opened the screen door with her foot. She was carrying two plates with slabs of pie upon them. It was like she could read his thoughts. All that was missing was the vanilla ice cream, but hey, you can't have everything.

Eleanor said, "I have vanilla ice cream inside."

After topping their pie with the ice cream, Eleanor sat beside him, her thigh touching his. "Your job description must be the longest anyone's ever seen, Winston Browne. You're a coach and sheriff, the coroner, and you deliver groceries. What else do you do?"

Winston had to think about this. "Well, I win at Scrabble a lot."

She laughed. "The incredible Winston Browne."

"But I haven't been playing lately. I'm probably getting rusty."

She scooted herself beside him a little closer. "Jimmy hates me too," she said.

"Ellie, I thought you told me it was over between you two."

"It is over," she said. "It's not my fault he won't listen to me." She took a bite of pie and made a sharp conversational turn. "You know, I don't remember Sheriff Branson ever doing funerals or coaching baseball."

"That old fool was too busy busting up whiskey stills to do anything else." Winston used the fork to negotiate the world's biggest bite. He closed his eyes and gave a complimentary moan. "Oh, Eleanor, this pie is . . ."

"Unbelievable?"

He laughed. Which led to a cough. The cold rain had gotten to him. "You don't have to be so modest on my account."

He took another bite. The frogs sang another chorus. The rain came down even harder. The thunder in the distance rumbled. If he weren't so busy dying, this would have been the most beautiful Floridian night of his entire life. Then again, every night had been like that lately.

"I like having Jessie here," said Eleanor. "She makes me feel useful. Like I have a purpose, you know?"

"You do have a purpose."

"I don't know."

"You're every parent's Sunday school teacher. Eleanor Hughes can reach the unreachable."

"No, I teach Sunday school because nobody else wanted to. And I haven't reached Jessie. Not like you. She lights up whenever you two talk about baseball or listen to it on the radio. All she can think about is the World Series."

Eleanor leaned against his shoulder. It made his body feel warm all over. He also felt himself struggling to swallow the brick in his throat, which was not due to the cough. This was nothing but boyhood angst. The kind of feelings that never leave a man.

"What's gonna happen to Jessie?" said Eleanor.

"If we win the Series, she's gonna be happier than a catfish in tartar sauce, that's what'll happen."

"I'm serious. What if we never find her parents? What then?" It was a loaded question. But Winston was a county man, not a dreamer.

"I've been making calls as far away as Montgomery. If she's from anywhere near here, we'll find her family. You need to be ready for that. How was school?"

"Mrs. Plum says she's a brilliant kid. She follows directions well." Eleanor hung her head. "But I don't know anything about her. If only she would talk to me. In our nightly prayers just now, she just asked the Lord to watch over someone named Duke Snider."

Winston half smiled. Duke didn't need prayer. He led the league in runs.

"She also prayed for someone named Ada. But she wouldn't say who that is."

They were silent for a few minutes, watching the rain. Winston came from a long line of rain-watchers. There was worry in Eleanor's whole being. He patted her knee.

"Don't you worry about Jessie. We're gonna make sure she's taken care of. All we can do is hope someone comes forward, pray for the best."

"What's the worst?"

He looked at his bootlaces. "Foster institution."

"An *orphanage*? No."

"No need to fret about that. We're not there yet."

He finished his pie and placed the plate beside him. He removed a pack of Luckys from his chest pocket and offered Eleanor one. After she put it into her mouth, he lit it. She used the ember to light his, then handed it to him. The smoke made him wheeze, but not enough to stand up. He didn't want to leave this woman. He took another drag, even though it made his throat close.

"Winston," she said, "that cough sounds like it's getting worse."

He took a long pull on his smoke and forced out a hard cloud, squelching another cough that tickled his throat. "Jimmy wants to kill me. You know that, don't you? He is not taking this well."

She didn't respond, and it made him feel like a fool. He was sorry he'd brought it up again. Eleanor stood without saying a word. She walked toward the door, clomping on the porch floorboards, stomping out her cigarette. She was leaving him. *Congratulations, Winston Browne, you ruined a perfect evening.*

"Ellie," said Winston. "I'm sorry. I didn't mean to spoil the moment."

"You didn't spoil anything," she said. "I'm just turning on all my porch lights so Jimmy can get a better look at us." She nodded toward a Ford truck sitting at the end of Evergreen Avenue, headlights off.

Then Eleanor walked toward Winston. She glanced down the street to make sure she had her audience. She held Winston's cheeks, stared into his eyes. "You're an answer to my prayers, Winston Browne," she said. Then she planted a kiss on his forehead. He wanted to respond with more, but it had been a long time since he'd been kissed.

Winston floated the entire way home.

Dummkopf

Midnight. Maria sat beside the Floridian Motor Inn's bright blue swimming pool. They had been searching Pensacola and Mobile for a long time, and she was tired. She had a headache from sweating so much in this horrid heat, combing through all the possible places a child could have gone after leaving a train platform. Noah sent two fools to help her, but Heinrich and his brother, Karl, were as slow and unfamiliar with the outside world as visitors from another planet, and they only made things more difficult.

She was cleaning up someone else's mess, that's what she was doing. The incompetent imbecile in Savannah had told her the child boarded the train bound for Mobile-Pensacola. But she wasn't sure the man could be trusted. Any man not smart enough to capture a small girl wasn't exactly the sharpest blade in the toolbox.

This was a goose chase. The child could be anywhere by now. And Maria was in a strange land, looking for a needle in a needlestack. She lit another filter-tipped Viceroy and watched the rippling light glow beneath the surface of the swimming pool's water. She had never seen a swimming pool before. Maria had never seen anything before. The bright blue water hypnotized her.

Karl stepped into the motel breezeway. He was wearing a

sleeveless undershirt and suspenders. Dressed immodestly. "Maria," he whispered.

"Over here," she said.

The young man walked barefoot on the concrete. He sat beside her and said, "*Warum bist du draußen, Schwester?*"

"English, Karl. You're not in Pennsylvania anymore."

He was embarrassed, she could tell. His English was bad. "It is too hot to be sit out here this tonight. I am sweat unto life."

"It's sweat to *death*, not unto life. *Death*."

He frowned. "I do not sweat *that* bad."

It was bad enough that she had to spend hours in a slow-moving vehicle with these goons looking for an elusive child, always searching, never finding. But these night hours beside the pool were supposed to be hers.

But Karl had not come to socialize. The young man was there to tell her something. "The *Bischof* was on telephone with Heinrich, and he says he has news."

"Why didn't you get me?"

"It is okay, do not worry, *Schwester*. We tell the *Bischof* you are relaxing by the pool with a *Zigarette*."

"*Zigarette*? You fool. You told the *Bischof* I was smoking?"

Karl looked confused. "But he smokes more *Zigarettes* than you."

"What did the *Bischof* say?"

"The *Bischof* says they have found your father's harlot."

Maria stepped on her smoke and stood. She balled her fist and popped the young man's snout. A fine trickle of red came from his nostrils. "*Dummkopf!* Don't you ever speak of my father that way again, or it will be you the *Bischof* is looking for."

And Every Boy Wore Blue

It was a Tuesday. In some ways it was like any other day in northwestern Florida. The air had become sharp with the first signs of cold weather. There was no traffic. No people on sidewalks. No women carrying grocery bags. No nothing. Only a few cars parked downtown. Moab proper had come to a dead stop because it was the most important day in the history of the world. At least that's what it was to Buz Guilford.

Pollen floated from the tall longleaf pines in thick yellow sheets, descending, painting the hoods of every car and ruining the lives of the perfectionists who had just simonized the old Plymouth. Anyone with seasonal allergies was doomed to suffer from a literal New Testament judgment.

Buz arrived at the mercantile just in time to see the third inning of the last game of the World Series on the large wooden television. Miniature ballplayers scrambled across a blueish screen about the size of an electric toaster. A group of men, women, boys, and girls huddled around the set. The television's single speaker was at max volume.

"Turn it up," said one old man.

"Shhh!" said another.

"You shhh!" said someone after that.

"Both of you shush!" said Jimmy.

All the men shushed. The children were quiet too, clad in their new Dodgers jerseys. Even the girls were hypnotized by the scenes on the television. Buz leaned against the counter for a better look.

P.J. was already there, wearing a satisfied expression on his face. "I thought you didn't care about baseball."

P.J. took a smug pull from an orange Nehi bottle. He looked at Buz with a half smile.

"What'd I miss?" Buz asked P.J.

"Nothing. Zero to zero. You couldn't stand it, could you? You had to see it."

"Shhh!" said an old man.

Three more shushes followed.

The boys shut their mouths and listened to the announcer, who spoke in the anvil tones of an evangelist. The voice called each play with the same kind of sincerity war reporters had used a decade earlier. Few in the mercantile dared to speak over the announcer.

Odie whispered in a flat voice, "We're struggling. Jackie's only hitting two-fifty-six this year."

"Shhh!"

"But he's Jackie," added Jimmy. "Besides, Snider leads the league in RBIs."

"Shhh!"

Buz could hardly see the player on the screen. He had to squint from where he stood just to make out who was who.

"Is that Jackie?" said Buz.

"Shhhhh!" said everyone at once.

The Dodgers had been to the World Series seven times and lost seven times. Seven. The boys in Moab had rooted for the team harder each year until they had reached the peak of their loyalty. And even though these boys were a thousand miles away, in a foreign world of

Southern accents, they would have fought anyone who spoke against Jackie, Duke, or Campy.

This World Series had started out as a heartbreaker. Right from the first swing. Brooklyn had lost the first two games, and it looked like it would be another bloodbath for the Bums. Until Game Three, when the tides had changed.

And then it was happening. It was *really* happening. Brooklyn defeated the Yanks, eight to three. Hope glimmered. But nobody had flown any banners. There was still a war to be fought. But Brooklyn had gone on to win the next two games, coming from behind like battered featherweights, punching anything that moved.

Then came Game Six. The Yanks clobbered Brooklyn hard. Everyone was constipated after that.

Now the Series was tied. And this tie gave Buz literal waves of nausea that would not quit. He had listened to all six games and had even watched Game Five at Tyler Randal's house, one of the only kids in town who had a TV. But this was Game Seven.

The Dodgers were hanging on by their pinky toenails. And even the pinky nails were starting to bleed. The line between euphoria and heartbreak was growing hairline thin. The fate of the free world rode on Game Seven. Buz wanted to vomit.

All Moab's shop owners had shut down for every game. Deliveries stopped. Mister Brannen's dry cleaning service quit taking orders. The filling station closed. The Franklin D. Roosevelt Elementary School closed, which was only right. Nobody would have attended school anyway. Everyone would have come down with a sudden case of cholera.

During the series every boy in Moab Township was wearing royal blue, except for the troublemakers who wore Yankee pinstripes. Those boys were begging for an untimely death.

Tensions had started to run high among local boys. Yanks fans against Dodgers patriots. Some boys had changed sides once the Dodgers won the pennant and pretended to be Dodgers sympathizers all along. Everyone loves a winner.

Fights broke out in the backyards on Evergreen, Peach, Azalea, and Hydrangea when the names of Jack Roosevelt Robinson or Roy Campanella were taken in vain. Freckle-faced Yankee sympathizers and Dodger allies had laid fists into one another for the pride of something that was higher than themselves. Tempers flared. And each boy, practicing the loyalty that baseball alone demands, forced his mortal enemy to "Take it back!"

Buz stood in the mercantile, just like all the other loyalists. The Nehi P.J. handed him went down easy and cut his nerves a little. A few more boys wandered into the store. Henry, Floyd, Carson, Arliss, and Craig.

Henry saw Buz and whispered, "Hey, what'd we miss?"

This time it was Buz who said, "Shhh!"

Winston sat on the back porch of his little house on Terrence Street, overlooking the pines in his backyard. He listened to a candy apple–red Philco Transitone radio, which had been a gift from the county for outstanding service. This was laughable. The truth was, Winston Browne was sheriff of Okeauwaw County because nobody else wanted the job. Nobody ever ran against him. Furthermore, he had no other occupational skills. After the war, he'd fallen right into county work.

He lit a cigarette and crossed his legs, leaning back into the wooden chair. He sat sandwiched between Eleanor Hughes and Jessie. The radio was on the porch railing, a long electrical wire stringing backward into his screen door. The flat, urgent voice of Vin Scully announcing each play hummed through the tweed speaker. Vin was in good voice today.

Winston sipped black coffee between drags. By the fourth inning, Eleanor had quit pretending to be interested in the game. She left Jessie and Winston alone and went inside to clean. By inning five, his house was cleaner than it had ever been.

He was glad to have Jessie as his partner. He explained each detail of the game of baseball to her while she stared at the radio with hawk-like interest. Winston had never known that sharing a game with a child could enhance the pleasure of it. But it did. It was wholly different from coaching boys on a field. When the girl put her arm around his shoulder, he turned into custard.

"How do you like going to school?" he asked her.

"It's okay."

"You're lucky. All the kids love Mrs. Plum."

Jessie shrugged. "She's all right."

The child was clearly more interested in listening to the game, so Winston kept his mouth shut. Inning by inning, Jessie leaned against him a little harder. One small move at a time, she inched closer to him, until she was sitting on his lap. Eleanor gawked from the kitchen window.

The girl reminded Winston of himself. She had grasped the game faster than any boy on his team. And somehow the Series had brought this little girl out of her shell. Jessie and Winston both wore home-made Dodgers T-shirts.

"Where are the Bums playing again?"

"The Bronx," said Win. "They're on Yankee ground, up in New York City, a long way away from here."

"Where's New York?"

"Practically on Mars."

The Flatbush neighborhood of Brooklyn was exactly 1,175 miles away. Winston knew this because he had once figured the mileage years ago when he'd threatened to drag Jimmy to a game. That was back before Jimmy wanted to see Winston Browne burned at the stake for being so neighborly with Eleanor.

"Mars?" she said.

"Yeah," he said. "Don't you know what Mars is?"

She shook her head.

"It's another world, sweetie. Just like New York. It couldn't be any more different from Moab if it was full of green men in space helmets."

The Lucky's smoke wafted upward through Winston's throat, making him cough. The fit lasted through half of the fifth inning so that Jessie had to stand beside the radio with her ear pressed to the speaker just to hear.

He was still coughing when she began jumping and shouting, "We scored, Win! We scored!" He let out a whoop, more for the girl's sake than his own. He was becoming dizzy from the hacking, and it was hard to cheer. Even so, a true fan never lets his partner rejoice alone.

"Are you okay?" said Eleanor through the open window. She was cooking now.

"I'm fine. It's just the pollen . . ." He coughed even harder.

"I still wish you'd just try the syrup I bought you."

She had no idea how sick he was. Neither did she have any idea he was taking a lot more than simple syrup. The doctor had him on every medication under the full moon. His insides were a chemistry experiment. The doctor advised him to quit smoking and start chewing navy plug. He tried it. He lasted one day before he opened a new carton of Luckys.

Eleanor brought the bottle of syrup to Winston. "Please, Win, try some for me."

He grabbed the bottle and spoon and made a big production out of swallowing the spoonful and then acting like it was killing him, for Jessie's sake. Jessie seemed to think this was marvelous.

The radio blared:

"And Berra stands at the plate, number eight is looking good, folks. And it's a loud night here in the park . . . Here in the Bronx . . . Here's the pitch . . . Berra swings and . . . misses . . . High and inside . . ."

Strike.

Jessie and Winston rejoiced. Berra was one of the bad guys.

"What's happening now?" said Eleanor.

Jessie shushed her. A true convert.

"Podres winds up again. Here's the offering. And . . . it's below the belt." The crack of a bat on the radio.

Winston almost swore, but he held it in.

"Oh no," said Eleanor. "Is that bad?"

"Bad?" said Jessie. "He just hit the ball. Of *course* it's bad."

Through the small tweed speaker, Yankee Stadium's sixty thousand fans screamed for their man, Berra, and almost distorted the little speaker.

"Berra hits it high into left, Amorós runs after it . . . Amorós takes off his glove, folks! Amorós puts it on his RIGHT HAND! And . . . and . . . Amorós . . . He . . . MAKES THE CATCH!"

Winston and Jessie shot to their feet and cheered. Winston held the girl in his arms and twirled her. He saw electric joy on her face. She was screaming louder than he was.

When the exuberance had faded, Eleanor said, "Was that good? Did something good happen?"

"Sweetie," said Winston, taking her into his arms. "We might actually win this thing!" He kissed her on the mouth. He hadn't meant to, but he didn't dislike the way it felt.

And he could tell she didn't hate it either.

Buz was wringing his blue ball cap in his hands. Not a single man in the mercantile would say a word to interrupt the game or he would have been shot. The sounds of breathing were all Buz could hear coming from the mercantile. The score was two zip, Dodgers.

The eighth inning was the longest inning of Buz's life. Brooklyn's victory was hanging in the balance. One wrong move and evil would win and the whole earth would explode.

Old men edged forward on seats. Even the girls were resting their chins on their fists. One lady looked like she was on the verge of crying.

Buz could hear his heartbeat in his ears. He reminded himself it was stupid to get this excited about a ball game. Utterly stupid. But he couldn't help it. This game had a strange power over fatherless boys. It lied to them, led them to believe that a bat made all men equal.

Time slowed down. The bottom of the eighth moved with molasses-like sluggishness. The Yankees threatened, but Johnny Podres stood cool on his mound, snuffing batters out one by one.

"One more inning to go," whispered P.J. "I think I'm gonna puke."

At 3:44 p.m. Winston Browne was holding Jessie on his hip, standing two feet away from the little red radio. His wheezing had subsided long enough for him to breathe. Or maybe it was that stupid syrup.

A starling was feeding from the backyard feeder he had refilled with seed that morning. The sunlight was getting a little dimmer while the afternoon crickets clocked in for their daily shift.

The last innings had brought an entire spectrum of human emotion. Total elation, followed by pure death. And . . .

Then it happened.

It all went by so fast, so easy, so effortless, so smooth that it almost flashed past him like a snake crossing the highway. The hits. The catches. The outs. The strikes. The victory.

The radio voice said, *"Ladies and gentlemen, the Brooklyn Dodgers are the champions of the world."* The radio voice did not shout this. It did not scream these words or use any inflections of deep emotion. It simply stated the fact. Brooklyn was the champion of the world.

Winston Browne felt a cold wave sweep over him. Then, without his permission, he felt his face bust open. He was overtaken by a sensation that was unfamiliar to him. He could not shout, he could not speak, he could not swallow or breathe. He was numb.

Jessie was jumping and cheering. Even Eleanor was cheering. There were the sounds of shotguns in the distance. The clanking of pots and pans came from Terrence Street and every street nearby. Local boys were running around screaming. Cars were honking their horns. The whole world was celebrating. But Winston was hushed and calm.

In his mind he saw his own life. Every piece of it, from the early days to the late ones. He saw summers spent rolling on outfield grass as a child. He saw the face of his father, leathery from the sun, beneath harsh sunlight in a peanut field, pitching a ball toward young Win. He saw his mother, calling him for supper at the edge of the field of summer wheat. He saw the hours, months, and years passed on the pitcher's mound, perfecting his four-seamer, his slider, and his dipsy doodle, with a young Jimmy Abraham behind the plate wearing a chest protector.

And he saw Katie. The woman he almost married. Who promised him she'd wait for him while he traipsed all over a bloodstained Europe carrying her and a rifle that bore her name engraved in the shoulder stock. And he re-felt the pain when she told him she'd married another in his absence. A preacher of all things. She'd married a dadgum preacher.

He relived the whole decade. The uneventful years and the ones spent alone as a bachelor, eating suppers in his undershorts, listening to games in his kitchen, passing the monotonous hours without the company of a woman or the brightness of a child or anyone to care for. He recalled each marathon county council meeting and the decade he'd wasted filling out miles of municipal paperwork. He saw it all.

But more than anything, he saw the family he never had, now here on this porch. He lost himself in the sight of these two females. He began to sob. He began to heave. It humiliated him so much he stepped off the porch and into the yard to cry in private. But nothing is private among people who love one another. Eleanor followed him. So did Jessie. Eleanor draped her arms around Winston and embraced him. Jessie threw her arms around both of them.

They stood in his backyard. A three-person sandwich. The radio blared:

"The field is covered in Dodgers, folks. Not a patch of green is showing. The Dodgers win the World Title . . . Everyone is on the field! Everyone is on the field!"

But Winston was here. In this little ordinary town, positioned alongside the Escambia River. He was sheltered within two sets of female arms, crying so hard he nearly ruined Eleanor's dress. Not because today was a beautiful day. Not because America's team of lovable Dodgers had made history. Not even because he had grown to love these two women more than his own life.

But because Winston Browne was not ready to die.

MOAB SOCIAL GRACES

BY MARGIE BRACH

Moab celebrated the Brooklyn Dodgers World Series victory with a spontaneous auto-vehicle parade.

Mr. and Mrs. Sam Allen returned from their Miami honeymoon. "Miami is wonderful," said Mr. Allen. This is Sam's second marriage.

A television party at Mr. and Mrs. John Wannamaker's last week hosted ninety-three people for the World Series.

Miss Mary Whipple has altogether recovered from her cold. "You can quit bringing me chicken soup now," said Miss Mary.

Miriam Boswell has raised the price of her hand-made Brooklyn Dodgers jerseys, now $6 apiece. "It's called supply and demand," said Mrs. Boswell.

Rev. Lewis has been called to a West Virginia parish and will be leaving Moab Methodist after two years of faithful service. Farewell party on Tuesday. Bring hot covered dish.

Moab Little League is holding practices nightly at Moab field. All interested boys see Sheriff Browne. Gloves can be provided.

Mr. Allen Bittle visited Mobile to purchase a new Chevy Bel Air. "It's got leather seats," said Mr. Bittle.

Mr. and Mrs. Lawrence Roney have purchased the Danielsons' home on Terrence Street. Said Mrs. Roney, "I'm just going to leave it the color it is."

The Women's Missionary Society annual trick-or-treat caravan will be meeting at seven p.m. at Miller's Drugstore. Costumes involving use of blood are not allowed.

Postmaster Jimmy Abraham says mail is backed up due to staffing issues.

Larry Herrington's red angus heifer took second place in the Okeauwaw County livestock competition. "I'm taking Red to the state fair," said Larry.

Mr. Martin Bass escorted Miss Laney McWilliams to the theater in Pensacola last Friday.

Mr. Tab Brayden and Miss Sherry Taylor happily announce their engagement. Miss Taylor is from New Jersey.

Alvin Baker has stocked Baker's Hardware with official Dodgers hats, $2 each. "They won't last long," said Mr. Baker.

Sheriff Browne escorted Miss Eleanor Hughes to eat at China King in Pensacola last Saturday evening.

Les Baxter Is a Chump

Jimmy sat on the porch of the mercantile. He was watching Allen Bittle show off his new car to the old men. The radio in Allen's car was playing a string-heavy song by the Les Baxter Orchestra. You couldn't throw a rock without hitting a person listening to a Les Baxter song. It was like being trapped inside a romance movie, minus the romance and the film crew.

The truth was, Jimmy loved cars. He was a car man through and through, but he'd never owned one. He had never needed a car in Moab. The town was small enough that the city-limit signs could both be nailed to the same post. But he had always wanted a car. Always. He knew exactly which make and model he would get—a Chevy Bel Air two-door hardtop with three-speed manual, the 215.5 cubic inch, 3.5 liter Thriftmaster with optional wood-grain trim around the side windows. But there are some things a fella learned to live without in a place like Moab. Not that he was bitter about it.

Within a few minutes of parking in front of the mercantile, Allen Bittle's new car had drawn a small crowd. Every geezer in the county was running his hands along the chrome trim, asking questions like, "How's she run, Al?" or "What kinda mileage does she get?" or "Does she have dual quads, Al?"

Allen Bittle had no idea what kind of quads she had, or if she had quads at all. So he was making things up, spitting now and then to make his remarks seem more official. It was Allen's first car. He'd driven to Mobile to buy it, then cruised home at a top speed of four miles per hour so as not to kick up dust and get her underside dirty.

Jimmy wasn't interested. Not this morning. He was too mad to care about cars or dual quads, or anything else for that matter. Ever since Eleanor had quit him, the rumors drifting around town about her had multiplied like a virus. And they were getting worse. Each time he heard one about her and Winston, it cut him to the marrow. *People in small towns can be vicious*, Jimmy thought. *But they can also be right sometimes.*

He attended the Methodist church and watched them from the back pew. Eleanor sat beside the traitor. She had begun dressing differently too. He had even seen her wear a skirt that showed *her knees*. Not the whole knee, but some of it. It was scandalous.

The effects of Jimmy's concussion were still lingering, though not as bad as before. He had been confused for a full month after the little girl hit him with that can of carrots. Sometimes he found it hard to speak and think straight. The doc said if the can of carrots had hit him three inches higher on his temple, he might not have lived. The doctor said these things could last for years sometimes. In other words, Jimmy and the girl had sort of traded concussions the same way schoolchildren trade baseball cards, marbles, or black eyes.

Things had changed between the postmaster and the sheriff. Winston Browne had quit playing Scrabble in the mornings. Jimmy had quit helping with the Little League team and was fantasizing about setting fire to Winston's house on Terrence Street.

The sheriff didn't even have the decency to be discreet. He'd been wasting every free moment with Eleanor. She was even accompanying Winston to baseball practice. Baseball. Eleanor Hughes didn't know the difference between a baseball and a ball of belly-button lint.

Thus, Jimmy was on the porch of his store, boiling inside, eyes locked on the courthouse across the street. He should have been out delivering mail, but he was watching to see that backstabbing, good-for-nothing, scum-sucking, high-horse-riding, dog of an elected official come walking out of the courthouse across the street, just so he could glare at him.

No sign of the sheriff yet. But the courthouse lights were on. Someone was in there.

Moab was baptized in the autumn sun, chilly and crisp. Cold enough for a jacket, but nobody in town owned one. The stringed melodies of Les Baxter's symphonic sap wafted from Allen's car. Jimmy wished he'd turn that stupid music off. Les Baxter was a chump.

Eleanor loved Les Baxter.

A few doors down from the mercantile, four women gathered inside Miss Herrington's dress shop. Chances were, they were discussing the recent marriage of Mary King, who was now Mary Steadhamer. Or perhaps their discussion was about Ray's neon sign. Everyone hated that sign.

If they hadn't already covered the topic, they were getting around to talking about Reverend Davis, the new Methodist minister from Connecticut. He was an odd man who greased his hair and talked with an accent that sounded about as affable as a Thompson submachine gun. The man was a baseball fanatic, so he had that going for him. But other than that, he was just plain weird.

Allen popped the hood to his car. He doused a rag in gasoline and wiped the engine down. Jimmy wondered how a young man could be so excited about a hunk of metal and four tires when there were so many other things to worry about. Who needed a stupid car anyway?

When it seemed apparent that no turncoat sheriff was going to exit the courthouse, the old postmaster gave up waiting. He decided to take matters into his own hands. Jimmy walked into the mercantile and lifted the candlestick phone from beneath the counter. He was about to call the courthouse, but he thought better of it. Instead, something in his gut told him to try Eleanor's house.

"Catherine," he said into the phone, "get me Eleanor Hughes."

The phone rang several times, but nobody answered. After a few minutes of ringing, he slammed the handset into the cradle. This was eating him alive. He was about to walk away, but he didn't. He lifted the handset and told Catherine to try her again.

The phone rang. It kept ringing.

Click.

There was a slight pause before Eleanor spoke. "What do you want, Jimmy?" No sooner had she said it than a husky voice in the background asked, "Where'd you put the sugar, Ellie?"

Jimmy felt hollow and betrayed. He replaced the handset onto the cradle. He wandered back out to the porch and sat in the chair, watching the old fogies swarm the Chevrolet Bel Air.

"Take off your shoes!" Allen Bittle was shouting. "You'll get my floorboards all dirty, Alvin!" So six old men kicked off their shoes and nestled themselves into Allen's car, shoulder-to-shoulder like a bunch of grade-A idiots.

"Are you coming for a ride, Jimmy?" shouted Odie. "Allen's gonna show us how she handles."

"Why should I care how she handles?" said Jimmy.

"I thought you loved Chevrolet Bel Airs."

"Well, I don't," Jimmy lied.

Eleanor watched the Hudson pull out of her driveway. She and Jessie were waving goodbye to Winston until his taillights winked out into the moonless night. Eleanor held a paper Chinese take-out container, pocketbook draped over her arm. When she stepped onto her porch, she screamed.

Jimmy was sitting on her swing, smoking in the dark. She could see the glowing red ember floating in the night. He startled her, but she was not entirely surprised to see him here. In fact, she had been wondering what was taking him so long.

"Jimmy Abraham," she said. "You scared me half to death, you fool."

"Whatcha got there, Eleanor?" he said. "Egg foo yung?"

"It's Peking duck. What're you doing here? You're skulking around like some criminal."

"Hi, Mister Jimmy," said Jessie in a quiet voice.

"Hi, yourself," he said.

"Jessie," said Eleanor. "Go on inside. I want to talk with Jimmy alone." She handed Jessie the container. "Put this in the fridge, please. I don't want it to spoil."

"No," said Jimmy. "You don't wanna let a good Peking duck spoil."

When the girl disappeared, Jimmy flashed her a wounded look, which made her feel almost ashamed. She tugged at her pleated skirt when she noticed him looking at the sliver of knee beneath the hem.

But it turned out he was not there to criticize. "I miss you," he finally said. And it sounded like the most sincere thing Jimmy Abraham had ever said to her. "I *really* miss you, Ellie." He looked into his lap.

She wished he would have cried. That would have made it better. But a girl can't have everything.

"Jimmy, I think you should go home."

"I messed up, didn't I?"

She sighed. "Jimmy, it doesn't matter *who* messed up. We've both made mistakes. Right now we need to be friends and leave it at that."

"Friends?"

"We're only friends. I think you've made that clear to me over the years."

"*Winston Browne* was my friend. Do you realize that? He's my enemy now."

They were interrupted when Jessie emerged from the house onto the porch, making a loud noise on the floorboards.

"Go on back inside, Jessie," said Eleanor. "Get washed up and ready for bed. I'll be in to say prayers in a second."

But Jessie did no such thing. The child wandered toward Jimmy. She stopped a few feet before him.

"What do you want?" Jimmy said to the child.

She held out her hand.

"What's that?" Jimmy said, staring at the hand.

"I'm sorry I threw that can at you, Mister Jimmy."

Jimmy's scowl broke. He shook her hand. "Well, you're forgiven, Jessie." Then Jimmy stood and fuzzed her hair. "But there's a lesson you'll learn one day. Not everyone forgives you in this life."

He locked eyes with Eleanor. "Some people will hold your mistakes against you, then they'll tear your heart out. Good night, Eleanor. Enjoy your duck." He stepped off the porch and walked away.

"Jimmy," she called after him.

But he did not look back.

Lions and Cowboys and Bears

Winston led a trick-or-treating parade of thirty children across Evergreen Avenue, Terrence Avenue, and Azalea Street. When they finished with those houses, everyone crossed Hydrangea with pillowcases full of licorice whips, jawbreakers, and Baby Ruths. He'd been leading this trick-or-treat expedition for the last ten years, ever since he returned from the war and been elected as county babysitter, and Jimmy had helped him every year. But this year Jimmy was nowhere in sight.

Of course, Winston knew he should have felt terrible about this. But he didn't. There are some things a dying man quits feeling bad about.

So Winston guided the procession of kids in costumes without the postmaster's help. He spent most of his night pushing a wheelchair that carried eleven-year-old "Hooty" McPherson, who was dressed up as a pirate. Hooty held a pillow sack on his lap that was twice as full as everyone else's. Having a broken ankle on Halloween night had its perks.

Jessie and Eleanor followed Winston. Jessie was dressed as Johnny Podres, the superhuman pitcher and world champion. Eleanor had planned on dressing up as Scarlett O'Hara, but Jessie talked her into going as a giant Hershey's Bar. Winston and Eleanor had stayed up all night decorating a cardboard box with glue and craft paper. Which suited him fine. He had been looking for any reason to be with her.

When they reached Hydrangea, most of the storefronts had replaced their bulbs with orange lights. Another yearly tradition in Moab. No sooner had they passed the mercantile than they were greeted by someone dressed in a grizzly bear suit. The bear removed its head. Winston laughed when he saw who it was. "So you decided to join us after all, Jimmy?"

Jimmy was not in good spirits. "What're you supposed to be dressed as, Win? Judas Iscariot?"

"Can't you tell? I'm dressed as an underpaid county elected official."

"Well, don't forget your thirty pieces of silver." Jimmy replaced the furry bear mask over his head. His muffled voice came from behind the costume: "If you want a war, Winston Browne, you've got one."

"What's that supposed to mean?"

"It means may the best man win, Win."

It took more than ten minutes for everyone to reach the east side of Hydrangea Street because most of the kids' costumes had eyeholes that did not line up with their eyes.

"C'mon!" Winston had to frequently holler to the parade of staggering children. "Let's hurry up! We don't have all night! That means you too, Milk Chocolate. Pick up the pace."

When they reached Frond Street, every porchlight was on, awaiting the hordes of costumed beggars. Houses stretched back to the horizon. And it looked like they went on forever—at least that was how it looked to a man whose lungs were infected from the inside out. A man who was pushing a wheelchair when he should have been the one riding in it.

At each house Winston had to lift Hooty out of his wheelchair and carry the kid up to the door. He couldn't afford to let Hooty put any weight on his ankle. Hooty was his only catcher, but until that ankle healed, Hooty was guarding the watercooler.

"Am I heavy, Sheriff?" Hooty asked.

"What do you think, Hooty? You're eleven years old. That's practically old enough to shave."

"I can walk, Sheriff. You can put me down."

"Oh no you don't. I need you behind the plate. The sooner you heal, the better."

The next house they reached was Bill Jackson's. Jimmy had already assumed the lead because he was hell-bent on being in charge tonight. The lopsided bear charged up the steps and knocked on Bill's door. The kids all formed a mob behind him. Winston carried Hooty up each cursed step.

"Are you gonna be okay, Sheriff?" said Hooty.

Winston was out of breath. "I'm fine . . . This is a lot of . . . steps to climb . . . Captain."

"I'm not a captain. I'm a *scallywag*."

"What's the difference?"

Hooty sighed.

Winston set Hooty onto the porch and then he sat down. He was feeling light-headed and his stomach muscles were fluttering from exhaustion.

"Just let me walk," said Hooty.

"Nope," said Winston. "Without a catcher, we don't have a team. Can you just imagine what the Dodgers would be without Campy behind the plate?"

"Okay, everybody," shouted Jimmy, ringing the doorbell a few more times for effect. "Here comes Billy. Do it just like we practiced last year. Does everyone remember?"

When the door opened, Bill Jackson stared at the clot of kids in homemade costumes. Then thirty-some children made loud raspberry sounds and filled the air with a spray of spit and half-chewed chunks of candy. Hooty's raspberry was one of the loudest. Winston could tell this by the sheer amount of saliva that landed on his face.

Bill Jackson wore a scowl. "You're supposed to say 'trick or treat,' you bunch of little hellions."

"Where's the originality in that?" said the grizzly bear.

Bill made each child do a trick before he or she could get any treats. So every kid had to come up with something impressive to do. Dixon Rogers didn't know any tricks, so he just sang "Fairest Lord Jesus." Many of the children listened to Dixon's song, and when he finished, they all agreed that Dixon was, in fact, a big old mama's boy.

Jessie had no tricks, and Bill wasn't about to let her have any candy without doing something. Bill suggested that Eleanor do something for Jessie by proxy, which delighted Winston to no end.

"What do you expect me to do?" Eleanor said to the old grump. "Tap-dance to a song from *Guys and Dolls*?"

"Do you really tap-dance?" said Bill.

Eleanor swiped a candy bar from the old man's hand and told him he ought to be ashamed of himself.

Before they left the porch, Jimmy reached into his satchel and handed Bill Jackson a huge stack of mail. "Happy Halloween, Bill!" Bill cussed him in return.

The group of trick-or-treaters hit every house on Water Street, Laps Street, and Park Circle until Winston's back was sore and he was all raspberried out.

Just to get through the night, he'd taken more medicine than he should have. His hands were shaking, and his heart was racing.

When they were finished for the night, Winston gave sixteen kids rides home. It was staggering how many kids could fit into the back of the Hudson when they used their creativity. Eleanor rode in the front seat with Jessie seated on her lap.

Dying was sort of an illogical thing. Winston had thought it would be total misery, but it wasn't all bad. The moments of mournfulness ebbed and flowed. Sometimes all he felt was a brilliant appreciation for being alive. There were moments when self-pity transformed itself into pure joy at everything around him. And sometimes the sensation would get so strong he forgot he was dying altogether. Tonight was one such night.

After dropping off the last kid, the night was officially over. The happy shouting was done. The children were all snug in their beds and the parents had visions of dental bills dancing in their heads. He drove the Hershey's Bar and the pitcher home. He said good night to the chocolate bar, who gave him a kiss. He felt his face get hot with embarrassment. For she was the loveliest woman ever to wear a refrigerator carton.

Before Jessie left him, he picked her up and held her on his hip and squeezed his favorite pitcher. "You know," he said, "you're a lot prettier than Johnny Podres." Then he pinched her nose.

"You think I can be a pitcher one day?" said the little girl.

He made her hold out her hand. He gave her three golden chocolate coins. "A million bucks in sugar says you can."

The rusted Ford pickup drove the dark gravel roads, moving slowly. The road zippered through the windshield at a snail's pace. No matter how many times Buz cleaned and reassembled the Ford's carburetor, the truck was always running too lean or too fat or backfiring like a howitzer. What the truck needed was a new carburetor.

Buz was at the wheel, dressed like a hobo clown, white face makeup and all. P.J. was fiddling with the radio dial. He was dressed like Frankenstein's monster, with a fine trickle of cherry syrup on the corner of his mouth. Buz had told P.J. this was stupid. Frankenstein's monster didn't suck blood. But P.J. said he thought the blood completed the costume.

The last week in October felt like winter was getting an early jumpstart on the Panhandle, trying to freeze it. Buz glanced in the rearview mirror. Nine full cans of gasoline were rattling in the truck bed and four empty ones. Every few seconds P.J. quit playing with the radio and looked through the back window.

"Would you quit doing that?" said the hobo clown. "You're making me nervous."

"Maybe we should get off the main road. If we get caught with you driving, we'll be in trouble."

"Pensacola police have better things to do, trust me. Just hush up and quit worrying."

P.J. clicked on the radio again. Static came through the speakers, followed by the sounds of classical music. He spun the dial left and right. Eddie Fisher sang "Watermelon Weather," a duet with Perry Como. Then static. A man yodeled a country song. More static. Classical music again. Hissing. Eddie Fisher singing "Lady of Spain." P.J. stopped scanning.

"Turn that off," said Buz. "Eddie Fisher's a dweeb. Only old farts like Eddie Fisher."

P.J. sighed and slapped the radio dial's knob. "Can you believe the Dodgers did it? It was so great that I feel sorta depressed, kinda like after Christmas morning is over."

Buz's family didn't do Christmas. Adam Guilford blew every dime they had on hooch. The closest Buz ever got to Christmas was when his granddaddy brought home a sack of oranges one year. Buz had no idea what a real Christmas felt like, but he did know what P.J. meant about the giddiness. It was almost too much to handle. The Dodgers had risen to the top of the heap and every boy felt a little different inside. And even though Buz didn't let himself entertain the thought for very long, it made him think that if *they* could beat the odds, a boy could too.

P.J. said, "I heard that right after the game, the telephones quit working in Brooklyn from all the phone calls."

Buz also heard that Western Union received the most telegrams in a few hours after the game than they did on Victory over Japan Day. The neighborhood of Flatbush had turned into a baseball circus, extending outward into the whole borough. Parades of automobiles roamed the streets of Brooklyn, and the skies overhead glowed with fireworks for a week. Or so the rumors said. Boys had been telling tales like this since the big win.

P.J. kept checking the mirror so often he could develop a sprain in his neck.

"Would you quit?" said Buz. "You're making me nervous."

"Can't we get off the main road?"

"We just stole forty-five gallons of gas, and you're worried about me driving?"

P.J. slumped in his seat. He brought his hat down over his head and pretended to be sleeping. "My daddy would kill me if he found out. He wouldn't let me be on the team. I'll feel a lot better when we get home."

"The team? What're you talking about?"

P.J. became very quiet.

Buz couldn't believe what he was hearing. "I thought we said we'd never play with those bunch of mama's boys."

"I never said that, Buz. You said that."

"You little turncoat. You didn't."

"Why not? Coach Browne's great, he brings a whole case of orange Nehi to practice. It's fun."

Buz swatted his friend. "You've already *been to a practice*?"

"You should join. If we had *you*, we'd definitely have a chance at winning a game—"

Buz shushed P.J.

Both boys stopped talking, bodies tense. P.J. sat straight in his seat and looked out the window. Buz glanced into the rear mirror and slowed the Ford's speed. And all of a sudden the inside of the truck filled with flashing red lights.

Halloween was fading to a close. Winston sat on the courthouse steps reading. The whole world had settled into tranquility. Tommy was in the courthouse with the doors and windows open, eating candy and reading a magazine. The sound of a Westinghouse fan made a high-pitched whir. The red dog curled beneath Winston's feet and slept.

Winston thumbed through pages of *Life on the Mississippi*, but he couldn't keep his focus on reading. His mind was too busy. He was thinking about *it. It* was always there, just beyond the curtain. Each day *it* came a little closer.

He surveyed the town. The little world was all buttoned up for the night.

"I'm going on patrol," he announced to Tommy, shutting the book and walking toward the Hudson. He kicked the tire of the busted Packard. Arty would never fix the clutch, he knew that. The stupid thing was nothing but a massive sculpture.

The red dog followed him and assumed his place in the passenger seat of the Hudson. The two partners drove along Moab's side streets for hours, sharing Baby Ruth candy bars. The porch lights had all clicked off. Moab was sleeping. He drove north, across the railroad tracks. Kids didn't do much trick-or-treating on the north side of town. They were too poor. But he did see a few teenagers sitting on porches. He waved at them, just to let them know a badge was still nearby.

Halloween was the biggest prankster holiday of the year, and he'd seen some doozies in his day. He'd even been accessory to a few classic pranks himself. Such as the time when he helped disassemble a small tractor and reassembled it in Clark Jensen's living room. That one went down in local folklore, a prank that had not been outdone since they pulled it many moons ago.

This thought made him laugh.

He found three cars parked at the bottle tree, all with steamed windows. The young lovers inside the cars were necking, doing what all kids were hardwired to do. To fall in love. He hated to ruin their moment, but he was obliged. Otherwise these teenagers would grow up without any good stories to tell, and everyone needed a good story. He extinguished their campfire and gave them a stern warning.

After that, he drove around Bell Park twice. Then he checked the back doors of all the shops on Hydrangea. He followed 29 toward the rural roads. He drove past all the local farms. It made farmers feel good to see the Hudson from time to time. He passed the Nyals' house, the Fordmans', and the Bryant place. He stopped when he got to the Pearson house out on Bigsby Road, a house that had been vacant for years.

There were lights on.

Busted

The deputy pulled the truck over beside a field of peanuts, just outside Pensacola. Buz sat with his head pressed against the back window. He was doing all he could not to lose his composure in front of P.J., but he was frightened.

"Oh man," said P.J. "We're done for."

Screwed was the word P.J. was looking for, Buz thought. But he didn't want to say it outright. Buz glanced into the rear mirror. He could see the deputy stepping out of the cruiser. It was a Ford Galaxie. A powerful car, but not a speed demon. Buz glanced across the dark field of peanuts to his right. He knew every square inch of the land between here and Moab. He knew the field butted up to Turner's pond, which led into Hal Lynn's cattle pastures, which were next to Mister Arnold's property, which would lead them right to Red Basin and finally to Highway 29. A fleeting thought raced through the hobo clown's head.

The truck was old, but the land between here and Moab was level for the most part, except for two hills. All he needed was a jump start. The cop would never be foolish enough to follow the truck across such terrain. That Galaxie was too low to the ground to overcome bumpy farmland. The deputy would give up, and they would be home free.

"Hang on," said Buz.

"What're you doing?"

Without saying another word, Buz threw the gearshift and gunned the engine in one choreographed movement. The old Ford screamed to life, backfiring like a Remington shotgun.

"What are you doing!?" shouted P.J.

"Just hold on!"

This was suicide. Even Buz knew this, but a kid doesn't always think rationally.

"Buz! You're gonna get us shot!"

In a few moments, the truck bounded down over a steep ditch into the peanut field. Soon they were clipping across the rows of peanuts, mowing down plants left and right. P.J. was bracing himself against the bumpy ride, hands pressed against the ceiling.

"Have you lost your mind, Buz?"

Yes. Yes, he had. But there was no going back now. Buz jammed his foot hard on the gas pedal. The gasoline cans in the back of the truck bed were rattling out and tumbling onto the ground. The truck was fishtailing through a pasture of peanuts.

Buz looked into the rear mirror. The Galaxie was right behind him, red lights blazing. The sound of a siren filling the night.

"This is crazy!" shouted P.J.

"I think I can outrun him!" Buz said.

The old Ford lumbered up the small grade that led to Tuner's pond, and he rode the thin trail that led around the pond. He expected the Galaxie to turn around, but it was doing no such thing. The Galaxie was taking the hill even better than the truck was. This deputy wasn't giving up. Buz could see him in the mirror, through the haze of black smoke spilling from his tailpipe. The policeman was driving like a professional stock car man. Buz was driving a jalopy.

P.J. shouted, "Buz! Watch out!"

Buz removed his eyes from the mirror and saw the pond rushing up at them. He'd lost control of the wheel. The truck raced forward and the headlights hit the water. It took a few seconds for the truck to begin to sink into the soft mud on the pond's scummy floor. The engine gurgled to a stop. The red lights were closer now.

"We're screwed," said Buz.

This was all wrong. There shouldn't have been any lights on at the Pearson house. The house should have been condemned. Daniel Pearson had lost both his sons to the war and moved away with his daughter to Kansas City several years earlier. The place was overgrown, ramshackle.

The Hudson rolled to a stop fifty yards before Pearson's old mailbox. Winston killed the lights. He threw the gearshift into neutral and tugged the parking brake. There was a vehicle in the driveway covered in a tarp. Definitely not a good sign.

Winston and the dog walked through the darkness along the edge of the Pearson property. He lifted the tarp. It was a black Dodge Coronet, no plates, no tags, no stickers. He cursed. He was in no physical shape for a confrontation. Not tonight. He was a weak man, dying, who could not stop wheezing, let alone be a hero.

The sounds of radio music were coming from the old house, drifting on the night air. He walked to the window and peeked inside. He saw a young woman seated at a dining table, hair disheveled and long, hands in her lap. There was an ashtray with a burning cigarette, and two handguns sitting beside it.

He swore again. He willed himself to stop wheezing, but that was just making it worse. He had an important job to do, and he hoped his body would allow him to do it. He knocked on the door with the authoritative knock of a county official. The music stopped. He heard footsteps on the floorboards, but nobody answered the door.

So he knocked again, this time louder. More waiting. More footsteps. A few doors slamming. The sound of a whispered conversation. Finally, a woman opened the door. This woman had her hair tied up in a bun. She was trim, wearing a black dress, barefoot. He looked behind her. No sign of the other lady.

He was the first to speak. "Good evening."

She was not smiling. "Good evening."

Coming up behind her were two others. Men. Young. Fit. Tall. They could fold Winston into a paper hat if they'd wanted.

"I'm Sheriff Browne. I just noticed your lights on. Are you folks related to Daniel?"

One of the young men came to the door and nudged the young slender woman out of the way. "Why, yes, we are related to Daniel, yessir."

The accent. Winston could not make it out. Dutch maybe, definitely not French. More German than English. Daniel Pearson came from run-of-the-mill hillbillies.

"Oh, that's nice," said Winston, flashing his voter-approved smile. "How is old Daniel doing these days? Haven't seen him in a few years since he took up full-time fishing."

The young man nodded and grinned like a fool. "Good, good. Daniel is doing good. You know Daniel." The young man was holding something behind his back.

"Ah, yes," said Winston, wheezing like a steam whistle. "I do know Daniel. Well, you be sure to tell old Daniel I said hello."

"Yessir, I will."

The sheriff looked past the young man's shoulder again. No handguns on the kitchen table anymore. He smiled, then bid them good night. He walked back to the car, feet crunching on the uneven dirt and gravel. Nothing was blacker than a country night.

His lungs were on fire from the short walk, and his abdominal muscles were sore from wheezing so hard. He lifted the radio receiver handset from beneath the Hudson dashboard and radioed Tommy.

"What is it, Win?" came Tommy's static voice. "Was just about to leave for the night."

"I need you to do something, Tommy. We have squatters. And I think they have a captive."

"A what?" There was a little excitement in the deputy's voice. "Where?"

"Pearson house, on Bigsby. They claim they're kin to Daniel, but I don't get a good feeling about them. Get in your truck and come down here right now."

Tommy's voice squawked back, "Don't have a truck. I walked to work tonight. Arty's fixing my truck."

Winston swore. "Then borrow someone's car, for Pete's sake."

"Everyone's asleep, Win. What do you mean, a captive?"

Winston slammed his hand on the dashboard. A county with one squad car and a siren that was as dead as ragtime. "I'm coming to the courthouse to pick you up. Grab the scattergun."

"Four-ten, Sheriff."

Clowns and Lawmen

The deputy had escorted the hobo clown and Frankenstein's monster into the jailhouse in Pensacola. It was two in the morning, and Buz was embarrassed to be dressed so stupid. He might as well have been sucking a pacifier and wearing a diaper. It was one thing to be dressed like a clown. It was another thing to be dressed like a clown in police custody. He had never felt more like a clown in his life.

This jailhouse was not like the one in Moab, which was primarily for people who practiced moonshining as a hobby or drank too much on Saturday nights. This place held bona fide criminals. The deputy led P.J. and Buz past a line of cells filled with grimy men wearing rags.

Buz had never seen an actual tattoo before. Moab people didn't believe in tattoos. If any man had them, he did not show them in public. Except for Mister Bob Limestone, who had been in the navy. Mister Bob had an illustration of a naked woman on his forearm. And sometimes, when he ushered at the front door of the Methodist church, he would show it to the boys. If the boys were especially good, Mister Bob would flex his forearm and make her dance. That was what Buz had heard, at least.

In the cell, P.J. had curled himself into the corner and was crying. Buz knew this wasn't because P.J. was scared of this place but because of what his father would do to him. P.J. would be doing hard labor until he entered his midsixties.

Before the deputy shut their cell door, he asked, "Can I get y'all anything? Maybe something to drink?"

This struck Buz as odd. What in the world was happening here? Buz didn't know what to say.

The deputy unlatched Buz's handcuffs through the bars. The young man said, "Water, juice? We even have 7 Up in the fridge. They're good and cold."

7 Up? Buz had never even tried one. Until now he had thought of this uniformed man as a kind of enemy, an opponent. For heaven's sake, he'd tried to make him eat his dust.

"Coffee," said Buz, just to see how the man reacted.

"I'll have to brew a new pot. How do you take yours?"

Take it? What was next, a shoeshine and a massage?

Buz said, "Black."

In a few moments, Buz had his coffee, and it was hot. P.J. was still in the corner. Before the deputy walked away, Buz said, "Can I ask you something?"

"Sure."

"I tried to outrun you. Why're you being so nice to me?"

He shrugged. "Remember, kid, we're the good guys. You want a little free advice?"

Buz didn't answer.

"That truck of yours needs a new carburetor. We pulled it outta the water, and I had our mechanic give it a once-over before they towed it back to Moab." The man looked at Buz's coffee. "Hey, you wanna donut to go with that?"

Buz hung his head. "Sure."

"Say," said the cop. "Just what're you supposed to be? A hobo or something?"

"Can't you tell?" said Buz. "I'm the world's biggest clown."

The Pearson House

Tommy and Winston approached the Pearson house in the dark. The old house sat in the distance, leaning a little. Squatty, rectangular, ugly. The home was low to the ground, with a flat roof. Daniel Pearson had built the house himself, board by board, back when dinosaurs roamed the earth.

The red dog followed after Winston, keeping his nose to the dirt. Winston felt awkward to be wearing a gun belt. It had been at least two years since the last time he'd worn one, which had been for the Sheriff's Association award brunch in Pensacola when he'd won the county's J. Billings Stratford Traffic Award for pulling over the most speeders.

They were ill prepared. Tommy carried a twenty-two gauge rifle, which was not the right gun for this job; it was just a peashooter. But Tommy had used the department's twelve gauge to take his nephews squirrel hunting a few days ago and left the gun at his sister's house. Tommy might as well have been carrying a water pistol filled with apple juice.

There were no lights coming from the windows anymore. No sounds from a radio. The driveway was empty.

"Looks like you scared them away," said Tommy.

Winston was disappointed in himself. He did not feel like a lawman anymore, just a shell of a man. The medicine made him jumpy, it slowed him down, and he did not trust his own reflexes. And now, because of his weakness, four deviants were on the loose headed for who knew where.

"I never shoulda left," said Winston.

"At least they're gone now."

"*At large* is a better term for it."

Winston had been prepared for professional failure ever since he'd gotten the news from the doctor. But he had not anticipated it would feel so humiliating. This was like forgetting the words to the national anthem.

"I feel like an invalid." He coughed.

Tommy said, "You couldn't have done anything on your own anyway, Win. You're just one man."

Tommy's pity made it worse.

They stepped inside the Pearson house. The home was foul smelling, like dust and old river mud. The years of humidity had swollen the wood and warped the walls. Winston pointed a flashlight into every room but found nothing. Mice scurried from the light. The basement door was wide open, swinging slightly in the air. Tommy was the first to hold the gun to his shoulder and aim it at the doorway.

"You wanna go down first?" whispered Tommy. "Or should I?"

"You go ahead," said Winston, still coughing. "I'll follow."

But the barrel of Tommy's gun quivered. And Tommy was making no moves to walk forward.

"Never mind," said Winston. "I'll go."

"Four-ten."

Winston crept down the stairs and said, "Hello?" into the stone echo chamber. His pistol was drawn, flashlight held below his gun handle. He'd seen men do this on TV and it had always looked very slick.

The dank basement floor was covered in a thin layer of mud, and the air tasted like mold. The room was empty except for a few barrels of rotted feed, a sack of mildewed grain, and some old tires. There were rodent carcasses and dead cockroaches galore.

"Look at this," said Tommy.

In the corner was a long length of chain, wrapped around a thick pine beam several times. A padlock lay on the floor, unlatched. The chain and padlock looked brand new.

"I think you were right about them having a captive," Tommy said. "Someone was tied up here."

Hamburger Steaks and Potatoes

Buz sat cross-legged on the concrete floor of the cell. P.J. was asleep on the cot, snoring like a transatlantic barge. It was stuffy inside this concrete room. The deputy in the Pensacola courthouse opened the windows to let the morning air fill the place, but it had only made the jailhouse cold, wet, and unforgiving.

In the next cell were two black men, singing together between sips from a pocket flask. They looked downright happy. When Buz looked at them, they were grinning at him. He felt foolish, dressed like he was, like a hobo. These men were the real thing.

In some ways, jail wasn't all that bad. For starters, prisoners were given lunch. A good one too. When the drifters received their hamburger steaks, they had to eat them with both hands and lick their fingers. They asked for more, and the deputies obliged them. The men ate three or four steaks apiece. At first Buz was too timid to ask for seconds. But when he saw the drifters do it, he followed suit. The officers gave the prisoners all they wanted, and it was the best meal Buz had eaten in weeks.

The deputy said, "I don't know how you can eat so much, Weary Willie."

"It's good steak," said Buz.

"Yeah? Well, believe me, they ain't so hot when you eat them every day for lunch for five years, because that's all Joe knows how to make. Gimme your tray. You want another one?"

"One more. Please."

When the deputy returned, three more steaks were on the tray. He slid it beneath the bars.

"How'd you become a cop?" said Buz.

The man leaned onto the bars. "Think I knew I wanted to be one when I was a kid. I knew I wasn't like everyone else, you know? They say you just know."

"Do you like it?"

He frowned for a moment. "What's not to like? I get to help people. I get free donuts and hamburger steaks. I've even delivered two babies, if you can believe that. I love it."

"I'm sorry I tried to outrun you."

The deputy reached his hand through the bars and slapped Buz's shoulder. "You promise me you'll shape up and we'll call it even. Now, you'd better hurry up and finish that food, kid. Sheriff Browne is downstairs waiting to take you home, and he don't look too happy."

One of the drifters whistled and said, "You gon' get it now, hobo."

Suddenly Buz wasn't very hungry.

Buz crawled into the front seat of the Hudson with his tail between his legs. The Hudson sat idling outside the police station, the back seat full of brown bags brimming with groceries. He was greeted first by the nameless red dog in the front seat. The dog recognized Buz and bathed his face with drool, smearing his clown makeup. Buz tried to push the dog away, but the dog won.

Through the windshield, Buz saw P.J.'s father guiding P.J. into a green Chevy. P.J.'s old man shook hands with the sheriff and drove away. It would be a wonder if the kid ever walked again. Poor P.J. would be simonizing that Chevy every afternoon until the second coming of Babe Ruth.

The sheriff climbed into the front seat, removed his beat-up fedora, and tossed it on the dashboard. Buz couldn't remember ever seeing a hat in such bad shape. The crown had holes in it and the brim was chewed up and floppy.

The old man turned on the heater and the car began to smell like burnt dust and metal. He coughed and it sounded like his chest was coming loose.

Buz was sick with anticipation. There wasn't a boy in Moab who didn't respect Sheriff Browne. Even the hoodlums. Everyone liked the baseball-loving sheriff. Some boys even worshipped him. To disappoint this man was like disappointing Abraham Lincoln and Gene Autry at once.

The sheriff said nothing of Buz's siphoning gas. "Well, I guess you and Huck already know each other."

"Huck? I didn't know this dog had a name."

The sheriff laughed. "Yeah, well, he didn't, least not until I gave him one. Your granddaddy shoulda named him. It's rude not to give a dog a name."

"Grandad said pet ownership was an artificial manmade construct invented by society to subdue the species and gain superiority."

"He would."

"Why'd you name him Huck?"

"After Huck Finn."

"Huck who?"

The sheriff's mouth gaped open. "You mean to tell me that you don't know Huck?"

Buz shook his head. He'd never heard of the man.

"You're a lot like him, you know. He's a good kid, just the last one to know it."

"I am?" Buz couldn't have been more confused if he'd woken up with his head glued to the floor.

They drove through the colorful lanes of Pensacola, past the iron balconies, the ornate streetlamps, and the cobblestone side streets. Sheriff Browne lit Lucky after Lucky with his dashboard lighter and seemed to be admiring the city. He didn't say anything for several miles, just coughed now and then. The haze would drift from his nostrils, filling the cab and making him cough more.

Buz kept waiting for the sermon. He expected a big one, too, about behaving, being a good person, following the rules, acting like an upstanding member of society instead of siphoning gas from the Pensacola truck stop. But the sheriff followed the long highway that led outside of Pensacola, crossing bridges, marshlands, peanut fields, cotton, and corn, without offering a single word. They crawled along the edges of the Escambia River until they were in the open country that surrounded Moab. Buz watched the grayish-green autumn fly past the windows and was too exhausted to appreciate it.

Finally, the sheriff said, "You know, when I was your age, I was a little like Huck too. There wasn't nothing to do in Moab except cause trouble."

Here it came.

"Yeah? Well, there's nothing to do *now* in Moab," said Buz.

The sheriff laughed, then hacked into a handkerchief and dabbed his mouth. "You have no idea how good you have it, Buz. There's a theater over in Layton now, and two theaters in Pensacola. They even have a Chinese restaurant downtown. You ever eaten Chinese food?"

"No."

Winston whistled. "The Chinamen can do things with ducks you've never even dreamed of."

"Ducks?"

"They got Peking duck, duck bone soup, duck dumplings."

Buz didn't answer this. Mainly because he couldn't speak with any authority about the subject of Chinese waterfowl. So he just offered a slight smile.

Winston went on, "See, we didn't have Chinese ducks when I was coming along. Moab was a one-horse town, and Pensacola was a million miles away by buggy. Shoot, Buz, there were only six cars in town when I was a teenager, and they all went one mile per hour. If you were feeling frisky, you could race the gopher turtles. No, we were all just generally bored and useless. We smoked a lotta cigarettes and chased a lotta catfish."

"Do they really have *two* theaters in Pensacola?"

"Yes, they most certainly do." He stabbed his butt end into the ashtray. "We oughta go sometime. I mean, if you ask me, it's a waste of time, sitting in a theater, but there're worse things a kid could be doing with his life."

He said that last part slow and deliberate.

Buz fell silent. A sermon could have been swelling on the horizon. But it never came.

The sheriff turned the wheel, and the car bounced off the pavement and onto the rural roads that cut across the golden farmland and sleepy pastures outside Moab. Dust from the gravel roads rose behind the vehicle.

Buz could almost envision his mother's face when her son came stepping out of a county vehicle. She would be angry. She would cry. But she would also be so embarrassed she would want to hide herself afterward. Everyone on his street would be on their porches when they saw the vehicle parked in his driveway. They would gawk and point, snicker. And Buz's mother would never show her face again in the grocery store.

The Hudson stopped at a four-way stop. The vehicle idled while the dust caught up with the car. The old sheriff stared out the windshield. So did Buz. They sat like this for several minutes, the stillness interspersed with coughs.

Finally, after enough time had passed, the old man held a hand out to Buz. The hand was trembling and Buz looked at it, perplexed, but too afraid to ask what this meant.

"Go on," said Winston. "Shake my hand, dang it. Don't be rude to an old man."

"Shake it? Why?"

The sheriff wore a little smile. "Shake it and find out, Huck."

Buz inched his hand toward the sheriff's. The old man gripped Buz's hand with his own. They pumped until Buz's shoulder was about to vibrate out of its socket. The old man said, "Right is right, and wrong is wrong, and a body ain't got no business doing wrong when he ain't ignorant and knows better." He released Buz's hand. "Samuel Clemens said that."

Buz thought about this for a few moments. "Who's Samuel Clemens?"

The sheriff just stared out the windshield and lit another cigarette. "You have to worry about this country." Then he tossed Buz a rag and said, "Wipe off your face, Weary Willie. We got deliveries to make."

Neither Hide nor Hair

Maria had used horse clippers to shave Ada's head in the motor lodge bathroom. Brown hair littered the floor like two cats had been fighting. Ada had been totally silent since they caught her. The young woman had not spoken to them since they caught her trying to slice the tires of their Dodge with a pocketknife. She hadn't said a single word.

The young woman was stronger than Maria thought she'd be. Even after they told her Johanna had given up information about the child. And Maria took it as her personal mission to break her. Though this seemed impossible. Between these women, only one had killed two men. And it wasn't Maria.

Ada wore a faint, disinterested smile. When the young woman finished removing Ada's hair, she told the young woman to sweep it up. Ada did not protest. She simply crouched onto her hands and knees and scooped up piles of her own hair and placed them into a wastebasket. She was not crying; she didn't even seem ashamed.

"Finish cleaning up and get to bed," Maria told her. "It's late, and I'm tired."

Ada scraped the last of the hair from the tile with her hands. Maria sat on the bed, trying not to nod off. She peered through the room window to see Heinrich and Karl fast asleep in the car. Heinrich's head was pressed against the passenger window. Karl had a hat placed over his face.

Ada crawled into the other bed. Maria watched her carefully, wondering what her father had seen in this young woman. She wasn't that pretty. She was just a plain temple woman. Maria couldn't understand men. Give them a little power and they lost their grip on reality, surrendered their good judgment, and became like fools. Every last one of them.

Maria clicked off the light in the room. She stayed awake until she heard sounds of sleep coming from Ada's bed. Sleep gnawed at Sister Maria like a hungry animal. They had been combing obscure Floridian places, looking for shreds of who knew what to find Ada's bastard child. And why? She couldn't find the reason for it all. Men in power. Heaven forbid anyone insult a man's pride.

She slept hard. And long. When she awoke the next morning, it was to the sound of birds chirping. At first she didn't think much about it. Then it occurred to her that this was unusual, birds in a motel room.

She opened her eyes to see the room brimming with daylight. The door to the room was swinging open with each gentle gust of wind.

Ada was gone. And she'd left only her hair behind her.

The Art of the Windup

Jessie watched the boys in Eleanor's backyard hurl the ball back and forth. It was the flattest yard in Moab, perfect for practicing. She had tucked her hair into her cap to make her look like less of a girl, just in case the boys needed an extra man. But they didn't. So she just watched. So did the gray cat.

On Eleanor's porch, a few children were roller-skating. Roller-skating seemed fun enough, Jessie supposed, but it was not baseball. The sounds of their wheels were like thunder on the floorboards. The skating kids begged Jessie to join them, but she was too busy rocking on the tire swing, sorting through mountains of Halloween candy, and watching the greatest game ever invented. For the last several weeks, she had been working on her curveball. Winston had helped her. But she couldn't convince the boys to let her play. Stupid boys. What did they know?

Today was no different. They acted like she had no business being in a game. They seemed overly serious about what they were doing, like they were performing surgery or something.

Eleanor kept telling Jessie to leave the boys alone, but this only ticked Jessie off. Why should she leave them alone? She lived here, and she had a right to be out in this yard just like they did. So she parked herself right there, on the swing. She made her presence known to the grubby little pukes and drilled holes into them with her eyes. They could tell her to buzz off all they wanted, but they couldn't get rid of her. Jessie was hard to get rid of.

Jacob Rogers was up. He rested his bat over his shoulder. Donny Anderson was catching, even though Donny wasn't on the team—he was a lot older than the other boys.

Donny yelled out advice, giving instructions to Jacob about batting.

"Let me play!" she said a few times, just to remind the boys she was still interested in case they changed their minds.

Benny Higgins started pitching. When he was in the middle of his elaborate windup, she started laughing at him loudly. He was so startled he lost control of the ball. They would be sorry they messed with her. Benny retrieved the ball and tried it again.

The moment before the ball left his hands, Jessie shouted, "Benny sucks pond water!" She wished she had thought of something more original, but under the circumstances, it would have to do. And it worked. The ball sailed a full fifteen feet above everyone's heads, straight into the woods. She laughed again, this time a little too hard.

Benny's face turned jawbreaker red. "Look what you made me do, you big dummy!"

"I'll get it!" announced Jessie, who was already bounding into the woods behind Eleanor's house. Because any chance to gain possession of the ball was a golden opportunity. They would have to kill her to get it out of her hands.

Jessie searched through the woods for a long time and ended up far from the house. She was surrounded by a world of greens and grays. She located the sliver of the white ball looking back at her through the tall weeds. The cat found it first. He was sniffing the thing. She picked it up, and the weight of it in her hands felt good. Something about a ball in the hand felt right. Then she practiced winding up. She kicked her leg upward. Her dress kept getting in the way so she tucked it between her legs.

She heard the sound of footsteps behind her.

Jessie lowered her leg. More steps. Twigs breaking on the forest floor. Leaves crunching. Rustling. She felt a surge of ice-cold fear sweep over her. She turned. In the distance, between two pines, was a woman. Ada. She had lost a lot of weight. Her head had been shaved, and there were bruises on her face.

They stood like this for a few moments, unmoving. Ada looked both directions, then placed a finger against her lips and shushed Jessie. In a quiet voice she said, "*Sie kommen dich holen*, Jessie."

It happened so fast that Jessie wasn't even sure it had been real. No sooner had she spoken than Ada disappeared, running in the opposite direction, like a wild animal. Jessie watched Ada until she disappeared. She had wanted to follow her, but she was too scared to move.

They're coming for you, Jessie.

Delivery Boys

The sun was high. The air was cold. Moab looked good at noon. Like a postcard, but with more color. Winston drove the Hudson with the window rolled down so the cool air could fill his lungs, but also so he wouldn't have to smell odors coming from the six rowdy Little Leaguers riding in his back seat, wearing their jerseys and blue jeans, all holding big grocery bags on their laps. Buz, the hobo, sat in the front seat with the dog. He looked tired, like he'd been up all night sitting in a jail cell. Which, of course, he had.

This kind of chilly weather was infectious. The boys were humming with energy. Except Buz.

"Sheriff?" said Dan Conroy. "You think we'll ever be good enough to beat Pensacola Baptist this season?"

"Yes, I do," said Winston. "I certainly do."

"Nobody beats Pensacola Baptist," said another kid.

"Are you calling us nobodies?" said Winston.

"But they're the best."

"They are not the best," Winston said.

But they were. Pensacola Baptist was *the* team in the area. The only team. Every boy in Moab who had ever been interested in playing baseball had to make a choice: try out for Pensacola Baptist or eat worms. But not a single child in Moab ever made the team because Pensacola Baptist was comprised of young men whose parents had golden toilets and paid for batting lessons from retired pros.

Buz took no part in the conversation. He sat still, staring off into space. There was something about this boy. He was nothing like his peers, a cardinal in a world of orioles. He wasn't a bad kid, just a good kid in bad circumstances. There was a difference. His face was smeared with traces of the white makeup, and he wore remnants of the painted-on five-o'clock shadow. Winston smiled at Buz to put the kid at ease, but it didn't work. The kid was exhausted from a long night of trying to outrun the law.

Winston clicked on the radio. The sound of an Eddie Fisher tune began to play. "Dungaree Doll." He liked Eddie Fisher. The young man was pure class, and he sang the way singing should be done.

It's funny how dying works. Winston didn't *feel* like he was dying. Most often he just felt winded, like he'd run a long way. Uphill. Against the wind. Towing a fire engine behind him. But other than that he felt as alive as ever. At first he had been avoiding taking the medications the doctor gave him, but now he was popping pills like candy. The Prednisone made him shake and swell up like a water balloon. But it did work a little. He held his puffy hand outward and watched it flutter against his will. His insides felt sort of the same way, as though at any moment his liver was going to quiver right out of his body and fall on the floorboard.

He heard the loud crunching of paper bags in the back seat.

"Hey!" said Winston, glancing into the rearview mirror. "Be careful with those groceries. Don't break the eggs. And for the love of Chrysler, who stinks so bad?"

The boys laughed, then exchanged punches.

Winston marveled at how the boys were so carefree. Boyhood carried such a lightness with it. Children, Winston thought, were much wiser than adults in many ways. Life was happening right now, right in this moment. There was no tomorrow, and yesterday was a photograph. And that was the essence of boyhood.

"Roll down a window back there," Winston said. "It smells like sourdough bread in here."

"It's Jacob's lucky socks! He never washes them!"

"When was the last time you washed those godforsaken socks, Jacob?"

"Kindergarten."

Winston turned onto Chorale Street at the edge of town. The uneven dirt road was lined with huge oaks bowing over the lane. At the end of Chorale, houses were replaced with shacks, overgrown fields, and deceased automobiles. He pulled into a small dirt driveway, past tall grass and dilapidated farm implements. He parked in front of an aluminum camper trailer with Christmas lights hanging on the trim.

"Where are we?" said one boy.

"Never mind," said Winston. "You boys just stay in the car." He leaned over toward Buz. "Except for you. You come with me."

Buz and Winston carried two bags of groceries up the crooked, overgrown walkway toward the trailer. Winston rapped on the flimsy metal door. In a few moments, the door opened and Mister Hackman appeared, still wearing his undershirt and trousers pulled up to his armpits. The old man hadn't changed out of these trousers since Winston and Tommy had made a grocery delivery last week.

He was smiling. Mister Hackman was always smiling, ever since he taught Winston how to use the English language in high school. He would be smiling when they laid him down.

They brought the bags inside, placed the items into the small cupboards above the sink, into the refrigerator, and under the kitchenette. The old man sat down on the sofa. He was listening to a radio.

"I just love Eddie Fisher," said the man.

"Everyone does," said Winston.

"What a singer, that Eddie," said the old man. "Who's your little friend, Win?"

"This is Buz, Mister Hackman. Buz, this is Mister Hackman."

The boy and the old man shook hands.

Winston said, "Mister Hackman used to teach me tenth-grade English, once upon a time."

"Worst student I ever had," the old man said. "He was rowdy, always getting into trouble. It's a wonder Win knows how to read at all." The man laughed. "It's a miracle he became sheriff."

Winston laughed too, because it wasn't entirely untrue.

"All it took," the old man went on, "was finding Samuel Clemens. The rest took care of itself."

"Buz doesn't know who Samuel Clemens is," said Winston.

Mister Hackman almost choked on his cigarette. He jabbed it into his ashtray and coughed. The cough sounded a lot like Winston's. "I'm gonna pretend you didn't just say that, Winston."

Winston whispered to Buz, "Mister Hackman has buried kids for less than that."

The old man was digging through a stack of books on his side table, beside an ashtray that looked like it hadn't been emptied since the discovery of Mount Shasta.

"This oughta cure your ignorance," said the old man, handing Buz three books. "I want them back, young man, in good condition."

Winston winked at Buz. "What d'ya say, Weary Willie?"

"Thank you, sir."

The kid had good manners. Winston had to give him that.

Mister Hackman smiled at the boy. He searched the room with his two brown eyes, and his face changed. Winston could see something overtake the man's being. It was in the man's eyes. A change that swept over him like it had been doing ever since he'd retired.

"What a singer, that Eddie Fisher," said Mister Hackman. "Who's your little friend, Win?"

"This is Buz, Mister Hackman."

"Oh, pleased to meet you, Buz. Your coach here was the worst student I ever had. I can't believe this man even knows how to read, let alone got elected sheriff."

"Don't forget to take your medicine," Winston said, rattling a brown bottle, then placing it on top of the radio. "Or else I'll make Tommy come over and force-feed it to you every four hours."

The old man laughed. "I will, Win."

"Thanks for the books," said Buz.

"What books?" said Mister Hackman.

They left the camper, following the trampled footpath to the car. Buz remained silent, and Winston interpreted this as a good sign. Winston popped the trunk of the Hudson. He could hear the boys inside the car having a disagreement, rocking the Hudson side to side. Winston dug around until he'd retrieved a ball glove. A catcher's mitt, cocoa brown, not yet oiled. It still had the price tag attached.

"I have a confession to make, Buz. When I heard you got locked up, I was a little glad about it."

"Glad? Why?"

He tossed the mitt toward Buz. "Because it means that as of right now, you're my new catcher until Hooty's leg heals. And if you don't come to practice, I'm gonna bury you *beneath* the jail."

"Catcher?"

"Practice is at four. You can walk home from here. I don't want your mama seeing you step outta this car."

The sheriff hobbled into the car and Huck jumped in after the old man.

Before he drove away Winston said, "And, Buz? I don't ever wanna hear you ask who Sam Clemens is again."

Sabrina

Eleanor walked to town like a woman who knew her own mind. That's how she was going to approach today. You don't wear shockingly modern clothes in public and act timid. You act bold. Confident. Foreign. A little buck wild.

Jessie was away with Winston for the day, and Eleanor was running errands. This morning, before she left the house, she had decided to undergo a complete self-transformation.

She was through pretending to be the quiet, mousy creature her mother raised, the old maid who wore tea-length skirts, pearls, and Peter Pan–collared blouses just to check the mail. Eleanor Hughes had been born an old woman, but she was through with that old biddy. Winston Browne had woken her from her sleep and made her believe things about herself she didn't know were possible.

It hadn't happened all at once. Over the last several months, she had laid parts of the old Eleanor to rest. She started wearing makeup more often, and skirts instead of just housedresses. She invested in a few new undergarments that caused her bodily parts to resemble pointed Soviet bullets. But by far her biggest leap into depravity was wearing pants. Today she wore black capris and a black sweater, three-quarter-length sleeves with a boatneck collar. Her hair was pulled back in an angular ponytail so that she looked like the love child between a beatnik and a cat burglar. Red handbag. Drugstore sunglasses. Red pumps.

She noticed people staring at her when they saw her walking through town. Eleanor could read their thoughts, since no woman her age had ever been seen in actual pants before, let alone a conical "bullet" brassier that was sharp enough to poke out a man's eyeballs. Sunday school teachers who made chess pies and ambrosia and who organized flowers for funerals were to be modest and bland and plain. They were not supposed to wear undergarments that made them look as though they were smuggling Mark-13 aerial torpedoes beneath their sweaters.

But this was not a Sunday school woman. No, sir. This was Audrey Hepburn. At least, that's where she'd gotten this outfit idea from. It happened when Winston had taken her and Jessie to the movies in Pensacola to see *Sabrina*. She'd overheard two young men in the row behind her refer to Hepburn as a "hot mama." Oh, she liked that. Long ago, such terminology might have disgusted her. But curiosity overtook her disgust, and all at once she was finished with being blasé as dishwater. Eleanor began reading *Hollywood Magazine* and *Screen Life* during her idle hours.

Soon, Eleanor had become entranced with the idea that there was a whole world of fashion out there that she had never even explored. She was looking at modern clothing catalogs in secret that she had purchased from a seedy bookstore in Pensacola. And she had come to realize that Eleanor Hughes had been so busy living up to everyone else's idea of her that she had forgotten to form her own opinion about herself. Old age was not a number; it was a way of thinking. And Eleanor had been elderly since she was twelve.

Well, not anymore. She went to Gayfer's in Pensacola to turn herself into Moab's own Perma-lift conical brassier spokesperson. She spent three dollars on this undergarment. And she had ordered two more like it. One in ebony and one in Hussy Red. She had spent thirty dollars on cigarette pants and boatneck sweaters.

She removed her sunglasses and walked into Herrington's dress shop to pick up the paper taffeta she'd ordered for Jessie's Christmas dress. The stares she garnered from the women in the store were downright nuclear.

Old lady Herrington herself almost had to be revived with cold water. She couldn't even find the words to say hello to Eleanor. Lisa Potts was even worse. "Eleanor," Lisa said. "You're wearing . . . You're wearing . . . What are you wearing?"

As though Eleanor were dressed in a Martian space suit.

Lisa Potts scurried out of the store. *Good riddance*, thought Eleanor. Lisa was an uptight woman married to the oldest Baptist deacon in town who preached against the dangers of "premarital relations" with the opposite sex because this might lead to dancing.

When Eleanor had paid for her taffeta, she left the store and carried the white box beneath her arm, traipsing down the sidewalk on Hydrangea, feeling a sense of adventure she'd never felt before. She was trying to light a filter-tipped cigarette when a group of younger men on the sidewalk passed her. All four of them removed their hats. And Mark Anderson offered to light her cigarette. They were all twenty years younger than she was. She taught three of them in Sunday school when they were still making mud pies in the backyard. Someone offered to carry her package of taffeta. She declined.

Next, she walked into the mercantile. Brazenly. The bell dinged on the door. Odie was behind the counter. She asked him for two things: baking powder and her mail.

"I haven't had my mail in four days," she added.

Odie looked like he was about to have a brain seizure when he saw her. He smoothed his white hair and hitched his pants up above his belly button. "Jimmy?" hollered Odie. "Will you come out here, please?"

"Keep your pants on!" shouted Jimmy.

Jimmy came from the back room wearing his green visor and mail-carrier shirtsleeves. His forearms were covered in ink from sorting mail. He was staring at a stack of envelopes in his hand. "Can I help you, ma'am—" said Jimmy before he caught himself.

"I'm here for my mail," she said.

There was a long pause. She was starting to feel a little embarrassed.

Jimmy made no remarks at first. Then, "You look so diff—"

She cut him off. "Do you have my mail or don't you?"

He blinked. He stuttered. *So help me,* she thought, *he's blushing.* Jimmy reached beneath the counter to dig in a parcel bag. He handed her a stack of mail that was thick as a brick. He smiled at her.

She spun on her heel to walk away. She could feel him staring, along with every other person in the mercantile. When she stood in the cool air of Hydrangea, she replaced her sunglasses and realized something she had never known before until this very moment. She was not a plain woman like she'd always believed. Eleanor Hughes was, in fact, a hot mama.

Still, even though she had been momentarily liberated, even though she had found an audacious piece of herself she never knew was there, she still felt her chest tingle when she saw Jimmy Abraham.

If she didn't hate him so much, she would have been downright in love with him. Maybe she was.

Pensacola Baptists

Pensacola Baptist's ballpark was nothing but pure fancy. It sat behind First Baptist Church and was several notches above Moab's brand-new field. But it lacked heart. Winston could tell. You could have fancy things, but without heart, that's all they were. Fancy.

Still, he was jealous over the public restrooms and the drinking fountains. The restrooms even featured fresh-smelling soap *in a hand pump.* He'd never seen such a thing. This town had everything. Modern cars, modern fashions, an airport, restaurants that served Peking duck, and pump soap. Astounding.

The Hudson sat parked at a distance, behind a few shrubs. Winston didn't want to be seen by the coach, not while he was committing blatant espionage. Jessie sat in the passenger seat. "Why are we hiding?" she said.

"Because," he said. "There are people in Pensacola I don't care to see."

"Can we get Peking duck tonight?"

"Probably not. You know that stuff's expensive. You're going to bankrupt me, Jessie."

Jessie shrugged and ate three handfuls of sunflower seeds until her face looked like a chipmunk's.

"Slow down on those seeds," said Winston. "You'll choke, and I'm not gonna be the one to resuscitate you."

"I'm hungry," said her muffled voice. "What's *resuscitate* mean?"

"It's Hungarian for 'you big greedy buzzard.'" Winston buzzed her with his fingers. Jessie did not laugh.

When Buz came strutting out of the bathhouse, he was smelling his hands. Winston understood this. He himself had been smelling his hands all night. The soap smelled like lavender and vanilla. Magnificent. Winston decided they would definitely build bathrooms with pump soap before Moab's first opening game, even if he had to build the restrooms himself.

Winston, Buz, and Jessie sat in his Hudson, passing around a bag of sunflower seeds, watching Pensacola Baptist's batting practice. They'd been doing this every night of the last few weeks. Winston had grown to enjoy Buz's and Jessie's company. Buz was more observant than any kid he'd ever known, and more like an adult than Winston was himself. Jessie was nothing but attitude and brains with freckles.

"Look at number forty," Winston said to the kids, "that tall kid with the blond hair. He'll give us trouble. He can swing a bat."

"There's no way we can beat these boys," said Buz.

The blond kid hit the ball so hard the cracking sound made the windshield vibrate. The ball arced through the air like it was rocket powered. And it was gone.

"I think you're wrong," said Winston, spitting seeds.

"Me too," said Jessie, spitting seeds in an unconcealed attempt to be just like the sheriff. "Why is he wrong again?"

"Because," said Winston. "Pensacola Baptist might play ball like a well-oiled machine, but they don't have heart." He thumped his chest. "Same reason the Redcoats lost the war to the Patriots. Heart."

"Yeah," said Jessie.

Winston wasn't sure who he was trying to convince. Pensacola

Baptist had muscled players who looked like they'd been held back in school since the 1920s. Their catcher was the size of a General Electric refrigerator, only with more chest hair.

Winston said to Jessie, "Notice how their pitcher never lets anyone see the ball until the moment it comes out of his hand? They do that in the big leagues too. When you pitch, try to keep the ball hidden."

Jessie was holding a baseball in her hand at this exact moment, experimenting.

The blond kid hit another one that went sailing all the way to Nevada. There was no way they could beat these boys.

Their conversation came to a halt when Charles Knowles exited the dugout and headed toward the Hudson. He was waving his arms at Winston.

"Oh, for heaven's sake," mumbled Winston. "We've been spotted."

"Who's that?" said Buz.

"Never mind, just stay in the car."

Charles Knowles was Winston's age, only shorter, and in much better physical shape. Some people never changed, no matter how old they got. Knowles was one of those people. He had always been deathly popular with the opposite gender and cocky. It was a wonder he became a preacher. He should have been a game show host or a toothpaste spokesperson.

"Winston Browne!" said Charles. "What on earth is the sheriff doing here?"

Winston brushed the sunflower-seed shells from his trousers, then shook hands with Charles in the hearty way that age-old enemies do—like they're trying to dislocate each other's shoulders.

"Hiya, Preacher," said Winston.

"Please, Winston, call me Reverend." Charles patted Winston's belly. "I can see you're still putting in plenty of hours at the Chinese restaurant."

Nope, some people never change.

The sheriff introduced Buz and Jessie to Charles, but only to be polite. He didn't want to prolong these false pleasantries any more than necessary.

"What brings you to the big city?" Charles asked. "You finally get tired of playing a banjo on the porch and swatting gnats?"

"Your boys look good," said Winston. "Who's the new pitcher?"

"That's my son, Matt. He's eleven this year. He's been playing with Mobile until this year. They got *real* ball clubs in Mobile, not the ragtag clubs in Pensacola. His mother babies him."

Winston's insides soured. Neither of the men spoke for a few moments. Old grievances returned. Hearts were rebroken. Nothing ever disappears from a man's memory, it just gets buried. The blond boy looked just like his mother. The same nose, same eyes.

"How is Katie, Rev?"

The pause seemed to last for ten years. "She's good, Win. I'll tell her you asked about her."

Another deafening stillness.

"So," said Charles, "what's this I hear about Moab having a new team? Is it true? Shoot, I can't find anyone in Moab to pump my gas, let alone nine boys to swing a bat." He laughed, even though it wasn't funny.

Winston was staring at the public restrooms. *Where would a fella buy pump soap if he were so inclined?* That's what he was wondering.

"Win?" said Charles. "Did you hear me? I asked if it was true. Do you actually have a team?"

"Yeah," said Winston. "We got a team, Charles, and we got a field too. A nice one. And we got one heck of a pitcher." He let his eyes sit on Charles Knowles, the man who had stabbed him in the heart. "We got talent enough to blow your boys to kingdom come." Winston didn't know where this was coming from. But it felt good. "And the Moab Dodgers are gonna beat you like a rented mule."

Charles laughed for a moment, but not entirely. "The Dodgers? Is that right?"

"Yes," said Jessie, leaning out the window. "That's right."

When the conversation ended, Winston got into the Hudson, slammed the door, and popped a Prednisone. He was having a hard time catching his breath.

"What was that all about?" said Buz.

"Never mind." Winston yanked the gearshift into reverse and spun the wheel. "Who wants Peking duck?" He emptied a handful of sunflower seeds into his hand and tossed them into his open mouth.

"Careful with those," said Jessie. "I'm not gonna be the one to resuscitate you."

The Joy of Cooking

Eleanor wore red fitted pixie pants and a tight red blouse, lower cut than normal. She'd had her hair styled in Mobile by a man who spoke with an Italian accent. She paid an arm and a kidney for this hairdo and sat beneath a hood hair dryer for forty-five minutes to get it just right. Her hair was shoulder length now, very modern and a little sharp. Pure sass. She glanced at her reflection in the hall mirror. *Not bad,* she thought. *Not bad at all, old girl.* If she kept this up, they would kick her out of the Methodist church for leading people into temptation. She didn't care. Eleanor felt better about herself than she'd felt in years.

Jessie sat in the kitchen wearing blue jeans and an apron. She kept staring out the window. Her mind was a million miles away. The two of them couldn't have been any more different if they had been born as different species. The child wanted to wear jeans and hold baseballs, and whenever Eleanor forced her to get dressed up for church, the girl seemed unhappy about it. Winston had made Jessie a member of the team, even though Eleanor didn't think it was a good idea, and now all Jessie did was spend time in the backyard, practicing her pitches. Until recently. Jessie had clammed up the last few days, and she seemed nervous about something. But the girl was hard to read; she could be tight-lipped and silent. No amount of probing did any good. But something was bothering her.

Autumn was in full swing in Moab, which meant nothing. Fall looked almost the same as summer except it was dimmer. Eleanor had always wished she could see a real autumn like they had up north. In fact, half of the jigsaw puzzles she owned were of autumn scenery. The other half of her puzzle collection was teddy bears and sailboats. Up north they had wild, vibrant colors. In northwestern Florida, you had the entire spectrum of mildew.

The only autumnish things any Moab person got to enjoy during the fall were food-related. Which happened to be her specialty. In the fall, a Methodist woman's food became rich, greasy, and borderline illicit, whereas summer menus featured fresh and crisp salads and the bright flavors of watermelon, cold corn, and pinto bean salads. In fall, the food was nothing but heart failure on a plate.

Thanksgiving was the World Series of cooking days for a cooking woman. It was the height of her year, along with Christmas, Easter, Fourth of July, Labor Day, Flag Day, Abraham Lincoln's birthday, Sir Walter Raleigh Landing Day, Librarian Appreciation Day, Bridge Night, and Wednesday church suppers.

Jessie was helping in the kitchen, wearing a checkered apron that used to belong to Eleanor when she was her age. She kept looking out the window.

"Jessie," said Eleanor, holding a hot enamel mixing bowl. "Move over. I'm about to put this bowl right there. And it's hot, hurry."

Jessie moved out of the way. Then Eleanor placed the bowl on the counter and shook her hands to cool them off. "What're you looking at?"

Jessie was not answering.

"So we're back to Little Miss Quiet?" said Eleanor. "I liked it better when you were chatty."

Nothing.

She gave Jessie a bag of flour and told her to dust the surface of the dining room table. Eleanor removed a new box of Blue Bonnet oleomargarine and placed it on the porch beneath a beam of sunlight to get soft. She could see Jessie in the kitchen window. There was no joy in Jessie's work; even Eleanor could tell this. It was clear this child was not interested in kitchen work. They had tried this several times, and every time the girl acted like she was having a tooth extracted, which was disappointing to Eleanor. She had always pictured herself having a little girl who wanted to learn to make lemon icebox pies, biscuits, jalapeño-cheese cornbread, and chocolate pound cake. But this child was all tomboy. She was 5 percent Shirley Temple, 95 percent Lou Gehrig.

"Are you okay, Jessie?" she asked. "You know you can talk to me."

Jessie quit dusting the counter with flour. She was obviously thinking about this. "Everything's okay."

The child was a terrible liar.

A Couple of Old Friends

Jimmy trotted up the steps of Eleanor's porch. He was carrying a paper sack of licorice, a bouquet, and her mail. He was the last to arrive and join the other people waiting on the porch, all dressed in nice clothes. It was cold, and everyone's breath made little clouds in the air.

"Right on time," said Winston Browne. He was holding a bottle of champagne.

"Who invited you?" said Jimmy.

"The same person who pitied you enough to invite you."

"Eat my shorts."

"You aren't wearing any."

Among the guests on the porch were Winston Browne, Buz Guilford, and Buz's mother. Also, elderly Miss Mayola and her sister, Miss Naomi. The two women were old enough to remember when the Dead Sea was just getting sick.

The six of them stood on the porch wearing heavy coats. Jimmy owned one jacket, and most years he never had a reason to wear it, which was why he smelled like mothballs.

Winston leaned close and sniffed. "What do you call that cologne, Jimmy? Eau de Attic?"

"How about you take that champagne bottle and—"

"Happy Thanksgiving!" shouted everyone else when Eleanor swung open her front door. Her hair was different, and her front side was a lot more pointy than usual.

"Let us inside," said Jimmy. "It's cold out here. I can't feel my hands."

Eleanor's house was decorated to the hilt just like it was every year. Garland adorned every surface. There were plastic poinsettias, lit candles, bells, cinnamon brooms, tinsel, porcelain tableaus, and stuffed pillows everywhere. Jimmy inspected all the decorations. He knew them by heart. He'd been the one to help her put them out every year since he could remember. But this year all the decor had mysteriously appeared without his assistance.

Bing Crosby music played in the background. The autumn pumpkins and squash made Eleanor's house look like a home.

Jessie was seated on the sofa wearing a plaid dress, hair in curls. She looked miserable. She was watching Jimmy.

"Well, don't you look like a pretty picture?"

"Hey, Mister Jimmy."

He handed her a baggie of licorice. "Happy Thanksgiving. Don't eat it all at once, it'll rot your teeth out."

He sat beside her and looked around the den. The corner furniture had been rearranged, making room for Eleanor's Christmas tree. Rearranging the furniture had always been Jimmy's job. Every year since forever, Jimmy had been the one to deliver her tree. It was an annual tradition with them. He would pick out a nice tree from the lot in Pensacola and deliver it a few days after Thanksgiving. But that was all over now.

"Who did this?" he asked Jessie, waving his arm in the direction of the empty space next to the couch.

"Winston," said Jessie.

"Did he now?"

Eleanor appeared in the living room looking like a walking advertisement for Gayfer's Department Store, modern-dressed. Wearing *pants*, for crying out loud. She asked if she could take Jimmy's coat. He removed it. She was leaving the room when he stopped her. "Why'd you invite me?"

She gave him a sideways hug and a pat on the shoulder. "We're old friends, Jimmy. Don't be silly."

"Friends? Why don't you just kick me in the shin and call me stupid?"

"Jimmy, don't make me regret that I invited you. Behave yourself. Which shin?"

"What've you done with your hair? I hardly even recognize you anymore, Ellie. You look . . ." He looked at the carpet. "You look magnificent."

She didn't respond, just turned on her heel and left the room. Jimmy glared at Winston, who stood across the den sipping his punch. He already had a crowd of admirers gathered around him. He had always been well-loved, admired. There was something about him. Whenever Jimmy was around Winston, it was like he ceased to exist.

Jimmy plopped back onto the sofa beside Jessie and stared at his hands. The red dog wandered through the crowd, looking for handouts. When the animal spotted Jimmy, it leapt into the seat beside him and willed him to rub his belly.

Jessie laughed. "I think old Huck likes you."

"Old Huck?"

The dog began licking himself in a deeply personal way.

"This dog never had a name."

Jessie shook her head. "Win named him."

"Did he now?"

Thanksgiving dinner was awkward. All Miss Mayola wanted to

talk about was the time it snowed in Moab, back in aught four. The old woman was a broken record. By the time she was rounding her fourth retelling, everyone's face had turned to wood. People chewed their food along to the monotone sounds of Miss Mayola's voice, which was powerful enough to make Jimmy hallucinate. But the food was delicious. Eleanor was an artist. He couldn't help but watch her all night. The woman had the face of an Italian painting. The new hair made her look like a movie star.

After supper, Jimmy offered to help with the dishes, but Eleanor refused him. She told Jimmy to stay in the living room to play with Jessie. "Entertain her," said Eleanor. "She likes you."

"But I always help with the dishes."

Eleanor was not listening to him. She had already wandered into the kitchen to resume her work and Jimmy wished he could disappear. So he took Jessie outside in the backyard. They sat on the steps for a few minutes, listening to the crickets screaming. A few frogs were having an argument. Jessie asked if he wanted to play catch.

"Catch?" said Jimmy. "In the dark?"

The girl nodded.

"I dunno," said Jimmy. "The last time you threw something at me, I couldn't remember my own name for three weeks."

Jimmy relented. They threw a ball back and forth in the dark until it was hard to see the ball, and the only telltale sign anything was happening beneath the moonlight was the sound of a ball slapping into gloves. Jessie's arm had been getting stronger over the past months. Rumor had it this child was going to be Moab's pitcher. And Jimmy could believe it. She threw hard enough to kill a man.

But he wasn't paying much attention to the ball. Jimmy was watching Eleanor through the glowing kitchen window, a yellow square in the night. She looked almost like a stranger to him now. And he was out here, in the cold, with the frogs. He saw Winston in the kitchen with her. They were washing dishes, laughing, carrying on like a couple of fools.

Jimmy lobbed the ball toward Jessie halfheartedly. His heart was sore. He realized Eleanor Hughes had forgotten about him.

That's when the ball hit him squarely in the forehead.

Onlookers

Maria and the others sat in the Dodge Coronet parked at the edge of Hydrangea Street. Maria was in the back seat, Heinrich and Karl in the front. They all watched the town of Moab through the windshield. It was a pretty town with people who were always busy. Not the same kind of busy as temple brethren. This was frivolous business. The secular world was nothing but frivolous business. Buying this and that.

Heinrich said, "That's the courthouse across the street. The lawman is in there right now."

Karl said, "We shouldn't be here. He'll see us."

"Shut up," she said. "You're the one who let Ada get away, *Dummkopf*."

"But Ada's not here," said Heinrich. "She's long gone by now. Probably all the way to Canada."

Maria said, "You know nothing of mothers."

They had been looking through the never-ending chain of rural hamlets surrounding Pensacola and Mobile, searching for the escaped woman. But they had ended up finding the child instead. It had been pure chance. Except it wasn't chance. The heathens believed in luck. Maria only believed in divine justice.

The lawman emerged from the courthouse. He was tall, wearing a tired brimmed hat, and there was a teenage boy with him. And a dog. The abomination child was with him too. She wore jeans and a striped T-shirt. Her hair was in braids. She looked just like Maria's papa. It wounded her to see this. And in that moment, she understood the fury her brother felt. This abomination child had no right to perpetuate the blood traits of the Prophet, nor his holy ancestors.

"Get down," said Heinrich. "They're gonna see us."

"Why haven't you tried to grab her yet?"

"I told you, she's always with *him* or with that woman who wears man clothes."

The lawman and the children disappeared down the sidewalk. The dog trotted behind them.

"Follow them."

They stayed four cars back from the lawman. The Dodge pulled into a parking lot slowly, tires popping on the gravel. A field was overrun with work trucks and men mixing mortar in wheelbarrows. In the distance, the work trucks sat parked around a half-constructed block structure, a small building without a roof. Workmen hauled concrete blocks, one by one, placing them onto a sand foundation. There were pipes sticking out of the ground.

"What're they building?" Maria asked. "Are those bomb shelters?"

"Bathrooms," said Heinrich.

The girl was on the green grass of the baseball field, playing catch with a few boys and the lawman. Had it not been for her braids, Maria would have mistaken the little brat for a boy. She could not look at the girl without feeling a mixture of hatred for the child and longing for her papa.

"That child is an atrocity," said Maria under her breath.

"Yeah," said Karl. "But she's got quite an arm on her."

"Show me where she's staying," said Maria, removing a gun from beneath the seat and ejecting the clip. "If you idiots can't take care of this child, then I will."

Adeste Fideles

The Moab beautification committee had already put up the Christmas decorations. Winston had seen Rob and Leroy perched upon ladders on Thanksgiving night, their wives barking orders from solid ground. Thus, the downtown was spectacular with its tinsel and the antique decorations Moab had been using ever since the Revolutionary War. The one glaring eyesore that clashed against all the finery was the glowing, vomit-colored neon sign suspended over Ray's Café. The thing got uglier every time Winston looked at it, blinking pea green and Pepto Bismol pink, like electric nausea.

In the window of the café, Winston could see Sarah Freeman, the town's only waitress. Ray's only needed one. He could see Ray himself behind the flattop, scraping the grill, smoking a cigarette. Sarah was seated facing the front door, reading a magazine, waiting for an early-morning visitor. Anyone.

Winston parked the Hudson in front of Ray's. Huck jumped out and followed him up the sidewalk. When Winston reached the door, he told Huck to wait outside. The animal did just that, but Winston could tell the animal wasn't crazy about the idea. The lawman walked into the café, removed his hat, and shook the cold from his shoulders. Nat King Cole sang "Adeste Fideles" over the jukebox, and Sarah's eyes warmed when she realized she had a customer. She greeted him. Ray mumbled a halfhearted greeting too but didn't look up from his stove.

"Hey there, Win," said Sarah. "You're in awfully early."

"Meeting a friend," he said. "We're meeting at the courthouse, but you looked lonely."

"I am lonely." Sarah shook her head and glared at Ray. "Since Ray found out he could make a few more bucks serving breakfast to anyone who wants to eat at the crack of dawn, we've been opening two hours earlier."

"Who eats breakfast at this hour? Suicidal truck drivers?"

"That tightwad is thinking of staying open twenty-four hours this summer just to make a few extra bucks."

"Good old Ray."

Win hung his jacket on his seat, then Sarah filled his mug with steam. Without asking, she dabbed his jaw with a damp rag. This surprised him, and he jerked backward.

"Sorry, Win," she said. "What'd you do, bite your tongue? You got blood all over your mouth."

The rag was stained with red. His cough was getting worse in the cold weather. Sarah nudged his coffee toward him.

"I guess I bit my lip or something," said Winston.

Ray hollered, "Make sure he pays for that coffee, Sarah. We don't give handouts."

"Good old Ray," whispered Sarah.

She asked if Winston wanted anything to eat. He said no, not until his friend arrived. So they passed half an hour in pure quietude. Winston read from his book. She read from her magazine. Ray scrubbed every flat surface in the place.

Sarah nodded toward the dog outside the window. "That old dog don't like being out there without you."

"Yeah," he said. "Old Huck and I have grown kinda attached."

"You named him Huck? I thought he didn't have a name."

"Everyone needs a name."

"He's just a dog, Win."

She was young and pretty, in a beautifully regular sort of way. Not the falsified kind of pretty with the bleached hair and fake eyelashes.

"You ever been in love, Sarah?"

She laughed. "Lord, no, I'm married." Young women and white-haired men did not often discuss this sort of thing.

"I mean before Billy."

"Yeah, I was in love once. But I was a fool. He fell in love with my sister."

Winston looked into his coffee again. He felt all the twinges of love inside his chest. And he also felt the old feelings of being cheated on at the mention of it. When you love someone, you trust them to hold your entire life in their hands, like a fragile object, like a vase, like crystal ware. When they leave you for another, they throw your vase against the floor. Vases are never vases after that. They can be reglued, but they won't hold water.

Ray had begun frying something on the grill, and the whole place started to smell wonderful. Winston felt the first pangs of hunger, but he was afraid to yield to them. Digesting made it hard to breathe. He took a few pills from his pocket and chased them with coffee.

"I was in love once," he said.

"You? I can't hardly believe it."

"I'm not that old."

"I didn't mean that. What happened to her?"

"She married someone else. I was over in France, marching for Uncle Sam. She was already married and pregnant with his child when I got back. I thought I was going to die. When I found out, I wished I would have died in the war."

Some things require no response. Sarah remained quiet.

Winston went on. "Ah, but her kids turned out beautiful and talented. Her husband's a Baptist preacher, everybody's happy. They belong on a dadgum magazine cover for the American family."

"I'll bet that preacher don't have a dog named Huck."

He laughed, then coughed. "Sarah, is there anything you've always wanted to do? You know, before you leave this world?"

She thought for a moment. "Do? Not really. I've done most of the things I wanted to do. But I always wanted to ride in an airplane. Does that count?"

"Yeah, that counts."

"What about you? Anything you want to do before you die?"

"Yep. Go to Flatbush, Brooklyn. I wanna see Jackie Robinson. I wanna eat a hot dog in Ebbets Field, the whole works."

"So why don't you go?"

"Can't, least not right now. The season's already over."

"There'll be plenty more seasons."

"Yeah."

A bell dinged. Buz Guilford walked in carrying a small box beneath his arm. The sheriff tucked his book into his jacket pocket. The boy plopped onto the seat beside the sheriff and said, "Sorry I'm late. Tommy said you'd be here."

Winston fuzzed the kid's hair. "Tommy and I have been working together too long. Did you bring it?"

"Oh, I brought it." Within seconds, Buz had unfolded a Scrabble game board onto the counter. "You're going down, old man."

And in Winston's heart, he knew the boy was right.

Casting Call

It was the first Nativity play rehearsal of the year. The fellowship hall was filled with the loud voices of children. Inside and out. Jessie was outside playing on the basketball court by herself. The girls had all formed their respective huddles and were talking about the same thing they always talked about: boys. The boys were dodging spitballs from the pews. It sounded like an atomic explosion of pure childhood, only with more giggling, some crying, and other bodily noises Methodists don't acknowledge.

The church kitchen was crawling with ladies who made the place smell like the world's largest Estée Lauder Youth-Dew bath powder convention. The women tended ovens and skillets. This was the church lady's calling during the Christmas season—to chop onions, grate blocks of cheddar, bake things in Bundt pans, and above all, prepare strange and exotic congealed Jell-O salads with unusual vegetables or Del Monte canned cocktail fruit embedded in the center. The buffet tables were loaded with pies and snacks to beat the band for the children's families to eat after rehearsal.

When rehearsal began, Eleanor herded all the children into the gymnasium and got their attention by rapping a pool cue against the podium. Where she'd gotten this pool cue, she couldn't remember, but it was a very effective visual aid when it came to young people. Rowdy boys thought twice about mouthing off when she held a pool cue. The room quieted to a dull murmur. She looked at the ocean of freckle-faced heathens. It was her duty to teach these children to perform onstage, speak their lines clearly, sing with their diaphragms, behave like revered holy Nativity figures, and most importantly, spit out their gum.

"Answer when I call your name!" shouted Eleanor, swatting the pool cue, calling roll.

First, Eleanor elected two teenage girls to be her assistants, a coveted position among the young volunteers. Then she doled out roles for shepherds and wise men, making notes on her clipboard. There was strict protocol when it came to casting. Only the most well-behaved boys qualified to be wise men. The shepherds were also expected to meet high standards. For example, any auditionee who used the word *ain't* onstage—even once—would be sentenced to the angel choir with Miss Terry, or worse, would be cast as one of the fruits and vegetables. Moab Methodist was the only church that featured fruits and vegetables during the birth of Christ.

Rehearsal was off to a rough start. During the Nativity blocking, Eleanor directed the herd of children. She walked to the back of the fellowship hall gymnasium to get a better look. She climbed onto a chair and did not like what she saw. This was no holy Nativity; this was a mass of bodies kicking and shoving each other.

"This simply isn't going to work," she said to Miss Terry. "Linda and Marcus have gone through puberty since the last time I saw them."

"But Linda and Marcus have played Mary and Joseph for the last two years."

"It's time for a change. Linda looks like she's a senior in college, and Marcus has a five-o'clock shadow."

Eleanor had no choice but to cast Linda as an archangel and

Marcus as a banana. Decisions were made. Feelings were hurt. But this was Eleanor's play; it had been her pageant for four presidential administrations. Eleanor alone was sovereign. Her obligation was to God and John Wesley, and she held the pool cue to prove it.

Ruth Ann, Linda's mother, marched up to Eleanor and pressed her finger into Eleanor's shoulder. "You think just because you keep steady company with the sheriff that you can call the shots?"

Eleanor was aghast. She tried to murmur a response, but nothing came out except, "You old heifer!" Not the most clever response, but it got the point across.

Ruth Ann took her children and left the fellowship hall. A few others followed Ruth Ann because this was how Moab worked. Whenever someone like Ruth Ann did something, her little toadies did it too. It had been this way since high school. If Ruth Ann had used a blowtorch to burn her eyebrows off, her friends would have shown up to church next Sunday with third-degree burns on their brows. Eleanor bid them good riddance and adjusted her Perma-lift.

Soon, the fellowship hall was a little less full.

Eleanor said to Miss Terry, "Well, that's several less costumes to worry about."

"But, Ellie," said Miss Terry. "Ruth Ann was our props manager. Who's manager now?"

"You are. You've been promoted."

"But Ruth Ann brought all those props from her house. I don't have any props at my house."

Eleanor patted her shoulder. "A pessimist sees the difficulty in every opportunity, but an optimist sees the opportunity in every difficulty. Winston Churchill said that."

The air was cut with the sound of a scream.

Eleanor hushed the children and scanned the crowd. Someone was missing. "Where's Jessie?"

Eleanor rushed out of the fellowship hall with the pool cue in her hand. She saw a black Dodge parked beside the basketball hoop, idling, then a woman manhandling Jessie, shoving the child into the back seat. In the woman's hand was a handgun. Eleanor's heart began beating fast and her body was flooded with a surge of adrenaline. She sprinted across the church lawn toward the basketball court, holding the pool cue like a bat.

When she neared the car, she saw two men in the front seat. "*Go!*" shouted the young woman in the back seat, who had her hand over Jessie's mouth.

Eleanor did not think. She simply reacted. Before the car moved an inch, she swatted the pool cue against the windshield several times and the glass shattered into a confetti of blue shards. The two men stared at her from the front seat with paralyzed faces. The young woman had dropped the gun. Jessie was kicking and screaming.

"*Get out, Jessie!*" Eleanor hollered, holding the pool cue like a cleanup hitter. She swatted it against the passenger window next.

The woman in the back seat grabbed Jessie by her hair and Jessie's arms waved like a windmill at the woman. Jessie landed several hits to the woman's face.

The car began to move forward. Eleanor was losing all control of this situation.

"Jessie!" shouted Eleanor, who was galloping beside the car. She swatted the pool cue against the glass window of the back passenger door, and it shattered. As she reached inside the splintered window to grab the door handle, the glass sliced her forearm like teeth. She yanked the door open, then grabbed Jessie's wrist with both hands.

Eleanor used every ounce of her body weight to pull the child from the vehicle's open door, using enough force to dislocate the girl's arm. Jessie came tumbling out of the moving car, rolling onto the grass.

The car snaked away, cutting two muddy ditches into the Methodist lawn, the back door still splayed open. She heard the car fall into low gear when it wheeled out of the parking lot and sped away. The woman in the back seat locked eyes with Eleanor until the car disappeared down Hydrangea Street.

When the car was out of sight, Eleanor dropped the pool cue, sat on the curb, and cried into her bloody hands. Her heart was in her neck, and her hands were shaking. "Who were those people?" was all she could ask Jessie.

But Jessie was not crying. Her hair was a mess, and she had a cut forehead that was starting to swell.

"That was Sister Maria," Jessie said.

The Truth Will Set You Free

They were in the courthouse. Winston tended to Jessie's scrapes and scratches with a cotton ball. Each time he dabbed her cuts it stung something terrible. Eleanor sat in a chair, her face still white with fear. Or shock.

Jessie told them everything. In some ways, it felt like taking in a full breath. A cleansing breath. It was honesty, plain and simple. It also felt humiliating. In the months she'd been there, Jessie had almost come to believe she was just like everyone else in Moab, almost normal even. But she was not normal.

Winston placed a bandage over her forehead, then he put one on Eleanor's arm.

Jessie felt ridiculous. She didn't want these people to see her as a freak. Since she'd been in this town she had become Jessie the Pitcher, Jessie the Tomboy. She was feared by the boys, respected by her teammates. She felt as though she had become the person she had always known she was, deep inside herself, the kind of person nobody at the temple ever would have let a bastard become.

"Do you know where this Ada is now?" said Winston, tending the gash on her shin. "Has she made contact with you?"

Jessie nodded. "I saw her."

"Where? When?"

"In the woods behind Eleanor's house, right after Halloween. She looked all beat up and skinny. I think they hurt her."

"Halloween? Why didn't you say anything?" said Eleanor.

The sheriff frowned and kept dabbing her shin with the cotton. "Did she say anything to you?"

Jessie started to cry. Not because she was scared, which she was, but because she didn't want to be Jessie from the Temple Community of Sanctified Brethren. She wanted to be just Jessie.

So the sheriff held her. He was good about sensing her feelings, and he knew when she was sad. "Did Ada say anything to you, Jessie? It could be important."

Jessie wiped her nose and nodded. "She said, '*Sie kommen dich holen*, Jessie.'"

"What's *that* mean?" said Eleanor.

Winston said, "I think it means 'They're coming for you, Jessie.'"

The sheriff held her again, patting her hair and speaking softly to her.

"Please don't send me back there," said Jessie. "I would rather die than go back there. I won't go."

"Don't you worry, sweetheart," said Winston. "You're not going back. Our team could never afford to lose you."

She began to sob into his shoulder. "I'm scared."

Winston touched her chin and brought her eyes to meet his. His eyes were like the color of tap water. "I was scared once. Back when I was in the army. It was a terrifying place to be, over in northern France and Belgium. Every morning you'd wake up and you'd think, 'Is this the day? Is this the day I'm gonna get it?'"

He dabbed her clammy cheek with his palm.

"I once had this major, Major Neidhammer, from Cincinnati," he said. "He was a nice man. Do you know what he always used to do?"

She shook her head.

"Major Neidhammer would always carry these stupid little gold coins in his pocket, made of chocolate. He'd always tell us boys the same thing, that he was giving us a million bucks in sugar. We were so far from home, so scared. It really was like a million bucks to us."

Winston reached into his pocket and handed Jessie a chocolate coin. "*Weine nicht, Liebes,*" he said with a horrible, almost comical accent. But she got the gist.

Don't cry, dear.

MOAB SOCIAL GRACES

BY MARGIE BRACH

Moab beautification committee is still installing Christmas decorations on Hydrangea and is sorry for any delays, but the reindeer were in bad need of fiberglass repair, and John Barry was out of town. Volunteers bring ladders if possible.

Mrs. and Mr. Sam Allen have decided to spend Christmas in Miami. "Nobody minds our business in Miami. I'm sick of seeing my name in the paper," said Mr. Allen. This is Sam's second marriage.

Ray's Cafe is now open at four a.m., serving early-bird breakfast specials.

The Boy Scouts visited Tallahassee on Monday for a field trip, led by Pastor Shelford. Jacob Adams shook hands with Florida Governor Johns. "He was so tall," said Jacob.

Moab Methodist Christmas Nativity play rehearsals began on Wednesday. But positions still need to be filled. Wear comfortable clothing. No blue jeans allowed. See Eleanor Hughes for more information.

Donations for Little League uniforms will be collected at the courthouse.

Mr. and Mrs. Lawrence Roney have painted their home on Terrence Street even though they initially said they would not. The shutters are forest green now.

Mr. Vern Alison visited his brother, Virgil, in Flomaton.

The Baptist Women's Coalition annual bake sale will be held Friday. Funds go toward new hymnals. "Our old hymnals are falling apart," said Pastor Shelford.

Larry Herrington's red angus heifer took first prize in the Florida state competition. "My heart is so full," said Larry.

Mr. Arnold Wilson escorted Mrs. Marigold Jeffers to Pensacola last Friday to play bingo.

Mr. Leonard Bradley and Miss Sylvia Grantham are engaged and are rushing the wedding.

Mrs. Eleanor Hughes accompanied Sheriff Browne to Saturday's city council meeting where electric-sign lighting ordinance proposals were discussed.

Postmaster Jimmy Abraham says mail will continue to be backed up through New Year's due to an unusual amount of holiday parcels.

The Far Country

A mailman had a different perspective on the world. He saw one person at a time, one porch, one storefront, one federal-approved mail receptacle at a time, one piece of gossip at a time. Jimmy Abraham crawled all over Moab each morning like an ant crawls along a beach ball, walking every inch of it, getting nowhere, hearing all the rumors at each front stoop.

The morning shadows were like a painting. The moss in the live oaks swayed in the gentle breeze. With the temperature at eighty-two degrees, it did not feel like winter.

Moab was full of rumors. It always had been. Rumors drifted through town like fluff from a cottonwood. There were rumors that someone had tried to kidnap Jessie. And there was the rumor that Eleanor had thrown herself in front of a moving vehicle to stop the attackers. But the biggest one was not about Jessie. And Jimmy was doing his best not to think about it. He was trying with all his heart not to believe that Winston would have taken up residence at her place and smeared a good woman's name. But people in Moab were saying they'd seen the sheriff's vehicle parked at her home at all hours. Even overnight.

Jimmy placed a stack of mail into the mailbox of the house he grew up in on Frond Street. One of the first Moab houses. Two story, white clapboards, green shutters. The yard was a work of art, manicured, trimmed, and primped. The Earnhardts lived here now. Jimmy remembered asking Eleanor to marry him on this porch when he was twenty-three. They had never set a date.

He sat on the steps and cussed himself for going through so much of his life as a biblical-style idiot. He looked in the front yard, at the swing still hanging from the oak. The same swing his father risked his life to hang from that tall limb.

Jimmy always held dreams of seeing the world someday. He didn't want to get married when he was a young man, and he didn't want to stay here in this town. He had never wanted to take over the store and post office, and he dadgum sure didn't want to be delivering U.S. parcel. But after his father died from tuberculosis, the decision seemed to make itself.

Delivering the mail would be the death of him. It was one of those jobs a man had to plan his life around. There was no room for anything else but the mail. And it wasn't easy getting the mail where it needed to go. He had hired two men, Luke Hopkins and William Cawper, in the past few months to help lighten his load. Luke lasted ten days. William simply didn't show up for work and quit returning Jimmy's calls.

He stepped onto the white porch of the Earnhardts' house. Pine garlands hung around the doors. Twinkling holiday lights wrapped around the porch posts. An American flag dangled in the breeze. A faint sound of a piano came from inside.

Lida opened the door. When Jimmy saw her, he tipped his safari helmet to her.

Lida was a pretty young woman who did not go unnoticed by young men in town. She gave piano lessons, and she always had plenty of students because when Moab boys reached the age of fourteen they suddenly developed an interest in Bach preludes.

"How're you this morning, Lida?"

"It's almost one o'clock, Jimmy." She grabbed her mail from his hand, then followed with a look. A classic face of moral disapproval. The same look Jimmy's father had worn every day of his life in this house. A look the old man wore even in his casket.

"Jimmy, I haven't gotten my mail in nine days. The world could be falling apart and I wouldn't know about it."

"Yes, ma'am. But you'll be glad to know that it's not falling apart, it's just corroding." A little humor never hurt anyone.

She shut the door in his face. And it struck him that he was not even a welcome person in the place that birthed him. In the space of a short period of life, he had lost his girl, his best friend, and his town.

After delivering mail all morning, Jimmy sat on the curb at the corner of Evergreen Avenue beneath a shade tree to catch his breath. He was drenched in sweat.

In the distance, he saw Eleanor's house, sitting at the end of Evergreen. Children were on the porch roller-skating. He could see Jessie in the front yard, pitching to Eleanor, who was crouching and wearing a catcher's mask. He missed her. Even from far away, and even from behind the mask, Eleanor was a beautiful woman.

She always had been lovely, and he had always been a fool.

The county Hudson passed Jimmy. Winston was driving. The car pulled into Eleanor's driveway and Winston stepped out of the vehicle. Jimmy saw Winston pop the trunk. He removed a suitcase and an army-green duffel bag, then jogged up the steps. And he didn't look like he was there to play patty-cake. Eleanor threw her arms around him. So did Jessie.

It was the first time Jimmy had cried in years. He hated this town.

It was early when Jimmy arrived at the courthouse. The lights were on inside the building. He found his old friend seated on the courthouse's back steps, a newly lit smoke hanging from the left corner of his mouth. He was reading a book.

Winston did not look up from his page. "Uh-oh."

"What're you uh-ohing?"

Winston shut the book. "Either you wanna kill me or you need money."

It was funny how friends made the best enemies, Jimmy thought. The two of them had been thick as tar for an entire lifetime, but now Jimmy's blood got hot whenever he thought about Winston Browne living at Eleanor's house. It disgusted him on a deep level.

Jimmy tried to think of something to say, but he'd forgotten his confrontational speech when he laid eyes on the sheriff. It had been a few weeks since he'd seen Winston up close. Winston was leaner, paler, and looked at least twenty years older than he had before.

Winston sounded nonchalant. "What is this about, Jimmy? I got work to do today."

"You know *what it's about*. Everybody knows."

"I'm not sure I know what you mean."

"I wanna know what's going on. The rumors going around town are filthy."

"I don't go in much for rumors."

"I oughta beat your butt right here."

Winston almost choked on his cigarette with his laugh. "What are we, fourteen years old?"

"I'm gonna ask you *one more time.*"

"You haven't even asked me the first time yet."

Jimmy was torqued. "So you're not even gonna deny it? You're just gonna go around ruining that woman's reputation, bringing her groceries, moving her furniture, *having sleepovers at her house?*"

"You don't know what you don't know, Jimmy."

"Don't gimme that. I saw you there last night. With my own eyes, like you were moving in." Jimmy cussed beneath his breath. "Your car was there all night."

"You don't know what you saw. I can't believe we're having this conversation. I can't believe I'm getting browbeaten by my best friend."

"I ain't your best friend. Don't call me that. Not ever again."

"You've been stringing that woman along since you were a young man, Jimmy." Winston was yelling now. "You don't give a flying flannel about that woman's heart, or how she feels, or about how great she is. All you care about is your own pride."

Jimmy didn't even take time to think. He slammed his fist into the sheriff's jaw. The man fell backward off the stoop and into the grass. Winston curled on the ground, clutching his chin. Jimmy was torn between helping his friend off the ground and throwing another punch. He did neither.

Jimmy just stared at his friend lying there, head in his hands. He felt a mixture of guilt and triumph. He noticed a small bottle on the ground beside Winston. It was brown, with a white cap. He picked it up and inspected the label. *Prednisone, 20 mg.* He pocketed the bottle and left the courthouse.

Prednisone

Winston tore up his desk looking for the Prednisone. He was gasping, wheezing, and his vision was dim, his jaw hurt, and his lip was bleeding from where Jimmy had coldcocked him. But he had bigger problems than his jaw right now. He felt like he was suffocating to death.

He knew the pills were here somewhere, for crying out loud. The medicine had become his crutch. Sometimes he wasn't sure if he was taking it because it eased his symptoms or his mind. It was the same way with the sleep medication the doctor gave him. Often it worked; other times it didn't. But he still took it every night because anything was better than spending the whole night seated on the edge of the bed, coughing blood into a napkin.

He felt his face getting hot from all the gagging for air, and his jaw throbbed and hurt to move. Not being able to breathe makes a man feel like a caged animal, desperate and trapped. He collapsed in his desk chair, and it was all sinking in at once. Winston Browne was not just dying, he was suffocating to death. And this was how it would happen. He tried to avoid these thoughts, but it didn't make them any less true. He was not long for this world, and any day could be his last turn at bat.

He emptied another desk drawer. The contents scattered all over the floor. He sifted through old receipts and piles of pencils looking for the bottle. Nothing. He emptied his jacket pockets. He dug through the bottom drawer. He slammed it shut and leaned back in the chair. His throat sounded like he was breathing through a sippy straw.

He was angry about the false accusations, of course. Angrier than he thought he would be. He never once slept inside Eleanor's home. He'd been sleeping in her backyard shed on a cot, just outside Jessie's room. He'd been using a battery-powered lamp to read Mark Twain each night, patrolling the perimeter of Eleanor's house on foot every few hours. He knew they were out there; he'd seen evidence of them in the woods. He did it because it was his fault that whoever was in the Pearson house was running loose and trying to either kidnap a child or worse. He did it because he loved Jessie like his own. He did it because he had come to love Eleanor.

Winston hadn't planned on feeling this way. He didn't even know that he wanted to, truth be told. Love was a wonderful inconvenience. Like rain. But you can't control rain. It does whatever it wants, whenever it wants.

He stared through the courthouse window at J.R.'s Mercantile. They were all probably over there right now, spreading their gossip around town like the Bangkok flu. They were as bad as a nest of old mother hens, perpetuating every rumor and embellishing it until it was fit for the front page of the *Messenger*. He rose from his chair. His chest felt tingly, like his legs often felt when they had fallen asleep. He marched across the street, getting dizzier with each step. Huck leapt from his bed and followed Winston on his warpath across Hydrangea.

The bell to the mercantile dinged when Winston pushed open the door. He found several old men seated at a table, playing their stupid board game. His hands were shaking something awful. Either from a lack of oxygen or from fury. Or both.

"What happened to you?" said Alvin. "You get into a fight with a brick wall?"

Winston said, "Give 'em to me, Jimmy." He could barely breathe. "Now. I'll count to five."

Jimmy didn't look up from the game table. "Uh-oh. Either you wanna kill me or you need money."

Winston became swollen with a rare feeling, a sensation more about the fear of collapsing on the floor than about Jimmy. This was desperation maybe. Nothing could make a man more desperate than dying. Or more angry. He was so infuriated he momentarily imagined himself using both hands to overturn the game table. He pictured the table sailing upward through the air with a thousand little wooden Scrabble tiles peppering the mercantile floor. But this wasn't in his nature, and he couldn't bring himself to do it. So he reached a trembling hand outward and wagged a finger in Jimmy's face. "Give them to me."

"Give *what* to you?" said Jimmy.

"Jimmy. Quit being such a horse's patoot." Winston was ready to be ungracious now.

But he didn't get the chance. Jimmy reached into his pocket and removed a brown bottle of pills. He rattled it. "My daddy took this same stuff for consumption, Win. How about you tell me what in the Sam Hill is going on?"

The men's ears became three sizes larger. Nobody even blinked.

Winston swiped the pills. He spoke not a word to Jimmy. He looked at the table again and briefly pondered putting an end to their game. But something else struck him in this moment.

He leaned over Alvin's shoulder and selected two wooden tiles from the man's rack. He laid them on the board and spelled *zoo* on a double-word score. "Twenty-six points," said Winston.

Then he left the mercantile without even saying goodbye. After all, Jimmy had said it earlier. They weren't friends anymore.

How Lovely Are Your Branches

None of the boys on the ball team had ever seen snow before. Especially not this much of it. Once, Buz had seen sleet. But it lasted for ten minutes, then was followed up by a hurricane. But this was real, honest-to-goodness snow. He wished it would have held off until Christmas Eve, or even better, Christmas itself. But people in Moab had to take what they could get. And snow occurring two weeks before Christmas was still welcome.

It was perfect. The snow made Buz feel like they were in the middle of a Bing Crosby and Fred Astaire movie. A few days earlier, it had been in the eighties, and Buz had worn a T-shirt. Now there were barrels of white stuff, falling in sheets, catching the moonlight, filling the night with actual winter. Welcome to the Panhandle, where the weather changes every three minutes, unless you want it to change. Then it stays the same.

The Hudson pulled into the Guilfords' driveway with Winston in the passenger seat. Tommy was driving. Buz was in back. Three other cars pulled into the driveway behind the Hudson.

"Have you ever seen snow before, Sheriff?" said Buz.

He nodded. "In France I saw it a lot. Didn't care for it then, don't love it that much right now either."

"It ain't natural," said Tommy.

The sheriff and his deputy wore homemade jackets with the embroidered team insignia on the front. Buz wore an identical jacket, as did every member of the boy's team in the other cars. The jackets had been made by Miss Ellie and given to the team earlier that evening as an early Christmas gift. She had fed the team pie, eggnog, peanut butter cookies, and tomato aspic. Everything was great except the aspic, which was about as appetizing as homemade soap. After snacks, Miss Ellie had given them the handmade jackets with official Dodgers logos and everything. Each jacket came wrapped in colorful paper and bore a handwritten note from the sheriff himself. They weren't short note cards either. Buz's personal note was two pages long, and it had made Buz blush to read the first few lines. So he tucked the note into his pocket to read later so he could blush freely without spectators.

The jackets made their team feel official. The Moab Dodgers. A real ball club.

Buz stepped out of the vehicle to look at his own ramshackle home dusted in the light snow. The roof was white. The field behind his house was blanketed in thick Barbasol. Neighborhood children were playing in their yards, dressed in sweaters and pajamas, forming pathetic snowballs of mud and weeds.

"I can't believe it," said Tommy. "Snow in Moab."

"It sure is cold," said the sheriff.

"It looks just like all the pictures," said Buz, noting how much like a dweeb he sounded. He stooped to gather a handful, just to feel it.

The sheriff laughed, then slapped Buz's shoulder. "You know what we used to say in the army, Buz? Don't eat the yellow snow."

"I don't get it," said Tommy.

"Never mind," said the sheriff. "C'mon, we got at least ten more to deliver tonight, and I'm not gonna live forever, you know."

Buz raced up the steps of his home, followed by eleven other boys and one girl in matching blue jackets. Buz marched into the kitchen, carrying a handful of snow. "Do you see the snow, Mama?" he said.

The redheaded woman was waiting for him at the kitchen table. She looked pale and tired. Her eyes were weary, and her hair was a mess. She'd either been up all night or had just woken up. There was no way to know; the mill kept her working odd hours.

"Where have you been?" she said to Buz. "I've been worried sick."

"Snow, Mama, look."

At that moment twelve more blue jackets filtered into the home, bearing gifts, groceries, and trinkets made from Sunday schoolers all over Moab.

His mother stood onto her polio-stricken legs. She balanced herself on the back of a chair. "What is all this?" she said.

Winston and Tommy came walking through the open door next, making heavy thuds with their boots when they entered the room. They carried a large tree in their arms. "Well, don't just stand there!" Winston said, holding the trunk. "Someone tell us where this thing goes."

They carried the fir into the den and propped it up in the corner. It was bigger than a Chrysler and twice as nice. When the tree was upright, Buz's mother covered her mouth and stared at it. Buz stood beside her doing the same thing. It was his first Christmas tree.

Tommy pulled out a harmonica and gave everyone a note. The mass of children huddled in the den like a coffee can full of tangled earthworms and they began to sing "Silent Night." It was the eighth time that night they'd performed this song, but it was by far the best performance. Jessie could even sing it in another language. Johnny Paul said the language was Latin. She had a lovely voice. The boys hummed with her, using every ounce of sincerity they had. Buz's mother even closed her eyes to listen. The children's voices were hoarse, young, and squeaky. But the sound made his mother's hard exterior turn to wax.

"Oh, Sheriff," she said. "It's beautiful."

Buz placed both arms around his frail mother and held her. The rest of the kids on the team added themselves to the group until it was one big mess of people with their arms entwined.

Winston was last to add himself to the group hug. "Don't thank me," he said. "This a gift from the Okeauwaw County Dodgers, ma'am. Merry Christmas."

Buz wondered what Winston had meant when he said that he wouldn't live forever.

Esteemed Ushers

Moab's streets were lined with automobiles with tags from other counties. The exiles were back for Christmas.

Moab Methodist was crowded this morning because Christmas was four days away, and this was the high point of the year. On any other Sunday, the church would have been half full with mostly old farts. But today it would be filled with everyone who lived within a four-hour radius of Moab. This made the town feel alive. Winston felt as though he were reliving the greatest moments of his childhood, seeing all these familiar faces again. Some men preferred whiskey; others were notorious gamblers; some were playboys. Winston Browne was a people person. It was his vice and addiction, the melodies of people's voices and the warmth of their handshakes.

Young women cackled outside the fellowship hall, preparing for tonight's Christmas social. People were walking across the street, dressed in their nicest clothing. Old faces had been flocking to Ray's for breakfast by the dozen. Ray, to show his appreciation for all the local business, had jacked up his prices.

That morning there was a long line trailing out the door of the church onto the steps and sidewalk. Winston and Jimmy were ushers, standing on both sides of the front door. Winston would have rather been paired with a rabid badger.

Ninety-eight people were in line, waiting to get inside. And that was just at Winston and Jimmy's door. The north entrance had an even bigger line. The Baptists across the street had a larger crowd than Moab Methodist. The Baptists had so many people they had set up a tent outside to hold the service since the sanctuary wouldn't hold them all. Pastor Shelford had been shouting and hollering Baptist-style sermons about hellfire and brimstone all morning until spittle came from his mouth and the vein on his head poked out. Merry Christmas.

The Methodists were amused at the sermons coming from across the street because, within the Methodist tradition, sermons were generally pretty warm and fuzzy, with a maximum of two jokes. Baptists did not believe in jokes, nor did they acknowledge the existence of fuzzy feelings.

"Well, don't you look fancy this morning?" Winston said to Jimmy, who was passing out bulletins on the other side of the doorway.

These were the first words exchanged between them since their last confrontation at the mercantile. Something was different about Jimmy today. The old postmaster had Brylcreem in his hair. In all the years Winston had known Jimmy, the man had never put anything in his hair but his own greasy fingers. And Winston could smell cologne all over the man.

"Jimmy, is that hair lotion you're wearing?"

Jimmy touched his hair. "So what?"

"I hope it ain't flammable."

Jimmy straightened his collar. "Why don't you make like horse flop and hit the road?"

"Can't we call a truce, Jimmy? It's Christmas."

Winston handed a bulletin to Mrs. Clyde and her teenage son. Her son towered over the sheriff by a full foot. A handsome boy with an athletic frame. "Clyde, I wish you were younger, then you'd be on my team instead of being a future football star."

The sheriff dug into his pocket and gave the kid a chocolate coin. The tall teenager accepted the coin but seemed a little embarrassed.

"What's this?" the kid said.

"A million bucks in sugar," said Winston Browne. "Don't spend it all in one place."

The kid's mother hugged Winston and told him she was praying for him. This took Winston a little off guard. He glared at Jimmy. There was no such thing as a secret in a small town. When the woman was gone, Winston said to Jimmy, "What'd you do, put it in the classified section?"

"Put *what* in the classified section? You ain't told me nothing yet."

"Did you hear what she just said to me?"

"Don't look at me."

Bess and Oney Williams came through the door next. The small elderly couple was smiling. They were always smiling. Winston hadn't seen them since he was a teenager, since they moved to Detroit. Pronounced *Dee*-troit. Both Bess and Oney were under five foot tall and old enough to remember when people in Moab still had to drive to Pensacola just to rent sunshine.

The old woman said, "Winston, why don't you let me make you a poultice? It helps with consumption."

Winston locked eyes with Jimmy for a moment. Then he smiled at her. "Thank you, Mrs. Williams, but I don't *have* consumption. Just a cough."

Larry and Helen Crenshaw came through the door next. They were a nice-looking young couple with a redheaded son named Dil, who was covered in freckles and missing two front teeth. They lived in Montgomery. Larry used to be a deputy, once upon a time. Winston shook their son's hand, then reached into his pocket for a chocolate coin. "Don't spend it all in one place, Dil. That's a million bucks, you know."

When they were gone, Jimmy said, "Everybody's tired of your stupid coins and your stupid jokes, you big goober."

"You're a sad man, Jimmy."

"You're ugly."

"I shoulda punched you back."

"You just go ahead and try."

Winston saw Eleanor and Jessie coming up the sidewalk. They were as pretty as a picture. Jessie wore a green print dress, her hair in big curls. He had rarely seen the child wear anything but jeans and T-shirts since he'd met her. Eleanor had on a plaid dress that fully—not partially—revealed her knees. She wore a green headband, red earrings, and a string of red beads. Winston stepped off the porch to greet them before anyone else. But Jimmy raced after him.

Soon the two men were moving in a controlled but fierce footrace across the church lawn with bulletins flying from their hands, nudging innocent pedestrians and helpless elderly people out of the way. In the end, Jimmy won because Winston was in no shape to compete.

When they reached Eleanor, both men were out of breath, and there was a long trail of church leaflets strewn behind them. Winston felt like his lungs were going to burst and his throat was closing.

"Win," said Eleanor. "Are you okay? You look sick."

"Hey, what about me?" said Jimmy.

"You always look sick, Jimmy," said Eleanor.

Winston said, "I'm fine. I wish everyone would quit worrying about me, for pity's sake. Everyone's treating me like I'm in a pine box."

But Winston was not fine. In fact, something was very wrong. More wrong than usual. He turned to stagger toward the church, trying his best to keep upright. But he could feel people watching him. *Rubbernecking* might have been the better word. His ears were ringing; the world was fading in color. His heart was in low gear, like it was ready to give out.

Winston hobbled into the men's bathroom and flashed a fake smile to Tim Hopkins, who was washing his hands. Tim gave him a strange look. Winston stumbled into the last stall, latched the door, sat on the toilet seat, and tried to breathe. He was inside for maybe thirty minutes before he left the bathroom. Church was already in session when he shuffled toward the Hudson, which was parked in the rear of the church amidst a gulf of vehicles. He crawled into the front seat, curled himself into a ball, and tried to make his lungs work. He felt himself pass out. It was like falling into a warm blanket. A very big, very frightening, very black, warm blanket.

When he awoke, church was over, the parking lot was empty, and Jimmy was standing at his window, staring at him.

"I think it's time you let me in on your secret," said Jimmy.

Clearing the Air

Eleanor's kitchen was swirling with a cloud of rich-smelling smoke. The ashtray in the center of her kitchen table was filled with a miniature Everest of gray ash.

Eleanor sat beside Jimmy, who sat beside Winston. Tommy stood next to the screen door, looking outside with a pitiful expression on his face. The coffee was hot. The cookies were fresh from the oven. Eleanor's outfit had come from Gayfer's, not that this mattered. Not right now.

Winston explained to them the worst. She had suspected something was wrong, but not this. Not death. The worst part was, Winston had said it so calmly, as though the fact that he was dying didn't bother him at all. Like it was no big deal.

He even made a few light remarks about it and chuckled at his own humor, choking on his own smoke. Nobody else laughed. Tommy cradled his coffee mug like a security blanket.

Nobody in her kitchen knew what to say, so they didn't say anything, they just smoked. Winston alone carried the weight of the morbid conversation. Sometimes Eleanor would ask a question, but he didn't answer right away without thinking about each response first.

Jimmy kept looking into his mug and shaking his head. Tommy was pinching the bridge of his nose, probably to keep from bawling.

"Does the girl know?" said Jimmy.

Winston said, "Nobody knows but you three, and I'd like to keep it that way."

"Too late," said Tommy. "Half the town knows something's up."

"And whose fault is that?" said Winston.

"Don't look at me," said Tommy. "I haven't breathed a word about this to nobody." He paused. "I heard about it from Jimmy."

Winston shook his head. "Telephone, telegraph, tell-a-Jimmy."

Eleanor was still too shocked to cry. And besides, she didn't want to make this worse than it already was. Not in this roomful of men. In her experience, the one thing men hated most was seeing a woman cry. It made them feel helpless and agitated. So she squelched her tears and did a lot of coffee sipping between drags on her cigarette. Winston tapped the ash from his Lucky and leaned back into his chair, releasing a cloud that gathered on her ceiling. His cough sounded like a honking horn.

Speechlessness fell over the room.

"What about final arrangements?" said Jimmy.

Eleanor gave Jimmy a hateful look.

Jimmy threw up his hands. "Look, I know nobody wants to talk about it, but we gotta know. When Daddy died, he'd never told anyone what he wanted for a send-off. I felt helpless, and I wasn't in no state to figure out his last wishes."

Eleanor was holding the tears back. She had to stand from her chair and consult her stove to keep from turning into a drizzling mess.

"Geez, Jimmy," said Tommy. "Sorry, Ellie."

Winston lit another cigarette. He pulled in a lungful and said, "I don't want anything special, Jimmy. Just gimme something regular."

More horrid bouts of quiet. Horrid, horrid quiet. The sound of the wind outside could be heard. It sounded so lonely. Eleanor felt the saltwater roll down her cheeks.

"You want Reverend Davis to do it?" said Jimmy.

"Good gracious," said Eleanor.

"No," said Winston. "I don't want him doing it. He doesn't even know me. He just wouldn't get it, he's from New York."

"Connecticut," said Tommy. "And he's a big Dodgers fan."

Winston said, "Well, since you put it that way."

"His brother works for the Dodgers organization," Tommy added.

The tension in the room was released for a brief moment. They all half laughed at Tommy, who was probably the densest deputy this side of the Blackwater. Laughter, however, was a welcome port in a sea of black grief. But it was short-lived.

Eleanor looked at the skinny lawman at her table. She cursed herself for not putting two and two together. She should have seen the signs: the persistent wheezing, coughing, and weakness. Maybe she had been so selfish she hadn't wanted to see it. Maybe she had been so concerned with her own love life that she had contributed to this man's death. Maybe this was her fault.

She looked at the filtered Camel in her own hand. She stared at the thin stream of white rising from the ash. She rubbed it against the side of the sink. She could see Winston watching her from the corner of his eye. He gave her a look that suggested he understood what she was thinking.

"What can we do, Win?" said Eleanor.

Winston's eyes immediately pinkened. His voice broke, and it stabbed Eleanor's heart. Jimmy bit his lip and closed his eyes. Tommy turned his back to the group.

"Nothing," Winston said. "Just don't forget me when I'm gone."

Cannulas

The New Year did not feel very new. It felt old and tired. And over the last two months, Winston kept writing the date wrong. But nothing stays the same. Especially the things you wish would stay the same.

A young man in white clothes walked across the room and checked the oxygen canisters and the patients' nasal cannulas at various intervals. Occasionally he would jab a victim with a needle the size of a javelin. They called this "a blood gas." It was anything but a gas. It was medieval torture.

The sterile medical room was done up in garland and little silver bells as though this cut the ugliness somehow. Women were sitting in chairs, knitting, hooked up to tubes, and old men attached to oxygen canisters were reading books. This was a place you did not want to find yourself in. It was a place where the dying experienced a brief layover between connecting trains.

The man who sat beside Winston couldn't have been more than forty. Maybe even younger. Sandy hair, pale skin. He didn't look good. Winston looked at his own scrawny forearm. Neither did he.

Buz sat on Winston's other side, quiet, reading *The Mysterious Stranger.* The boy read sluggishly, a lot like Winston did. Winston could spend an entire day reading one paragraph. His teachers had called him a daydreamer. His father called him lazy. He was neither. He was just a bad speller.

The only thing people did in this room was breathe. Nobody talked because they didn't have the wind for it. In a way, it was a pleasant repose from daily life. For Winston, the job of Moab's elected officials was to be amiable, impartial, cheerful, chatty, and whatever the heck else anyone expected from their government. This ability became more obligation than anything.

"So, are you from here?" the young man beside him said. "Pensacola?"

Winston closed his eyes. *Dadgum it.* He did not want to talk. But there was no way to avoid a direct question. Winston turned to face the man. He was going to tell him he couldn't breathe, let alone chitchat. He was going to tell the man all he wanted was some time to catch his breath. But the sheriff in him said, "We're from Moab."

The young man nodded and frowned. The international reaction of people who had never heard of Moab.

"You'd have no reason to know it," added Winston.

"Small town, huh?"

"We were nine hundred and twelve people, but we had two births this week. So we're at nine-fourteen now."

"Is this your son?"

Winston rested a hand on Buz's shoulder before the boy could speak. "Yes."

The man smiled. "You two look alike. Well, I'm from Florida too, but not Florida-Florida. I'm from Florida, Missouri."

"I didn't know there was one," said Buz.

"No reason you should. Although we do have one claim to fame." The man tapped the spine of Buz's book. "Sam Clemens was born there."

Winston turned in his seat to face the young man. The words lingered in the air, almost like the smell of disinfectant that was all around them. There were moments in his life when it felt as though the universe was crashing into itself, like a celestial traffic jam. Either that or the heavens were teasing him. This was one of those moments.

"You're joking," said Winston.

"I never joke."

"Mark Twain?" said Buz, the recent convert.

"The one and only," said the man.

Winston slumped in his chair. "What a small world. You've never met a bigger Twain fan than me, well, except for Buz here."

"Everyone thinks I'm a fan because I lived in his town, but it's not true. Just 'cause we're from the same dirt don't mean nothing. He's okay."

"What brings you to our part of the world?" said Winston.

"Army air corps, though now it's called the air force. I've been everywhere."

"Me too. I was in the army during the war."

"Europe?"

"Ninth Infantry. I was a captain."

"Infantry. Jeez. You doughboys were the real heroes. I was in France too. What a small world."

It really was a small world. And it kept getting smaller.

Winston wanted to know all about Florida, Missouri, but he didn't have the wind. Neither did the young man, who kept having coughing fits that sounded identical to Winston's episodes.

The man said, "A captain, huh? You were the guy who was always yelling at me."

"I was the old man trying to save your life."

The young man clammed up. Some subjects were hard to talk about. War was one of them. Then again, it seemed so harmless compared to the inevitable.

"Family?" said Winston.

"A wife, a thirteen-year-old, and a five-year-old." In a few seconds, the man was showing photographs from a small leather photo wallet, the way every man who ever warmed a foxhole did. "These are my girls."

"What're their names?"

"Heather and Catherine."

The man coughed, then flagged for one of the orderlies and asked for more oxygen. The orderly apologized and gave a response that sounded almost rehearsed: "I'm sorry, sir. I can't give you any more. It will do more harm than good."

"You tell me that *every* time," said the young man, tugging at his collar. "I feel like I'm choking. If I wanted to choke, I'd just stay at home and die instead of coming here."

"I'll see what I can do." The man in white went to the canister. He pretended to turn the nozzle, but it was all for show.

"You said she was thirteen," said Winston. "Does that mean she was born when you were still overseas, or just getting back?"

"I was in France, and on the day she was born, I got shot in the armpit." He laughed, then coughed. "I was working on a Flak-Bait, under the wing, arms up like this, wrench in my hand. Next thing I know, people were screaming, I was bleeding. Don't remember much after that. Probably sounds like a paper cut compared to what you boys in the Ninth saw."

Winston didn't respond. He could hear Missouri in the man. Winston once had a kid under his command from Joplin. "You miss Missouri?"

He slumped in his chair. "Miss my mom. But I can't bring myself to go and see her after I came down with this junk in my lungs. It's gonna kill her. We talk on the phone."

"What's wrong with you?" said Buz.

There was a beat between the question and the answer.

"I'm a classic blue bloater," the man said. "Least, that's what the doc calls it. Just a fancy word for cancer. Said I could have months, maybe weeks. What about you, Captain? What're you in for?"

"Same thing. Only the doc called me a pink puffer."

"Has the doc tried to get you in a wheelchair yet? That's when it really gets fun. When they shove you in a wheelchair, it all starts to sink in. You'll be against it at first, but you won't have no choice."

The young man stared straight ahead. Winston could tell from the look on his face exactly who he was thinking about. The same people all dying men thought about. His girls.

Winston considered the young man lucky. In fact, he was envious. But when he looked at Buz, reading that book, he wondered about things. He wondered if perhaps this was the reason his life had played out the way it did. Maybe this was why he had been so lonely for so long. Maybe he had been waiting for Buz Guilford.

A trail of water formed on the young Missourian's cheek. The man closed his eyes. Winston had seen this sad face on almost every kid who had carried a rifle. Scared of dying, but tired of trying. Just enough boy in them to need someone to hold their hand. Just enough man to be embarrassed about it.

Winston rested his hand on the young man's hand and squeezed the man's fingers.

"You know," said Winston, "I'd like to see where old Samuel was born. I wish I coulda visited Missouri."

The young man sniffled a few times, then wiped his face. "Wish I could go home one more time too, to see Mama." He covered his face.

Any man from any war will tell you the most common last word uttered by any dying boy is *Mother.* In every major war. In every country. On every side.

They didn't speak after that. They simply breathed. Winston released the man's hand and reached into his pocket. It was almost instinct. He handed the young man a foil-wrapped chocolate coin.

The young man looked at the gold coin. "That's funny."

"What's funny?" said Winston.

"I had a major in France who always carried these. He gave 'em out all the time, everyone knew he had 'em."

"Major Neidhammer?" said Winston.

"You knew him?"

"Wow, it really *is* a small world."

And it kept getting smaller.

Bobby Pins and Buckets

Ada sat on the floor of the dank, wet basement. She had walked right into their grasp when they got too close to Jessie. It was only partly accidental, for she was more angry than afraid. Ada had put up a hellacious fight too, leaving a stunning set of bloodred fingernail marks across the man's forehead.

The light from the basement's only window above her turned the whole cellar a moonlit blue. She had been looking at this window for hours, considering its size. She wondered if she could fit through the window. There was no way she would ever know if she couldn't figure out how to break the chain that was keeping her attached to the wooden beam.

She could still smell the chloroform. She knew the smell because she had used the stuff once. She never could have made it to Florida without chloroform's magical properties. Or without taking the lives of two men.

She was not afraid of what they would do to her. She deserved whatever punishment came next. But Ada knew they were after Jessie. And she knew what they would do to the child. The same thing they had done to the others.

She spent hours using a bobby pin on the lock that bound her wrists and ankles. She knew it was a worthless endeavor, but she kept trying. She could not coax the spring-loaded latch to budge. The bobby pin was too feeble, and it was too dark to see.

But she persisted. Until her hands were sore. Until her fingernails were bent and bleeding. Until she felt as though she was going to crack inside.

She stopped fiddling with the lock and slid the pin into her pocket again. She began to cry. Death inevitable. They would kill her, of course. The only reason they hadn't was so they could find her "bastard" and kill her too.

Ada blamed the entire mess on herself. She had lain with the *Bischof*, she'd had his child in secret, she'd denied her own flesh-and-blood daughter. And then, as if she hadn't made enough trouble in this universe, she sent her own child away. And would end up getting them both killed in the process. There was more than a little blood on her hands.

She was paying for each of her sins. One by one. A just God would not let her get away with her crimes.

Ada rested her head against the stone wall and wiped her tears. Crying was not helping anything; neither was scolding herself. She forced herself to stop with the self-pity.

Her bladder complained. She reached for the galvanized tin bucket they'd left her. The metal scraped against the hard floor, making a loud rattling noise. That was when she noticed the wire handle of the pail. The handle was a short, looped, sweeping piece of thick metal wire. Its diameter was smaller than a pencil but thicker than a bobby pin. And the handle was coming loose.

It took another hour, at least, for Ada to work the handle free from the bucket. Then she wasted no time inserting its bent end into the padlock. It was the perfect fit. Ada negotiated the spring-loaded mechanism upward and felt a small pop inside the padlock. The latch lifted. Her chains fell to the ground.

And as it happened, the basement window was not too small after all.

MOAB SOCIAL GRACES

BY MARGIE BRACH

Mrs. Jeanne Allen is in Cleveland to visit her sister, Flossy Bentley, indefinitely.

Mr. Sam Allen is at home. This is Sam's second marriage.

First Baptist is holding their annual Easter egg hunt behind the fellowship hall this year. Last year too much foot traffic ruined the front yard grass. "It took a year to regrow in some places," said Pastor Shelford.

Miss Tilly Hood called upon Miss Cynthia Pines for tea and ham salad sandwiches on Thursday.

Rev. Davis, from Connecticut, was a guest of Mr. and Mrs. A. F. Blake, who are also from the North.

Negotiations are pending for the appearance of a vaudeville entertainment show in the Masonic Temple in Pensacola.

Okeauwaw County Fair is to be rescheduled for second week of April, as many volunteers complained the fair was too close to Easter. "It was an oversight on our part," said city councilman Robert Menchen.

Mr. Frank Tuckett, 17, of Franklin D. Roosevelt High School, intends to apply to medical school in Alabama.

Mr. Morgan Manning has somewhat recovered from his recent illness. Manning is one of the town's best citizens.

Mr. and Mrs. James Otts officially have one of the largest fine Jersey cow herds in West Florida. "You never expect to receive such an honor like this," said Mrs. Otts. The second biggest herd is in Okaloosa County.

Moab Dodgers are set to play their first game of the season April 3. Boys interested in trying out are to apply at the courthouse.

F. L. Hood & Sons have erected a new feed mill equipped with gasoline engine and are prepared to do custom and buckwheat grinding. They are also general dealers in grain and mill supplies. Mr. Hood for years has been a prominent businessman and a steadfast member of the Layton Church of Christ and does not tolerate the use of foul language on his property.

Sheriff Winston Browne has announced that he will not run for reelection next term.

Jackie Is Everyone's Favorite

Jessie sat in the passenger seat of the Hudson wearing her new blue-and-white ball cap along with her periwinkle Sunday dress and black patent leather shoes. The windows were down. Church was out, and most people in Moab were chewing the fat on front porches.

But Winston was doing busywork like he did every Sunday. And Jessie was his sidekick. Eleanor had told her to be *very careful* in this new outfit "or else." Jessie didn't know what "or else" meant, but she had already ruined two dresses by roughhousing with impossible boys. Eleanor told her if she ruined another dress she would be going to church wearing a potato sack without arm holes.

Winston wore a starched white shirt and trousers and had not bothered to change before doing odd jobs for local elderly people and widows. He delivered a few sacks of groceries. He helped the Devon boys remove a baseball from their gutter and saved their weekend. Before he left them, he took the time to teach them to oil their mitts with axel grease.

Jessie had helped him all afternoon, holding sacks of produce, handing Winston tools, laughing at his stale jokes, and taking care not to ruin her dress.

She adjusted her ball cap and leaned out the window to get a glimpse of herself in the side mirror. Her braids stuck out beneath her hat, whipping in the wind. She took a sip from an orange Nehi soda and wiped her mouth with her forearm.

"Be careful with that dress, Roy Campanella. Eleanor will kill me if you so much as wrinkle it."

She plopped backward into her seat, taking more sips. "I don't want to be Campanella. I'd rather be Jackie."

"Well then, I'd suggest laying out in the sun a little longer."

She thought about this. "Lay in the sun?" she said. "Why?"

"Jackie Robinson is black."

Well, this put a new light on things. She'd only ever heard Jackie's name spoken on the radio. *"Jackie singles to right!" "Jackie golfs it to center!"* But she'd always envisioned him as a seven-foot-tall man who looked like Moses, or maybe Samson.

"Jackie's my favorite," she said.

"Jackie is everyone's favorite."

She darted her hand out the open window and formed it into a flat airplane. When the car came to a long stretch of highway and built up speed, she made her airplane move up and down. It was very satisfying, feeling the wind under her hand. Then a quick burst of air whipped her hat from her head and sucked it into the current, flinging it into the daylight.

"Hey!" she said. "I lost my hat!"

Jessie poked her head out the window and looked behind them. A tiny blue cap was airborne, sailing across the sunny highway, end over end, until it landed in a scalped field far behind the vehicle.

Winston downshifted and made a U-turn on the vacant highway. "I can't take you anywhere," he said.

He eased to the side of the road and offered her his sternest warning. Which was a little humorous because Winston was not a stern person. "Stay in this car."

Jessie crossed her heart.

Winston trudged through the tall grass, high-stepping over puddles and uneven patches of dirt. She watched him through the open window, hiking across the stubble until he reached the hat. He picked it up, brushed it off, and started back for the car.

She could hear his cough, even from so far away. And she could see him coughing. And it wasn't getting any better, only worse.

Jessie leapt out of the car and jogged across the field. When she reached the sheriff, he was still coughing, doubled over, hands resting on his knees. He had dropped his cigarette and the hat, which both lay in the dirt beside him.

"Are you okay?" she said, touching his shoulder.

He couldn't answer her. He only held his hand upward as if to say, "I'm fine." But he wasn't fine. So she stood beside him and rubbed his back. Sometimes this was all you could do for a person.

She sensed there was something deeply wrong, but she didn't ask about it because she knew he didn't want to talk about it. After all, in the time he'd known her, he had never probed her about things she didn't want to talk about. He had asked where she'd come from and why she'd arrived in Moab in a strange black dress. But when she didn't respond, he had respected her silence, and she did the same to him. Sidekicks did that for each other.

When he finished his whooping fit, he took a few wheezing breaths. His face was pink and his eyes were bloodshot. His voice was so weak his words warbled. He straightened himself and gave her a deeply disappointed look. "Jessie," he said. "Your dress."

She looked at herself only to find that she was covered in stickers, sandspurs, and streaks of red-clay mud. Her shoes were even muddier.

He brushed her dress with his hand but only made it worse.

"I'm a dead man," he said.

And he meant it.

Easter Bonnets

It was the end of March, and the town was covered in a never-ending drizzle. The rain hung around all day. Even when it wasn't raining it seemed like it was raining. The skies were always gray. The humid air was so wet it turned men's trousers into soggy brown paper.

The mercantile was flooded with customers buying yardage for Easter dresses. Jimmy loved this time of year. Moab's women always bought fabric from J.R.'s, even though they could have gone into Pensacola to find a bigger selection. This was their tradition.

Their mothers had bought Easter-dress yardage here. Their grandmothers had done the same—back when girls still wore bonnets. And they would follow the convention if it killed them. Which was why Jimmy marked the prices sky high.

Reverend Davis, the reverend from Connecticut, brought his young wife into the store. She was a Yankee and talked very funny, just like him. People still didn't fully embrace Davis or his wife. They had big-city hairstyles, and the reverend dressed more fashionably than ministers ought to. Even so, everyone liked his sermons; he was a good speaker. This covered a multitude of sins. That's just how Methodism goes.

The floorboards creaked beneath the combined weight of so many mother hens and customers inspecting fabric prints. Jimmy could close his eyes and hear all the women's voices saying the same things: "Isn't that cute?" and "Isn't that darling?" and "I swear, I could just eat that child up." Jimmy hoped no child-eating would be taking place today. That was reserved for Halloween.

A small fire was burning in the potbellied stove. A hundred years ago Jimmy's father used the stove during humid weather in early spring. It produced just enough heat to dry the air out inside the store, but not enough to heat it up. The stove made the entire mercantile smell like burnt cobwebs and rust. Jimmy loved this smell. It was the smell of his youth.

Winston Browne walked into the mercantile accompanied by Buz Guilford. The two had not been seen apart from each other for months. Buz had quit his job with Mister Arnold and begun working as an unofficial errand boy for Sheriff Browne. Buz did odd jobs around the police department, sometimes even working underneath the hood of the patrol car, cleaning the carburetor or adjusting the serpentine belt. Or trying to repair the broken siren.

Word had gotten around that the sheriff was dying, and Jimmy felt terrible that he'd been responsible for such gossip. Still, this was Moab. Word would have gotten out one way or another. Secrets did not exist here.

Winston Browne looked awful. Like a skeleton with hair. Those who didn't know he was sick asked why he wasn't running in the upcoming reelection, but he was a well-noted professional when it came to ignoring questions. Jimmy watched the man smile at the townspeople and ask how their kids were doing.

Winston approached the counter. "Got a second, Jimmy?"

"I'm kinda busy. What's up?" Jimmy didn't stop sorting the mail.

"It'll only take a minute."

"No dogs allowed in this store, Win, you know that. Get him outta here."

"Who, Huck? He ain't hurting nobody."

"I don't care what kinda dog he is. He ain't allowed unless you're here to buy some yardage for your summer dress."

"No, I'm here for Buz."

Buz was wandering around the store, the dog following him.

Jimmy stopped sorting. "Buz? What color of fabric are you gonna put him in?"

Winston placed the newspaper cutout from the *Moab Messenger* classifieds onto the counter. "I thought he'd make a good candidate for your open position."

Jimmy pushed it away. He didn't want to know where this was going.

"I thought Buz was working for you, Sheriff."

"He's plenty old enough to carry letters, and you oughta see him hit the ball."

"I don't care *how* he hits, that ain't got no bearing on being a federal employee. The answer is no."

"Now, you haven't even heard my proposal, Jimmy."

"I don't have to. I've been through five mail carriers in the last six months. I've heard more than enough proposals, and not one of them was worth a cuss. I don't wanna hire your little second baseman."

"He's our catcher, Jimmy. If you came to practices, you'd know that."

Jimmy eyed the kid from a distance. Buz was so wiry and lean he looked like he would've had to run around in the shower just to get wet. He had never seen a kid so scrawny. "*That's* your catcher?"

"He needs a good job, Jimmy, and you're a good man. Mostly." Winston's chest began to rumble. He covered his mouth and hacked. The cough drew the looks of people in the store. Soon he was almost gagging.

Jimmy removed his reading glasses. "You expect me to hire one of the Katzenjammer Kids to deliver the U.S. mail?"

"He's gotta work. You know the Guilfords, you know what kinda fix they're in. Besides, he's keeping me company."

Jimmy replaced his glasses and resumed sorting. "Don't you remember what you were like when you were fourteen, Win? Use your head."

"Sure, when I was fourteen I was fit, healthy. I could walk all day without getting tired. I coulda delivered the entire town's mail before noon and still had time to go get a lemon phosphate from Miller's Drugstore."

"You were chasing girls and baseballs, just like I was."

"He ain't like that, Jimmy. Besides, I love that boy." Winston began to hack again. This time it was worse. When he covered his mouth with his fist, his hand was shaky.

"That Prednisone ain't working anymore, is it, Win?" said Jimmy.

Winston ignored this remark. "Give the boy a chance. I'm asking you as a friend. I wanna do right by him. He needs something permanent. When I'm gone, the new sheriff won't owe Buz anything."

The words lodged in Jimmy's ears and stayed there for a few seconds. Jimmy looked back at the boy, who was leaning on the counter like a telephone pole with legs. "Dadgum you, Winston Browne."

They both had tears in their eyes. "I'm strict. I catch him messing around on the job and . . ."

"Yes, absolutely."

Jimmy came from behind the counter. "And this is only an evaluation period, mind you. He's gotta prove himself. If he's more concerned with baseball than he is with his duties, well, he's got another thing coming."

Winston wrapped both arms around him. It was a full-body embrace. Jimmy could hear the wheezing in the old man's chest.

"Lemme go," said Jimmy.

"Oh, Jimmy, Adam Guilford's dancing a jig, wherever he is."

Jimmy worked his arms through Winston's bear hug and shoved the tall, gangly man away. He didn't mean to shove so hard. The sheriff lost his footing, collapsed backward onto the floor, and knocked over a magazine rack. Jimmy was stunned. He waited for the sheriff to move, but he didn't. His best friend lay on the floor coughing.

"Don't just stand there," Jimmy shouted. "Go get someone! He can't breathe!"

Buz Guilford ran from the store, and his feet only touched the ground twice.

King of England

The sunlight hurt Winston's eyes. It gave him a headache something fierce. He found himself lying in his own bed, but he was disoriented. How did he get here? Who brought him here? The light was shooting through his window, illuminating all the dust in the air. It looked like pink fog. He saw three faces staring back at him.

He blinked his eyes several times. The first face he recognized was Reverend Davis, leaning close to him. Oiled hair, pointy features. Pure Yankee. "Mister Browne?" the man said in his northern accent. "Are you with us?"

"Are you here to bury me, Rev?" said Winston, rubbing his eyes. "What happened to me?"

"You passed out, Win," said Eleanor, whose was standing beside the preacher. She said her words slowly. "You blacked out at the mercantile."

"I *know* that, I'm not senile. I just don't remember details."

Eleanor's eyes were bloodshot. Winston noticed the minister had been crying too, which was bizarre. He didn't even know this man, let alone consider him a close enough friend to warrant crying.

Winston tried to sit up again, but he felt his elbow scream in pain. He looked at it. The arm was bandaged and red.

"You cut your elbow," said Jimmy. "I shoulda let you bleed out on my floor, but I bandaged it because I'm a very good man."

Winston laughed. "You shoulda let me bleed out. I'm tired of wondering how it's gonna happen."

"Next time," said Jimmy.

Winston wished Davis would leave the room. Then again, he felt sorry for the man. It was hard injecting yourself into a small town. Especially if you had once asked the church ladies if they ever served bagels. After a stunt like that, he was lucky anyone in Moab made eye contact with him.

"What is it?" said the minister.

And even though it was none of the man's business, he told him. "Cancer. My lungs. Same thing the king of England had." He forced a laugh. The others did not join him.

"What do you need right now?" said Eleanor.

"I need for this sapsucker to keep his promise and hire Buz."

No response from the room.

Nobody knew what to say, and Winston couldn't blame them.

Jimmy was the first to leave. He turned on his heel and walked down Winston's hall and out the front door. Reverend Davis followed after Jimmy. Winston saw them both through his bedroom window, crossing his front yard, walking down Terrence Street. Davis was trotting after Jimmy, who was covering his face with his hands.

"That preacher's weird," said Winston.

"He's a nice man," said Eleanor.

"But a weird one. He talks funny."

"He loves the Dodgers."

"Maybe he's all right."

After a few moments of silence, Eleanor knelt beside his bed. She was looking at Winston with mournful eyes. He hated this sad look she'd been wearing ever since he'd told her about his lungs. It was pity. He'd never felt like more of a dead man than he did when she pitied him.

He patted her hand. "I'm not dead yet, Ellie," he said. "I just fell, that's all."

"I know," she said.

He left his hand on hers. He closed his eyes and felt a warm trail of saltwater form on his cheek. He didn't want to look at her. It was too honest. This woman had been a balm to him. She had given him the feminine version of joy. He had never known the companionship of another human, not like this.

When the war ended and Winston came home to find that the woman he loved—the same woman whose photograph he'd carried against his chest during the campaign across northern France—had married someone else, Winston had married Okeauwaw County instead.

But then came Eleanor. It was not merely a romance. Winston did not want a romance. He had wanted something deeper, higher, wider. He had gotten it, but he wouldn't live long enough to hold it.

Before he opened his eyes, he felt the warm lips of Eleanor Hughes pressed upon his own. When he did open his eyes, he saw that she was closing hers. She smelled of citrus and vanilla. And her hair was so stylish. This woman was too much for Moab. It could not contain her.

When their kiss ended, he said, "I'm sorry, Eleanor. We coulda been great, couldn't we?"

She kissed him again. This time harder. Their tears were mingling together. He could feel them, hot and slippery. He could even taste their salt on his lips.

"We were," she said. "And we always will be."

Real Men

Buz stood before the stove, stabbing at the skillet with a fork. The ham steaks hissed. When they were browned, he removed the steaks, then poured a slurry of flour and leftover coffee into the pan drippings. He scraped the bottom with a fork until the mixture had darkened into mud. He salted it, then added spoonfuls of pepper.

Men do not cry. That's what Buz kept reminding himself when he felt like he wanted to let it all go. *Men don't cry.*

The skillet cornbread was almost done. He opened the oven and removed the black skillet with a dishrag wrapped around the handle. He broke one of the straws from a broom, stabbed it into the bread crust, inspected it, then licked it. The bread wasn't finished yet so he placed the skillet back into the oven.

His mother walked into the kitchen, rubbing sleep from her eyes. "What's all this about? You're cooking supper early tonight."

"I have to hurry," he said. "Baseball practice is in a few minutes."

She looked confused. His mother lived in a state of sleeplessness and exhaustion. All she did was work and sleep. Her hair was still tied atop her head from a full shift in the mill office the night before. She sniffed the air. "Ham? Are you making ham? We can't afford ham."

The tears were getting too much to hide. They were gathering on his eyes and falling onto his shirt. Buz wiped his face, nonchalant, with his sleeve. He didn't want his mother to see him behaving like such a child.

His mother crossed her spindly legs in the kitchen chair. The woman's misshapen calves were often hidden by her thick stockings, but not right now. "Are you all right, Buz?"

"I'm fine."

It's funny how life works, Buz thought. This should have been a great day. He'd gone from being a dropout flunky to a federal employee overnight. He would be carrying the U.S. mail, earning more money than even his mother made. Life would be a lot easier for them, and there would be a lot more ham steaks. But before he could enjoy this new phase of life, the good Lord required blood. Nothing was fair in this world. Nothing. It made him so angry he could have kicked something. Or cried. But *real men don't cry.*

"I have a new job, Mama," he said, sniffing again.

"A new *what*?"

"A new job. I was waiting to surprise you with the news tonight."

"Buz, Mister Arnold pays you better than anyone should pay a kid your age. We can't leave him high and dry. He's been good to us."

"Well, things are gonna be even better now." Buz reached into his pocket and placed sixteen crumpled dollars and a few nickels onto the table. He slid the stack of change to his mother. "An advance on my paycheck."

Then Buz left the room. He went into his bedroom and put on the uniform. When he looked at himself in the mirror, it felt like a hollow victory. Buz returned to the kitchen wearing slate-blue trousers and a pressed button-down shirt with a white circular badge on his shoulder that read "U.S. Postal Service Dept. Letter Carrier."

"I'm a government man now," he said.

His mother's mouth gaped open. Buz had never felt as much like a child as he did right now. A baby wearing man's clothing. A kid without a father tries so hard to be a man before his body agrees with his efforts. By the time puberty was finished, Buz would be eighty inside. That's how it worked. But right now he felt so young. He wanted someone to squeeze him and tell him it was only a bad dream. He wanted life to go back to the way it was. Why did everything always have to change? Why did people have to die?

"Buz," his mother said. "You look so handsome."

Buz darted out of the house and into his truck. He sped across town and parked next to the tree so adorned with bottles it looked like it was going to fall over. When he was sure he was alone, he bawled until he had a headache. Because even though real men don't cry, boys do.

A Connecticut Yankee in Moab

The knock on the door startled Eleanor, who was arranging her laundry according to colors. She was alone in the sunshine of her backyard. She hadn't been by herself much in ages, not since Jessie had become her permanent houseguest. When the girl wasn't at school, she hung around Eleanor like a baby kangaroo. But in this rare moment she was alone. She had too much nervous energy. So she folded clothes, placing them into respective piles of red, blue, green, and white.

The knocking persisted, which meant whoever was at the door was not familiar with Moab ways. Only Jehovah's Witnesses and salesmen used the front door. Her friends would have come around to try the back door or left the casserole dishes they'd borrowed on the porch.

But this person was still knocking.

She slammed her hands into her lap. "Okay! I'm coming!" she shouted.

Her entire world had fallen apart in the past days. She knew she loved Winston Browne, all right. It was not a question of if but of how much. This thought alone made her feel guilty. She knew her love for Winston was not the same kind she felt for Jimmy, which had matured over the years. Like a houseplant. A very dehydrated and moderately diseased houseplant. But they had formed a companionship, with all the easiness and security that went with it.

With Winston she felt young again. Excited. The thrill of being desirable. Winston was the best of men and she loved him. But not the way she loved Jimmy. You cannot erase your own history, and she had written a lot of her own with Jimmy. This, of course, made her feel so guilty her chest hurt. Jimmy was her lifelong swain, whether he knew it or not. And she was his lifelong whatever she was. And even though it was not exciting, it was love. And even though sometimes she regretted loving him, a person cannot control who will be the beneficiary of one's affection. They can try to convince themselves to follow logic and common sense, but the soul knows nothing of logic. And it has never been interested in common sense.

She opened the door. It was Reverend Davis.

"Reverend," she said. "You coulda just let yourself in."

But he was not that kind of a man. Ever since he'd arrived, Davis had seemed uncomfortable in their small-town world. The big-city man who talked funny and wore a strange-smelling hair lotion. A man who had never heard of grits or okra.

"Are you all right, Eleanor? I've been worried about you," he said. "You missed the floral arrangers' planning meeting."

"I didn't feel like going."

The man followed Eleanor through the house and sat on the back porch step beside her. He unbuttoned his blazer and adjusted his wire-rimmed glasses.

"Where's Jessie?"

"She's with the sheriff. Would you like some coffee?"

"Sure, why not?"

This man was unbelievable. No *Yes, ma'am*, no *Yes, please*, or *Thank you, ma'am*. Just *Sure*. Yankees.

"Help yourself," she said, waving a pair of blue jeans at him. "It's in the kitchen." She didn't have the time or the wherewithal to deal with him.

The man returned with a mug, and soon he was helping her fold laundry. For all his faults, at least Reverend Davis knew how to fold a towel correctly.

"This is excellent coffee," said Davis.

She did not look up from folding. "It's a family recipe."

"For coffee?"

"Yep, I use chickweed with a touch of cinnamon. My mother taught me. She learned it when she lived in New Orleans."

"Is that where your family's from?"

"Goodness, no. I'm a fourth-generation Moabite. Mama was a cleaning woman for the McDavids, here in town. They had a second house in New Orleans. Mama lived there for the summers, tending their family. That was before she had me."

The minister placed his coffee on the porch. He rested a hand on her shoulder. She stopped folding. "Ellie," Davis said. "You just folded that shirt twice."

Eleanor was embarrassed, and a little offended. Her chin was trembling, she could feel it. But she was not about to cry. Not in front of this man.

She flipped his hand away. It was rude, she knew this, but she didn't want to be mollycoddled. And it was important for him to know that. What she wanted was for life to go back to normal. What she wanted was for Winston Browne not to die. What she wanted was not to feel so guilty for knowing that she loved two men at once.

The minister placed his hand upon hers, and she began to weep.

"I'm sorry, Reverend. I'm so sorry. I don't know what's come over me. I'm just so . . ."

"Ellie, that's why I'm here," said Davis. "I came here today because I want to talk about the Dodgers."

"The what?"

"I saw a Dodgers flag flying from the Moab courthouse. I know the sheriff is a fan."

She had made the flag after the World Series. "Everyone in Moab is a fan," said Eleanor. "We get games on the radio from Mobile."

Davis killed his coffee and placed his mug on the porch railing. "I know that, but you see, Eleanor, my brother-in-law is the equipment manager for the Dodgers, in Flatbush."

"Okay," Eleanor said. "I don't follow. What does that have to do with anything?"

"I introduced him to my sister. I'm the reason they're married, and he would do anything for me."

"Reverend, I'm afraid I don't know what you're talking about."

"Ellie, I think this town could use a little cheering up. Do you know if Moab's field is regulation size?"

Biscuit Queen

The kitchen was a wreck. Jessie had made a mess. Flour peppered the cabinets and the counters like the aftermath of a wheat explosion. The radio was playing a song Jessie had come to like, "By the Light of the Silvery Moon." Though the song did little to cheer her up.

Jessie couldn't help but feel as though her life was falling apart. Tonight she was by herself while Eleanor was away at a church meeting. It was the first time Eleanor had left the house in days.

Tommy sat out front beneath the dim glow of a single porch light, rocking on the porch swing, but Jessie found it impossible to talk to him.

She had never seen a woman as sad as Eleanor. Until recently she had only known the diligent and busied version of the woman. The woman who was always baking, always bossing someone around. Eleanor was always in charge, organizing something or fixing flowers. But now she was a corpse. She did her chores and kept the house in perfect order. But she was quiet and hadn't demanded Jessie brush her hair or take her shoes off at the door. Jessie decided maybe seeing her in the kitchen would make Eleanor happy.

So Jessie decided to be useful too. She turned up the radio and tied an apron around her waist.

Eleanor had once shown her how to make biscuits, but Jessie couldn't find the recipe and she had messed them up pretty badly. The biscuits came out looking like little black rocks when she removed the smoking skillet from the oven using her baseball mitt. So she tossed the biscuits into the backyard for Huck to eat. Huck obviously thought they were marvelous.

The dog had been sleeping in the backyard shed where Winston had been living before he got so sick. Now it was Tommy who kept an eye on the house, and she missed her old friend. So did Huck.

Huck stood in the yard, wolfing down the scalding hot biscuits. Jessie placed the hot skillet on the porch steps. She heard Tommy laugh. He must have found her failure amusing. She wandered to the garden shed. The night had already fallen, and the crickets were out. She opened the door and looked into the dark room. It felt so empty without Winston.

Jessie used to look out her bedroom window to see Winston on patrol around Eleanor's yard, the bright red coal from his cigarette bobbing through the night. Every night she would visit him in this shed and listen to his stories, or they would play cards or tic-tac-toe, or he would read to her. She had never known what it felt like to have a father, but Jessie imagined it couldn't have been any better than being Winston Browne's friend.

She sat on his cot and flipped on the lamp next to his bed. The orange light cut through the darkness. On the wooden walls were rakes and garden hoes. There was a rocking chair, a rug, a washbasin. There were even pictures on the walls and a vase with lilies in it. That was all Eleanor.

Jessie was about to leave when she heard footsteps outside.

She stopped breathing to listen, stood still in the center of the shed. The sounds stopped for a moment. Then she heard them again. Slow steps. These feet were getting closer. Jessie felt her body start to shake against her will. Her insides felt loosened from fear. She removed a garden hoe from a hook, trying not to make a sound. Jessie held the implement like a Louisville slugger during the bottom of the eighth.

The door opened, slow and curious. The little potting shed was filled with the blue light from the night sky and the songs of crickets.

A silhouette stood before the open door, backlit by the glow of the moon. Tall and lean. And feminine.

"Jessie," said Ada. "They're coming."

Hell on Wheels

A few lightning bugs hovered in Winston's front yard.

The old men sat on Winston's porch looking at the wheelchair like a science-fiction oddity, clouding the atmosphere with bitter smoke. Doc Howard was relighting his pipe. Someone's radio played gentle music in the far-off distance. The lights from the Parkers' house across the street were clicking off. So were the lights from the Dollarhides' and the Hansons'. Life moved at such a dirge-like tempo. Dying, on the other hand, happened at a breakneck speed. It didn't seem fair.

Jimmy was sitting in the wheelchair, rolling it in circles like a third grader. Alvin Baker was sipping from a Dixie longneck and skimming through Margie Brach's gossip column, making remarks about who was getting married and who was having babies. "I guess Sam Allen's gonna be on to marriage number three if Jeanne don't come back soon."

Winston was holding a Lucky in his fingers, shaking his head at the wheelchair beneath the glow of the porchlight, which was attracting half the gnat population of the Southeast. "I'm not riding in that chair," said Winston. "I'd rather die than be seen in a chair."

Jimmy was freewheeling the chair on the porch. "Little hard to steer, but once you get the hang of it, it's very comfortable, Win."

Alvin Baker did not look up from the paper. "Did you know the Otts have the biggest herd of Jerseys in West Florida?"

Doc Howard said, "Win, I want you to keep the chair. You don't even have to pay for it, it's on the house."

"That's very kind of you," said Winston, "but no."

Jimmy said, "Hey, how can it be so bad if it improves the quality of your life and makes you more comfortable?"

"Stop saying that word," said Winston. "I don't want to be comfortable."

Jimmy stopped rolling. "Well then, what do you want? You wanna be miserable? Is that it? Would that make you feel more self-righteous, Saint Winston? Or is it just your own pride?"

Alvin lowered his paper. The air became a little tense.

"This is my life, Jimmy," said Winston. "You can sock me in the jaw all you want, but you can't tell me what to do."

"Can I have that in writing?" said Jimmy.

"Keep the chair nearby," said the doc. "Just in case."

The chair made Winston angry. Not at life, not at himself, not at his friends, and not even at God. It was something else, something unnameable. A man watching his own body fail was one of the hardest things he would ever do. A man spends a lifetime learning how to run the machine that is the human body, and just when he gets the hang of it, it breaks.

Winston took a pull from a sweaty bottle. It was the first beer he'd had in what seemed like fifty years. The beer had amplified his medication and made him dizzy, but the familiar taste made him feel half normal. He would miss beer. He peeled the wet label off the bottle with his thumbnail.

He wanted to do things before he died. Little things. Silly things. He wanted to eat more flavors of exotic ice cream, such as pistachio or butter pecan. They had twenty-eight flavors at the orange-roofed

Howard Johnson restaurant in Pensacola. Winston had only ever tried chocolate.

Winston wanted to know what a symphony sounded like. One time in Belgium he'd heard a string quartet play. It had moved him and made him curious about a full symphony. He wanted to put things right with the lover who'd hurt him long ago. He wanted to go to Flatbush, Brooklyn, to eat a hot dog at Ebbets Field.

"I just don't feel like I'm done," said Winston.

"So tell us what you want, Win," said Jimmy.

The men on the porch looked at their shoes.

"I don't know," Winston lied.

Finally, Doc, Alvin, and Odie excused themselves and wandered home. The night was over, and these men had lives to get back to. *Lives. How lucky those men are.* But Jimmy stayed put. He was sitting on the railing of the porch, his arms crossed, leaning against a post, staring at the moon. The sounds of bullfrogs and the choir of cicadas were like a symphony in their own right.

"Why're you still here?" Winston said. "I thought you hated me."

Jimmy didn't answer, only let his attention focus on the ash of his cigarette.

"I don't want your charity, Jimmy. I'm not an invalid."

"The truth is, Win, I do still hate you. But you can hate someone and love them all at the same time."

"Jimmy, I'm sorry," Winston said, and he meant it.

They sat for a long time, watching the little yellow dots fly around beneath the oaks. The lightning bugs swirled in elaborate airborne whirlpools, making connect-the-dot patterns in the dark. Then all of a sudden they winked off, as though someone had flipped the divine light switch. It was staggering how little time the bugs lived. He'd read a book once that said lightning bugs live two months after they become adults. He wondered if they knew this going into it. He wondered if lightning bugs ever fell in love. If they did, did they ever break each other's hearts?

Winston flicked his cigarette butt into the yard and exhaled a gust of fog. "Take me for a drive."

"What?"

"You asked me what I wanted. There's something I need to do."

Going by Memory

The first thing Jessie did was rush to the front porch to alert Tommy, but he was not there. All she found was an empty swing, barely swaying back and forth in the moonlight. She darted inside and dialed the number for the courthouse, which was written on a piece of paper stuck to the refrigerator. Nothing. Called Winston, but no answer there either.

"I can't get anyone," said Jessie.

"We need to hurry," said Ada. "I've been watching your house. When I saw them circling around yesterday, I knew they'd found you."

A pair of headlights blared through the front window of the den, illuminating the furniture in the dark house.

They tore out the back door and off the back steps. In a few moments they were jogging on the pavement of Evergreen, heading toward the distant glow of a Methodist steeple.

"Where are we going?" shouted Ada.

"Just follow me."

When they had put some distance between themselves and Eleanor's house, Jessie paused to glance behind her. She saw the embers of taillights on the street against Eleanor's curb. The car wasn't moving. Jessie doubled over to catch her breath.

"The church is just up the road," said Jessie. "It's not far." The car began rolling along Evergreen, the high beams shooting straight at them. Jessie could hear the engine humming and the rubbing of tires on the pavement.

"Quick!" said Jessie, turning left into a driveway, dragging Ada by the hand. "I know a shortcut!"

They cut through a backyard and leapt over yard ornaments until they came to a fence that was too tall for Jessie. Ada hoisted her upward. Jessie tumbled over the fence and hit the dirt hard. She had begonias all over her shirt and she had cut her palm. Ada fell over the fence next, hands first. Jessie heard her whimper.

"Are you okay?" said Jessie.

"Just go, *Kleinerin*."

They cut across two more yards, all littered with more yard ornaments. What was it with these people and their iron dwarves? Jessie became confused, especially in the dark. They were facing what might have been the Parnells' yard, or it could have been the Tillys'. She wasn't sure. Jessie looked in all directions, trying to get her bearings, but she was turned around. She couldn't see the steeple behind the ocean of rooftops. Not from this angle.

"Which way now?" said Ada.

"I don't know."

Jessie chose a direction, but she wasn't sure it was the right one. Any direction was better than standing still. They trotted past white clapboard houses that looked dark gray in the night.

Between the homes, they could see the car, driving along the side streets, keeping pace with them. Then the car stopped. They heard the automobile door slam, followed by the sound of rapid footsteps.

"Go!" said Ada.

In the distance Jessie finally saw the church.

"There it is!" Jessie said. "I know where we are now!"

Together, they ran until Jessie's thighs burned and her lungs were working triple time. She felt a surge of relief wash over her when they reached the parking lot. They were going to make it. She arrived at the back door of the Methodist fellowship hall and threw her fists against the door.

"Help!" she shouted. "Please!"

But nobody was answering.

Jessie turned to see Sister Maria and a very tall man. The man threw an arm around Ada, then held a rag over her face until she fell limp. Jessie tried to run, but Maria was faster. The woman caught her and pressed a damp cloth over Jessie's mouth and nose. The last thing Jessie saw was the light of the silvery moon.

This Is Stupid

Win, you're right, this is downright stupid," Jimmy said, throwing the gearshift into neutral, hauling back on the Hudson's parking brake. "We shouldn't be here. Especially at this hour. She probably don't even remember your name. Are you sure you ain't drunk?"

"I had one beer."

"Well, maybe I'm drunk then, because this feels crazy. You haven't seen her in years."

"Ten."

Jimmy was right, of course. It was not just stupid, there was no real point to it. It was late. Pensacola people were in bed, and Brent Lane was dark. Winston hadn't been on this street in ages. It was nicer than he remembered, lined with fine houses and streetlamps. Call it a compulsion. Call it the remains of a youthful obsession. Call it the aftermath of his first heartbreak, which a man never really gets over.

Winston leapt out of the squad car and hobbled toward the beautiful home that towered above him like a Victorian showboat. It was so lovely, so big, and so ornate it could have passed for a funeral home. He clomped onto the porch. He was calm, his hands steady. The medicine was working, and he could feel fresh oxygen in his lungs. A welcome sensation at this stage of life.

The crickets were screaming. The moss in the live oaks was moving slightly in the breeze. The stars were out, and not a single cloud obscured them. Oh, he would miss this. He would miss everything. The way the humidity felt on his taste buds, the sound of a breeze rustling leaves.

He knocked on the door. She answered and took his breath away.

He hadn't seen Katie in a hundred years. She was even lovelier than Winston had remembered. Dark hair. Lean features. That same easy smile. He stood before her front door with his chewed-up hat in his hands. He was hoping for her to speak first since he didn't know what to say. But life doesn't usually work the way you want it to.

Nobody spoke for a few moments.

On the drive over to Pensacola, he had sat in the passenger seat, preparing what he would say. He had decided to start with something lighthearted, humorous, and he would try his best just to make her laugh. But all his plans had flown out the window when he saw her. She wore her bathrobe, and he was beginning to feel like a toad in her presence.

"Katie," he said. Just like that. No hello. No cordial stuff. No apology for knocking on her door so late after years of hatred. And he had hated her for what she'd done to him.

Katie gave him a strange look, a look that suggested she didn't fully recognize him. That was what cut him. The years had altered him. This last year had changed him even more. He had lost all the fat from around his face; his frame had grown so gaunt that Eleanor had to alter his uniform. Twice.

"Winston Browne?" she said.

The way she said his name hadn't changed. There was a moment of uncomfortable quiet while the crickets took another chorus. He didn't want to come right out with it. So he didn't.

"Oh my word," she said. "What's wrong?"

He had to laugh. He was standing in a county uniform on her porch. He must've frightened the poor woman to death. "Oh, nothing's wrong, everything's fine. I just had to stop by to—"

"Charles is at prayer meeting tonight. He's on his way home. Did you want to wait inside?"

"No, I didn't come here to see him."

She looked confused now. Winston looked back at the idling Hudson in the driveway. Jimmy had been right. This was a stupid idea.

She crossed her arms like she was getting chilly.

Way to go, Winston Browne, he thought. *You are the foremost man in Okeauwaw County, but right now you are an idiot.*

He almost lost himself looking at her. Not because she was beautiful, which she still was, but because she was part of his past. When he saw her, he saw the young version of himself. A young man who was, in many ways, dead. Just like the old version of himself was soon to be. He felt nothing but affection for her on this porch. And this surprised him. He thought he'd come here to forgive her, to quit hating her. But he didn't hate her. And you don't quit loving someone. Not even after they leave you. Romance can dry up, the steady stream of kisses can quit flowing, but love carves a ditch into a man's soul.

"I just wanted to see you," he said.

"Are you okay, Win?"

He forced a weak smile. "No."

Silence.

"I suppose . . . ," he said. "I suppose I just wanted to say I'm sorry."

"Sorry? For what?"

"For not understanding you, for being young, and for being so stupid."

"Oh, Win."

They were interrupted by a car pulling into the driveway.

Headlights cut the darkness like aircraft lights. It was her husband. And Winston knew that in a few moments, Charles Knowles would come sauntering up the sidewalk behind him. The preacher would shoot out his hand toward the sheriff and say something polite. So Winston had a few seconds to get it out before the man came.

"I loved you," said Winston. "And in a way, I still do. With all my heart, I want you to be happy, Katie. I just wanted you to know that."

Then Winston bid her good night.

Jimmy and Winston didn't speak on the ride home. Winston was in no mood for conversation. He wasn't even well enough to drive his own squad car. Jimmy had asked him twice what he'd said to Katie, and he hadn't answered. He was too lost in his own thoughts.

The dark road loped past them at a slow speed. The black fields had been scalped for spring foraging grass. The peanut fields were newly planted. The river was warming up. Summer was on the move. Life was coming back to normal. And he was going to miss it.

"So, what's Katie been up to?" said Jimmy. A variation on a theme.

Winston chain-smoked for an hour and endured each cough that resulted from each puff. They had helped kill him, Lucky Strikes. He knew this, but it didn't make him hate them any more or love them any less. It was just a fact. Just like when lightning strikes a tree. You don't hate the lightning. It just happened.

Lucky Strike cigarettes were distributed among the troops during the war, complimentary. Every man in the Ninth Infantry Division got five packs per week. Each Thursday Winston would open crates of Luckys and pass them to his men like he was distributing gold. They didn't last long. It was rare for a young man not to run out of cigarettes after two days of marching across Belgium. Tobacco was precious. Sometimes the Luckys were the only thing that kept a man from feeling like a soon-to-be corpse in uniform.

In his left hand he was holding his crumpled beaver pelt hat. It's funny what's in a hat. More than just sweat and oil stains from outdoor labor. This hat was an extension of him. He'd been wearing that same buckskin-colored thing since he bought it in New Orleans when he was in high school, on a senior trip. Jimmy was with him. He had been so proud of that thing at first. Young men wearing hats could be like that.

In its lifetime, the hat had endured fishing trips, outdoor baseball games, river water, hours of sunshine, church socials, a world war, elections, lung cancer, and arteriosclerosis. In the army, the hat had lived in the bottom of his footlocker. It had traveled in his duffel bag through Belgium, the woodlands of France, and across the bloodied hedgerows of Cherbourg. When he'd gotten back home, by then it had completely lost its original shape. It was an ugly fedora. But it was loyal and sincere. And it represented him.

The radio beneath the dashboard hissed.

"Hello?" said the tinny voice.

It was Tommy. The urgency in his voice was unsettling. Chances were it was nothing. Tommy radioed the sheriff whenever he so much as washed the courthouse windows.

"Hello? Hello? Sheriff? You there? Over."

Winston made no attempt to reach for the radio right away. It was probably about something ridiculous. He was not in the mood.

Jimmy stared at the speaker, then looked at the sheriff as if to say, "Are you gonna get that?" But Winston didn't even make eye contact with Jimmy. He was still looking at his hat.

"Win?" said Tommy's voice again. "Hello? Pick up if you're there, over."

"Win?" said Jimmy. "Shouldn't we answer that?"

Winston sighed blue smoke out the open window. The fog got sucked out by the wind current. He replaced his hat and took the handset in his hand. "What is it, Tommy?"

The static voice squawked again, louder this time. "I swear, I only left for a few minutes. I wasn't gone for more than ten minutes, tops."

"What?" said Winston. "What're you talking about?"

"I went to get a magazine from my house. I was only gone for a few minutes, I promise. I wasn't gone that long."

"Slow down, Tommy. Tell me what's happened."

"It's Jessie. She's missing."

The Horrid Blackness

It was a strange place. Deep in the woods. That much she could tell. She could hear the frogs, even through the thick walls of the house. At least it looked like it used to be a house. In the glow of the oil lamps, Jessie could see the furniture was dilapidated, covered in thick dust and cobwebs.

Jessie struggled against the duct tape that bound her wrists and ankles, which had cut off the circulation to her hands. They had put Ada in the basement.

One of the brethren was in the kitchen, cooking something that hissed in a skillet. The tall man was seated on an ancient sofa, his long legs crossed, reading a *Life* magazine. The magazine itself would have been grounds for excommunication. It had a woman in a one-piece on the front. The man read the magazine and didn't even attempt to hide it.

Sister Maria fumbled with a long chain and a padlock and swore beneath her breath. "I can't get it loose, Karl. Get off your butt and help me."

The tall man didn't answer her. Bad move on his part. Sister Maria threw the padlock and chain at the man. It slammed into his chest. He dropped his sin magazine and uttered something under his breath.

"And turn that light off," said Sister Maria. "Do you want them to find us again?"

"Nobody's gonna be looking for us tonight. The lawman left town with his friend, and the other lawman doesn't even have a car." This made the tall man laugh.

"You idiot," she said. "The whole town is probably looking for her. *They* have cars."

The tall man leaned forward and extinguished the lamp. He made a big show about it. Soon they were all in the dark. The whole place smelled like beefsteaks.

"This padlock needs some oil," said the man. "Maybe there's some out in the shed." He rose from the sofa and left the house. The screen door slapped behind him.

"You'll never get away with this," said Jessie. "He'll find me."

Jessie did not expect to hit a nerve, but she must have, for Sister Maria focused her beady eyes on Jessie. The woman's face had the warmth of a snow-covered rockslide in January. Even in the midst of this horrible place, in the horrid blackness, with the conflicting smells of hamburger and dust mites in the air, Jessie's heart momentarily soared because she could tell the woman believed her.

"You do not know anything, *Kleinerin*," Maria said. "That is your problem, that has always been your problem. You don't even know who you are."

"He's looking for me right now. The sheriff is gonna find us, and you are gonna be . . . screwed." It was the strongest word Jessie could think of. She'd been saving it for just this moment.

Maria smirked. She stepped toward Jessie and slapped her. It was the kind of slap the sisters gave at the temple school for using filthy language. It was not personal. This was just part of child rearing.

"*Kleines Mädchen*," said Maria. "The only one who should be worried is you."

Bigsby Road

Buz, P.J., and Tommy followed the old rural road where they had found fresh tire marks in the dirt on Bigsby Road. Buz had almost missed it, but Tommy pointed at the tracks and said, "There," and Buz yanked the wheel left, almost throwing everyone from the vehicle.

Tommy was in the passenger seat, loading a rifle between bumps in the road. "Keep the wheel steady, Buz," said Tommy. "You're gonna kill us before we get there."

The road snaked off the main highway into a muddy darkness, the tall longleafs blocking out the moon. Three other unmarked rural roads shot out from Bigsby. Buz followed each road until it dead-ended and found nothing except old hunting shacks, a few abandoned campers, and ramshackle barns.

When Tommy finished with the rifle, he started loading his pistol. Riding on the old county roads was like going over a miniature mountain range. The truck threatened to rattle apart with each violent jolt.

At the end of the last unmarked road was an old house. A light was on in the window.

Tommy said, "There they are. I didn't think they'd be stupid enough to go back to the Pearson house. You boys stay in the truck."

Buz cranked the engine off.

"No way. You can't go alone," said Buz. "You don't know how many there are."

Tommy didn't argue. The deputy appeared to be having a moderate emotional breakdown. He cussed loudly. "I don't know what to do, boys. I wish the sheriff were here."

"Gimme a gun," said Buz.

Tommy didn't answer at first. "I can't do that, Buz. You ain't grown."

"You can't carry them both," said Buz.

Tommy shook his head.

"I *know* how to use a gun, Tommy. For crying out loud."

Tommy hesitantly placed the cold, heavy steel in his hand, and Buz felt himself transform into Gary Cooper in *High Noon.*

"Don't make me sorry I did that," said Tommy.

Buz became a cool piece of iron.

The Pearson house sat in the distance, low to the ground and flat-roofed. Boats were scattered everywhere, covered in moss, with heaps of weeds growing from the hulls. The roof looked like it was made of thatch it was so covered in decades of fallen pine straw.

"This is suicide," said Tommy.

P.J. and Buz stuck close to the deputy, crossing the open field toward the house.

"We should have stayed in the truck," said P.J.

But Buz knew better. He was in better shape than Tommy and P.J. combined. This was *his* moment. A boy could wait an entire lifetime for the electrifying opportunity to be Billy the Butt-Kicker.

"I can't see anything," whispered Buz, trying to look through the window. The light had gone out. Everything inside was pitch dark.

Tommy leaned against the clapboards. He was breathing heavily.

Buz heard someone in the shed. It sounded like someone digging around through tin cans and clanking tools.

"Hide," said Buz.

They scurried off the porch and threw themselves into the nearby bushes. A tall man came striding out of the shed, shaking a spray can of something.

Tommy whispered, "This is ridiculous, Buz. You two shouldn't be here. This ain't the same as stealing gasoline."

Buz rested his eyes on a Dodge Coronet parked in the distance. Black, reflecting the moonlight. The Dodge Coronet was a well-built car. "What'd you say, Tommy?"

"I said this ain't the same as siphoning gasoline."

Buz could have kissed Tommy.

The clouds blocked the moon, the thick layer of humidity making the entire world look like parking-lot tar. The Pearson house sat in the distance as Buz and P.J. sprinted across the open field, falling into action like trained hoodlums, lugging the paraphernalia of true siphoning professionals. A hose, three large gas cans, a backup hose, and P.J. held a baseball bat.

"I really gotta pee, Buz," said P.J.

"You'll have to hold it. There's no time."

When they reached the Dodge Coronet, Tommy stood watch while the boys did the hard work. P.J. was nervous and moved with all the grace of a seasick musk ox. Buz inserted the hose into the tank and pressed it to his lips. He sucked once, then spit out a mouthful of rich gasoline. "Tastes good," he said.

"Shut up," said P.J.

"Relax," said Buz. "We're not dead yet."

"Don't use that word. Why are we filling these cans? Why don't we just let it run all over the ground?"

"Their windows are open," said Buz, pointing toward the house. "They'd smell it, dummy."

Soon came the welcoming sound of fluid filling the can. They had removed two cans of fuel when they heard a screen door slam.

"Listen!" said P.J. in a whisper. "Someone's coming."

Buz placed one hand over P.J.'s mouth and with the other plugged the hose. One of the cans fell sideways and a puddle of gasoline formed a fragrant river around their feet.

They heard someone pacing on the back porch. They heard him spit. Then they heard the unmistakable sound of a man making water. Buzz looked around and couldn't find Tommy.

P.J. began bouncing on his knees in the international gesture for "I gotta pee like a Russian racehorse."

The man didn't go back inside right away. He walked through the overgrown yard of tall grass, then wandered toward the river until he was out of sight. Buz and P.J. slid their bodies beneath the Dodge to hide themselves.

"I can see him," said P.J.

They could hear him too. He was whistling. It was an eerie sound under the circumstances. "I've gotta go, Buz," said P.J.

"Then do it," said Buz. "Just quit whining."

"Right here?"

"Shut up."

The man lingered by the bank for what felt like an age, then he finally began walking toward the house again. They could see his dark shape coming through the grass.

P.J. was trembling beside Buz, clutching him as tightly as he could. The man's footsteps stopped and faced the Dodge for a brief moment. Buz could see shoes from beneath the vehicle, several feet away from them. They moved closer. Stopped again. More whistling. A few more steps closer. Buz aged a hundred years.

"Hello?" said the man. "Who's there?"

Nothing. The feet were not moving. Buz was not breathing.

The man started whistling again, then the feet turned toward the house. When they heard the screen door slap shut, Buz felt the huge sigh from P.J.'s chest fill the air.

"He's gone," said Buz. "C'mon, hurry. We gotta get all this gas back to the truck."

"Buz," said P.J. "I think I peed my pants a little."

Pure Adrenaline

"Shouldn't we use the siren?" said Jimmy. Winston knew he had always wanted the thrill of running a siren.

"No, just drive."

Winston was in the passenger seat, ignited by pure adrenaline. Adrenaline was more effective than the Prednisone the doctor had him taking. If doctors ever got serious about dilating someone's airways, all they needed to do was scare the ever-loving bejesus out of them.

They were several miles outside Moab, almost to Highway 29. They never should have gone to Pensacola.

"We have no idea where they are," said Jimmy. "What do we do once we get back to Moab?"

"We'll cross that bridge when we get there. Just hurry."

"You're sure I shouldn't use the siren?"

"For the love of Mike, the siren doesn't work. Arty said he was gonna fix it, but he hasn't gotten to it. Buz has been working on it all week, but he can't even get it to light up."

"Arty's as worthless as a white crayon."

Jimmy flipped the siren switch anyway. Nothing happened except a faint low-pitched growl that ended after a few seconds. It was pitiful.

"Sorry to disappoint you, Jimmy."

They rushed through the gravel roads that connected Pensacola to Moab, and when they finally hit Highway 29, they were stopped by a street crew patching a pothole on the highway. Large machines rolled through the dark, lit by tower lights blaring overhead. Men in jumpsuits raked hot asphalt over the notorious potholes that had almost ruined every car in Moab.

"Pull over," said Winston.

Jimmy came to a stop beside one jumpsuit. Winston rolled down the window and shouted over the machinery, "Did you see any black Dodge traveling east?"

But the men could not hear over the loud noise. One jumpsuit indicated this by patting his ears, so Winston removed the badge from his shirt and held the golden star outward.

"Shut it off!" the jumpsuit shouted to his partner who was mounted on the behemoth machine.

The loud noise died. The men in jumpsuits gathered beside the Hudson, leaning onto their brooms and rakes.

Winston said, "Did you see a black Dodge on this road, traveling east?"

"Which way's east?" said one young man.

"Heading that way."

The men looked at each other. Each shook his head and one said, "You're the first car we've seen tonight, Sheriff."

Winston looked at Jimmy. "I think I know where they are."

And as if by magic, the siren started to work.

Hold On

When Tommy finished helping them load the gas tanks into the truck bed, he cocked the rifle, then handed a pistol to Buz and told him not to shoot his own hand off. The handgun was much heavier than it looked. Buz needed two hands to hold it outright.

Tommy and Buz sidled toward the house, bent at the waist, just like they did in the Roy Rogers Westerns. When they arrived on the doorstep, Tommy took a few steadying breaths and forced his shoulders back. "Are you ready?" he said.

Buz could only manage a nod.

Tommy Sheridan kicked the door so hard it came off its hinges and splintered. It was a heroic move. Buz wished he would have thought of it first. Buz held the pistol in front of him, double-handed, crossing behind Tommy. He caught a glimpse of the sweat rolling down Tommy's face.

In the room were two men and a woman. The woman was slight and hard-featured, like a bird, but less attractive. Her hair was pulled back into a tight bun.

"The basement, Buz," said Tommy. "That's where they are."

Buz moved toward the basement door, training his sights on the tall man, like Tommy had told him to.

"Buz," said Tommy. "The keys are on the table."

When Buz lifted the keys from the table, the woman whispered to her two goons in another language.

"That's enough outta you two!" shouted Tommy. His voice broke like a kid going through puberty.

Buz descended the basement steps and saw something that made his blood turn milkshake cold. A slender woman with a shaved head. And Jessie, who was beside her.

"Hey, Buz. Boy, I sure am glad to see you."

They were chained to the stone wall. Buz unlatched the padlocks and led them past Tommy, who still had his rifle trained on the men who were now standing in a corner.

"Get them outta here," said Tommy. "Then come back and help me cuff 'em."

Cuff 'em? Just like in the movies. If it hadn't been so terrifying, and the threat of actual death was less imminent, this would have been pretty wild.

They ran across the dirt driveway like a band of escaped convicts. The Ford truck came ripping across the gravel toward them with P.J. at the wheel.

The truck screeched to a halt, and Buz helped Jessie and the woman into the bed.

"What about Tommy?" said P.J.

"He said to—"

A gunshot.

Three more gunshots.

The sound of a man screaming. Tommy.

Two more shots.

The screaming stopped.

"Go!" shouted Buz, who was leaping into the moving truck.

P.J. drove across every bump on the neglected dusty road. With each lurch of the vehicle, they bounced upward, along with the air-borne gas cans.

"Hold on!" shouted P.J. from the front cab.

Buz was helping Jessie and the women find a grip on something sturdy. "Don't fall out," was his sage advice.

When the tires hit the smoother dirt of Bigsby Road, Buz felt the back of the truck fishtail. The rear slip differential of old Ford pickups; it was the model's one weakness.

"We hit something!" said P.J. "We're in a ditch!"

The tail section of the Ford sank by a foot. They were at a stand-still. The Dodge lights were coming straight after them. Buz cussed openly, watching the two bright lamps approach. He looked under-neath the truck and saw the rear tire spinning but going nowhere.

"I'm sorry!" P.J. yelled. "I didn't see it!"

"Everyone out!" shouted Buz. "We gotta push!"

The two lamps from the Dodge were charging forward like some-thing from the pit of Hades, and the Dodge engine was revving like an animal screaming. Dodge made great engines.

"I thought they were out of gas!" P.J. screamed.

"They've still got some fumes!" Buz said. "Give it a few seconds."

Buz, Jessie, and the woman who looked like she'd been in a con-centration camp shouldered themselves against the rusty pickup and heaved. "Hit the gas, P.J!"

P.J. gunned the engine until it sounded like the Ford was going to explode. Buz could hear the transmission switch into low gear. The whine of the tires against the soft dirt and sand was loud enough to drown out his shouting. He wished he had replaced that carburetor.

The Dodge's high beams were getting closer.

"Push harder!" shouted Buz.

Jessie lost her footing. She slipped and fell face-first into the dust, and the back tire sprayed her with a blast of sand and grit. Buz tried to lift her but fell atop of her. The spinning tire kicked up a mist of debris that cut Buz's face and eyelids.

Buz lay helpless in the dirt watching the hairless woman use her entire weight to push. It was just enough to make a difference. Before Buz had even gotten to his feet, the truck had gotten a bite on the loose earth and shot forward. P.J. leaned out the window and shouted, "We're free!"

Buz grabbed Jessie and threw her into the truck bed, then he and the woman leapt in after her. The truck rocketed forward, and the distance between them and the Dodge became greater.

Buz looked at the woman in the darkness, the draft of wind and gravel whipping around them. "Remind me never to make you mad."

Jimmy was speeding down the western portion of Highway 29 heading toward Bigsby Road. He passed deer waiting on the shoulder and willed them to stay put on the side of the road when he passed by. He hadn't killed a deer this season, that's how busy the post office kept him. He couldn't remember the last time he'd shot a decent redhead duck.

The patrol car's siren was wailing, and the Hudson was the most powerful car Jimmy had ever driven. It had made him want to give up on the idea of buying a Chevy Bel Air altogether and go for a Hudson. Almost.

Winston was sitting in the seat beside him, loading a shotgun. He latched it shut and checked the barrel of his sidearm, which he had removed from the glovebox.

Jimmy took in a deep breath just to keep himself breathing. He was not the steadiest person under pressure.

When Winston had finished loading the weapons, he holstered his handgun and said, "I told her I was sorry."

"What?"

"Katie. I told her I was sorry."

The radio beneath the dashboard began to hiss and pop. It was garbling like the sound of someone talking underwater. It was a woman's voice, but it was unclear. Winston lifted the handset and yelled into the mic. "Say it again. I couldn't hear you!"

He waited. Nothing.

"Eleanor, is that you?" he said. "Please repeat yourself. There's interference. Eleanor? Hello? Over."

Hissing. Crackling.

"Dottie Donaldson just called," said Eleanor's tinny voice. "She said she heard gunshots out near Bigsby Road."

"And it ain't deer season," said Jimmy.

P.J. flew down the county road, weaving around the bumps and potholes. Buz had been expecting more gunfire, but it never came. Still, he told everyone to keep their heads down. It was instinct, or maybe it was the dime magazines he read. Whenever "lead started to fly," Gary Cooper always told people to keep their heads down in the Westerns.

Only feet behind them, the Dodge roared, kicking up a cloud of county dust behind it. The old Ford was no match for a Dodge. Buz felt a genuine wave of awe and admiration wash over him when he looked at the Dodge, running on fumes but still charging harder than anything made by Henry Ford. The car was missing a windshield. Buz could see the splintered glass around the edges.

"Faster, P.J.!"

But it was not working. The Dodge was inching closer.

Buz could hear the Dodge's engine faltering from lack of gas. He heard it cough a few times before regaining its momentum.

Then came the shots. Only a few at first. The tall man was leaning out the busted windshield, aiming at the truck's tires. The shots came slow, like the man was taking careful aim.

"Gimme one of those gas cans!" Buz said to the woman. Before Buz had even finished his sentence the lady had lifted a can and shot-putted it toward the Dodge. Jessie did the same thing, hoisting a can onto her shoulder and hurling it forward.

The first can hit the hood, bounced through the open windshield, and went into the back seat. The Dodge swerved momentarily but found traction and charged the truck again. The second can sailed through the open windshield frame and hit the tall man in the chest. Buz could hear him howl. A few more gunshots. One shattered the back window of the Ford. Buz ducked and covered. They weren't aiming at tires now.

The third and final can was thrown by the slender woman. She put her whole body into it. The can's cap came loose, midair. Pungent gasoline sprayed into the night, misting Buz and the others in the face. It hit the driver square in the head. The Dodge veered, then rocketed down a steep embankment, across a ditch, and into a tree. Buz watched the automobile slam so hard into the pine that the mighty tree wavered sideways.

"Stop, P.J.!" shouted Buz.

P.J. hit the brakes. The truck came squealing to a stop. Bodies flew against the sides of the truck bed.

Buz could see the Dodge catching fire. The flames tripled in a matter of seconds until the steady inferno in the Dodge's cab had overtaken the entire car. In a few seconds, the vehicle was a gasoline-fueled blaze.

A red police siren was approaching in the distance.

"How do you like that?" said Buz. "I guess I fixed the siren after all."

Cuts and Scrapes

The Methodist church was quiet. Jessie and Ada watched Eleanor arrange flowers. The night before was still a blur to Jessie. She had never seen a car burn like that before. She had never seen people die.

Miss Adeline walked into the chapel and sat behind the piano. She waved to Jessie and Ada, who sat shoulder-to-shoulder in the first pew, like mother and daughter. Jessie waved back.

The old woman began to play, and the whole room was filled with a mournful melody that made Jessie sad.

Ada had bruises on her smooth cheeks, and her arm was in a white sling. Ada had declined Eleanor's offer of hot tea because tea was a vice among the brethren.

Jessie had almost forgotten about vices. In her time in Moab she had grown to love vices like jawbreakers, wax soda bottles filled with what tasted like cough syrup, sourballs so incredibly sour your face would actually be sucked right into your mouth, and of course Mary Janes. She had also grown to love television, colorful clothes, world geography, long division, comic books, music, and the Brooklyn Dodgers. Hallowed be their names.

But these things were all off-limits to the brethren. She couldn't have been any more different from Ada if she'd been born into the animal kingdom. And it suddenly occurred to Jessie's young mind why Ada had sent her away.

Ada bowed her head and listened to the piano. She seemed to be enjoying the music, which surprised Jessie, since temple people did not believe in the sanctity of song from earthly instruments.

Jessie watched this woman who had given birth to her. A woman she could never bring herself to call Mother. Not after all that had happened. It was a title Jessie would never use. Not with any human being. Not ever. The woman's cheekbones were high, smooth, and well-formed. Jessie couldn't help but notice similarities in their physical features. Only Ada was considerably more beautiful.

Ada opened her eyes. "She plays very well."

"Yeah," said Jessie. "And she's just practicing."

Miss Adeline practiced for Sunday service like this every Saturday while Eleanor organized flowers as though it were a matter of national security. Eleanor used the same carefulness that a beaver uses when he builds a dam. She would stand and stare at her arrangement for a long time, holding her chin, waiting for divine inspiration to hit. She took flowers seriously. Jessie liked this. She liked almost everything about Eleanor.

"Music is beautiful," Ada said. "I wish I heard it more often."

"Yeah," said Jessie, who was a veteran in the secular hedonist world. "Miss Adeline's a good old gal."

Eleanor paced before the pulpit, staring at the flowers. She fussed with them several more times. Jessie tried very hard to see whatever Eleanor saw in the flowers.

Ada massaged her shoulder and winced.

"Does your shoulder hurt bad?" asked Jessie.

"It's only a fracture. The doctor said it'll heal in a month or two. He used a very big needle on me."

Jessie nodded. "Yes, you have to watch out for their needles."

Ada rested her two ocean-blue eyes on Jessie. "Jessie, I prayed for you every moment of every day. I never stopped. Not even for a second. I asked heaven to watch out for you."

She put her hand on Jessie's. Jessie only looked at it. This woman had abandoned her. Her mother, but a stranger nonetheless. Jessie didn't know how to feel about her.

Jessie forced a weak smile. "Thanks."

The piano music was interrupted by the sound of male voices entering the room. Jessie turned to see Winston Browne walking into the rear of the chapel, joined by four men, all wearing suits, with nice shoes and plain neckties. Ada shifted in her seat, then stood.

Jessie wanted more time. In some ways, she wanted Ada to be with her forever. Not as mother and daughter but as friends. She needed more time. Jessie could see what a child Ada was herself. The woman was so skinny, so young.

"How old are you, Ada?"

"I'm twenty-four."

Jessie began to cry. She didn't mean to, it just happened. Ever since she'd joined this new world of piano-loving, jawbreaker-eating Methodists, she had become more tender. "Why didn't you tell me who I was?"

"Jessie." Ada touched her cheek.

Jessie drew back. "You never told me anything."

"I was a girl when I had you. I was a stupid girl. And I believed keeping your identity a secret was the only way to keep you safe. No matter what you think of me, you were born out of love, and I only want the best for you."

"The best," said Jessie.

Ada wiped Jessie's eyes without permission. She kissed her on the forehead. Like a mother would.

"Where are they taking you?"

"I don't know."

"What did you do? Did you steal something?"

"It was a crime against God, but I would do it again if it meant you would be free to think for yourself and be who you want to be."

Jessie had so many things she wanted to ask Ada. She had a whole library's worth of questions.

The suits came loping down the aisle and placed steel bracelets on Ada's wrists. They spoke to her in the official voices of lawmen. They placed Ada into an ugly automobile. And it all happened so fast.

"Wait!" shouted Jessie, chasing after them. Her thighs were sore from the night before, and they felt weaker than limp cookie dough. "Wait!" she said, running harder.

When she reached the car, she was winded. She pounded on the window until it was rolled down.

"I love you, Mother!" It was the first time the word had ever passed through Jessie's lips. And for all Jessie knew, it would be the last.

When the unmarked Ford took Ada away, the girl watched until the vehicle disappeared on the pink horizon. The car became smaller and smaller until it was nothing. Almost as though the car and the people in it had never existed at all. Jessie quit waving.

She was a strong girl.

Winston kept his two arms around her, though his arms had lost much of their size and all their muscle. In fact, his arms were chicken bones. But they had the same amount of love in them.

"Where are they taking her?" Jessie's voice sounded hollow. Winston wasn't sure exactly how to tell her that her mother had killed two men just to keep her safe.

He chose his words as gently as possible. "Sweetie, your mother did some things she's got to answer for."

"What did she do?"

"Doesn't matter. She did what she had to do, as a mother. Whether she was in the right or the wrong, the law is the law, and those lawmen have jobs to do too."

The sheriff could see the thoughts forming in this girl's head like miniature clouds. She leaned against the sheriff.

"Are you gonna send me away next?" she said.

Winston stooped low. He exerted every bit of strength he had left to squeeze her, which wasn't much. He did not let go.

"Hush," he said. He wished he could have said more. He wished he could have alleviated every one of her fears, but the county and the state had the last word.

He kissed her hair. "I would never send you away. I need your right arm too badly."

If he'd had a chocolate coin, he would have given it to her. But he was fresh out. So he gave her a kiss instead. Because that was a million bucks in sugar too.

MOAB SOCIAL GRACES

BY MARGIE BRACH

Mr. and Mrs. Sam Allen have reunited and are moving to Montgomery for peace and quiet. Said Sam, "We are ready to have our privacy." Sam has been married twice.

Deputy Tommy Sheridan is recovering from a gunshot wound to the leg during an impressive display of heroism. Tommy said, "The doctor says I'll be up and around in no time. Jessie is safe, that's the important thing." Said Sheriff Browne of his deputy: "Tommy Sheridan is a man with hair on his chest."

Buz Guilford and Peter James Griffith Jr. were awarded for outstanding citizenship on Friday. "I'm so proud," said Mr. Griffith Sr.

J. G. Lennox and LaMonte Lennox attended the Interstate Fair in Birmingham on Monday. "I got sick on the whip ride," said LaMonte.

Mr. Ben Vanetta has left for Kansas City to spend time with his daughter.

Mrs. Martha Washburn inherited her Eternal Reward on Tuesday. Memorial service will be on Friday, four p.m., at Moab Methodist.

Next Sunday the Moab Dodgers will play Pensacola Baptist. Last May Pensacola defeated them 3–1.

Municipal council meeting will be on June 22 at the Baptist fellowship hall, to discuss updated commercial signage rules and restrictions.

At the residence of George W. Folke last Saturday, Mr. John Wood of Andalusia was united in marriage to Miss Coral Folke by Rev. Davis.

Mr. Fowler of Myrtle Grove has an award-winning pig for sale to good home. "He's a good pig. He took the blue ribbon three years ago."

Sheriff Winston Browne is not well as of this writing and has announced his resignation to city council members, who denied his request. We hope to see him restored to good health soon.

The June Classic

The summer mornings in Moab sounded like a bird sanctuary. Moab was pure melody in the hours when the sun was rising, making crisscross shadows on the narrow gray river that was the Escambia. The sky was electric blue. The weather was humid. Steam was rising in the forest. Not fog, but steam. This happened in the summer when the humidity descended on the hot soil.

The yellow flies were out, and they were biting, causing Jimmy's and Eleanor's various exposed body parts to swell.

And the birds. The birds owned this town. They came from all over the world to sing to Moabites. It was one of the greatest pleasures found in living away from big cities. The birds.

Long ago—the same year Lindbergh made his flight to Paris—Florida elected the mockingbird as the state bird. Jimmy's father was ticked off about it. Fourteen people from Moab had been on a committee that tried to overturn that infamous decision. They thought the great white egret should be the official bird. And they had a point. Egrets were always high-stepping on the banks of the Escambia, blindingly white, wearing that serious look all herons wear. In the end Jimmy's father lost his fight. But the old man was not sorry he tried. When the *Moab Messenger* quoted Jimmy's father in an article from

1927 about his efforts, the headline read "Thomas Abraham Has No Egrets."

"This doesn't make any sense," said Jimmy, looking at his watch. "Why aren't we at the baseball park? Why are we meeting here?"

"Don't worry," said Eleanor. "Be patient."

"Patient? Everyone has probably gone to the ballpark like sensible people while we're here watching birds poop on a statue."

"Would you just trust me for once in your life?"

"I just don't see why we couldn't meet at the ball field."

"Relax," said Eleanor, patting his hand like he was four years old.

Jimmy tried to relax. He closed his eyes, leaned back on the park bench, and listened to the birds in Bell Park. This woman was impossible when she wanted to be. She had always fancied herself a surprise artist. She was always trying to plan the perfect little party, complete with flower arrangements and coasters. He wouldn't be surprised if she'd put flowers all around the ball field. Maybe made pear salad and punch for the players.

All he'd wanted was a community game for his dying friend, but this woman had to turn it into a tea party.

He looked at the bronze statue of John R. Bell, Moab's founder, covered in bird poop. He thought about how the entire town, and an entire way of life, had been founded on a giant fool who hadn't *found* anything the Muskogee hadn't already discovered. How is it that fools often get themselves immortalized in bronze or have parks named after them? Meanwhile the people who really deserved to have such credit were seldom noticed publicly.

"I wanna change the name of the mercantile," said Jimmy.

Eleanor frowned. "Really?"

He nodded. Yeah, that was exactly what he wanted. He wanted a change.

A bird landed on the bench armrest. He didn't move. He only stared at it before it flew away to join the choir.

The whole town looked golden in the early light. No traffic, no crickets, no voices. Just birds and the occasional noise of a sacred river. And the life-threatening, almost deadly bite of a yellow fly. The sound of lawn mowers in the distance brought the faint smells of cut grass. This was the quintessential smell of Moab, a town famous for its summer lawn care. When nine hundred–some people were obsessed with their front yards, all you smelled was their clippings.

The first men to arrive at Bell Park were Robert Lockland and Denny Franklin. These two men were used to waking up early in the morning since they'd been collecting the town's garbage in their pickup trucks and taking it to the Pensacola Municipal Dump ever since the dump opened. They were still wearing their jumpsuits from the morning's work.

"Hi, Jimmy," said Robert.

"Why're you smiling like a gut-eating possum?" said Jimmy. "Where's your glove? How does anyone expect to play baseball without gloves? What year is this?"

Robert only smiled.

More people arrived. Men and women, a few teenagers. Soon the park had a small crowd of about thirty-five people, stragglers showing up every few minutes.

Eleanor wore jeans and her hair was pulled into a ponytail behind her head. Her mother would have turned over in her grave if the old woman had seen her dressed like this. Jimmy had never known Eleanor's mother to wear anything but the attire of a laboring nun. Cotton dresses. The eternal apron. Silver hair atop the head like a giant hair-biscuit.

"I've never seen you in jeans before," he said to her.

She ignored him. The woman had changed since her life had been marked with the friendship of Winston Browne. Everyone's life had.

For the past months, Jimmy, Eleanor, and Jessie had been living at Winston's house. Eleanor and Jessie had been sleeping in Winston's spare bedroom. Jimmy had been sleeping in the den on the sofa. Together, Eleanor, Jessie, and Jimmy had been keeping the sheriff's daily life going ever since Winston had started to go downhill. Buz Guilford was at the house almost every waking hour that he wasn't delivering the U.S. mail. Buz would sit in the sheriff's bedroom beside his bed, reading aloud or just talking. Tommy held down the fort at the sheriff's office. Everyone did their part.

Jimmy and Eleanor swapped shifts, and oddly this had brought them closer together. It had restored something between them that had been lost. Jimmy took the sheriff on his patrols and helped him file paperwork. He handled things like bathing, bathroom matters, and grooming. Eleanor handled anything regarding food, house upkeep, and domestic sanitation. Jessie and Buz were Winston's entertainment. Caregiving had aged Eleanor. Her hair had become grayer, and her eyes looked tired.

"Look." Eleanor pointed. "Here come the boys." Buz and several teammates were walking toward them. Buz was still wearing his mail carrier uniform from his route that morning.

Jimmy was hot. "Why isn't anyone dressed to play? Why doesn't anyone have their dang glove?"

The boys only shared a knowing glance.

"What're you grinning for?" said Jimmy. "If you got something to share with the rest of the class, come out with it."

A few of the boys had on the same mail-carrier uniform as Buz. In the past months the delivery of the U.S. mail had fallen to Buz and thirteen members of the baseball team since Jimmy had become a glorified nurse. They had done a better job than any mail carriers

Jimmy had ever hired. They were fast, efficient, spry, and—this was their best feature—cheap.

It had been eight days since Jimmy had even stepped foot into the mercantile, and he'd trusted Odie not to bankrupt the place. And he'd really let the place go. Sales had not dropped, but the general appearance of the store had. No old men lingered there anymore. They all congregated on the porch on Terrence Street, the house where the sheriff was clinging to life.

The people in the park milled around with steaming mugs and thermoses of coffee, waiting. "Shouldn't we start heading over?" Denny asked.

"He's right," said Eleanor, standing and adjusting the waistband of her jeans. "Let's get started."

"Get started?" Jimmy said. "This isn't a church ice cream social, it's a baseball game. Never should have left it to a woman to organize a baseball game."

"That's rude. You don't know a thing about me, Jimmy Abraham. I played softball in college."

"You were the bat boy."

"Bat *girl*."

Eleanor clapped her hands to get everyone's attention. Then she gave what Jimmy assumed was her version of a pep talk. She was calling today's fundraising game the Winston Browne Classic. The name had a nice ring to it, Jimmy thought. After all, the name had been his one and only contribution to the event. He'd tossed around a dozen or so names but settled on something unassuming. The game was to raise money for Sheriff Browne's bills and offset some of the minor medical expenses, but it was more for the ceremony. Winston Browne had not been able to see the first game played on his own ball field. Jimmy wanted his friend to see something wonderful happen. But now he was frustrated that Eleanor Hughes seemed to have turned it into a finger-sandwich social.

Eleanor had taken over planning and irksomely had kept Jimmy in the dark. No matter how much he begged, she was mum on all the details. Infuriating woman. All he knew was that it would be a doubleheader and there would be food. Tickets were a dollar per family or fifty cents for an adult. The first game would be played between the Little League Moab Dodgers and their parents. The second would be played by local amateur players—the Milton Millers—and a group of Moab young men. That was the extent of his knowledge. Even though the whole dang thing was his idea, this tomboy was calling the shots.

"Okay, can we go now?"

"What're you so worked up about?"

"Oh, I don't know. Maybe that we've got two garbage men and several mail carriers who look like they slept in their clothes last night. Didn't you think to tell them to wear their uniforms? Honestly, Ellie."

She patted his hand. "Would you calm down? Give me a little credit, Jimmy."

Eleanor had been on the phone all week with Reverend Davis, lining things up. She'd been making trips to Pensacola with the minister, and she said they had even found a Dixieland band from Mobile to play.

Above all, they were keeping everything a secret from Winston, which wasn't that difficult, since he was either being driven around in his squad car or lounging in his bedroom. But somewhere along the way, she'd started keeping things a secret from Jimmy too.

"Why don't you lead us in prayer before we walk over, Jimmy?" said Eleanor. Jimmy swallowed his pride and led everyone in what might have been his first communal prayer in forty years. Everyone removed hats and bowed their heads. The boys closed their eyes. Before the prayer even started, Eleanor held Jimmy's hand.

Her hand was warm. And so was she. His prayer sounded more

like a public brain seizure because he was thinking about her. This woman. How could he not realize how wonderful she was? Eleanor Hughes had been one of the great themes of his life, though at times he had been too foolish to recognize it.

When the World's Shortest Prayer was officially over, people chirped their amens, and Jimmy led everyone from the park to the ball field like a tiny army of ants on the sidewalk.

"I wish you'd learn to trust me," said Eleanor again, marching beside him, arm hooked through his.

"I do trust you, Ellie, just not with baseball stuff."

"Why not?"

"I know this is hard for you to accept in your new jeans, but you're a girl."

The sun was climbing above the tree line now, and Moab was painted a cool orange. Every shop was closed today. Jimmy had convinced the businesses on Hydrangea to shut down in honor of the occasion. The Moab men carried hickory bats over their shoulders, the women held picnic baskets, and children were riding bikes.

Jimmy heard a sound in the distance and stopped walking to listen. It sounded like a diesel engine. He squinted at the horizon and moved his hat back on his head.

"What in the . . ."

He saw a fire truck parked by the field.

He released Ellie's arm and broke into a light run. His knees hurt. The closer he got, the more he could see.

The Moab field was overtaken with hordes of people, automobiles, families on blankets, kids playing tag, men selling hot dogs, dogs chasing dogs, people playing catch, the Dixieland band warming up, and people in their summer pastel colors and pongee shirts.

There must have been four hundred vehicles, like an ocean of chrome, rubber, and steel. People cooking breakfast on gasoline camp stoves. Fathers and sons tossing footballs in the outfield. He counted eighteen pup tents in the Walkers' nearby vacant lot. Eighteen. Transistor radios were playing music. Everyone was murmuring with a kind of excitement. The band started playing "Honeysuckle Rose."

"I forgot to tell you," said Eleanor, adjusting her waistband. "I had a friend at the *Pensacola News Journal* advertise in the paper last week. The story got picked up by several other newspapers."

"Newspapers?" said Jimmy. "What're you talking about?"

"They loved the story. Papers ran the story as far away as New York."

"Story? What story?"

Eleanor didn't answer. She squeezed his hand, then pointed toward the east. "Oh look, that must be them."

Them?

A tiny silver dot was approaching on Highway 29. When it got close enough, Jimmy heard the hiss of the bus's air brakes and the sound of an enormous engine working double time to make it up the final grade that ushered them into Moab.

"*Them*?" he said. "Who's *them*?"

She shrugged. "How should I know? I'm just a bat boy."

Moab Proper

The Hudson traveled through the outskirts of Moab, Winston riding shotgun. Doc Howard was driving at a snail's pace, careful not to let the car exceed four miles per hour because Doc Howard was an old geezer and this was how geezers drove. The doc was trying to be helpful, but they would never finish the morning patrol at this pace. Huck was asleep in Winston's lap. The dog never left his side.

"Doc," said Winston. "We can drive faster than this, you know. You oughta let me take the wheel. I feel pretty good today." He was not a complete invalid. Some days he could even walk to the kitchen without passing out.

But the doc did not even acknowledge the sheriff's request. He drove the car up Frond Street, across Evergreen Avenue, then all the way to east Moab to the railroad tracks. Winston never patrolled east Moab in the early mornings. He tried telling the doc this, but the old man ignored him.

It was almost like the doc was deliberately trying to keep Winston out of Moab proper this morning.

Winston looked at the driveways in east Moab. There were no vehicles sitting before the houses. He saw nobody in their front yards.

"Is today a holiday?" he asked the doc.

The doc said nothing.

He marveled at the quiet. On a weekend morning like today Moab's population was often operating tiny gasoline engines, cutting their grass, trimming their hedges. He only heard a few lawn mowers in the distance.

"Maybe they're all at the beach today."

Winston looked sideways at the old man. "The beach?" Now he knew something was up.

After spending an hour in east Moab, they began heading toward town again. Winston watched the manicured homes lope past his windows. He admired the pretty yards, the magnolia blossoms, the magnificent blue sky framing it all as though it were a painting. He would miss this place.

When they reached the ball field, Winston sat bolt upright. The doc looked forward, gripping the wheel with both hands.

"What in the world?" said Winston.

The first thing Winston saw were big red fire trucks. They lined the road, ladders extended, American flags waving from the tops of each ladder. Behind the trucks were squad cars with "Pensacola Police Department" emblazoned on the doors. Lights were flashing. Officers were positioned before their Fords with hands behind their backs, standing at military-style attention. When the Hudson drove past them, they showed full salute. Winston hadn't saluted anyone in years. But he still remembered how.

Cars upon cars upon cars. Upon cars. That's what he saw. The vehicles were parked cattywampus, scattered in all directions, extending to the tree line. Nash Metropolitans, Chevy Bel Airs, Studebakers, Oldsmobiles, Plymouths, they had all spilled over the curbs and onto the grass.

Banners were hanging from back windows. One read "We love our sheriff!" Another: "Thank you, Sheriff Browne!"

The doc drove over the outfield grass, through the throngs of people who were now swarming the vehicle. Kids were patting their hands on the windows. People were hollering in happy voices. Doc Howard shut off the engine and said, "Do you wanna walk on your own, Win? Or do you need help?"

Winston could not speak. He could not understand what he was seeing. "I can walk." As soon as he said it, he felt a surge of strength shoot through him like whiskey. He kicked open the door and stepped out of the car.

The applause was deafening. Screams, cheers, shouting, music from a band.

He followed Doc Howard, walking toward the field with hobbled steps. He leaned onto his cane and limped forward one shuffle at a time. The dog followed. His lungs didn't hurt so bad. The mind could be a powerful thing, he thought. He was no less sick than he'd been ten minutes earlier, but right now he felt like he could walk to Mobile and back.

He cut through the massive crowd, which was only getting louder. He didn't wave and he couldn't smile—he was too overwhelmed. All of Moab was here. Past and present. Young and old. Current residents; old friends who had moved to big cities; members of his graduating class in their high school colors; old deputies; the sheriffs of Escambia County, Santa Rosa County, Okaloosa, Walton, Holmes, and officers he'd never even met; and Eleanor Hughes, standing front and center. He saw Katie sitting on the bleachers with her beautiful family all waving their hands in the air, cheering.

"Doc," said Winston. "Did I die and you just forgot to tell me?"

"No, son, you're more alive than anyone who has ever lived."

The applause spread. Mark Laughlin was standing on the mound, presenting Winston the game ball. "What do you think of the old field, Sheriff?" said Mark. "She looks pretty good, don't she?"

Winston nodded.

The catcher approached the mound wearing full catcher's gear and a face mask. When the catcher flipped his mask above his head, Winston saw that it was Jimmy Abraham. Winston began to laugh when he saw his friend. They embraced.

"You wanna throw the opening pitch?" said Jimmy.

"I don't think I have it in me."

"You never did," said the postmaster, flipping his mask back over his face. "But that never stopped you before."

Jimmy didn't wait for Winston's answer. He jogged back to the plate and crouched behind it. Soon the applause had died down. Winston could feel fourteen bazillion eyes resting upon him.

He massaged his bony shoulders and rubbed his creaky elbows. He loosened his wiry arms. But he wasn't thinking about pitching at all. He was thinking about the huge halide lights suspended above him, un-illuminated, proud in the morning air. He was thinking of the tight green grass of the outfield behind him, grass he had babied into conception. He thought of his red infield, with its crisp white lines, straight as a preacher's collar and brilliant in the sun.

It struck him all at once. This was his. It was all his. Everything. The people. The dirt. The grass. He looked into the stands again and saw Jessie, smiling and waving at him. And in this moment she looked older than before. It was in the eyes. He could practically see the child's future, and it would be a good one. Beside her sat a young man in a mail carrier's uniform. He was skinny and big-eared and beautiful. And a Mark Twain convert.

He forgot about his own end for a moment. He was no longer a county official. Neither was he a coach, nor a peace officer, nor a coroner, nor a lifelong Methodist, nor a dying man. He was here.

"I must be outta my mind," mumbled Winston. He nodded once to Jimmy. "It'll be a wonder if I don't dislocate my shoulder."

He adjusted his crumpled brown hat. He straightened himself, then coiled his muscles in the familiar way he'd done long ago when he was nineteen. He hiked a knee outward, kicked out his foot, lunged forward, and threw the ball as hard as he could.

His shoulder snapped. The ball zipped through the air like a white javelin and hit Jimmy's glove with a slap. It was a little high and inside. But it landed in the mitt.

The cheers hurt Winston's ears.

Jimmy rejoined him on the mound. He was laughing. "You still can't pitch worth a cuss," he said.

Together they left the mound. Winston felt the emotion hitting him like a dozen freight cars at once. He felt his chest swell.

Winston lifted his ugly hat to them, like all courteous pitchers do, and waved it. They cheered even louder, until the treetops fluttered.

As he approached the dugout, the adrenaline Winston had been feeling began to fade. He was looking for a place to sit and catch his breath. He was greeted by a large group of young strangers. Winston didn't recognize any of them, but he wasn't paying much attention—he was too preoccupied with breathing. Then he noticed a collection of little boys gathered around the fence, faces pressed against the chain link, eyes as big as washbasins. He looked around, noting the men in the dugout all wore matching jerseys. Blue and white. With blue ball caps. A few of these men were stretching their muscles, performing the calisthenics of professional athletes.

The first person to shake Winston's hand was a tall, broad-shouldered, middle-aged black man who said, "It's a pleasure to meet you, Mister Browne."

"Win," said Reverend Davis. "I'd like to introduce you to Jackie Robinson."

Some Glad Morning

The radio was blaring on the windowsill of the courthouse. It was hot inside this morning. Like a stagnant puddle. Kamikaze flies and mosquitoes clung to the walls since the windows were open. Winston Browne was sweating something awful.

Ever since the Brooklyn Dodgers played an exhibition game against the Mobile Bears on Moab's little ball field, the little town had become world famous. News reporters had been in and out all week, darting through each shop on Hydrangea, conducting interviews, throwing cigarette butts on the sidewalks, eating their meals at Ray's. Ray made a small fortune.

The whole town had been glowing after Jackie Robinson and his all-stars lit it on fire. Little boys wearing blue and white rode bikes with their rears not even touching the seats. Women marched toward home carrying bags of groceries, dressed a little nicer than they normally would have been. Men raked every single play from the exhibition game over the coals in their minds.

The Dodgers were family now. Winston listened to the games with a different affection than before. Each time he turned on the radio, he felt like he was checking in on his cousins. He could see Jackie when he closed his eyes. What a man. He had hit four home runs during the Moab game. He slid into home twice. The man had skidded into home like his life depended on it.

Winston wasn't even listening to the radio game. He was half sleeping. Through the open courthouse windows, he could hear the sounds of distant children hollering and laughing. He heard water from the water tower striking the pavement, flooding the street. He heard the sounds of heavy automobiles.

A brown starling had been trapped inside the courthouse all morning. Winston had been watching it flutter from one side of the room to the other from where he sat in his office chair. Tommy had been trying to get the bird out, rushing back and forth on his crutches, his entire leg in a white cast. He was trying not to let his wounded foot touch the ground.

"Leave that bird alone," said Winston.

Tommy chased the bird for half an hour longer before opening a window in one of the cells. When he cornered the bird, it flitted through the prison bars and flew away. Tommy congratulated himself but did not shut the window fast enough. After a few seconds, the bird returned. The stream of swear words pouring from Tommy's mouth was like artwork. He used clever combinations of swear words that Winston had never even heard before. Pain made a man do unusual things.

Winston was too tired to care about the dumb bird. Not just tired in the body. It was more than exhaustion; he was tired of being a weight on people's shoulders. Jimmy and Eleanor had no lives of their own since they'd moved into his home. Tommy had been managing an entire town, single-handedly, on one leg. For crying out loud, boys were delivering Moab's mail. And they had a little girl helping them.

There were no two ways about it, it was time to resign. He had tried twice, but the council would not allow it. But it was too late. His body had already resigned. The radio announced the seventh-inning stretch. He turned the volume down and noticed something about his own hands. His fingertips were growing numb. Everything was tingling. His nails were bluish purple. Soon this odd feeling was spreading to his feet and legs. And his chest was beginning to feel the same tingling way, like his whole body was falling asleep.

"Tommy," he said. But the deputy didn't hear him, he was too busy with that bird.

His heart was pecking out a weak rhythm, irregular and faint. He forced another breath inward, but his chest didn't cooperate. His ribs did not expand, his belly muscles didn't move.

"T-T-Tommy," he said. "I can't . . ."

Winston forced himself to calm down. The seventh-inning stretch was over and he was struggling to find a breathing rhythm. Nobody ever tells you that dying is difficult; nobody tells you that it is a full-time job. It consumes you, exhausts you and everyone you love. And it is godless work.

The sounds of Vin Scully on the radio played in the background: *"There's the pitch, Campy swings, hits a single into right, fielded on a hop, and he's . . . Not in time . . ."*

"Tommy."

Winston had closed his eyes for what felt like only a few moments. But when he opened them, a crowd of men was standing around him. Lots of people with concerned faces. Jimmy was at the forefront. Buz was there too.

"Winston!" someone shouted. But the voice sounded like he was a lifetime away. *"Breathe, Winston!"* In this moment it was almost comical to him. Breathing.

He closed his eyes again. When they reopened, men were carrying him. Young men, old men, and Jimmy Abraham and Buz. He saw the ground moving beneath him as though he were on a merry-go-round. He heard voices, but he could not make many of them out.

"Hang on, Winston!" Tommy's voice. He sounded like he was all the way in Canada.

Winston caught a glimpse of the brown bird, sitting on the windowsill of the jail cell. It leapt once, spread its wings, and passed through the cold iron bars.

Awake

When Winston opened his eyes, he heard the hissing sound of a large machine beside his bed. He was lying in his own room. Eleanor Hughes was beside him, holding his hand. The windows were dark.

"How long have I been out?" His voice sounded like sandpaper on the driveway. But it was not loud enough to wake Eleanor.

A nasal cannula was draped around his ears, shunting cold air into his nostrils. He could feel it working its way into his lungs. He could breathe, but not as freely as he would have liked.

Eleanor was warm. He didn't want to wake her. So he closed his eyes and willed himself to drift off. It wasn't hard to do. It's funny how little the outside world and all its riddles seem to matter when you're in a bed attached to oxygen. All the things he'd always wanted to figure out and all the schedules he'd kept running within his mind's calendar, they all disappeared and he felt free. It wasn't altogether unpleasant.

Winston slept for several hours. He had odd dreams about people he hadn't seen in a long time. About old friends. And old dogs. He was awoken when he heard heavy footsteps down the hall. Eleanor was no longer beside him. Now it was Jimmy Abraham who sat in a chair next to Winston's bed, reading the newspaper.

Winston swallowed the gravel in his throat and said, "What day is it?"

Jimmy lowered the newspaper. "Tuesday."

"My word," was all Winston could say.

Jimmy was wearing saturated clothes and sweating to beat the band in the summer heat. Two floor fans in the bedroom were aimed at Winston. He waited for strength so that he could speak to his friend, but his diaphragm was tired. All his muscles were sore; even his neck muscles hurt.

"In the courthouse safe . . . ," said Winston.

Jimmy folded the paper and leaned in closer. "Say what?"

"The safe," Winston said with phlegm obscuring his words. He barked out a grunt to clear his throat. The effort about killed him. Literally. "The safe is under the desk in the courthouse. Tommy knows where it is, he can open it—" He coughed again, struggling for the wind to finish the sentence. "There are letters, and other things . . . I want you to make sure people get . . . them."

"Of course, Win, anything you want."

Winston sighed when he realized Jimmy understood him. "I want you to make sure Buz gets it all."

"Sure, Win."

"I want you to make sure he doesn't blow the money on a fast car or some girl." This made him laugh. The pressure from the laughter hurt Winston's face and eyes. "As soon as I'm gone, give 'em this house. There are keys in an envelope, and I paid the property taxes in advance."

"Of course, Win."

"And make Tommy . . ." Coughing. "Make him get that dang Packard fixed, even if he has to arrest Arty. That no-good, lazy son of a gun . . ."

"Okay, Win. I will."

Winston reached his hand outward and took the hand of his friend. "How'd we do today?"

"What do you mean?"

"The Dodgers, how'd they do?"

Jimmy clasped his hand firmly. His eyes were pink and bloodshot. "The Cardinals murdered them, six to thirteen."

Winston laughed himself to sleep.

Gallant and Brave

It was a hot night, and the sounds of music wafted from the fellowship hall behind the Methodist church. Buz arrived dressed to the nines. He wore a salt-and-pepper suit, a red hand-painted necktie, and enough hair product to make his head look like a piece of plastic.

Buz had borrowed the old suit from a friend. Buz's mother had to take the ancient suit in a little bit, but she said he looked handsome. Buz knew the truth, though. He looked like a walking advertisement for the 1890s. Still, he was proud.

The stage on the lawn outside the Methodist church was decorated with streamers and patriotic bunting. Old women wore white summer dresses, big hats, and corsages on their breasts. Young men walked around in busy circles, clad in seersucker and linen, doing whatever the hens told them to do. Buz was glad for the busywork. It kept his mind off the impending death of Winston Browne. The truth was, Buz did not want to be here. Not tonight.

Buz helped three old men hang Eleanor's large banner above the bandstand, standing on a very tall ladder while three church ladies barked commands at them from a distance. The banner read "Happy Forth of July," with no *u* in *Fourth*. When Buz saw it, he almost told someone about the misspelling, but he decided it was none of his business. Emotions ran high before church socials.

The band arrived next in a large red bus that parked behind the fellowship hall. Buz helped them unload their instrument cases, some of which were heavier than the stage had been. Especially the vibraphone. The guitarist asked Buz to carry his amplifier. Buz agreed, but wished he hadn't. The thing was so heavy it gave Buz a backache. But he was taken with these musicians in their snazzy suits and with exotic Yankee accents that suggested they'd been to places much better than Moab. They asked him to take their photograph with their Eastman camera. Buz positioned them in a large group and told them to say "Money!" on the count of three. He took three pictures, just to be safe.

The guitarist thanked him, then asked Buz to hit an A on the piano.

"An A?" said Buz. "I don't know which one that is."

Becky Jernigan came behind Buz and said, "Here, I'll do it."

She was dressed in white, with no sleeves. Her hair touched her shoulders and bounced slightly when she moved. She pressed one of the white keys on the piano. All the musicians began playing one long tone, but they were watching Becky.

Then twenty-four musicians launched into "Somewhere Beyond the Sea" and the music ricocheted off the gymnasium walls loud enough to hurt Buz's ears. It was lively and quick, and it swung. Buz watched Becky bob her bare shoulders to the music. She walked away, still keeping her shoulders in rhythm.

Buz wasn't thinking about her; he was thinking about how unfair life could be to good men. He was thinking about how the salt-and-pepper suit still smelled like his old friend. He was thinking about how the Forth of July was a lot more fun when it had a *u* in it.

"Go ask her," said the voice beside him.

He turned to see P.J. dressed in a checkered suit, his hair looking like it was being held in place with industrial pump lubricant. "Ask her." Then P.J. shoved him forward.

Thus, imbued with the strength that only a magic salt-and-pepper suit could give a man, Buz walked across the floor, swallowing and tugging his collar. He approached Becky. But he was still thinking about heavy things that had nothing to do with dancing.

"Would you, uh . . . ," he began. "Well, that is . . . Would you . . . like to . . ."

And somehow it worked. The girl finished his sentence, and soon he was holding her. Or was she holding him? He couldn't tell the difference. Her hand was soft and a little clammy. And his insides had turned into Twinkie filling. They strode to the center of the dance floor. Every eye on the church lawn was on them. Buz could see his cheering section, three old men standing on the sidelines. They were watching, not out of curiosity but to give him courage. P.J. was grinning—literally—to beat the band. Tommy was seated, his casted leg propped on the chair next to him.

Buz placed his arm around Becky's waist the way a good man had once shown him to do. No. A great man. A man who had once been foolhardy enough to love Buz Guilford like a son, who once taught him a thing or two about moving his feet. And Buz began shuffling his shoes in the short shuffling steps of a sluggish foxtrot.

She laughed. "Don't go too fast, Buz. I don't dance so good."

Buz spun her. He twirled her. He tossed Becky backward in a dip and said, "Don't be silly, Becky. Anyone who can fog up a mirror can dance."

The Strong Girl

Jessie sat beside Winston. Her face was stained with tears. He could tell she'd been crying. But she wasn't crying now. Not this strong little girl. Jimmy had helped Winston sit upright in bed. His head leaned against the headboard.

"Jessie," he said. "I wanted to talk to you."

The girl wiped her eyes.

"It's about your mother. She's gonna be away for a long time. You won't be seeing her for a while."

"I don't really feel right calling her my mother."

"Fair enough."

"Where's she going?"

Winston decided to speak to Jessie as though she were a full-grown woman. He didn't have the stamina to beat around any bushes. He hoped she was strong enough to handle it. He gave it to her straight and withheld nothing. He told her how Ada had suffered when she'd tried to leave the compound. And he told her about how she'd killed two men to help Jessie escape with Johanna. He told her Johanna and the boys had been found by the temple brethren and taken back to Pennsylvania, and how Sister Maria and her two goons had held Ada for months but how brave she had been to keep searching for Jessie. He told her about Ada's plea of self-defense but that she would still be in prison for a long time.

It took him a long time to convey the facts to her because each sentence took a monumental effort. When he finished, they were both quiet and still for a while.

"Are you okay, Jess?" he asked.

All she said was, "What about Sister Maria?" There was no emotion in her voice now.

"She's gonna make it, but she's burned pretty bad, almost died."

She didn't say anything. She reminded him of himself. He wondered if this was how parents felt when they looked at their own children. He could see the look of loneliness wash over her face. He knew this look because he saw it in the mirror sometimes.

"Come here," he said.

She crawled into the bed and lay beside him, rested her head on his shoulder. She soaked his sheets with her tears. She was heavy on his chest, and he began to have trouble breathing. "Jessie, your mother . . . I mean, Ada wants me to ask you something, and that was what I wanted to talk to you about." He coughed. "I need you to think carefully about what I'm going to say."

She stopped crying but didn't lift her head from the sheets. "Carefully about what?" her muffled voice said.

"Oh, it's just . . . well . . . Ada wants you to be happy, and . . . Sweetie, how would you like to live here, in Moab, forever? How would you like to be Eleanor's daughter?"

Jessie lifted her head. Her hair was a mess; her face was even worse. "Eleanor wants to adopt me?"

"That's right." He reached onto the nightstand and grabbed a small folder containing a slab of papers. "Ada has already signed these, and if you agree, Eleanor will sign them too, and that's all there is to it. You would be Eleanor's legal daughter."

The child looked at him. There was no resounding yes. No major reaction at all. She just answered with: "What about you?"

"Me? What about me?"

"Will you adopt me too?"

He tugged one of her braids. He pulled the child closer. Few things on planet Earth are sweeter than the hugs of a little girl. "Oh, sweetie, you're too late for that. I adopted you a long time ago."

Samuel Clemens

Jimmy had been sitting with Winston for thirty-six hours. It was not unpleasant. In a strange way, it was gratifying to be right here with his old friend.

The sunlight stabbed through Winston's bedroom window and right onto the body of Jimmy's friend. Outside the windows, the blue-skied, puffy-clouded, happy day was beginning. The mockingbirds were singing. The mosquitoes were gathered on the screens of Winston's window looking for a way in.

It seemed ironic almost, this weather. It seemed as though there was some kind of divine joke to it all. As though God was either happy about something or indifferent to it. Jimmy thought his friend deserved rainstorms and dark clouds and, at the very least, a good hurricane. But he got sunshine and flowers.

Jimmy had spent most of his light-sleeping moments thinking about how ever since the second grade, Winston's mother used to say that Jimmy and Win were "joined at the hip." And they were too. They had liked each other, hated each other, tolerated one another, leaned on one another, been jealous of each other, changed each other's tires, loaned each other money, been drunk together, lost and won games together. They had engaged in a fistfight exactly twice. Once over a girl. The other time was over a card game wherein someone might or might not have cheated. That someone might have been Jimmy. The punch Jimmy threw at the courthouse months earlier didn't count because Winston hadn't fought back.

The hardest part of watching a man die was feeling something but not being able to feel it all the way. Jimmy wanted to weep, but he could not. Something in him wouldn't do it. There would be plenty of time for weeping later, and his brain knew that.

When Winston opened his eyes, he smiled. But it wasn't a long-lasting one. Jimmy removed a book from his jacket pocket. He cleared his throat and said, "I brought you something." He held up the book.

"What's that?" whispered Winston.

"What's it look like? It's your old buddy Sam."

That got another smile from Winston. He said in his mangled voice, "I didn't know . . ." *Gasp*. "I didn't know . . . you could read, Jimmy."

Jimmy didn't even dignify this remark. He simply put on a pair of reading glasses, then adjusted them low on his nose. He opened the book to a place that had a dogeared page. He figured it must have been important to Winston.

"Don't do that," said Winston.

"Don't do what? You don't want me to read?"

"No . . . I mean . . . Don't . . . don't feel sorry for me."

Jimmy shook his head and began reading aloud.

"'Now when I had mastered the language of this water and had come to know every trifling feature that bordered the great river as familiarly as I knew the letters of the alphabet, I had made a valuable acquisition. But I had lost something too. I had lost something which could never be restored to me while I lived. All the grace, the beauty, the poetry had gone out of the majestic river!'"

Jimmy paused to let Winston finish a cough. It sounded like the cough was breaking ribs with each explosive burst.

"'There were graceful curves,'" Jimmy read, "'reflected images, woody heights, soft distances; and over the whole scene, far and near, the dissolving lights drifted steadily, enriching it every passing moment with new marvels of coloring.'"

Winston was already asleep when he finished. The lawman's chest was rising and falling.

"How could I ever feel sorry for you? You were beautiful."

Silly Boyhood Things

Eleanor was serving breakfast and Buz tried to eat but couldn't. The bacon made Winston Browne's kitchen smell alive, and it made the whole house feel less grief stricken. Bacon had a way of doing that. And they could do with all the happiness they could get this morning. But nobody was eating, including Eleanor.

Everyone stabbed at their food. The eggs went cold, the bacon got hard, the grits congealed. Buz's glass of Ovaltine was unappealing. He was running on fumes. He sat at the table dressed in his carrier blues and struggled to keep his eyes open. He'd been out all night for the third time in a row. They should have been the greatest nights of his life. Instead, he had wept openly in front of Becky Jernigan more than a few times. The girl had held his head on her bare shoulder. Last night had not gone the way he wanted it to. There was no kissing. No necking. Just a grown boy, crying. And a beautiful girl holding him.

Breakfast was awkward and quiet. There was nothing to talk about. No events to discuss. No joys to share. The whole world seems trivial when someone is dying, as though the world's problems have always been trivial, but people have been too preoccupied to notice how silly they are. All the things that were once so important became dust. Boyhood things like ball games, budding romance, or hopes of success. They were silly with a capital *S*.

It was Jessie who pushed her plate away first. "I'm not hungry."

Buz slumped in his seat, using his fork to swirl his grits and egg yolks until it became a yellow and white mess.

"What's Jimmy doing?" said Jessie. "Why isn't he eating with us?"

"He's helping Win, sweetie. Feeding him a milkshake."

Buz placed his fork on the table. He hated this. He hated the feeling inside him. It was a kind of halfhearted sadness mixed with elation from the night before. Also, he was mad. He wasn't sure what he was mad at. But he'd never felt anger and romantic passion at the same time. They conflicted with each other.

"Buz," said Eleanor. "Aren't you hungry?"

He dropped his fork. "Not really, ma'am. I'm sorry. I just feel sick. It was a long night."

Eleanor removed his plate. She picked up Jessie's plate and her own plate too, since she hadn't eaten a bite. She scraped all the food into a big tin bowl. She opened the screen door and placed the bowl before Huck, who was waiting on Winston's porch.

Huck ate with little concern for the black bereavement that surrounded this kitchen. Buz was envious of this animal. The dog hadn't mourned for his grandfather, and it likely would not grieve for Winston Browne. Dogs did not lament. Were dogs smarter than man? Or were they just oblivious?

Eleanor sat at the table and placed both her hands on its enamel surface. She lit a smoke and tapped the ash into the tin ashtray, which was shaped like the state of Florida. Nobody said anything. They could hear the sounds of Winston coughing from the back room. They heard the gentle voice of Jimmy Abraham.

"When my mother died," said Eleanor, "I wanted to scream, I

wanted to yell, but all I could bring myself to do was clean her house. So that was what I did."

"You cleaned?" said Jessie.

"Yep. I cleaned for sixteen hours, floor to ceiling, until I was about to pass out. My daddy just left me alone because he knew I needed to *do* something."

More coughs from the back room. It sounded like the old man was choking to death.

"But after a whole day of cleaning, Daddy came to me and he gripped my wrists and said, 'Sweetie, what if you've been looking at death all wrong?' He said it just like that, so reasonably. Like he was talking about one of his goats or something. I've never forgotten how he said that."

"Looking at it wrong?" said Buz. "How many ways can you look at it? There can't be more than one."

"What if there are two or three? Or fifty? You know, what if we don't understand death at all? What if it's the same as birth? Nobody understands birth either."

"There's nothing to understand," said Buz.

"Sure there is. One minute you're *not* here, the next minute you *are* here. It's a miracle. That's what everyone calls it. What if death is a miracle too, but we're too simpleminded to see it?"

Nobody said anything else. Jimmy emerged from the hallway carrying an empty milkshake glass.

"He's resting now. I finally got him to eat."

"Would you like some breakfast?" Eleanor asked.

He collapsed in a chair. "No thanks, I ain't hungry."

They sat in a kind of painful reflection for three more cigarettes. After several minutes of listless gloom, Eleanor stabbed out her Lucky. She stood, wrapped a dishrag around her hair, then tied an apron around her waist. She opened the cabinets below Winston's sink and began removing bottles and buckets. She opened the pantry and removed a mop and a broom. She filled the bucket with water and suds.

"What're you doing?" asked Jimmy.

"I can't just sit here," said Eleanor. "I have to do something."

The makeshift family watched her scrub the floors and baseboards and clean light fixtures. They didn't move from their seats, not for a long time.

Two Ways of Seeing a River

The muscles in Winston's neck struggled against his own throat. His eyes opened. He could see Buz sleeping in the chair beside him. Snoring. He wore a mail carrier's shirt. Blue slacks. Black shoes. He looked like a government man. Winston remembered what he first felt when he saw his own reflection wearing an army uniform. It was intoxicating.

The suffocation started behind Winston's sternum. Then his abdomen locked up. Soon he was filled with a feeling different from anything he'd experienced. It moved through his ribs, then upward to his head. Emptiness, that's what it felt like.

At first, instinct kicked in. A kind of animal reaction. It was almost as though his body already knew how to handle what was happening to him. Like eating, or sleeping, or going to the bathroom.

He closed his eyes. When he reopened them, he was watching his body from another angle. He was looking down on it. As though he were in the corner of the room as a spectator. He could see his own face: tense, mouth gaping open. No breath was coming in or out.

He felt the room get brighter, bigger, taller, heavier, broader, and more surreal.

There was a pageantry to what was happening that he hadn't expected. Sort of like the same fanfare that goes with a child being born. Everyone stands in the delivery room and rejoices even though a birth is not grandiose nor poetic. In fact, Winston had birthed three babies in his career as a lawman. Birth is messy and traumatic. The room looks like a hog killing took place when it's all over. But it was beautiful nonetheless. And nobody is ever sad in a delivery room.

Buz was still asleep in his chair. Winston wanted to get his attention, but there was no way. It was already starting.

For a moment he was sucked back into himself. He opened his eyes and he was lying on the bed. The pain returned. His chest was throbbing. Then he had the strange sensation of falling. He closed his eyes, and the world became pure light. Wonderful, sacred light.

He saw an ocean made of clouds. Long, flat, icy clouds. Like they were made of snow and ice cream. And in one moment he felt his breath return to him. Or maybe it was leaving him. He couldn't tell. Either way, the sensation was cold, refreshing, and windy. Glorious wind. Inside his lungs, outside his body. It was so fulfilling. For the first time in a long time his body felt rejuvenated. Everything relaxed. And he was done striving.

Life itself was striving. He could see that now. He'd never seen it before. Life was the constant tensing of muscles, adjusting to an unkind world around you, reacting, spinning, working. It was one continuous fighting against the unseen. But not now. When he drifted past the clouds, he could see the gentle Escambia and its easy water, snaking across the miles of his homeland, weaving past his house on Terrence Street. The color of the river looked almost grayish brown from so high above. He saw it all. The rooftops of a small town that gave birth to him. The golden hues of its sunlight, falling on the main street. The endless labyrinth of roads and avenues all Moabites could navigate with their eyes closed. Home.

And in this moment, dangling above the beautiful earth, somewhere beneath heaven and the clouds, he realized he had been wrong about life. He had been wrong about the whole thing from start to finish. At times he had believed life was a kind of walk. Like the walks he used to take on the cow paths when he was on his way home from school. But he could see now that life wasn't a journey; it never had been. It was art. Like a flower. All a daisy has to do is bloom and be pretty. There was nothing to accomplish, there was no path to follow, there were no mile markers. Life was a blossoming thing, vivid and lovely in the sunlight.

How could a man be so mistaken? Winston Browne had known the greatest thing that ever was, and he felt so incredibly grateful. Whatever you called *it*—life, existence, being, the human experience—he had known *it*. He had touched it. He had held it. He had loved it. It was wild. It was pretty, sad, remorseful, exciting, dangerous, terrifying, lonely, full of angst, peaceful, rewarding, cruel, sorrowful, interesting, gentle, surprising, and full of people.

Oh, the people. They were the best part of it all. Hands down. Better than the rivers, or the sunrises, or the smell of fresh-cut grass, or cold beer, or Scrabble games, or good music, or the taste of clean air, or the hope of romance. They were like the salt on the crisp, warm tomato of life.

He drifted over the skyline of his gentle town, momentarily returning to the little bedroom on Terrence Street. He had a choice. He could stay for a little longer, or he could go on and have an adventure. He didn't even have to think about it. For he'd been here long enough, and it was time to go somewhere else.

Once more he found himself in the corner of his dreary bedroom. He was staring at Buz. He saw his young friend stir awake. He heard

Buz call his name. Winston watched while his friend started shouting. Winston saw the lump in the bed beneath the sheets. Its chest wasn't moving anymore. Buz Guilford was crying.

It had all been his. A temporary possession, but a possession nonetheless. Like the little toys Winston's father used to give him. That's just what life was, and he could see it now. It was a gift. A birthday present from On High. The greatest gift that ever was. The greatest gift that ever would be. But now, here in this abysmal room, he knew it was time to give the gift back.

And Winston Browne went on to Glory.

Route 29

The North Florida night air was brisk and cool, which was rare for a June evening. The McDonald's sign glowed in the darkness with a golden halo around it. The Moab water tower in the distance behind it was releasing its monthly overflow onto Hydrangea. Next to the McDonald's was a Pizza Hut. They were godawful signs. The entire town hated these signs. People wrote op-ed articles about them in the *Moab Messenger.* Council meetings were held about these signs. But then, people didn't hate the signs enough to quit buying Big Macs and supreme pizzas.

The Crown Victoria was humming through Moab's dark streets like the mechanical workhorse that it was. These Fords were the greatest cars ever to be made. To a lawman, they were almost flawless. Easy to work on, inexpensive to maintain, dependable, indestructible, comfortable, smooth-riding, powerful, and most importantly, unattractive.

County cars were supposed to be ugly. It was an unwritten law.

The two peace officers patrolled Frond Street, Evergreen Avenue, and Hydrangea. They went out to Red Basin and pulled over at the Bottle Tree where a Chevette was parked, steamed windows, filled with two necking teenagers. Buz told them to get lost. When they were gone, he tossed a stick at the old bottle tree just to hear the noise it made.

Moab's frogs were warming up their voices. The stars were out to play in the sky. The dewy air fell upon the world, suffocating the deputies in their own sweat and bodily fluids. He crawled into the car and began heading toward Moab proper.

"You think anyone will actually be there tonight?" said John, the new deputy.

"You don't understand, John, this game's a big deal. The whole town shows up."

"Why?"

"Tradition."

John was still new to the job, and young. Young enough to be drugged by the thrill of the forest-green county uniform he wore. He was still a little bit taken with himself, a confidence Sheriff Guilford had never possessed. Then again, it was hard to blame the kid. Buz did in fact know how hard it was to get over seeing yourself in a government uniform. It changed a man. Some people never got over it.

The scanner was broadcasting more hissing messages from dispatch in nearby towns. Messages that were piped across the tri-county area. The Okeauwaw County Sheriff's Department was small, the lowest-funded in the state. But Route 29 was a hot route for crime when it happened. A few weeks earlier Buz had busted an Oldsmobile carrying twenty pounds of narcotics. But tonight was a quiet night, and Buz thanked the stars for this.

The Crown Vic rolled through the manicured neighborhoods. The houses reflected the headlights of the cruiser, displaying their quiet glory. Each home painted in grays or browns or yellows. Buz could remember when these houses were white and off-white only. Back then it would have been a sin to paint them another color, but times had changed. The world had changed with them. Every house had been updated, and each residence had cable television.

All was well on Hydrangea. The downtown was doing good

business this weekend since so many of the exiles had returned. The Open signs were all off for the night, and the lights in the windows had been turned off. All except Ray's Bar and Grill, its neon adding an air of nostalgia. Everyone loved that sign. A developer had tried to tear it down when he took over the building, but the city fought him and won. The sign was declared a historical landmark.

The mercantile was still in business, but the shelves were not as well stocked as before, and most of the coolers had been unplugged long ago. Everyone did most of their shopping at the new Piggly Wiggly on the edge of town now. Nobody bought flour at a mercantile when you could get it for a buck cheaper at The Pig.

When the squad car reached Browne Memorial Field, Buz saw vehicle upon vehicle parked in haphazard patterns. They were scattered in every direction. Law and order had not been observed, and this warmed the sheriff's heart. All available patches of grass were covered with Fords, Nissans, Mazdas, and Chevys.

"Here," said Buz, handing John a jersey from the back seat. "I think this one's about your size."

"You want me to play? I'm not much of a baseball guy. I'm more into football."

"Not tonight," said the sheriff. "There's no way you're going to miss the fun of watching a bunch of old men pull their groins sliding into home. Did you refill the hand-pump soap in the bathrooms?"

"I did that this morning."

A woman approached the vehicle and rapped on the window. Tall and beautiful, carrying a blond baby on her hip, her hair in braids, Jessie was wearing pleated jeans and a striped shirt. Buz almost choked himself with his seatbelt leaping from the vehicle. He hugged her in the glow of the vehicle dome light. She hugged back.

He could hear the Dixieland band in the distance. They were playing "Meet Me in Saint Louis."

"And who's this little guy?" Buz said, touching the baby's chin.

"This is Winston," she said.

Buz fuzzed the child's soft hair and marveled at the infant. He felt the moisture build in his eyes. They held each other again. They stood like this for a few minutes. No matter how old a man gets, he will always be a boy around some people.

The ambient sounds of the small-town symphony were swirling around them like old music. The memories got so thick Buz had to swat them away like gnats. The chirping tones of voices on the field. The melody of laughter. The happy trickle of joyful voices that accompany the God-given blessing that is baseball.

Baseball-wise, the whole world had altered itself the moment Winston Browne left this world. One year after his passing, the Brooklyn Dodgers had been sold to Los Angeles. Brooklyn had become a graveyard almost overnight. The radio station in Mobile quit broadcasting games. Jackie Robinson retired. Men with wrecking balls demolished Ebbets Field to build apartment complexes. A few years later the Milwaukee Braves moved to Atlanta, and the South got a real baseball team. Though the town's interest in baseball was not what it had been during Buz's childhood. Children were more interested in football now. Some Moab parents even took their children to Pensacola to play a sport called "soccer." What the heck was soccer?

"How's Becky?" said Jessie.

"She's good," said Buz. "Her stomach is out to here." He made the international sign of a pregnant belly. "She swears this is our last, but she said that with the last one."

More cars were arriving at the field. Dozens of them. He had not expected such a great turnout. This little town could surprise you.

"And how's Greg?" Buz asked Jessie.

"Good, just busy."

An elderly woman and man hobbled toward the Crown Vic.

Eleanor wore a loud shirt with geometric designs on it, neon green pants, and white tennis shoes. She held her hands outward. "There's Granny's little man!" She took the child from Jessie and kissed his fat cheeks. Buz exchanged hugs with Eleanor and Jimmy. Jimmy Abraham, small and frail, looked like he would live forever.

Eleanor held Buz just a little longer than normal, the baby sandwiched between them. She whispered into Buz's ear, "I have something for you. I found it yesterday."

The old woman pulled back, reached into a paper Piggly Wiggly bag Buz hadn't noticed she'd been carrying, and removed a crinkled brown hat with a soft brim. Buz held it in his hands and—it was a reflex—smelled it. It smelled like smoke.

"Well, don't just look at it," said Eleanor. "Try it on."

Eleanor covered her mouth. Jimmy bowed his head. "It suits you," Jessie said.

Eleanor pulled Buz into another embrace and he saw something over Eleanor's shoulder. It was a dog, sniffing around the dumpster behind the insurance building. A reddish dog with a black snout. He'd seen this dog a few times before. It was a dog that didn't belong to anyone. Not even to the dog himself. For nobody could own a life.

The dog seemed to be on a mission. It sat in one place staring at Buz from across the nighttime haze that separated them. Then it turned, sniffed the air, and waltzed down Hydrangea Street, past the town's proud little storefronts, into the residential area. Who knew where the old dog was going? Maybe the dog was heading to someone's porch. Maybe it was going to find someone who needed the company of a friend. Or maybe the animal would follow the shoulder of rural Highway 29, a scenic two-lane road, well maintained, that meandered alongside the gentle Escambia River, which cut downward through South Alabama, slicing through the western Panhandle straight through Moab. A town about as wide as it was high. Which wasn't very high. Seventeen feet above sea level. A river town, full of humidity, pine trees, good people, millworkers, and insatiable gossip. This place didn't look like much, but the Brooklyn Dodgers once visited this place. Jackie Robinson had played on this very field. Still, even the fantastic, nearly unimaginable feats of Jackie Robinson faded in comparison to the man who had laid the field's foundation.

For nobody was more incredible than Winston Browne.

Acknowledgments

I'd like to thank Alex for perpetually believing in me, even when I don't. And Julie, one of my editors, who believes in me almost as much as my own mother.

And the people at Thomas Nelson. Listen, I've had a lot of jobs in my life. I've done everything from hang commercial roofing to scooping ice cream. The publishers at Thomas Nelson have been the best "bosses" I have ever worked for. I am eternally grateful for their patience with me, waiting on a manuscript that was overdue by about nine years.

Lastly, my wife is my everything. She made not only this book possible, she makes me possible. I am nothing without her.

Discussion Questions

1. The opening line of the book informs readers that Winston Browne is dying. What effect did this knowledge have on you as you read the book?
2. What did you think of the Moab Social Graces column interspersed throughout the book? How does it advance the narrative? Discuss how it create the atmosphere of a small Florida town in the 1950s.
3. Winston reflects that he "had married Okeauwaw County." What does he mean by this? Winston has no biological children, but how is he a father figure as the sheriff? Discuss the significance of family, both biological and created, in the story.
4. How does Eleanor's character evolve throughout the story?
5. At Adam's funeral Winston quotes Mark Twain's *Life on the Mississippi*: "No, the romance and the beauty were all gone from the river. All the value any feature of it had for me now was the amount of usefulness it could furnish toward compassing the safe piloting of a steamboat." What parallels does this quote have to Winston's life and death?
6. What did you think of Winston's decision to keep his terminal diagnosis to himself for much of the book? How might the

story have played out differently if Winston had told Eleanor and Jimmy of his condition earlier?

7. What character affected you the most, or which character did you see yourself in? Why?
8. The author uses a lot of symbols throughout the story: cars, Mark Twain's books, golden chocolate coins, the dog Huck, the bottle tree. What do some of these symbols represent? Did you notice others while reading?
9. As Winston approaches death, Eleanor says, "What if death is a miracle too, but we're too simpleminded to see it?" What do you think she means?
10. What did you think about the closing chapter, when the story's characters reunite at the annual Winston Browne Classic and give readers a glimpse into their future lives? Was there any particular character not mentioned in this chapter you wished you knew what happened to?

About the Author

Photo by Sean Murphy

Sean Dietrich is a columnist and novelist known for his commentary on life in the American South. His work has appeared in *Newsweek*, *Southern Living*, *Garden & Gun*, *Good Grit*, the *Tallahassee Democrat*, *South Magazine*, *The Bitter Southerner*, *Thom Magazine*, the *Birmingham News*, and the *Mobile Press-Register*. He has authored twelve books.

A mediocre sailor and fisherman, a biscuit connoisseur, and a barbecue competition judge when he's not writing, he spends much of his time aboard his fourteen-foot fishing boat (the SS *Squirrel*) along with his coonhound, Thelma Lou.

Visit Sean online at seandietrich.com
Instagram: @seanofthesouth
Facebook: @seanofthesouth
Twitter: @seanofthesouth1